# THE ORCHID ROOM

## CHRISTOPHER SWEET

OTHER DOOR PUBLISHING

Published by The Other Door Publishing

*This one's for Lara*

# THE ORCHID ROOM

# PART 1

1

Sweat oozed from underneath Farren Murakami's helmet; charted a path along her eyebrow, down her cheek, and into her mouth. She blew out, spraying saliva and half-ingested sweat onto home plate. With a swish and the quick smack of horsehide on leather, the first pitch blew past her. The umpire called the strike a split second later.

"Wake up, Murakami!"

Farren could just barely see Coach Lorenz in her peripheral vision, tearing his ball cap off in exasperation, wiping imaginary sweat from his brow, then ramming the hat back onto his head. Farren didn't have to see Coach's face to know it would be an unflattering shade of scarlet. It was only the first pitch of the at-bat, but even she had to admit she'd been daydreaming a bit. She tightened her grip on the bat and dug what stood for her left foot into the hard-packed dirt surrounding the plate.

Sixty feet and six inches in front of her, Carla Werner adjusted her own grip on the ball and rolled her shoulders.

Carla was tall, deceptively lean, and one of the best pitchers Farren had faced in the three years she'd been playing varsity baseball for the Maggie's Knee Ultras. But Carla had a tell.

The shoulder roll was such an obvious giveaway Farren had a hard time believing no one had trained it out of her, but there it was.

The second pitch started out looking like a fastball up high but Farren trusted her instinct and maintained her stance. Sure enough, in the split second it took to fly from Carla's palm to home plate, the ball dipped low and to the outside, exactly where Farren had anticipated it would go. She swung hard and low, fighting the instinct to lift the ball upward. The contact was dead on and the satisfying crack of bat meeting ball reverberated up her arms.

She watched for half a second as the ball sailed off the tip of the bat, over the head of Alicia Bruce on first, and into the shallow outfield, too far in front of Keira Pratner in right field for her to dive for.

Farren knew a race to first when she saw it. She sprang off with everything attached to her left ankle, sprinting for all she was worth. Darla Hoffman, the first base coach, was waving her on. Had Keira fumbled the play? No time to look. Farren rounded first, barely maintaining her footing in the dirt, and sprinted for second.

"Down! Down!" Darla shouted from behind her.

Farren dropped, left leg extended, and slid into second plate.

She had no idea she'd slid into Jess Hutchinson until the second baseman fell on top of her. It took an extra few seconds for Farren to realize Jess was wailing and the ump was calling time.

"Freak!" Jess cried as Farren rolled out from under her. "Your cyborg foot broke my ankle."

Both teams were moving in to surround the girls at second base.

Darla knelt next to Jess and eased her foot up, probing around the ankle and heel. "It's definitely not broken."

Jess shoved her away. "Don't touch me. I'm done playing with her." She lifted her chin toward Farren. "Totally unfair she plays with that thing on her leg."

Lindsay Ellis, catcher for the Ultras, helped Farren up.

"Yeah, completely unfair she plays with only one foot," Lindsay shot at Jess.

"Please don't," Farren muttered, feeling her face grow hot.

Jess stood, favoring her injured ankle. "Unfair if she's going to assault us. And we all know she gets extra spring from it when she runs."

Lindsay said, "You really think being an amputee is an advantage?"

"It is if her foot costs more than my mom's car."

"Stop!" Farren shouted before she even knew she was going to say anything. "I'll leave. Just stop talking about me like I'm not here."

She turned to find Coach Lorenz standing in her way.

"You can't leave the game, Farren," he commanded.

Farren brushed past him. "Last inning anyway. You'll need a runner in for me."

When she reached the dugout, she glanced over her shoulder, half expecting—or maybe hoping for—someone to have followed her across the diamond to talk her into staying. Both teams were still gathered at second base, though. Two of Jess' teammates supported her as she hobbled off the diamond, an arm slung over each of them. Farren tossed her batting helmet into her bag, tore off her batting gloves, and carried her stuff out of the dugout without bothering to change out of her cleat.

Most days she could ignore it. In fact, most days, she wore a completely different prosthesis, one that resembled an actual foot and fit into her shoe. Now, though, the sound of her prosthesis clicking and scraping against the asphalt was all she could hear.

She normally walked confidently, with only the most imperceptible of limps, but today she felt like she hobbled as she crossed the parking lot and hit the sidewalk. The energy-storing carbon fiber blade that had replaced her left foot did indeed give an extra spring to her step, but unless she wanted to walk like someone out of a Monty Python sketch, she had to control the extra force, something that had taken her almost a year to get the hang of. The extra control forced her left leg to work harder than the right, giving her thigh the slightest bit more muscle right above her knee. She was the only one who'd ever noticed this but today she felt as though the disproportions made her look and move exactly like what Jess had labeled her as: a freak.

She rammed earbuds into her ears and selected a Tool playlist on her phone, then cranked the volume until she could no longer hear her foot against the sidewalk.

Z

THE HOUSE WAS empty when Farren arrived home twenty minutes later, which was perfect. Only Bonzo, their lab-shepherd mix, greeted her with a single low bark when Farren came through the door. The bark was followed by the clicking of nails on the hardwood floor as he came trotting to the front door to verify it was her. She reached down to give him a rough scratch around his ears and under his collar. The big dog pushed his head into her, letting her know she could never scratch hard enough.

When her arms grew tired of giving affection, Farren lugged her baseball gear to her room and dumped it on the floor. Melinda would have something to say about it but Farren couldn't give two shits what her stepdad's wife thought today. In fact, she almost hoped Melinda would pick a fight.

Smirking at herself, she sat on her bed, aware that her dirty baseball pants were another thing for Melinda to get her panties in a twist over, and set about removing her prosthesis. Once it was off, she scratched the ankle where it had been sitting, almost as hard as she'd scratched Bonzo. She counted to ten, slowly, then forced herself to stop. When she'd first received a prosthetic foot as an eleven-year-old girl, seven years ago now, she'd scratched at her leg so much she'd caused it to bleed. This happened frequently and each time she would have to wait for her leg to heal before she could attach the prosthesis again. Finally, her physiotherapist, Anika, had advised her to allow herself ten seconds of scratching—and *only* ten seconds—whenever she removed the limb. It took some discipline, but soon became a habit and, since then, she never scratched for more than ten seconds, no matter how badly it itched.

Anika had been integral to Farren's long road to recovery after losing her foot. There were days during her physiotherapy Farren had loathed her physical therapist, but the superficial hatred would melt away after the painful sessions and she would embrace Anika as the friend and mentor she had become.

From Anika, Farren learned how to cope with the pain, how to redirect the energy she spent thinking about it, and, best of all, how to meditate. Starting with simple breathing exercises, she helped Farren train her mind to almost completely leave her body behind and go somewhere else while the pain was at its worst. Now, at eighteen, Farren could put herself into a peaceful trance almost immediately in even the most distracting environments. These days though, instead of using meditation to cope with physical pain, she used it to deal with her anger and the fathoms-deep depression that were her constant companions.

Farren shoved off the bed and took a giant, leaping hop across her room, where a single titanium crutch leaned in the corner. She snatched the crutch and got it under her arm in one fluid motion, then used it to propel herself out of her room. As much as she hated using the crutch in public, she enjoyed how much longer her stride became with it. She took the hallway in two long steps, pivoting on the crutch and swinging her body through the bathroom door.

She caught a glimpse of herself in the mirror on the way to the shower and had to laugh; her face was still covered in fine brown dust from her slide into second base. She rinsed her hands under the faucet and swiped at the dust, revealing clear skin of almost the same sandy shade. Rivulets of dirt-darkened water ran down her cheeks and dripped off the strong jaw she'd inherited from her mother, like so many more of her looks. Only her eyes, large and almond-shaped, and skin tone came from her father. The rest of her looks—her straight, almost regal nose, her full lips, her lean build, and her hair—were all copy and pasted directly from her late mother. Darya Murakami had been a goddess to behold, and even though Farren didn't typically enjoy indulging in vanity, she secretly loved catching glimpses of her mom in her own face.

In the shower and under the hot water, she allowed herself to reflect on the baseball game. Part of her regretted storming off, as she often regretted actions inspired by her temper, but no one would hold it against her. She only wished she'd stuck around, at least from a distance, to see the outcome of the game. None of the girls on her team would go out of their way to text her the score, but at least it would be uploaded to the school's varsity website by the next morning.

It wasn't that Farren had no friends on the team, only that she'd managed to passively isolate most of them, as she had everyone else in her life. It was a habit started after the death of her father and cemented in her when her mom died a few years later.

She turned her face up to the hot shower spray, attempting to wash thoughts of her parents away.

Bonzo's anxious bark pierced the noise of the shower. It was the one he reserved for Melinda. He seemed to be the only one who felt the same way about her that Farren did. Her stepdad's wife never made an attempt to hide the fact that she loathed Bonzo, which only solidified Farren's contempt for the woman, never mind that she was an intruder in Farren's shattered life. She had never given Melinda a real chance but, to Farren's credit, Melinda had never proven herself to be anything more than an entitled leech.

"Farren? That you?" the voice came from right outside the bathroom door.

*Of course it's me*, Farren thought, directing poisoned mental barbs at Melinda, wishing they would stick for once.

"Sweetie?"

"Don't call me that," Farren mumbled into the water.

"What was that?"

The woman had ultrasonic hearing.

"Yes! It's me!" Farren hollered, hoping the annoyance in her voice would cut through the water and the door.

"Oh, good," Melinda said. "I was afraid it was some sicko. Ridiculous of course. Can never be too careful though. All those kids going missing. Mayor Hatfield had better start acknowledging what's going on. Raquelle, from my yoga class —I had such a wonderful session this morning—thinks he has something to do with it. Can you believe it? That man has no more cunning than Bonzo."

Silence. Farren knew Melinda was waiting for her to say something, in defense of her dog perhaps. But she wouldn't give Melinda the satisfaction. She did agree, though, that the idea of Byron Hatfield being behind the disappearances was ridiculous.

"Anyway," Melinda said after a pause that would have been awkward with anyone else, "I'll let you shower in peace. I'm going to make myself a smoothie." She said something else but her voice faded as she walked away from the door.

Finally.

Using one of the half-dozen grab bars affixed to the shower wall, Farren turned her back on the spray and poured a glob of shampoo into her hand. She scrubbed her hair with one hand while the other held the bar to stabilize herself.

She'd once had a full head of thick, black hair that other women had ooed and awed over her whole life; another gift from her mother. All that hair had proven to be a hassle in the shower. She'd slipped and fallen over in the tub four times while balancing on one foot to wash her hair with both hands. After the last time, shortly after her mom died, she'd gone to the salon and had her hair chopped to a pixie cut. Gordon, her stepdad, had cried when he saw what she'd done. Said her mother would have been ashamed. That had been the beginning of the end of their already fragile relationship.

Now Farren could juggle in the shower without her prosthesis if she wanted to, but she'd grown used to the convenience of short hair and admittedly still relished the hurt it caused her stepdad.

She lingered in the shower until the water started to cool, then slammed the tap off, wrapped a towel around herself, and went straight to her room.

Z

THAT NIGHT, Farren had the train dream:

*The tracks are the same ones* her *train traveled on, but this landscape is vastly different. Her spot is surrounded by tall pine trees. This dream track is in the middle of a vast desert; nothing for as far as the eye can see. The ground she walks is made up of smooth, round, interlocking white stones. She is barefoot, both legs intact. In her dreams, she always has both feet.*

*She walks alongside the tracks, not knowing where she is headed, only that she has to keep moving.*

Dad wants me to keep moving.

*The thought is accompanied by the deafening shriek of a train's whistle, unlike any sound real trains make. This one sounds as if it comes through suffering human vocal cords. It conveys agony, pain, misery. Death.*

*She runs, knowing in the logical part of her brain she is safe as long as she stays off the tracks. Except when she looks down, she sees she is running on them.*

*She veers to the left. The tracks turn with her. She tries the other direction. Same result. They remain underfoot no matter which direction she turns in.*

*The train shrieks its terrible whistle again. A hot wind pummels her back.*

*Too terrified to look over her shoulder, she forces herself to run faster, makes her legs pump harder. They are so tired. She is so tired. All she wants is to lie down and let the train take her.*

But Dad says to keep going.

*The train screams a final, deafening whistle before it overtakes her.*

"Control to Farren! Come in!"

Mr. Hurley's voice jerked Farren back to reality. Judging by her classmates' laughter, it wasn't the first time he'd called on her.

She'd been deep in a daydream, reliving the fragments she could recall of last night's nightmare. The shriek of the train's whistle, the most memorable aspect of the dream, had carried over into waking life with chilling clarity.

She looked up from her desk to see a dozen faces turned toward her, amusement in their eyes. How long had Mr. Hurley been calling her name?

"Sorry," she muttered. "I was thinking about geography."

A smattering of laughter followed this.

Mr. Hurley—who many of the students referred to as Shaq, thanks to his imposing size and bald head—twirled a pencil between his fingers and gave Farren a look of dry amusement tinged with a hint of concern. He'd always made the wellbeing of his students his primary interest, a trait that was as endearing as it was bothersome, for Farren anyway.

"Did your thinking happen to include what the layer beneath the lithosphere is?"

"Asthenosphere," she replied immediately.

The teacher's eyebrows went up in unsurprised approval. He rambled on for a little while longer, reminding the class about the test that would be conducted at the end of the week, and encouraging them to get a good start on their end-of-term assignments, though it was still only April.

Farren was making her way to the door with the rest of the class when Mr. Hurley called her name.

"What's up with you?" he asked when the class had emptied out.

He leaned against the chalkboard, heedless of the line of white dust that would imprint itself on the backs of his thighs the way it did on the butts and backs of much shorter teachers. He twirled his pencil between his fingers as he watched her. He'd once confessed to the class that if he didn't keep something in his hands to fiddle with, he'd start tapping and drumming on whatever surface was nearby, which unfailingly aggravated everyone in earshot.

Farren shrugged and sat on the closest desk to her. "Didn't sleep great."

"Heard you did some damage in yesterday's game."

"Was that in the box scores?"

Mr. Hurley coughed out a light laugh. "You this evasive at home too?"

She didn't answer that.

He gave her a look that told her he intuited much more than he let on. "Just know that if you need to talk or yell at someone, I'm always around. And if that's weird, I can assure you Mrs. VanWyn is a helluva guidance counselor."

"Thanks, Shaq."

"Stow that Shaq stuff. You know he makes guys like me look bad, moving like he don't weigh over three hundred pounds."

Farren gave him a chuckle that was only partially forced.

"All right, get moving now," he said. "You come find me or shoot me an email if you need me."

Farren said she would, then stepped out into the hallway.

She had her lunch period now and went to her usual spot to eat, sitting back against one of the pillars under the main stairs. It was the closest she could get to a completely isolated spot without leaving the grounds, which would take way too much time from her lunch. Once she was comfortably seated with her prosthetic foot—this, the one she wore in her day-to-day life, resembled an actual foot, and allowed her to wear a left shoe—tucked under her, she pulled a peanut butter sandwich and a battered paperback copy of *Dune* from her bag.

"...take them to Huggy's and boost a car," a guy's voice said from nearby.

Farren looked over the top of her book without moving her head. Two boys from her year, Garrett Mews and Pat Healey, had taken a seat at the bottom of the wide staircase. From the looks of it, neither of them had spotted her, which was why she liked this spot so much.

Garrett, a handsome kid whose dad was a private banker and made loads of money, shook his head. "Let's just have some drinks in the park. Last time we went joyriding we almost got busted."

"Pussy," Pat said, shoving his friend. "It's barely even illegal. If someone leaves their keys in the car, they're asking for it to be stolen. And we put the car back, with hardly any damage to it."

Garrett always seemed nice enough to Farren but Pat was a douchebag of the highest order. The things she'd overheard him say to some of the girls, especially freshmen, were disgusting. He'd tried giving her a hard time about her foot when they were both juniors and she'd smashed his kneecap with the handle of her crutch, which she was still using pretty regularly at the time. He'd gone to the ground with tears in his eyes but didn't say anything more to her on the subject. In fact, he'd barely so much as looked at her since that day.

"You knocked the driver's mirror off the last one we took," Garret said with a hint of a whine in his voice.

"Fine, man, whatever. But if those girls don't put out, we're getting ourselves a ride and doing burnouts on the bridge."

"We've got booze and weed," Garrett said, "they'll put out."

So maybe not the gentleman he pretended to be.

The boys fell into silence as each got lost in his phone and Farren couldn't help shaking her head at them. She had a phone, same as everyone else, but could not understand the appeal of staring into them, neck bent at a brutal angle, endlessly scrolling through polished snapshots of other people's lives and getting off on the number of likes and views and shares that tallied up on whatever the last thing you posted was. She knew she wasn't much better, having her nose stuffed in a book whenever the opportunity presented itself; she was essentially doing the same thing as everyone with a phone, only there was no one on the other end of what she was staring at. Her fulfillment came from story and tantalizing prose rather than pictures of food and thumbs-up icons.

Farren used her phone strictly for information and to stay in touch with the few people she spoke to, mainly her stepdad, teachers, and a few of her teammates.

Social media was something she just couldn't get behind—which was funny since Maggie's Knee was home to the offices of the biggest social media platform on the planet, and funnier still because her dad, her real dad, once worked for KnowMe in its upper echelons.

The bell rang, signaling the end of her lunch. Too soon, as always. She tossed the book into her backpack, crammed the last bite of her sandwich into her mouth, and made her way to her next class.

3

That Monday night found Garrett Mews propped up on his futon, noise-canceling headphones wrapped around his ears, and eyes glued to the big screen hanging across from him on his bedroom wall. He'd been so absorbed in *Kill 'Em Up*, the game he'd been absolutely slaying at, he almost didn't notice his phone vibrate with a message alert.

He finished the round he was on, cursing when he saw he'd come in second place by a lousy three kills, pulled off the headphones, and checked his phone, keeping his ringing ears open for any indication that his parents were still awake. The message, as he'd known it would be, was from Pat Healey, his best friend since grade school.

*We here. U cuming?*

The message was followed by half a dozen eggplant emojis. Most of the messages Pat sent were riddled with innuendo. They were seniors now, mere weeks from graduation, but Pat had never really exceeded the maturity of a thirteen-year-old, which suited Garrett just fine. Most of the time he found Pat hilarious to be around.

Pulling on his jeans and a clean T-shirt, Garrett hoped his friend would reign it in a bit tonight, hilarious as he was; they were meeting up with Katie MacDonald and Priya Bakshi at Finchview Park. Apparently they were already there with Pat. Girls tended not to appreciate Pat's humor the way a lot of guys did. Katie and Priya both knew Pat though, so it wasn't as if it would come as a surprise if he was no more refined this evening than on any other day. Still, Garrett thought he should get there as soon as possible.

Garrett had fostered a crush on Priya since her family moved to Maggie's Knee last year. With less than two months before graduation, he'd finally gathered up the courage to ask her to hang out and had been floored when she agreed. It came as even more of a surprise that Katie was willing to come along as Pat's date. She even seemed sort of excited about it.

Sneaking out of the house was easy enough. Garrett's parents slept like corpses in a dark, soundproof room. Still, he took every precaution; this would be the absolute worst night to get busted.

Free from the house and standing at the foot of his driveway, he realized he'd forgotten to steal one of the bottles of liquor his parents kept in the cupboard above the fridge, as if they believed it was still too high for Garrett to reach. He considered sending Pat a message to ask if he brought anything to drink but decided against it, he didn't want to delay anymore. Besides, Pat said he had a couple of doobies rolled, which should be plenty. Lots of girls got horny when they smoked weed.

Kildeer Road was completely silent and Garrett's footsteps

echoed off the houses set far back from the street as he plodded toward Sunpath Avenue. The sound set him unreasonably on edge, like his parents might hear and know it was him. But even if they did bust him, what was the worst they could do? He was old enough not to have a curfew.

He was turning onto Sunpath when he noticed his shoelace was undone. He stopped to tie it and froze in mid-crouch. There'd been a sound.

And again. The unmistakable scrape of a shoe on asphalt. He stood. Turned in a quick circle.

The street was empty.

He thought of calling out, decided he was being paranoid, and took a knee to finish tying the rogue lace.

It had to be Pat screwing around. He'd apparently decided to intercept Garrett and screw with him along the way. Garrett could imagine the girls standing off in the shadows, watching the shenanigans with patient smirks on their faces.

The moment he bent over, the footsteps returned. Running. Getting louder.

He looked over his shoulder. A black shadow streaked toward him.

Garrett tried to say something clever but only managed to get out the first syllable when an arm wrapped around his chest and an acrid, burning smell invaded his nostrils, making his eyes sting. He had a second to wonder what exactly Pat was trying to pull before darkness took him.

4

A few days later, Farren was on her way to her last class of the day when she noticed the poster taped to every fourth or fifth locker. The face taking up the middle of the page was familiar. There wasn't any need to read any of the accompanying text to know what it was about. She skimmed the text anyway:

*MISSING SINCE MONDAY NIGHT: GARRETT MEWS. IF SEEN, PLEASE CONTACT MAGGIE'S KNEE SHERIFF'S DEPT. REWARD OFFERED.*

Another one gone missing. Farren doubted the reward would turn up any solid leads. She wasn't exactly the first one people ran to with news, but she was certain she'd have heard something about it if all these missing kids were involved in some kind of coordinated exodus, which, according to her step-dad, was the running theory in the mayor's office. During one of their increasingly rare chats over breakfast, which could only occur when Melinda was out of the house, Gordon had lamented that Byron Hatfield, mayor of Maggie's Knee, was in denial about what was going on.

"He thinks it's a TikTok fad," Gordon had said, sipping from coffee so hot it made Farren wince. "And he doesn't want anyone saying anything different. He's afraid it'll eat into the tourism, that folks won't want to make the day trip out to take selfies on Jessop's Bridge anymore if they find out over fifteen kids have gone missing in the last couple years."

Garrett Mews made number eighteen, though, and Farren had to wonder how many more it would take before people in charge started taking it seriously. She had no trouble imagining why someone would want to run away, she'd considered it herself on enough occasions, but so many kids disappearing without a trace had to be unusual. Wouldn't some of them have come back or at least popped up on social media if they'd simply run away? And Garrett came from a wealthy family. She didn't know him well but from what she'd seen, he didn't want for much. Would he really give up all of his comforts for a bit more freedom?

Someone called Farren's name from behind her, startling her out of her thoughts.

She turned to see Holly Werner jogging to catch up with her. Holly pitched for the Maggie's Knee Ultras and was one of the few people Farren chatted with in the dugout. She and Holly weren't especially close but the pitcher spoke non-stop and would focus her attention on whoever was within earshot. Holly was also one of the few people who could make Farren laugh, often by making jokes at the expense of whichever team they were up against.

"What's up, Holly?" Farren said, unconsciously stealing a glance at the digital clock on the wall. She hated to be late to class, mostly because it meant everyone staring at her as she made her way to her seat.

"Coach wants to get in some fielding practice tonight. Can you make it after school?"

Farren rolled her eyes. Coach Lorenz was often calling impromptu practices for one reason or another and a lot of the girls on the team were convinced it was because he had no one else in his life and needed the company.

"I'll have to go home and get my blade first," Farren said, already heading in the direction of her class.

Holly hurried to keep pace. "You can't play with that?" she asked, pointing at Farren's left foot.

The foot Farren wore for regular walking around was a fine prosthesis and would probably hold up for a light practice, but Farren didn't have a matching cleat for it and didn't want to damage it if she needed to do anything much more strenuous than jogging a few steps. That and it felt different; the blade she used for sports had a unique feel and she didn't want to practice with something she wouldn't be using in an actual game.

Instead of explaining all this to Holly, she said, "No. See you at practice. Tell Coach I'll be a bit late."

Holly gave her a companionable slap on the shoulder and turned to head in the opposite direction while Farren continued to her class.

z

GORDON NOBLE SIPPED from his stained mug and grimaced. The coffee was ice cold and had been too bitter from the first sip. He put the cup down harder than he intended and cursed when the contents splashed over a couple of forms laid out on his desk. The paperwork meant little but the spill was frustrating nonetheless. He reached behind himself and pulled a handful of tissues from the box he kept on one of the shelves lining the office, then pressed them to the puddle, which had already mostly soaked into the papers.

"Sheriff?"

Barb's voice startled him so badly he almost knocked the cup over with the hand cleaning the spill. He made himself take a deep breath before looking up.

His receptionist, a cheerful, rotund spinster in her sixties, had one plump foot in the door and looked ready to evacuate if his response wasn't favorable. Was he becoming that ornery in his old age? Was forty-eight considered old?

"Yes, Barbara?"

She cleared her throat. "Franklin Mews here to see you. Again."

His frustration must have shown; she visibly flinched from him before he could respond. Her painted-on eyebrows were raised in an exaggerated look of supplication that made him simultaneously want to hug and throttle her. Barb was a good woman, if a little tiresome. She was always pleasant, even in the face of his increasingly frequent outbursts.

"Send him in."

Barb disappeared and, almost immediately, Franklin was standing in her place. His eyes were red and underscored by puffy bags of darkened, sagging flesh. As a successful financial consultant and private banker, Franklin Mews was normally well put together, dressed to the nines, not a hair out of place. This man was something else entirely; he wore faded jeans with an untucked flannel shirt, days' worth of stubble shadowed his cheeks, and his dark blond hair was greasy and uncombed. Seventeen kids had already disappeared without a trace. Seventeen kids still at large. And now Garrett, number eighteen.

Gordon wouldn't bother trying to appeal to Franklin's optimistic side. He stood and gestured to the padded chair in front of his desk. "Franklin. Have a seat."

The banker didn't sit so much as collapse into the chair. He hunched forward, looking like he was planning to beg for the life of his son. Gordon prayed it wouldn't come to that.

"Suppose you're here for an update," Gordon said.

Franklin spread his hands, palms up, as if to say there was no other meaning to life. And who could argue? Only son gone missing, likely never to be found. Gordon could only imagine how he'd feel if Farren fell victim to the same fate as the eighteen other missing kids, even if, as she loved to remind him, she wasn't his biological daughter. Melinda would probably rejoice, in her subtly cruel manner.

"Rose and I thought we could help organize a search party," Franklin said.

Gordon shifted in his seat. "I want Garrett to be found as much as you and Rose do, but you know it's going to be near impossible to gather enough bodies to do a thorough search."

It was worse than that, though. Nobody would show up for a search party. Nobody had for the last five or six kids who'd disappeared. The whole town had turned up for the first couple who had gone missing, but fewer than a dozen volunteers came out for the last three searches. People had just become too discouraged by the lack of success. None of this was helped by the fact that Maggie's Knee was bordered by the

Alleghenies and nestled in miles of dense, hilly woodland, much of it uncharted.

Franklin sniffed. "I know it's going to be tough, that's why we'll do all of the organizing. I'm sure I can call in some favors, I've made a lot of folks in this town pretty wealthy. We just need a few of your people to join us."

There it was.

"I'm not sure I'm going to be able to make that happen. You know Byron's not keen on allocating any more resources than absolutely necessary to runaways."

"Goddammit, he didn't run off!" Franklin shouted. "He's not some punk like half those kids. He's a good boy. He likes to have some fun but he's got a solid head on his shoulders."

"I know that," Gordon said, keeping his voice mild. "The mayor's made up his mind, though. All missing kids, unless we find incontrovertible proof there's been foul play, are to be treated as runaways."

"You know how fucking insane that sounds?"

Gordon sipped from his bitter, cold coffee. Today was one of those days that he hated his job.

Franklin shot up out of his chair. "Never mind. Waste of my time coming here. You can tell Byron he's got a lawsuit the size of Texas coming down on his head for this. It's unconstitutional, Gordon. Him I expect it from, but you're supposed to stick up for us little people." He stormed out of Gordon's office, stumbling over and knocking down the chair on his way. He slammed the door behind him hard enough to knock a framed certificate for something or other off the wall.

Barb appeared in the doorway a second later. "Another happy customer?"

Gordon sighed. "Never thought I'd hear Frank Mews refer to himself as little people."

Barb smirked. "I'm going to get some good coffee from across the street. You want?"

"God, yes. But I don't deserve it." He slogged the rest of the hours-old sludge from his mug, pushed back from his desk, and checked his watch. "Give Byron a shout before you go. Tell him I'm coming by for a visit. He'll be at the country club."

"You sure he's going to want to see you during his leisure hours?"

It was Gordon's turn to smirk now. "No. But that's the point."

Z

FARREN MADE good time getting home and figured, since she was already going to be late for practice, she had time to make herself a snack. Only Bonzo was home when she came in so, after giving him his requisite scratches, she cranked her favorite death metal playlist. The music, which she preferred to have pounding through big speakers or her headphones, sounded pathetic and tinny coming out of her phone speaker, but it was nice to be able to play it without any grief from Melinda.

After sticking a Pizza Pop in the microwave, Farren headed to her room to fetch her blade. She was just sitting down at the kitchen table with her snack when the front door slammed and Bonzo lost his shit. Seconds later, Melinda strode into the kitchen with a shopping bag on each arm. Bonzo followed at a distance, his barking having resolved to a frustrated growl. Farren's appetite died with Melinda's arrival.

"Turn that trash off," Melinda said, dropping the bags on the counter.

In spite of her lost appetite, Farren took a bite of the Pizza Pop to prevent herself from saying something nasty. Her phone sat at her elbow but she didn't make a move to stop the music or adjust the volume.

It took Melinda a full minute to clue in to the fact that her orders hadn't been obeyed. "Excuse me," she said with all the haughtiness she was capable of, "are you deaf too?"

Farren swallowed. "What do you mean, 'too?'"

"You know what I meant." Melinda turned away from her and set about transferring items from her bags to the cupboards.

"No, I'm not sure I do. You mean, am I deaf as well as crippled? Or is this about you thinking I'm gay?"

Melinda kept her back turned and said, "Turn off the music, Farren."

Now it was a matter of principle. Farren wished she could turn it up louder just to spite Melinda. She opted for taking another bite of her pop instead.

Melinda turned to face her and, for a long moment, the two only stared at each other.

"What do you want from me?" Melinda asked.

Farren shrugged.

"Do you enjoy getting on my nerves?"

Shrug. Bite. Chew.

Melinda's face went red. She slammed her hands on the counter in front of Farren. Her reddish-brown hair—normally kept rigorously in check by hundreds of dollars' worth of product and treatment—came loose and hung in her face, which was probably turning red underneath the dense layer of foundation she wore. Farren stared into Melinda's pale green eyes and thought her stepdad's wife might actually be pretty underneath all the makeup she slathered on each morning. She was in good shape, especially for a woman in her forties. Still, she came nowhere close to Farren's late mother. How the hell could Gordon have gone from her mom to this horrible, self-obsessed, status-driven action figure?

"You can't treat this house like your own personal domain," Melinda hissed. "Other people live here. People who contribute."

"What exactly do *you* contribute? Did your business finally take off in the last twelve hours?" Farren fought to keep her voice level. "I'm not the one who barged her way into someone else's life."

"Gordon got down on his knee and asked me to join *his* family. So here I am. If you're not happy with his decision, you can find another family to live with."

"Why?" Farren shouted. "Because mine all died off? Because you forced Gordon to purge the house of all traces of my mom? This was *her* house! My dad's house! *My* house! First Gordon came and that was all right because he made my mom happy. Then we lost her and suddenly you're here with your attitude and adjustments and all your talk about this imaginary business I'm pretty sure you perpetuate just to excuse your all-day boozing." Farren's eyes burned with tears.

"From what I heard, your parents both died by pretty preventable means," Melinda said in a perfectly calm voice. "You have to wonder what it was they were trying to get away from. Maybe life with you isn't as perfect as you'd like to believe."

Farren seethed. "Rot in hell."

A giant police officer, ranger hat still atop his head, stepped into the kitchen at that moment—Gordon in full uniform, bearing paper bags with *LUCKY CHINESE FOOD* stamped on their sides.

"Excuse me?" he said, pinning Farren to her seat with his best cop stare and setting the bags on the counter. "You'll apologize now."

Hot, angry tears spilled down Farren's face. "Didn't you hear what she said? About Mom? About Dad?"

"I heard what mattered," Gordon said.

Farren stumbled off her seat, knocking it to the floor. She snatched up her phone, still blaring tinny death metal, and accidentally knocked one of the bags of Chinese onto the floor. A carton broke open and fried rice exploded from it, covering the linoleum. Bonzo was there in a flash to gobble it up.

Melinda uttered a horrified gasp.

Farren yanked her equipment bag from the floor, slung it over her shoulder, and stormed out of the kitchen.

Gordon placed a hand on her arm as she passed. She stopped but ripped her arm away.

"I really need you two to get along," he said.

"Don't you miss my mom?"

He looked seriously wounded at that—a grizzly bear of a man stuffed into a brown and tan police uniform, looking like he'd just been stabbed in the heart. For a brief moment, Farren felt bad for him. Then he cast a glance over at Melinda and Farren could see her forbidding him from even acknowledging the question, which was just too much.

"Forget it," Farren said. "I just wish she was worth at least hanging onto a photo of."

"Farren."

"It's cool. I know it was her." She tossed her chin at Melinda. "My mom loved you, almost as much as she loved my dad. I hope she never knows how you just erased her from your life."

Deflated, Farren turned her back on them and headed for the door. She wanted to stomp and yell and throw things but the fight had gone out of her. Why bother trying to make Gordon understand how she felt? It was obvious where his allegiance was. Despite her anger toward him, she still harbored some love for Gordon in her heart. Which was why it hurt so much that he seemed to have completely moved on from her mother.

Farren could hear Melinda starting her case against her as she made her way to the door. She didn't bother calling out that she was going to practice. Let them figure it out.

5

J asper locked the door to the Bunkhouse, jiggled the knob to make sure it was secure, then sauntered down the short path leading away from it. He whistled while he walked, trying to match the tune of one of the many birds singing their bedtime songs to drown out the screams coming from within the building.

New recruits were expected to put up a fuss, but this guy was especially feisty. Even the knockout rag wasn't as effective against him as it had been against the others; it had taken twice as long for their newest recruit to fall unconscious and he'd begun to stir well before they'd returned with him.

Most recruits started to come around after one or two days. It was, Jasper assumed, a big part of why they were hand-picked. But this guy still hadn't calmed down in the slightest a full three days after they'd picked him up. He was safely locked up now, and far enough away that he would no longer be disturbing anyone with his noise. Still, it never sat well with Jasper when one of the recruits put up a good fight. This one was on track for a one-way trip to the Orchid Room, which Jasper did not look forward to.

Someone was waiting for him on the path ahead. Even if he didn't recognize her silhouette in the dusky gloom, made darker by the thick forest surrounding them, he'd have known it was Sasha. No one else in their motley tribe possessed the air of menace that surrounded her. He'd only known her for a few years and had met her less than six months before coming here, but he was very aware of how much she'd changed, especially over the last year. She'd always had a mean streak, but lately, her meanness had twisted and changed to something beyond cruelty. If he'd been raised to believe in evil, he would have used that word for her.

"What is it?" he called.

Silence.

Crap. That almost certainly meant she was in one of her moods, which didn't bode well for anyone. He wasn't in the frame of mind to deal with her after single-handedly escorting the new recruit to the Bunkhouse and making sure he was secured within. All Jasper wanted was to go home and pass out reading a book.

He drew near to Sasha and studied her face in the dying light, trying to gauge how she was feeling by her pout. Sasha scared him, but she had the most ridiculous habit of pooching out her bottom lip when she was unhappy, which was most of the time. The worse her mood was, the further out it protruded.

She was staring toward the bridge crossing Eagle Creek, profiled against the dusk sky. Her lip was sticking out from her face almost as far as her nose.

"*He* wants to see us," she said as he drew up close.

Jasper didn't have to ask who she meant. "Already? We literally just brought someone back. Don't tell me it was the wrong guy."

The thought that they'd somehow messed up made his balls shrivel up into his stomach. But there was no way; they were always careful and hadn't screwed up yet.

Instead of answering him, Sasha started off toward the little footbridge.

Jasper was frozen in place for a moment.

They'd always waited at least three weeks between recruits. That was one of the rules they'd established back when this whole business had first begun, before they'd even named this place and its myriad outbuildings.

He jogged to catch up. "You sure?" he asked when he was within earshot.

She stopped and spun around to face him. "You think I somehow got that wrong?"

Her eyes blazed and it took all of Jasper's willpower not to look away.

"I didn't say that. But you know how weird this is. It'll draw unnecessary attention if we recruit too many at once. "

She turned her back on him and continued across the footbridge, which was little more than two dozen worn planks nailed to some four-by-fours two feet above the bubbling brook one of them had dubbed Eagle Creek at some point in their relatively young history. The hard-packed dirt path at the other end of it forked in two directions and Sasha took the path bearing left, the one that led to the Museum.

Jasper hurried to catch up with her, avoiding looking at the building at the end of the path to the right. Both structures, and their inhabitants, creeped him out, but the Orchid Room felt like an entity unto itself and Jasper was sometimes certain it, or something within it, was returning his gaze.

As always, the moment he crossed the bridge, all sounds of life died out. Nothing lived over here. It was as if the gently burbling creek acted as a barrier that blocked out all sounds of life from the other side of the bridge. Of course, it had nothing to do with the creek itself and everything to do with the two buildings on this side of it.

He caught up to Sasha just as she reached out to grasp the handle of the Museum door, a ruse if there ever was one. Neither of them went into the Museum alone. As tough as Sasha wanted everyone in the tribe to think she was, both buildings on this side of the creek scared her as much as everyone else.

Jasper felt the urge to hold back, to see how far she would take the bluff. Would she open the door? But even as he had the thought, he knew he was bullshitting himself as much as she was. He was as terrified of her showing up in the Museum without him as she was of going in alone. The consequences were one thing, but if she was going in by herself, it could mean he was being cut out. And that scared him more than anything.

Sasha pulled the door open and stepped inside with the casual air of someone walking into a shopping mall. The familiar, musty aroma of the aging exhibits invaded Jasper's nostrils as he followed her in, allowing the door to swing shut behind him. Sasha was already halfway down the hall, still behaving like she didn't care whether he followed her or not. It would serve her right if he turned around and left.

All at once the urge to do so was almost overpowering. He really could just leave. It was the sanest thought he'd had in almost two years. He could run and leave all of this behind. Let Sasha deal with the twisted madness that dwelled within these walls. Let her hear that grating voice in her head. Let her drag back the next unwitting kid on her own. See how far that lip stuck out then.

He shoved the thoughts from his mind and strode past the shadows of the smaller exhibits dotting the foyer, slipping down the adjoining hall to catch up to her, ever the follower. He pulled up next to her and she shot him such an accusing look he was convinced she could hear every one of his thoughts, something he was coming to suspect more every day, absurd as it sounded. And if she'd heard his thoughts, there was no doubt *he* had heard as well.

That would not bode well for Jasper.

They came to a halt in front of a double set of steel doors with a sign over them that read *MAIN HALL*. Sasha placed a hand on the crash bar of the left door and raised her eyebrows at him in a question. He placed his hand on the right bar and nodded.

Together they pushed through their doors and into the cavernous dark beyond. As was custom, they paused just inside to allow their eyes to adjust to the gloom.

For Jasper, this was the worst part. He was certain he could make out shapes moving in the dark, some no larger than a squirrel, some impossibly huge. He'd never seen this room with any more illumination than what seeped in from the hallway, dimly lit by a single emergency light. The windows had already been blacked out when they'd come to this place. Even after their eyes adjusted, only the vaguest shapes of the shadows filling the large room could be distinguished. He thought it was better that way. There was a reason this room had been kept in the dark since who-knows-when.

He heard Sasha move ahead of him and hurried to keep up. Couldn't stand the thought of being in any part of this building by himself, certain if he was ever caught in here alone he would be whisked away by something nightmarish.

They knelt in the same place as always, a dozen or so feet from the vague, man-shaped form that presided in the center of the room. In the darkness, its form was hard to lock onto. It seemed to frequently change size and shape; at one moment humanoid and the next, something gigantic and insectile.

In the parts of his brain dedicated to logic and reason, Jasper knew it was the lack of light that made the figure's size and shape waver. But this was no place for logic or reason, that had been made clear from the start.

*She's ready*, the words came as something scratching at the inside of his skull, playing it like an instrument, hitting just the right places to articulate what it wanted him to understand. He'd never discussed this sensation with Sasha but expected it was much the same for her. She was never in a good mood after they'd spent any amount of time in here. Neither of them were.

"So soon?" Jasper asked, knowing Sasha would be furious over him daring to be the first to speak.

Something shifted to his right. Something big.

*You have something else to do?*

"No," he sputtered, "we just came back with a recruit is all. Just checking."

*The time is right, regardless of your compunctions or cowardice.*

"I'm not—"

An abrupt, searing pain erupted in his head like forks being shoved into the backs of his eyes.

He bit his cheeks to keep from shrieking, knowing it would invite further torment. The sensation disappeared as swiftly as it had arrived.

"Just show us who," Sasha said.

And *he* did.

6

Whether or not it was because of the extra practice earlier in the week, the Maggie's Knee Ultras swept the Pinedale Raccoons 7 - 0. Farren didn't score any runs herself, but she did have three RBIs, one of them a double in the fifth inning.

Sweating, slightly sore, and covered in dust kicked up from the diamond, Farren crept into her house, managing to escape Melinda's attention. Gordon's wife was sitting in front of the television, tapping away at her phone while a talk show played on the screen. Farren showered, dressed, strapped on her everyday prosthesis, and left the house again without a word. If Melinda noticed her presence at all, she gave no indication.

An hour later, Farren meandered down the sidewalk leading into "downtown" Maggie's Knee, which was no more than a mile-long stretch of Main Street populated by restaurants and boutique shops. Some of the storefronts maintained their original facades with faded signs and drooping awnings, but the majority of the businesses were fewer than ten years old, having moved in when word came that KnowMe would be building their new technological park in pretty little Maggie's Knee. Farren couldn't remember the town looking any different. They'd moved here with KnowMe, her dad having been promoted to systems and network architect. The town had been on the verge of financial collapse before KnowMe had decided on Maggie's Knee as their new base of operations. Apparently Jeremy Hrongar, the company's founder and CEO, had been smitten by the small town that was now one of the top day trip destinations in Pennsylvania.

All of a sudden someone was directly in front of her. Farren walked into them, stumbled, and would have fallen on her backside if the person hadn't grabbed her by the elbows. She looked up to apologize and was treated to a grin full of blackened teeth surrounded by lips of a violent shade of pink, themselves ensconced by lightly stubbled cheeks.

"Hey, you gorgeous Japanese goddess," the owner of those teeth, lips, and cheeks said.

Farren smirked. "Only half Japanese. How's it hanging, Stacey?"

She realized she was standing in front of the Maggie's Knee Mission, where no fewer than a dozen people, mostly men, smoked cigarettes and drank out of paper coffee cups.

Stacey still held her by the elbows and Farren gave him the briefest of hugs. If she had a real friend in this world, it was this man, who she now noticed was wearing a bright blue tutu over black and white striped leggings, a knit sweater that could have originally been brown or gray under its current layer of filth, and tattered Converse shoes. His long, blond hair was slicked back and partially hidden under a trucker cap with the words *LUV DIK* plastered across the front in a hot pink that almost matched his lipstick. For all his feminine wardrobe choices, Stacey staunchly identified as a man, and, as his hat advertised, he very much preferred the company of his own gender, at least as far as intimacy was concerned.

"You okay, girl? You look kinda like you belong here with the rest of us today." He released her elbows and swung an arm around her shoulders.

"I was thinking about my dad."

Stacey gave her a squeeze. "The sheriff still married to that hell-bitch?"

Farren laughed and said he was, not bothering to correct Stacey about Gordon being her *step*dad.

"That woman needs a lesson from Stacey in how to behave like a lady," Stacey said.

Farren said, "No offense, but I think she might set herself on fire before taking lessons from you."

"And that's exactly what's wrong with that bitch," Stacey huffed. "Wanna buy your friend Stacey some lunch?"

His brazenness and no-bullshit attitude were two of the things Farren adored about Stacey. He didn't hesitate to ask for what he wanted. If she said no, he took that as the final answer and wouldn't revisit the subject. And she'd had to say no on a number of occasions, either because she had no money, no time, or no interest in some of the more illicit things he'd asked of her. Once, last fall, Stacey had explained to her that he'd fallen out with his dealer and needed Farren to go pick up for him. She didn't know what it was he was trying to buy, but it wasn't pot. She'd adamantly refused and that had been the last time Stacey had asked anything like that of her.

Farren took Stacey across the road, where they grabbed a table on the patio of a diner called Bred n' Stu. She never understood the name but loved everything on their menu. Farren ordered a grilled cheese with extra fries while Stacey got a burger with broccoli soup on the side. The place bustled with Saturday diners and day drinkers, many of whom gave Stacey and Farren undisguised looks of distaste when they made their way to their seats.

"Got kicked out of my residence again," Stacey said between mouthfuls of his burger, which he dipped in his soup before each bite. He didn't quite close his mouth all the way and the food he chewed resembled diarrhea.

Farren focused her attention on the mound of fries on her plate. "What for this time?"

"Missed curfew." Dunk, chomp. "And I was wasted. And they found stuff on me."

Stuff probably meant meth. They had a deal that Farren would be there to talk about anything Stacey needed, but didn't want to hear the details of taking the drugs; it grossed her out and made her sad. She knew her friend's life expectancy was probably down to months and not years if he kept up his current habits.

"Where are you staying now?" she asked, trying not to watch as Stacey dunked his burger for another bite.

"Got a little place by the river."

"A tent?"

"Better. Donny Bombs helped me with some tarp and poles. Stacey got himself a nice little yurt on the waterfront."

"And what are you going to do when the weather turns?"

Stacey popped the last hunk of burger, dripping with green clots of broccoli soup, into his mouth. "I'll be back in res before then. Don't you worry."

Farren had no idea how Stacey wound up on the street or

what sort of life he'd led before then. It was a subject he vehemently refused to even come close to talking about. Anytime Farren expressed concern over his situation, he steered the conversation in another direction.

"What about you, honey?" Stacey asked.

"What about me?"

"What are you going to do? About Melinda?" Stacey put a cold, calloused hand over hers. "You can't hold all that pain in you. It's gotta come out somehow."

Farren twirled a fry around in a puddle of ketchup on her plate and shrugged. "For now, I'll just deal with her. I graduate this year."

She had no plans to attend college, had no idea what she'd study if she did. Gordon had been understanding about this, not wanting to force her into studying something she wasn't passionate about.

"Graduating don't mean you're free from all your woes. The opposite, actually."

"Maybe I can get a job working a night shift somewhere. Then she and I won't have to see each other. I'll save up and get an apartment or something. Maybe in Philly."

Stacey frowned at that but didn't push the matter any further.

When they'd finished lunch, Farren walked Stacey back across the road to the Mission. Even though he was banned from the residence, all his friends were there. For a relatively small town, Maggie's Knee had a thriving population of homeless.

As they came up onto the sidewalk from the street, Stacey bumped into a guy in his twenties wearing designer jeans and a shirt that hugged his considerable biceps.

"Watch it, faggot," the guy said without breaking stride.

"I'll be watching that sweet ass while you keep walking, honey," Stacey teased.

The guy, who had been continuing on his way, turned now and got in Stacey's face. Farren made a move to interfere but Stacey used a surprisingly strong arm to push her behind him.

"How about I knock your teeth out in front of all your friends?" the guy said.

"Mmm then I can take care of that stiffy you're packing in those tight pants of yours?" Stacey took a step toward the guy. "Don't think I didn't notice."

The guy's face shook and Farren was certain he would kill Stacey right then and there. Instead, he spat in Stacey's face and stormed off, dodging traffic to cut across the road.

"What a fucking asshole," Farren shouted, hoping he'd hear her.

Stacey wiped the spittle from his face. "It's all good. He'll be back to make up."

Farren burst out laughing. "You're insane."

"Just call 'em like I see 'em. You gonna be okay, honey?"

"Sure," Farren said, "just going to avoid home for the rest of the day. Maybe go for a hike."

Stacey's face, normally jovial, turned serious. He grabbed Farren by the arm and pulled her up the sidewalk, away from the crowd gathered at the Mission.

"Maybe best you stay out of the forest for now," he half whispered.

Maggie's Knee was bound on all sides by dense, hilly woodland; it had originally been a mining and forestry hub before morphing into the go-to tourist spot for people day-tripping from the city.

"Since when are you so opposed to a little fresh air?" Farren asked. "Didn't you just finish telling me you'll be tenting it by the river all summer?"

"It's a yurt and it's just up from Jessop's Bridge."

The covered bridge was one of the town's most photogenic spots and background to a billion social media posts. It crossed the fifty-foot width of Widow's River, nicknamed Old Maggie generations ago. The town's name was based on the jagged bend in the river that led into town—those who referred to the river as Old Maggie called that bend Maggie's Knee, or, after a few beers, the Bitch's Knee. Widow's River received its name based on that bend, which could prove deadly to anyone traveling the river without the knowledge or skill to navigate it, especially during the rainy season. Exact figures changed from storyteller to storyteller but it was said no fewer than one hundred souls had perished on that bend in the last couple of centuries. To Farren, it was a convoluted sort of history for the name of a small town.

"So, what's the story?" Farren prompted. "One of your friends flashing young girls out there?"

"You know all about them disappearances," Stacey said, his voice still low.

"The missing kids? Mayor Hatfield says they're all runaways."

"You believe that, do you?"

Farren admitted she did not.

Stacey pulled her further up the sidewalk. "You know Pietro?"

"Which one's he?"

"Dude always wearing the hat with the feather in it."

Farren scanned the crowd of homeless outside the

Mission. She spotted Pietro easily enough; he wore a gray stovepipe hat with a bright yellow feather sticking out of the band, as well as a matching gray dinner jacket over a soiled white T-shirt, and tan Bermuda shorts.

Stacey went on, "He's seen them."

"The missing kids? He should tell my ... the sheriff."

"Not the kids, the ones who took 'em."

"All the more reason to get Gordon involved."

Stacey shook his head. "Ain't no sheriff or anybody else gonna believe what Pietro has to say."

"But you do?" Farren was growing weary of this game.

Stacey shrugged noncommittally. "Says they were taken by shadow people. Kidnapped in the middle of the night."

"Shadow people? For real?"

Stacey raised his hands, palms out. "Just repeating what I heard."

Farren said, "Okay, well, it's broad daylight now. Should be safe."

"Just promise you'll stay out of the forest for a while. At least at night."

Farren took Stacey's face in her hands. "I promise I'll be careful."

They parted ways after a few more warnings from Stacey and a few more half-hearted promises from Farren to watch her back.

Farren was surprised by how concerned Stacey had been over what had to be some kind of hobo rumor. Stacey was normally pretty level-headed, even for someone who was deep into a chemical drug addiction. Maybe that sort of thing wore on you, though. The more she thought about it, the more concerned for her friend she became. She wished there was something she could do to help him, but knew by now that any decision to go clean had to come from Stacey himself.

Still, maybe she could do some research and talk him into at least considering trying to sober up.

She checked her phone—barely after lunchtime. Still most of a day to kill before heading home if she wanted to avoid Melinda. She decided she'd head to the baseball diamond in hopes there would be someone playing a game she could watch. Shoving her earbuds in and cranking the metal, she sauntered back up Main Street.

As she walked, she happened to glance down one of the few unkept alleyways in Maggie's Knee. It was nestled between Laundry King and the only empty storefront on the strip, a For Lease sign plastered in the soaped-over display window. The alley seemed to reject daylight, which was odd since the sun shone directly into it at this time of day.

Something in the shadows made her pause. At least, she thought she'd seen something. She backtracked a few steps and, similar to one of those holographic images, a word appeared, graffitied onto the brick wall in black spray paint.

*ZIIS.*

The S was painted with hard angles, as opposed to gentle curves, giving it the shape of an inverted Z. The idea was obviously so that the word would appear the same in a mirror, whatever the point of that was. She had no idea what it meant but it gave her an uneasy feeling, as if she had a legion of spiders crawling up her back.

As soon as that comparison popped into her head, she felt, for an instant, as if she could actually feel hundreds of arachnid legs scrabbling up and down the skin of her back. She shook her shirt and danced a little jig on the sidewalk, but the feeling left the instant she took her eyes off that strange word.

She glanced back into the alley but the graffiti was once again invisible. She took a step backward to see if it would reappear.

The blaring of a car horn followed immediately by the squeal of brakes shook her out of a fugue she didn't realize had come over her.

Though she could have sworn she'd never left the sidewalk, she now found herself standing on the road. She turned around to see an SUV idling inches from her. She'd almost been hit by it.

"You gonna move?" a woman in her forties shouted, sticking her head out the driver's window.

Farren stepped back onto the sidewalk without a word and the driver of the SUV gunned it, probably hoping it sounded more intimidating than its eco-friendly engine would allow. Farren watched it turn down Miller Road before continuing on her way. Maybe she'd head home after all. She could suddenly use a nap.

7

Gordon eased his cruiser, an aging Crown Victoria, to a stop along the curb in front of Town Hall, ignoring the *No Parking* sign posted directly in front of him. When he was not on the clock, he obeyed every street sign and traffic ordinance he came across; he was a firm believer in setting the example. When he was wearing the badge, though, he knew it was almost expected that he use his impunity to traffic laws to expedite matters of the office.

He checked his watch and saw he was fifteen minutes early for his meeting with Mayor Hatfield. Thursday's attempts at pinning Byron down at the country club had been less than fruitful. His Mayorship had been in the private lounge when Gordon showed up and, while his badge would get him through the doors of the exclusive Pine Sunset Golf & Country Club, his authority seemed to falter when it came to the inner cloisters of the wealthy and powerful. Namely the Cedar Room, the club within the club. He'd known better than to cause a scene, ever mindful of this year's looming election.

But he told the concierge to pass the message on to Mayor Hatfield that he could expect a visit the following day. The mayor's secretary had called Gordon's office later that afternoon and had set a lunch appointment for this afternoon instead, stating the mayor would be tied up on Friday. Which probably meant he planned on fishing all day.

Gordon slurped the last of the coffee from the ancient, plastic thermal mug he'd used every day on the job since graduating from the academy. The mug had been a gift from his girlfriend at the time. At one point in history, it had boasted a golden police shield with the clever title *Officer Sexy* stenciled within. The logo lasted much longer than the relationship. Now, after years of use, it was simply a polished, white travel mug. It did nothing to keep his coffee warm, but it carried a certain talismanic comfort for him; not that he held to such things. He set the mug back in its cup holder and promised to find a replacement, a vow he'd broken countless times over his twenty-five-year career in law enforcement.

The municipal building was a ghost town, as was to be expected on a Saturday. Gordon passed a janitor he didn't recognize swishing a mop around the tiled floors of the foyer and bobbing his head to whatever was playing through the giant headphones he wore. The main reception desk was unmanned but Gordon needed no one to point him in the right direction. Politics and bureaucracy were a necessary, if frustrating, part of his job, so he found himself in this building more often than he wished, though he limited his meetings with Byron as much as possible.

He often found himself turning down invitations to social mixers, tee times, and "private functions." Part of his refusal to accept these invites was because of the optics associated with joining the mayor in his frivolities. Mostly though, he didn't like Byron Hatfield. Obviously, the voters of Maggie's Knee didn't share his distaste for the man, so he kept his opinion to himself. Only Melinda and Farren knew his true feelings about their mayor.

His thoughts circled Farren as he shoved through the door that led to the stairwell. She'd never come right out and said it, but he knew she blamed him for her mother's death. Her moods were so volatile lately he was positive the accusation was imminent.

It was obvious part of her outbursts had to do with Melinda. He loved his wife, but not a day went by that he didn't regret how quickly he'd moved on to his second marriage. Farren had still been mourning the loss of her mother, which was understandable, especially given the nature of her death. He too missed her dearly, though he wasn't sure he could ever convince Farren of that.

Talking about Darya was strictly verboten in their household—Melinda was fiercely jealous of her. And Gordon understood why; his first wife had possessed a striking and undeniable beauty of both body and spirit. He used to keep pictures of her around the house but Melinda had put a swift stop to that, almost certainly one of the reasons Farren despised her the way she did. Gordon still kept a couple of photos around, without Melinda's knowledge. His favorite was tucked into the visor of his cruiser and featured Darya laying back in a beach chair, Piper Lake stretched out behind her, still and blue. In the photo, she wore a sheer, powder blue blouse over a black bikini, her perfectly sculpted, bronze legs stretched out in front of her in a way that still drove him crazy, something he felt strangely conflicted about. Her thick, black hair was undone and blew wildly in the breeze. Farren had possessed the same stunning hair until she'd decided to chop it all off, which had broken his heart. Not because his step-daughter looked bad with short hair—she was stunning no matter how she styled herself—but because it had reminded him so much of her mother.

Farren was in the photo as well, an out-of-focus pink blob floating close to the water's edge in a rubber dingy. They'd lost Darya about thirty yards out from that spot a couple of years after the picture was taken.

Gordon reached the top of the stairs and paused before the handle of the door leading to the fourth floor, taking a deep breath to compose himself and tuck the memories of his late wife away. Maybe he'd revisit them over a glass of bourbon later that evening.

The office was empty, with the exception of Nyla, Byron's secretary, who hunched over an iPhone at her desk. She didn't look up as Gordon moseyed past.

"Afternoon, Nyla," he said out of politeness.

"Go on in," she mumbled.

Melinda had shown Gordon the secretary's Instagram account a few months ago and, based on her online photos, he was confident she hadn't been hired for her administrative capabilities. He had to admit she was gorgeous, but her attitude and ineptitude turned him off completely. That and she had to be at least twenty years his, and Byron's, junior.

Gordon pushed the office door open to find Byron in a similar position to Nyla, slouched in his chair with his face in his phone. Did no one just look out the window anymore?

"Gordon, how the hell are ya? Sorry, I've got nothing to offer you. I'd asked Nyla to order us some lunch an hour ago but seems she forgot." Byron shot up from his desk and shook Gordon's hand.

He was a handsome man in his fifties, almost as tall as Gordon, who stood over six-and-a-half feet, and possessed all the charm of a snake oil salesman.

Gordon waved him off. "I had a late breakfast. Seems you could've told her to stay home if I'm your only meeting."

Byron fed him a shark's grin and said, "She's done her part today."

Gordon decided not to ask what that might mean.

"So," the mayor went on, "word has it you've been trying to pin me down. You know I'm off the clock when I'm at the club."

"Is the mayor ever really off the clock?"

Byron gave Gordon a look that said he should know better.

Gordon said, "Franklin Mews came to see me."

"Poor guy. Rose too. How they holding up?"

"How can they be? Their kid disappeared in the middle of the night and, by all appearances, nobody gives a shit."

Byron plopped into the plush chair behind his desk and gestured for Gordon to take the seat in front of it. Gordon made no move to comply.

"Is that what we're talking about today?"

"Eighteen kids now, Byron."

The mayor held up a finger. "Only eleven of those are actually from Maggie's Knee. Those other townships can deal with their own runaways."

"So we're still going to stick to that narrative?"

"You're damn right," Byron said. "I took an oath to look out for this beautiful little town's best interests, and I am. Even before I was in office, I played a significant role in bringing the

KnowMe offices out here, which, pardon my Français, was a fucking lifesaver for this town's economy.

"We brought in an expert in PR to drive the day-trippers and tourists and fucking influencers all the way out here and, Gordon, it's worked. The town hasn't thrived like it is now since back when the mines were open and before those tree-hugging snowflakes put a stop to our foresting industry. Now we've got a few kids who have decided to up and run off, no doubt to live a better life in the city, or to stick it to their parents, or because they're too woke for this place anymore. And I say God bless 'em and protect 'em. But let's not pretend there's some conspiracy going on out here.

"There's no dark cabal kidnapping our kids and eating them up in the mountains. No mutants sucking them into sewers. No Bigfoot taking them home to meet his family. Kids everywhere run away all the time. Maggie's Knee is no different. Now look, I'm starting to sweat, you've got me so damn worked up." Byron got up and paced the office, fanning his shirt against his chest as if the air conditioning didn't keep the room at a perfect sixty-eight degrees.

Gordon watched the mayor and took a few deep breaths, a self-calming trick he'd picked up from Farren.

After a minute of pacing, Byron flopped back into his chair, in a slouch akin to a petulant teenager more than mayor of a thriving town in the forests and hills of the Alleghenies. "Volunteers only. I don't want this to be a big budget item."

"Can I assume you'll be one of those volunteering?"

"Goddammit, Gordon. Can't you just take what's offered to you?"

Gordon leaned forward and placed his palms on the mayor's desk. "Byron, how do you think it'll look if we not only have to lead a search strictly with volunteers but then this town's beloved mayor also decides not to show up?"

"Fuck's sake, you know how to get to me," Byron said with a smirk. "I knew it was a mistake backing your nomination."

"We'll see you there then. Sunrise tomorrow. We'll gather at Morton's Trail." Gordon turned and sauntered to the door.

"You're a son of a bitch, sheriff."

"And you're one hell of a mayor, Byron. See you in the morning."

Gordon didn't bother bidding farewell to Nyla, who appeared to be taking a selfie when he came out of the office. He took the stairs back down to the lobby with a hint of a spring in his step.

He didn't need the mayor's permission to rally a volunteer squad to comb the forest surrounding Maggie's Knee, but having his endorsement, and presence, would go a long way toward motivating the rest of the town to show up. If Mayor Hatfield was going to be there, Gordon could count on at least a couple dozen people from the community coming out. And even though it was technically supposed to be a volunteer team, Gordon would have as many deputies as he could spare out stomping grass with the rest of the town. After all, he was up for re-election in the fall as well.

8

Farren woke with a shuddering start and only barely managed to prevent a cry from escaping her lips. She'd been having that same, terrifying dream again; the one in which she'd been fleeing from a screaming locomotive. Had her dad's voice been present in this one? Couldn't recall.

She'd come home from her lunch with Stacey and, still feeling a bit dazed from nearly being run over—not to mention the weirdness with that word she'd seen spray painted in the alley—had lain down for a nap. She hadn't been sure she'd be able to fall asleep but had apparently dozed for a couple of hours according to the time on her phone.

As she roused herself from the comfort of her bed, she heard raised voices coming from down the hall, probably the kitchen; Melinda and Gordon arguing. Again.

She fought the rising hope that he would finally kick her out; there was no way Gordon would ever be the one to end his marriage. He was whipped by the women in his life. When her mother had been around, Farren found it endearing. Now she was disgusted by it. She fully recognized this opinion was because of her dislike—okay, *hatred*—of Melinda, but she couldn't grant Gordon any quarter. He'd made his choice and it had clearly not been in favor of the family he'd committed to when he married her mom.

She pulled on her pants and attached her prosthesis, straining to hear what they were arguing about. No doubt it was over one of their two favorite topics: Melinda's work or Farren. And since Farren hadn't yet had the opportunity to do anything to upset Melinda today, she could only assume it was Melinda's so-called business that started the fight.

Gordon's wife described herself as an entrepreneur and business owner, and was seldom more specific than that. The only thing Farren had ever seen her do in this capacity was messing around with one of those do-it-yourself website platforms. In a rare moment of humility, Melinda had asked Farren to help her with it, claiming she was building a website for her business. When Farren inquired about the nature of the business, Melinda had grown cagey and before long they were arguing so viciously Gordon had to step between them to break up the fight.

From the sound of the argument going on now, it was about money. It couldn't be easy to be the sole provider for the family on a small-town sheriff's salary. Add to that Melinda's regular business meetings, which took place over brunch or cocktails at one of the trendy places on Main Street, and the stress was understandable. Even though they'd grown apart, Farren felt bad for Gordon. She knew she wasn't the easiest person to get along with and could only imagine how tough it must be to have to deal with her *and* Melinda.

She slipped out of her room and only had to take a couple of steps down the hall to make out what was being said.

"... don't get to ask for that," Gordon was saying.

"She's not even going to know it was missing," Melinda said. "It's a business loan. I'll pay it back with interest if you're going to be such a nazi about it."

"What you're asking is illegal. It's Farren's inheritance. Hers alone. I'm not allowed to touch it except for the small amount of maintenance it requires. Even then, Franklin Mews deals with all of that for me."

"Then tell Franklin it's a matter of maintenance. Or for school," Melinda was almost shrieking.

Farren had heard enough. She didn't care if they knew she'd been eavesdropping. She stormed into the kitchen.

"Who do you think you are?" she said to Melinda, glaring at her, pouring as much hate as she possessed into the look.

Melinda was standing in the middle of the kitchen, arms spread in exasperation. Gordon sat at the table, holding his head in his hands.

"Farren," he said with unmistakable regret.

"Of course you've been listening in," Melinda said to Farren. "Can't ever mind your own business."

"You're a witch," Farren said, keeping her voice level.

Gordon slammed his hand on the table. "That's enough! Farren, let us continue the discussion we were having in private."

"Fuck that," Farren said, ignoring Melinda's feigned gasp. "Why is this the first I've heard of any inheritance?"

Gordon rubbed his eyes with one large hand, running it back through his short sandy hair and bringing it to rest on the back of his neck. "I wasn't hiding it from you. It's yours when you're twenty-one, no question. I guess I didn't want you asking me to try to get it out earlier."

"But there was no problem telling *her* about it, right? It's okay for Melinda Watkins-Noble, entrepreneur of the fucking year, to hear all about my family's money but I can't even know it exists?" Farren felt tears burning in her eyes and hated herself for it.

But in that moment, she hated Gordon more.

"I'm his wife," Melinda said, raising her chin at Farren.

"You're a fucking leech!"

"Farren!" Gordon's face had gone as red as the lipstick Melinda wore.

Farren turned on him. "And whatever small amount of trust I had in you was obviously misplaced. I don't know what my mom ever saw in you."

Satisfied with the hurt in his face, she shoved out of the kitchen and back down the hall.

She didn't bother shutting the door when she got to her room. Instead, she shoved her phone, a sweater, and all the cash she had into her backpack, then headed for the back door.

Let her be added to one of the missing for a while.

Number nineteen.

9

Jasper leaned against the bridge abutment in the spot Sasha had chosen for them to hide while they waited for their next recruit to come along. He'd just spent the last fifteen minutes watching a group of kids—none of them older than twelve or thirteen—tossing rocks over the other side of the bridge into Widow's River. While he hadn't been concerned about the kids finding the pair of them hiding, he *was* worried about their parents showing up. Slim chance anyone around would recognize either of them but they couldn't take the risk; it would all be over if they were discovered.

He looked to his right to see Sasha staring at him with raised eyebrows, impatience wafting off her like a stench.

"They're gone," he said. "Took off toward town."

She didn't relax, never did, but her shoulders lowered by half an inch, which was enough to tell Jasper she was appeased, at least for the moment.

Sasha leaned her head back and closed her eyes, inches from where he sat. She almost looked pretty with her eyes closed and her mouth shut. He couldn't quite bring himself to be attracted to her anymore but often found himself admiring her, remembering how it used to be between them. Too much had happened now to go back to the way things were, but every now and then he would let his imagination wander.

He looked at his watch and groaned.

Without opening her eyes, Sasha said, "She'll be here."

"It's almost six. I don't want to miss supper again."

"Then go back."

That wasn't even an option. He'd sit out here with her until the sun rose the following morning if necessary. To go back without their recruit would be to sign their death warrants. For reasons he couldn't figure out, this time seemed especially important. Sasha acted as if she knew the significance of it but he saw through the performance; she was as clueless as he was. Nice to be on equal footing for once.

They'd never been asked to bring in a recruit less than three weeks after their last one, had always been cautioned against it. In fact, it was common for entire months to go by without them bringing someone in. The more frequently they drafted, the more attention people would start paying to the disappearances. It would only take a couple more kids to go missing for folks to go on high alert. For them to take two in less than a week seemed reckless. But he could never say that, he'd suffered enough just asking simple questions.

"Light me a smoke," Sasha's voice startled him from his thoughts.

She still sat against the abutment with her eyes closed,

only now her lips were slightly parted, waiting for him to place the filter of a lit cigarette between them. For a split second, he thought about shoving his dick in her mouth instead but swiftly decided against it. She was apt to bite it off.

He lit a smoke from his backpack and dutifully stuck it between her waiting lips. She accepted without a word of thanks and took a long, deep drag.

"I was expecting your cock," she said, exhaling a blue cloud, eyes still closed.

He had to force himself not to do anything more than snicker. What he wanted to do was grab her by the shoulders and demand to know if she was reading his mind. More and more she would voice exactly what was going through his head. Sometimes he was able to pass it off as the result of spending so much time together—this could be one of those occasions. Other times, though, she would echo his thoughts as if he'd just spoken them aloud. On some occasions, she'd even articulated what he was thinking better than he understood it himself. In those instances, he was certain it had to do with what dwelled in the Museum, the thing they'd been serving all this time. It had to be affecting them.

He watched her. Wondered what she might be thinking about. Was she as afraid of the thing in the Museum as he was? Did she have the same nightmares he did after meeting with it?

This recent meeting had been the most intense yet. The images of their targets weren't so much shown to him as they were crammed into his skull. It felt as if this new recruit's entire life had been concentrated into an instant and then mainlined into his gray matter. Already, most of the details Jasper had been shown were gone from his mind, similar to what happened with dreams, but he remembered feelings of loneliness, sadness, and anger. All things the shadowy presence in the Museum seemed to cherish. He wasn't sure why but Jasper feared this newest recruit. Her coming seemed to herald a change.

A pressure on his arm startled him out of his thoughts.

"Someone's coming," Sasha whispered, lips brushing against his ear, smokey breath filling his nostrils.

Jasper pushed himself into a crouch, groaning at the stiffness in his legs from sitting still so long. He peered over the barrier and spotted a shape coming toward them from the other end of the bridge, the evening sun bathing her in orange light. He dropped down and pulled his backpack close.

"It's her," he said.

"Finally." Sasha flicked her smoke into the river and watched for a second as the current took it downstream. "I'll get the sled."

Z

FARREN HELD a hand up to shield her eyes against the reddening light of the setting sun as she stepped onto the walkway of Jessop's Bridge. The river was quiet today, likely because of the unseasonably dry spring they'd been having so far. On days following a rain storm, the white noise of the river could get loud enough to drown out oncoming traffic, making it a dangerous place to walk inattentively. Today, only a gentle gurgling sound echoed off the gabled roof of the covered bridge, accompanied by the staccato of Farren's footsteps on the sidewalk spanning the north side.

She had the bridge to herself this evening, which she was glad for. On nicer days, especially in the summer months,

Jessop's Bridge attracted a lot of pedestrian traffic. Tourists from the city would come to take selfies on the south side with the picturesque rise of the Alleghenies in the background, the river winding up toward them, a cobalt serpent in a sea of deep green.

Mountains at her back, Farren swung up onto the old, wooden barrier of the bridge and sat with her legs dangling over the river. She slid her backpack off her shoulders, letting it drop onto the walkway behind her, and watched the lazy flow of the river, considering what to do next. She didn't have much of a plan when she slipped out the back door of her house, just needed to be as far away from Gordon and Melinda for as long as possible. At least for the night.

At first, she'd planned on paying Stacey a visit at his new yurt on the river but when she arrived at the place he'd told her about, there was little more than a hole-pocked tarp strung up across a couple of trees. No sign of Stacey, or anyone else, save for a filthy shopping bag filled with what might be garbage or someone's personal effects. She'd left immediately, worried that the place might belong to someone other than Stacey. The people who lived in tents by the river were typically less than welcoming to visitors, and for good reason; unwelcome guests tended to either be kids who wanted to trash the improvised homes, or deputies of the sheriff's office delivering one of countless unheeded eviction notices signed by her stepdad.

Gordon. Angry as Farren was at him for keeping the fact of her inheritance from her, never mind sharing that information with Melinda, she felt bad for what she'd said to him. She didn't hate him. He tried to do right by her and she'd deliberately been pushing him away, allowing Melinda to carve a chasm between them.

She wondered how much her parents had left her, whether it would be enough to take her far away from this hole of a town. The speculation was almost immediately overshadowed by guilt. How could she be looking forward to receiving money that came from the deaths of her parents? It made her sick to think about.

Maybe she would donate it all. What good would it really do her anyway? She had no plans after graduation. No aspirations. No future.

Sitting high above Widow's River, she felt a familiar loneliness settle over her, weighing her down. When the only person who cared about you was a forty-something junkie who lived in a lean-to by the river, it was hard not to feel forsaken.

She leaned forward until she felt the insistent pull of gravity coaxing her toward the river. A little over fifty feet below, Old Maggie flowed on, indifferent to whether or not she was part of its traffic. She could lean forward just a few more inches and bring a swift end to the anger and isolation she'd been feeling lately. It would be over instantly if she landed on her head. They'd find her mangled body weeks from now, miles downriver, and Gordon would know it was his and Melinda's fault.

In the darkest corner of her heart, the idea kindled, grew brighter, more appealing. She felt herself canting downward and, when she was on the precipice of being pulled all the way down, stiffened her muscles. She leaned out over the river, almost facing directly into it and, for the first time, gave actual consideration to ending her own life. It would be a quick resolution to her pain. No more worrying about her prosthesis, no more misery at home.

Her abs ached as she hung over the drop, arms shaking

from the exertion. She considered again the pain it would cause Gordon if she were to take her own life and found she regretted wanting to hurt him. He was far from perfect, and he'd never replace her own dad, but he'd also worked his ass off to make sure she was taken care of, even if he did betray her mother by marrying that bitch.

Funny enough, it was the thought of Melinda that made Farren decide perhaps suicide was not for her. Did she really want to give that woman the satisfaction? Melinda would think she'd won. Even if Farren ran away, which was what she'd been planning on doing, at least for a day or two, wouldn't that be giving in? This was her life and there was no way she'd allow someone like Melinda to get the upper hand over her. She would go home and face whatever consequences there were for her outburst. Let Melinda deal with *her* from now on. Then, when she turned twenty-one, she could take her inheritance and rub it in Melinda's face before leaving for good. She could stick it out another two years, especially with that to look forward to.

Feeling much better, she eased herself backward, stomach muscles screaming out for relief.

Strong, rough hands grabbed her suddenly from behind. An acrid reek burned through her nostrils, slicing its way into her brain. She struggled, but dizziness was already overtaking her. The world went dark. She fell into the blackness, helpless to stop herself.

*No!* she thought. *I changed my mind!*

Then she must have died.

Z

PIETRO LEANED HIS HEAD BACK, stuck his tongue out, and upended the empty Jim Beam bottle over his mouth. He closed his eyes while he waited, not able to bear watching the rim of the bottle to see if a droplet formed there; it was too much to hope for. He'd polished this bottle off himself just that afternoon.

A drop hit the tip of his tongue and lit his synapses on fire.

"Fuck yes," he moaned.

He slapped the bottom of the bottle, knowing he was pushing his luck. Two more drops splattered onto his tongue. His mouth filled with saliva, craving more, needing more.

He needed more.

Judging by the setting sun, it had been a few hours since his last real drink. Far too long for the sensibilities of Pietro Bernasconi. But it was Sunday and the odds of finding someone to buy him a bottle, or even a drink, at this hour were not in his favor. The few drops he had squeezed out of the bottle did nothing more than inflame a thirst that never fully went away.

He staggered out of his hut of sturdy tarp and took a leak into Old Maggie, fixing his stovepipe hat as he did so. He wished fervently that he hadn't woken up from his nap, that he'd slept through the night until morning when he could find some sympathetic soul to buy him a damn drink.

The setting sun lit flying insects on fire as they buzzed through the shafts of light streaming between the trees. Pietro watched them for a while with his penis hanging out of his pants, grateful for the distraction. Not much besides the drink made him very happy these days but even he had to admit creation was one beautiful mind-fuck of a work of art.

He was shaking off and zipping up when he spotted them.

*Shadow people.*

He'd never seen them in the light of day before but he was certain this was them. He recognized their gait and they pulled the same sled they had on the last two occasions he'd spotted them. Some poor soul was strapped into it again, already dead, he was sure. He'd seen them carry two other bodies into the woods on that sled over the last few months.

Now that he could see them in the light of day, he realized they were just kids. Miserable specimens by the looks of them. Pietro shook his head at the state of the youth of today. Soft, entitled, mewling babies, the lot of them.

A lean, long-haired guy who looked as though he'd been on the street almost as long as Pietro himself was pulling the sled, followed by a rail-thin young lady who sort of resembled a couple of coke whores he used to hang around back when he had a solid roof over his head.

Pietro recognized the girl on the sled. He didn't know her name but she was all chummy with that fairy, Stacey. At least he thought it was her. His mind could play some pretty nasty, pretty convincing tricks on him if he wasn't careful.

He took his hat off and held it to his chest, mourning the soul of the poor thing the shadow people carted off on their sled. What did they do with the carcasses? Eat them? He shuddered, pulled his hat back on, and staggered back to his tarpaulin house. The thought of going after them didn't so much as flit through his mind. They may look like kids during the day, but shadow people were still shadow people and not to be trifled with.

He spotted an empty Jim Beam bottle lying on top of his bedroll.

"Now who left you there?" he muttered at it.

He sat cross-legged on the bed, unscrewed the cap of the bottle, and held it upside down over his mouth. It was too much to hope for, he knew. He was pretty sure he'd polished off the bottle himself that afternoon. He held his tongue out and waited.

10

Farren watched the canopy of the forest drift by overhead as she slid along the earth, apparently carried on some kind of travois. The sun had gone down almost entirely and the sky above the trees and beyond was a striking shade of deep blue, more typical of the sea. Her head ached and every little bump sent jolts of fresh pain from the back of her skull to her eyeballs.

She'd come to only moments ago, at first worried she was drifting along Widow's River. She tried to sit up. Couldn't. Something held her in place. She could hardly even lift her shoulders.

Gritting her teeth against the pain in her head, she lifted it as much as she could bear. Someone was walking ahead of her. Pulling her. In the dying light, she could barely make out a rope, stretched taught, that went out from in front of her feet, over the shoulder of the person ahead. He—at least she thought it was a guy—hunched forward against the strain of pulling. Where was he taking her?

Farren remembered the bridge then. She'd been leaning out over the river.

And she'd fallen. She could remember the sensation, but not the actual experience. Must have cracked her head pretty good when she'd landed, which explained the headache. And why this person was pulling her. He was a paramedic and she was strapped to a gurney. She must have been carried pretty far downriver; looked like they were deep in the woods.

How long had she been in the water? Based on where the sun appeared to be, dipping below the horizon, it had to be around seven-thirty, which meant she'd been in the river for at least an hour. It could have taken her pretty far in that time. Incredible she hadn't drowned. Even more so that she'd been found. Her body felt dry, certainly not as if she'd been tumbling down the river for over an hour. The paramedic would have stripped off her wet clothes, she supposed.

But something felt off. Maybe it was the bump she'd taken on the head.

She opened her mouth to ask her rescuer how long she'd been out and where he'd found her, but her throat was so dry she couldn't utter more than a faint squeak.

"She's up," a female voice said from behind her.

The gurney came to an abrupt halt. She heard the male paramedic's footsteps coming toward her.

"Want me to dose her again?" he asked.

What did he mean by that? Had they needed to sedate her?

"Don't bother. We're almost home."

"We should probably give her some water."

Footsteps coming closer. A figure hunched over her, face hidden in shadow. It stuck something hard against her lips.

"You've gotta suck," the guy said. "It's got a straw."

Farren put her lips against the nozzle of the water bottle and drank, feeling her throat open up to it. She drank until he pulled the bottle away, spilling water on her throat, the cool drops raising goosebumps on her skin.

"Who are you?" she croaked. "What happened?"

The guy walked back to the end of the rope and resumed pulling without another word. Now that she knew the girl was there, Farren could make out the second set of footsteps behind her. She wanted to believe these people had saved her, but what the girl said about being almost home had her worried, especially since they seemed to be headed deeper into the woods.

"Where are you taking me?" Farren demanded, arching her head back to try to see the girl. All she could see were more treetops, and only barely now that the sun had almost completely set.

Her questions went unanswered. All she heard were the footsteps of what she had thought of as her rescuers—who, she was terrified to admit, may actually be her captors—and the scrape of whatever she rode upon as it slid along the soft forest floor.

She tried not to let herself worry. These people might have been part of a recovery effort. Gordon would organize a search party for her if he noticed she'd gone missing. Which meant she must have been out for much longer than just an hour. Maybe she'd been wrong about the time—as many as twenty-four hours might have passed for all she knew. These two had to be search volunteers.

She coughed and a chemical taste filled her mouth, as if she'd swallowed paint thinner.

The memory of the hands grabbing her came back in a flash. That horrible stench in her face.

No. That had to be something she'd dreamt after hitting her head. People didn't get grabbed from behind and knocked out like that in real life. These two were here to help her.

Then why hadn't they answered any of her questions?

And what did the guy mean when he'd asked if he should dose her again?

This was no rescue effort.

Farren sucked in a breath as deep as her restraints would allow then braced against the straps with all her might, rocking herself from side to side as she did so. She couldn't tell exactly how many straps held her in place but she could feel them biting into her shoulders, chest, hips, and legs. Her hands were bound to her legs and were no help at all.

The guy stopped pulling and turned to watch Farren struggle.

Something cracked underneath her and she thought she'd felt a fraction of an inch give in her restraints.

A sudden, hard weight fell upon her and ripped the wind from her lungs. One of her escorts had a foot planted on her chest. She fought harder, hoping to hear that cracking sound again, wishing she had her hands free so she could twist this person's ankle until bones snapped.

"She's strong," the girl said from directly above her. She pulled her foot from Farren's chest and knelt next to her, watching.

Farren could already feel the strength leaving her body. Her head throbbed and now the rest of her ached from the pointless struggle.

"We done?" the girl asked.

Farren stared straight up into the growing dark. If they wouldn't answer her questions, she sure as hell wouldn't answer theirs.

There was a click and then a beam of light shone on them both. It barely lit up the girl's features, made her look horrible and terrifying. She had hard, sharp features curtained by straight lengths of blonde hair that hung over her face.

"You mind not killing my night vision, Jasper?" the girl barked.

The light moved away from them immediately, once more steeping them in darkness.

After a long silence, the girl stood and said, "Let's go. She fights again and I'll break her nose."

The gurney resumed its motion, scraping against the forest floor.

Farren fought the nagging voice in her head that whispered what she knew in her heart: *Shadow people. These are the shadow people Stacey told you about. You're as good as dead.*

Farren closed her eyes to prevent herself from crying.

z

SOMETIME LATER, maybe half an hour, maybe twice that, Farren heard voices. New ones.

Neither of her captors had spoken since her outburst, which was unsettling. At least when they were talking to her, she could get some sense of their mood or intention. The silent marching was ominous, spooky. It took every ounce of her willpower not to ask them questions, to try to get them to tell her what their plans for her were.

She'd fallen into a sort of trance as the one called Jasper pulled her across the rough terrain of the woods. Not quite at peace but she had discovered a sense of calm acceptance. Forcing herself to relax, the restraints felt just a little bit looser. Not loose enough to slip them, but enough that they were no longer cutting into her.

The voices shattered her tranquility the instant she heard them. They came from far off; sounds that belonged to a schoolyard, which was ridiculous given how late it was and that they were somewhere in the depths of an enormous forest.

It sounded like a bunch of kids.

She cracked her eyelids, not wanting to let her captors see her looking.

The beam of a flashlight bobbed over the ground foliage next to her head. Further up, she could see Jasper's light shining in a straight, steady beam in front of him. Not too far ahead, appearing through the breaks in the trees, were more lights, big ones. They were approaching some kind of structure. The voices grew louder as they approached and, in spite of the dark, Farren had a hard time believing they weren't coming up on an elementary school at recess.

There was an orderly, almost regimented sound to the voices, which was all that dispelled the illusion they belonged to children at play. In fact, the more she listened, the more it sounded like a work camp than a playground.

"Sounds like we missed supper," Jasper muttered from up ahead.

"Kip will make you a sandwich," the girl said. "Let's unload before the bend and avoid making a scene coming in." She knelt next to the gurney and shone her flashlight up at her own face. Dark, almost black eyes peered down at Farren. "I'm Sasha. This is Jasper."

Sasha flashed her light on the guy. They were both young. Jasper barely looked older than Farren herself. He was tall and lean with dark, longish, shaggy hair held back by the headlamp he wore. He might be sort of handsome in a rugged way if it weren't for his apparent proclivity for abduction. He offered a lame wave that was cut short by Sasha bringing the light back to her own face.

"We're going to unstrap you," she said. "I'm not supposed to hurt you if I can help it, so don't try to run. Cool?"

She pointed the light into Farren's face, blinding her. Waiting for an answer.

Farren nodded slowly, though she had every intention of running as soon as she was free. She could take this girl, she was sure, probably him too. Her best bet, though, was to run. She didn't have a doubt in her mind she could outpace them both. The guy was wearing combat boots for one thing, terrible to run in. The girl, Sasha, was obviously in charge but didn't appear to have much going for her in the way of physical strength. She was skin and bones under her black denim jacket and skin-tight jeans. And Farren smelled cigarette smoke on her breath, which meant her cardiovascular system was probably shit. Good.

"Um, Sash?" Jasper said from the end of the gurney.

By way of response, Sasha shone her light in his face.

He was looking down, shining his own light on Farren's feet. "Come look at this."

Sasha stormed over to where he stood. "What is so—oh shit."

"Do you think *he* knows?" Jasper whispered, nowhere near quiet enough for Farren not to hear.

"Let's just get the straps off." Sasha stomped her way back to Farren and knelt over her once more. Loosened the straps around Farren's shoulders, then moved down to those across her chest. "How do you get around with that?"

At first, Farren had no idea what the girl was talking about. "With what?"

Sasha raised her eyebrows in what looked like cruel amusement.

Farren might have slapped herself on the forehead if she had a free hand. They were talking about her prosthesis. It surprised her Jasper had noticed in the dark; many people were surprised when they found out her left foot wasn't made of flesh and bone, unless she was playing sports or running and had the blade on. Outside of her athletic life, Farren almost exclusively wore her prosthetic foot, which appeared lifelike and was practically indiscernible from a real one when she had her socks and shoes on.

"My prosthesis?" Farren said.

Sasha barked out a laugh that made her sound as if she was gagging. "The fucking stump where your foot should be."

Farren pushed herself up with stiff arms and followed Jasper's headlamp beam, which illuminated the ankle of her left leg, where it ended. Her jeans were flopped over the stump and covered in mud, apparently having been dragged along the ground for the duration of their journey.

"Jasper, did you lose her foot?" Sasha laughed.

Farren couldn't take her eyes off her left ankle. She might still be able to take the girl on, but fighting both of them wouldn't be possible. Running had been taken off the table.

"I swear, I had no idea it was missing until just now," Jasper said, the beam of his headlamp darting back and forth as he looked between the two girls.

Farren barely heard him. Had her prosthesis fallen off on the bridge? While she was being dragged? What were the odds of finding it again, even if she did manage to get free of whatever was happening to her? For the first time since waking up in the gurney, fear completely overtook her, paralyzing her limbs, muting her voice, dulling her mind.

They got her unstrapped and hoisted her to her feet. Her foot.

She saw the gurney they'd been conveying her on was actually a long, flat, heavy-duty plastic sled.

Jasper put an arm around Farren to support her for the rest of their walk. She tried to shove him off but almost fell over in the process, and relented when Sasha offered to strap her back into the sled.

"And if I have to do that, you'll spend the night in it," Sasha threatened.

Without having any idea what to do to help her situation, Farren allowed Jasper to take some of her weight and hobbled alongside him down the remainder of the path. Her body was still weak from whatever they'd knocked her out with and she had to lean on him much more than she wanted to. Still, she felt that between her captors, he was the lesser of the two evils.

The trail they followed wound through dense trees and brush. As they followed it, the voices of young people grew louder. Light accompanied the noise and by the time they'd rounded a sharp bend, the path was lit up as bright as day by lamps that hung from branches of trees crowding around them.

Eventually, the path opened up again into a small clearing, at the end of which stood an enormous wall constructed of upright logs with a door cut into it. The voices and sounds of activity came from the other side. Bright lights shone down on them from above the door, accompanied by two security cameras, each with a little red light blipping under its lens.

"Where are we?" Farren asked Jasper.

Sasha shoved past them and rapped on the door. "Home."

There was a delay after her knock and Farren got the feeling they were being scrutinized by whoever was on the other end of the cameras. Less than a minute later, the door swung open, held by a kid who looked no more than thirteen or fourteen. He took Farren in with wide eyes, registered that she was leaning on Jasper, and looked down at her truncated leg.

"How'd dinner go?" Sasha asked him.

The kid pulled his gaze up. "Fine. Is she hurt? I can go get Ramses."

"She's just handicapped," Sasha said.

The kid's face went red and he stepped back, holding the door open.

Farren barely heard the exchange. Her attention was caught by what was beyond the opening in the enormous wall. She allowed herself to be led through the door, which closed behind them with a heavy *thunk*.

Her mental image of a work camp was immediately dispelled. Cabins and cottages dotted what she could see of the far interior. Closer to her, several larger buildings lined the dirt path leading into whatever this place was.

The building closest to them, on their left, was the biggest of these. It took Farren several long seconds to notice the words written on the big display window of this one. Once she did, a veil fell from her eyes.

Gigantic, ancient oaks and maples grew all over the grounds. Outbuildings of varying shapes and sizes stood among the cottages and cabins. On their right, five or six buildings lined the path like a small strip mall. Kids were everywhere and would have made the place look like a summer camp if it weren't for the fact they were all hard at work.

A heavyset teenage boy ran past with a tub full of dishes, a young girl who looked to be about twelve carried an armful of firewood out of a shed. Many more bustled from place to place like worker bees.

"What is this?" Farren asked again.

Sasha said, "Take her to the Sapling Hut. I'll get Kip to make us some leftovers." She marched off toward the strip of buildings to the right.

Farren pulled her arm from Jasper, stumbled back from him, and almost fell on her ass. He made a halfhearted move to grab her but stopped when he realized she wasn't going anywhere quickly.

"Will you please tell me where we are?" Farren pleaded with him. She pointed up at the big building, the words written across its large window. "What does that mean? How can this place be here? Why does it feel like a summer camp? Why did you abduct me?"

She needed an answer, some kind of touchstone in this strange place.

"Later," Jasper said, not unkindly. "For now, I'm going to show you where you'll be staying for tonight. We'll bring you some food too. I know this is scary but pretty soon you'll see it's actually really cool here. Everyone here was once in your position."

"I'm not going anywhere with you," Farren said.

"There's not much choice," he said. "You can come with me on your own, I'll even get you some crutches if you want, or we can put you back in the sled. But like Sasha said, you'll spend the night tied to it. I don't want that for you."

His eyes told Farren he was telling the truth. He might be a good liar but she had the feeling he was being honest, that he really didn't want to hurt her.

Instead of answering, she lowered her eyes in defeat.

Jasper grabbed the shoulder of a kid walking by, a tall boy who might have been fifteen or sixteen.

"Go ask Ramses if he still has a set of crutches and bring them here," Jasper said to him. "Fast."

The kid ran off and entered the building at the end of the short strip, disappearing through the door. In about a minute, he came sprinting out with a set of metal crutches in his hands. He passed them to Jasper, gave Farren a smile and a wave, and took off again.

Jasper offered the crutches to her, eyebrows raised. She reached for them and he pulled them back, just out of her reach.

"You're locked in," he said, looking her in the eyes. "If you run, you'll waste a lot of energy and it won't end nicely. You'll spend the night in the sled, probably with some kind of injury to keep you awake, and without anything to eat. Nobody here wants to hurt you, but if it comes down to that or letting you run off, we'll do what's necessary."

Once more, she got the feeling he was telling the truth. She would go along to get along for now and, hopefully, lull them into thinking she was going to be easy to contain.

She reached a hand out for the crutches once more. He let her grab them but held them firm.

"You understand, right?" he said.

Farren nodded and he relinquished them. They were almost a perfect fit for her, but she held them slightly askew, not wanting Jasper to see how agile she could be. The idea was to convince him she was all but useless on crutches. Gordon had once told her, anecdotally more than anything, that if she was ever kidnapped she should play stupid and helpless so her captors would let their guard down.

Jasper gave her a smile. "Cool. Let's show you where you'll be staying for the night."

Z

JASPER STOOD LISTENING outside the Sapling Hut, a tiny cabin they had set aside for new recruits' first night. Not every newbie gave them a hard time but it helped to give them at least one night on their own to become acquainted with their new surroundings, their new home. Once they were no longer a flight risk, which tended to happen a lot faster than he would have bet before getting involved with whatever this had grown into, they were moved to one of the residential cabins, of which there was no shortage. Four still stood completely empty and one was used for storage. Only a handful of cabins had more than two people staying in them, and each housed six comfortably. To even call some of them cabins was dramatically downplaying their size.

The new girl wasn't making a sound, wasn't even moving

in there as far as he could tell. Not that there was a lot of space to move around in the Sapling Hut, but most recruits at least tried the doorknob after a few seconds. She probably heard him lock it.

He held his breath, pressing his ear tighter to the wooden door. It was a small shack, just big enough for one person to stretch out on the brand-new sleeping bag laid out by whoever had been on cleaning duty that day. At one point in this place's history, the hut had been used for wood storage. When they first arrived, it had been stacked to the roof with ancient hardwood, split into almost uniform logs. He and Sasha burned it all on the second night they spent here. Built it into an enormous pyre in the stone circle that served as a fire pit. The wood was so old and dry, it had caught fire in an instant and only took a few hours to burn through. The coals stayed hot for days, though.

It was incredible—and terrifying—how far they had come since first settling here, a little over two years ago. Back then he'd been doing little more than chasing tail, falling in what he thought was love, then finding himself ensnared in something far bigger than he ever imagined being a part of.

A sob, barely audible, came from behind the closed door. Good sign. Crying was much better than screaming or trying to bust the door down. Satisfied she wouldn't be trying to break out, Jasper trudged back up the path toward the dining hall, where Sasha was waiting for him.

Pushing through the door of the building where they all gathered to eat at least twice a day, he almost collided with Kip, who appeared to be in a hurry to get out of there. No need to ask why.

Jasper liked Kip. The friendly, husky seventeen-year-old

had seemingly been born for the role of chef in this place. He'd been one of the first kids they'd recruited, two summers ago. And had been one of the most difficult to break. Kip had sobbed and blubbered for days on end, utterly inconsolable. They hadn't been using the Orchid Room then, hadn't even known about it yet—that nightmare would come the following winter—or the poor bastard would probably have been tossed in there, never to be heard from again. The only times Kip had taken a break from crying were when Jasper brought him his meals, which led to the epiphany some culinary responsibility might soothe him. This in turn had led to the early revelation that recruits were easier to break—Sasha's term—if they were given a role as soon after arriving as possible. It was a game-changing discovery.

"She in a mood?" Jasper asked in a low voice as Kip squeezed past him.

Kip shrugged, ever the diplomat. "She's got a lot on her mind."

"We all do."

"The new girl ..." Kip trailed off.

"What about her?"

The young chef's face reddened. "She's pretty. I don't think Sasha likes her."

"Because she's good-looking?" Jasper smirked.

Kip only stared at him. That was exactly why Sasha didn't like her. One reason, anyway.

"I know I shouldn't ask," Kip said, "but why so soon? After that last guy, I mean?"

His apprehension was understandable, it was a dangerous question to ask. Much safer to ask Jasper than Sasha, though. In theory, they shared equal authority, but everyone knew who was really in charge, and she had very little tolerance for questions.

"We follow orders, you know that."

"But she's different."

Not a question. Kip looked him in the eyes—not typical behavior from the kid. He wasn't nervous about asking a question, he was downright scared of something.

"What is it?" Jasper had much more patience than Sasha but it was starting to wear thin.

Kip averted his eyes again, straightened his shoulders. "Nothing. Just tired. Night."

Jasper watched him shuffle out into the night and off in the direction of his cabin.

Now that was a weird exchange. Ever since Kip had accepted his role here, he'd been one of the steadiest guys they had. Never questioned orders, rarely complained, and always worked hard. Sure it was strange to bring a new recruit in so soon, Jasper could admit as much, but it was certainly not cause for the kind of concern Kip displayed.

Jasper found Sasha sitting at the same table she always sat at, in the far corner of the room, staring at him over steepled hands.

"What did Kip want?" she asked as he took a seat across from her.

"Usual excitement over a new girl."

Sasha narrowed her eyes. "Does he like her?"

"How should I know? Ask him."

"I don't think he likes me much."

Jasper let the statement hang.

"I need you to take care of the new kid," she said, a distant look in her eyes, voice taking on a dreamy tone.

"I just left her. She's fine."

"Not her. The one we brought before her. Garrett."

Shit.

"You don't want to give him another couple of days? It hasn't even been a week."

Sasha shook the table, startling him. Mustering all of her ugliness, she stared poison-tipped arrows at him. He'd grown used to these looks and was much less frightened by them than he used to be, but he recoiled nevertheless. She'd only grow angrier if he didn't act intimidated by her, which he was.

"He isn't needed," she said, voice even.

"We could bring him back," Jasper ventured, knowing what the response would. Needing to try anyway. "He was out the whole way here, has no idea where we are. I can knock him out again and take him back tonight."

"That's a stupid thing to say, Jasper. You really think he isn't going to talk about what he went through?"

"Nobody would believe him."

"If they did? What if they decided to come looking for this place?"

"I thought we were protected. Kept hidden."

The slap came out of nowhere, right across the mouth. She packed a mean wallop, especially for a skinny bitch. Stars danced in his vision. For a rage-filled second, he was certain he wouldn't be able to stop himself from hitting her back. And if he started, he wasn't sure he'd be able to stop.

She shoved a finger at his face. "You can doubt me all you want. It is never permitted to doubt *him*."

"Okay. Sorry," he said, chastened and hating himself for it.

She was right. It would be stupid to send the kid back home after bringing him here. The alternative would give

Jasper nightmares for a week, as it did every other time he had to do it. They had rules though, orders to keep things running smoothly and to keep *him* satisfied.

"Before dawn tomorrow," she said, pinning him to his seat with her eyes. "Right now I need you to join me in my cabin. I have an itch."

Without waiting for a response from him, Sasha shoved back from the table and sashayed out of the cafeteria in what he was sure she thought of as an enticing strut. Jasper looked away, thinking of what had to come the following morning. It made him sick to his stomach.

He lifted himself from his seat and followed her out the door.

11

In the twilight hours of the following morning, Sheriff Gordon Noble pulled his Crown Vic into the tree-lined public parking lot at the head of Morton's Trail and parked next to the only other vehicle, a cherry red SUV. His wheels barely stopped turning when the door to the SUV popped open and Barb rolled herself out, balancing a tray full of steaming coffee cups in one gyroscopically sound hand the way only experienced assistants and restaurant servers could achieve. She bumped the door shut with her ample posterior and waddled around to Gordon's door, liberating one of the coffee cups as she went. For all the frustration he often directed toward her, Barb was one of the sweetest, most nurturing people he knew. Her birthday was coming up, he'd have to remember to get her something extra nice.

"Morning, sheriff," she said, passing a coffee through his open window, little clouds of her breath visible in the predawn chill.

"Might as well get in," he said, accepting the piping hot

coffee. "It's damn cold out and it'll be a while before anyone except maybe Franklin and Rose show up."

She shuffled back around the car and eased herself into the passenger seat, resting the coffee tray on her stomach.

Gordon nodded at the drinks. "Who're the rest of those for?"

She gave him a sly smile. "I got us each two, figured we could use it. Was that selfish? I should run back and get something for the Mewses at least."

"Next you'll be getting donuts for the whole party."

"Should I—?"

Gordon cut her off by making a T with his hands. "Slippery slope, Barb. Do we know how many are showing up?"

She sighed, shifted in her seat. "Twelve said they'd be here for sure, thirty-eight were a maybe, a little over a hundred gave some form of a heck no."

"You called a hundred and fifty people?" He was impressed but not at all surprised.

"Two fifty if you count the folks who didn't pick up or call back."

"I need to clone you," he said. "Anyone from our office?"

Barb was just opening her mouth to answer when headlights washed over the cruiser, reflecting in the rearview mirror, and blinding Gordon. A silver Acura pulled in several spots over.

"That'll be Franklin and Rose." He popped his door open and hauled himself out to greet them.

A second set of lights washed over him seconds before a cube van pulled in and parked next to Franklin's Acura. *KPLT ACTION NEWS* was plastered in screaming letters across the broad side of the van, the news station's logo shining in the background. A fit-looking, thirty-something-year-old guy hopped out of the driver's seat and gave Gordon a wave. He strode around to the rear doors, popped them open, and set about assembling camera equipment and strapping expensive-looking devices to himself.

An attractive Black woman, who was either in her mid-twenties or rocking her thirties, stepped around the side of the van, and immediately locked in on Gordon. She wore tight jeans with a navy blazer over a white blouse and stood with an authority that had probably done as well for her career as her good looks. The cameraman passed her something with a wire coming out of it. Still watching Gordon, she reached behind herself, fastened the thing to the back of her pants, expertly fed the wire through her blazer, and jammed the end of it into her ear.

"Sheriff Noble?" she called.

Gordon didn't like this at all. KPLT was by no means a national news giant, but they had significantly more viewers than the local Maggie's Knee station. It took him a moment but now he recognized the reporter who was still waiting for a response from him, though he couldn't remember her name. He turned back to the cruiser and signaled for Barb to roll down the window, which she did.

"Call Byron and tell him to get his ass down here. I'm not covering for him on TV," he called to her.

Barb gave a thumbs up and had her phone in her hands a second later.

Gordon turned his attention back to the reporter and wasn't surprised to see she was striding toward him, brandishing a handheld microphone. The cameraman had worked swiftly and was following behind with a sleek-looking camera attached to a harness he wore over his shoulders. The cameraman flicked a switch on the camera and Gordon was bathed in soft, white light.

"Sheriff Noble?" the reporter asked again.

He said, "Don't suppose you're here to help with the search?"

"Actually, we are," she said with an obnoxiously triumphant smile. "We'll be filming the whole thing."

"I didn't get your name," he said, hoping to dent her pride on camera.

The reporter was unfazed.

"Mara Garrow, lead correspondent for KPLT Action News," she stated in a strong, silky-smooth voice. "You're leading the search today, is that right?"

"Correct."

She stuck the microphone out at him. He recoiled but she didn't miss a beat, following him with it as if she had expected the move. She was probably used to evasive maneuvers in her line of work.

"Can I ask why you arrived in uniform?" She jabbed the mic closer to his mouth.

He knew exactly where this was going. Franklin Mews must have called the news to get back at him for not mustering more of his forces to look for Garrett.

"This is a volunteer search, is it not?" Mara pressed.

Gordon sighed, loathing himself for showing exasperation so soon. "The Maggie's Knee Sheriff's Department wants to find Garrett Mews, and all the other missing kids from Maggie's Knee and surrounding townships. We're dedicating every resource we've been allowed to the search efforts today."

"So, your secretary is on the clock right now? Does she

work every Sunday?"

"She's volunteering her time this morning."

"How many deputies will be joining the search?" The reporter didn't seem to be able to keep a predatory smirk from her face.

Gordon had to fight to keep his anger in check. She'd done her homework and had likely spoken to someone in the department. That would need to be looked into. He made himself count to five.

Mara waited.

"We've dedicated all resources granted to the department," he said. "Mayor Hatfield will be here shortly, at which point you're welcome to ask him any questions you have about budgetary items like law enforcement staffing."

He turned his back on her before she could ask another question and forced himself not to look back until he reached the cruiser. When he opened the driver's door, he looked over his shoulder. Mara and her cameraman were back at the van, putting their heads together about something. With any luck he'd successfully passed them off to Byron. He didn't like that they would be joining the search for Garrett, but couldn't refuse the extra help.

He looked at Barb in the passenger seat, questioning her with his eyes.

"Mayor Hatfield is scheduled to arrive by nine," she said in a small voice.

"That's almost three hours after sun up," Gordon said through clenched teeth.

Barb made a tiny noise, no doubt worried he'd take his frustration out on her.

Gordon turned away from her. Barb shouldn't have to

suffer his anger. She was a volunteer too, after all.

Across the parking lot, Mara stared at him with a knowing smile.

Z

JASPER CRUSHED his cigarette out in the enormous glass ashtray on the antique bedside table, thinking about Garrett Mews. He shifted under the heavy, goose-down comforter and adjusted the pillow beneath his head. Sasha snored lightly next to him on the California king mattress, a full three feet away, blankets pulled almost entirely over her head.

He turned away from her. The sky through the window was still fairly dark but he knew it must be close to six by now, if not a little after. He hadn't been able to sleep at all that night. After fifteen minutes or so of rough, passionless sex, Sasha had smoked a joint with him and passed out. He'd tossed and turned for a while but eventually gave up and smoked one cigarette after another for the rest of the night, trying not to think of the task before him, and failing miserably.

He slid from under the covers, out of bed, and picked his way through the large, unlit room, hunting for his clothes. Sasha had the largest and nicest living space of them all, an arrangement that would never be contested. She had claimed the VIP villa, once referred to as the Silver Birch Lodge, long before they'd brought in their first recruit. It was the biggest waste of resources in the camp; the house had the potential to serve as a commonplace and could comfortably accommodate eight. The only rooms Sasha used were her bedroom and the adjoining bathroom—her house was exclusively for sleeping and the occasional conjugal visit.

After fumbling around in the dark for a few minutes, Jasper got himself dressed and slipped out of the room, then the house itself. The morning was frigid. Pulling up the hood of his sweater, he stood listening to the forest come alive with the first tentative bird calls of the day.

He fetched the sled and made his way to the Bunkhouse, then stood outside it for a full five minutes, listening. How much of his time did he spend listening at doors? Too much, he guessed. He gently twisted the doorknob, counting on Garrett being asleep. They'd left his hands tied, but the kid could put up a fight. If he was awake, it meant there was bound to be a struggle.

Jasper was relieved to find Garrett asleep on his side on the sleeping bag he'd been provided. The air in the Bunkhouse was ripe with the stench of shit, the bucket in the corner obviously having been used to its full potential. With practiced silence, Jasper brought the sled through the door and set it next to the sleeping boy. He grasped Garrett by the shoulders and rolled him onto the sled, fastening the shoulder and leg straps.

Garrett groaned and Jasper tied a gag around his mouth before he could start making a racket. That got him moving. Garrett rocked and strained against the straps binding him to the sled, but there were a lot of them and Jasper had tightened the most important ones already. He ignored Garrett's thrashing as he fastened the rest. Once the kid was secured to the sled, Jasper tied his thighs and ankles together to make things easier for himself once they reached their destination.

Pulling Garrett toward the bridge that would take them across Eagle Creek, Jasper regarded the longhouse on the other side, watching it as one approaching a sleeping bear.

It had been dubbed the Orchid Room long before they

realized what sort of place it was. Someone—he thought it had been Hannah or Morgan, one of the girls anyway—had given it the name based on the faded and peeling pink paint that clung stubbornly to the walls in a wiry coat.

Like the Museum, the Orchid Room's entrance faced away from the small creek, its door opening onto the single road that ran between the two buildings. On the other side of that dirt lane, dense trees went back for about twenty-five yards, the wall just beyond them.

Once across the bridge, Jasper's guts clenched. Garrett went still and quiet, obviously getting some sense of what dwelled on this side of the creek.

Jasper smoked two cigarettes while he waited for the rising sun to give him some natural light, which sometimes helped a bit. When the sun peeked over the treetops, he forced himself to take the overgrown stone path the rest of the way to the creaky wooden steps of the Orchid Room. Garrett was a big dude with an athlete's build, and Jasper was grateful there were only three steps to pull him up.

At the top of the stairs, he held his breath and listened. Silence. No bird calls over here, ever. As if they sensed what was inside. Even the spiders, who blanketed every other inch of the grounds in their silk, avoided this building.

Steeling himself, Jasper grasped the knob of the old wooden door and twisted—there was no need to lock the Orchid Room, anyone in their right mind would rather die than step foot inside.

Garrett, apparently grasping what was to come, started to scream beneath his gag, thrashing uselessly in the sled.

Jasper peered into the shadows of the place, knowing he wouldn't be able to see anything beyond a small strip of ancient wood floor dimly lit by the rosy glow of dawn. All he saw, all he ever saw in here, was blackness; deep, endless dark that stretched on forever.

The Museum terrified him, but at least he knew what to expect in there. The Orchid Room, though, was an endless hole filled with horrors his mind could only guess at.

He took a second to visualize what he would have to do, shook his hands out, then pulled Garrett inside. At the edge of the scant daylight, he set about undoing the straps holding Garrett to the sled.

Arms and legs still bound together, Garrett thrashed and kicked. The heel of his foot clipped Jasper in the jaw, dazing him. Jasper didn't mind. The kid deserved to get in a few good shots considering what was coming.

Straps untied, Jasper grasped the edge of the sled, dumped its cargo on the floor, and headed for the door. Behind him, Garrett screamed into his gag.

From somewhere in the dark, over the muted screams, came a deep exhalation. It exuded hungry anticipation.

Jasper's bladder threatened to let go. He made it to the door, pulled the sled through, and blindly reached for the doorknob.

He didn't look back. Never did. All he knew was once someone was locked in here, they were never seen again. Nothing to clean up; no muss, no fuss. It was a terrible convenience.

After a few seconds of groping behind him, he realized he must have shoved the door open farther than usual—his hand couldn't seem to locate the knob.

He spun around, looking for the door, and was unable to resist glancing at Garrett. The boy screamed and writhed on the floor, staring up and into the dark. Jasper grabbed the door-knob. Hesitated. He didn't want to see what was going to happen, but couldn't tear his gaze away.

Something colossal, something that blended into the dark of the Orchid Room, something that shouldn't exist, reached out from the shadows. Jasper's mind told him he was seeing an appendage, maybe a hand. He couldn't fixate on any aspect of it. Didn't want to.

Garrett's screams reached a pitch that tore at Jasper's heart, raising gooseflesh on his arms. He'd be hearing it in his sleep.

The thing reaching from the gloom closed down upon Garrett, muting his screams further. It pressed down on the boy, slowly, inexorably. The muffled screams grew louder. Became a squelching groan that didn't quite cover up the sound of bones being crushed. The thing in the dark pressed Garrett flat, then dragged him into the dark, smearing his remains across the floor.

Jasper yanked the door shut and ran until he was back at his own cabin with the door locked and barricaded.

Z

FARREN SCRATCHED her leg and counted to ten under her breath, staring straight ahead into the darkness of the shed Jasper had stuck her in, what he'd called the Sapling Hut. She'd only had about half a minute to orient herself by the light of his flashlight before the door was closed on her. In that regard, she was lucky the hut's amenities were spartan. A sleeping bag, which at least smelled clean, was spread out along one wall of the hut. In the corner of the opposite wall was a plastic bucket she presumed was to be used as a bedpan.

She had no idea how long she'd been in here but had an idea it must be close to dawn, or past that already, judging by the faint bird calls she heard from outside.

Occasionally, throughout the night, someone would walk past outside and Farren would have to exercise all of her willpower not to hammer on the door and scream for help. She assumed she would get no comfort from whoever was out there.

Jasper had assured her, if she was well-behaved, this would be the only night she spent in here, which could be utter bullshit. Part of her wanted to rebel, to throw herself against the door of the hut until it gave way or she fell over from exhaustion. The more rational, canny side of her, however, told her it would be best to try to play it cool for as long as possible. The way Jasper was talking, she was being invited to be a part of what he referred to as a tribe. She had no intention of being a part of any group that kidnapped their members, but if they thought she was buying into whatever they were selling, maybe they'd let their guard down around her.

For a few hours throughout the night, she had legitimately questioned the reality of where she was, nearly convincing herself she had fallen into the river and this was all something she was dreaming as she passed from life into death.

It was bizarre how normal and happy everyone here appeared to be, at least at a glance. None of the dozen or so kids she'd seen last night seemed to find it strange she'd been brought here against her will, which led her to believe the same thing had happened to all of them. And it hadn't taken her long to recognize several of the kids as some of those who had gone missing from Maggie's Knee over the last couple of years. But how had they all been roped into a cult?

And it *was* a cult. Had to be. How else do you convince this many kids to join your crew, after kidnapping them? It had something to do with brainwashing, which, to her, was more frightening than being locked in an old woodshed. She'd seen some pretty messed up documentaries on cults, many of them about perfectly reasonable people who were sucked in, preyed upon, and changed forever. She pictured the leader of this cult, Jasper and Sasha's boss, as a shoeless hippie kind of dude who wore a hooded robe and took the most attractive young women as his wives or consorts.

She took a deep, meditative breath, the way Anika taught her. Easing the breath out, she tried to let go of her increasingly panicked speculations. Her focus drifted to her bladder. She did not want to use the demeaning bucket left for her in the corner, but she had to pee so bad it was painful. At this point, it was use the bucket or wet herself.

No longer able to take the discomfort, she crawled around in the dark, groping about until her fingertips found the makeshift bedpan. Jasper had made her leave the crutches outside the hut as if he'd been afraid of her using them to MacGyver her way out of the little prison. She found the bucket, pulled down her pants, and braced herself against the walls in the corner as she lowered herself over it. Urine splashed back at her naked underside as she peed and she cursed herself for not thinking about that ahead of time. At least they'd left her a partial roll of toilet paper, which she cast about for now, awkwardly balancing on her foot.

As she was wiping herself off, she heard someone running toward the hut. The footsteps came from what might have been a few dozen feet away, thumping on the hard-packed dirt path that snaked around the grounds. The person, it sounded like a guy, was saying something. As he got closer, it sounded more like he was crying than talking. The sound resolved to a whimpering jabber when he ran past.

Sounded almost like Jasper's voice.

What had him so upset? Wild animal? A bear, perhaps? A girl could dream.

She lowered herself to the floor and sat cross-legged. Closed her eyes, even though she was already immersed in darkness, and focused on her breathing, on the muscles in her body, on what she was in control of. When she did this, she was able to feel her left foot as if it was still there. That feeling had scared her at first, upset her so much she'd refused to meditate anymore. Anika helped her overcome this, as she had helped her overcome so many physical and emotional challenges. She'd insisted Farren embrace the feeling and enjoy having some time with her lost appendage, that there might be something to learn from it. Farren never had any ghost-limb-related epiphanies, but she grew used to the feeling over time. Even came to enjoy it.

Breathing deeply, she receded into herself. Gradually, the floor disappeared from underneath her, the walls from around her. The songs of birds grew silent, and even the smell of her own urine in the bucket drifted from her senses. She floated in nothing, finding peace in her breath, feeling the pure, elemental nature of her existence.

And waited.

12

T hree sharp knocks ripped Farren out of the meditative state she'd been in for, judging by the stiffness in her body, close to an hour. She rolled her shoulders and neck, stretching out her tired muscles. The meditation refreshed her a bit, but she still wished she'd slept last night.

"Hello?" a young girl's voice called from the other side of the door. "I'm gonna come in. Please tell me if you're pooping or something and I'll wait."

Farren sat back against the wall, legs stretched out in front of her. It was tempting to ignore the voice at the door but she desperately wanted to be let out of the dark confines of her sleeping quarters.

"Come in," she called.

A key rattled in what must have been a padlock and then daylight was dazzling her, leaving her completely vulnerable to her visitor. Farren raised her hands to block the glare. She could just make out a small pair of feet outside the door. Gradually, her eyes adjusted to the light and she lowered her hands.

A young girl stood beaming at Farren from the door, hands clasped in front of her, golden hair scrunchied in a ponytail. Dressed in denim overalls and a dark T-shirt, which added to her cuteness, she couldn't have been older than eleven or twelve. Why take kids this young? What could this girl possibly have to contribute to this bizarre colony?

The girl's gaze dropped to Farren's diminished left leg, then to the bucket in the corner. Her eyes widened and she gave Farren an almost adorable look of astonishment.

"Oh my gosh," the girl said, voice dripping with sympathy, "I'm so sorry. I can't believe they just left you with a bucket when you, you know." She looked down at Farren's stump again.

Farren shrugged, already feeling herself liking this girl, against her better judgment. This was how they thought to win her over, by sending in an adorable kid to show her how magical and lovely this place could be. What a load.

"It would've been a lot easier to manage if I'd had a light," Farren said, allowing a bit of an edge to creep into her voice.

The girl's eyes widened again, eyebrows shooting up to her hairline so fast Farren almost let a smile creep onto her face. Her visitor reached a hand out and flicked a switch next to the door. A light came on overhead, barely perceptible in the morning light, but there.

Now Farren had to laugh. She was so exhausted and terrified and here came this sweet little girl to make her problems go away, hours too late, but better late than never.

"You could probably use a shower, right?" the girl asked. "You can use my bathroom. We have time before breakfast. I can get you some clean clothes too if you want. Yours are all muddy."

Farren said, "You seem nice, but I'm not going anywhere with you."

The girl's smile faltered. She looked genuinely hurt.

"I want to help make this easy for you."

"Make what easy?" Farren asked. "What is this place? Who do Jasper and Sasha and all the rest of you work for?"

The girl scrunched up her nose. "We don't work for anybody. It's just us. Jasper and Sasha are our leaders, but they're not super bossy. Okay, Sasha can be a bit abrasive, but we don't even really hear from her unless something big's going on."

Farren was caught off guard by the way the girl spoke, not at all like an elementary school kid. "How old are you?" she asked.

The girl rolled her eyes in a way that suggested she was used to hearing the question but was good-natured about it. She seemed to be pretty good-natured about everything.

"I know," the girl said, drawing out the second word and turning it into a groan. "My older brother and I both look way younger than we are. I'm actually fifteen. I'm Sadie McCallister." She held her hand out to Farren but remained at the threshold.

Farren sighed, rose, and took two hopping steps across the hut, sticking her own hand out and grasping Sadie's. For a brief second, she thought about yanking the girl into the cabin with her, holding her hostage, using her to get out of this place. But the plan swiftly died in her mind.

Without her prosthetic foot, she could do little more than pin the girl down and keep her in the hut. Even if she had her prosthesis, what would the next step be? How far would she be able to take such a plan? Could she inflict violence on an innocent-looking girl, deceptive as her looks may be? No, she absolutely could not.

Farren could be assertive on the ball diamond and could throw her weight around pretty well on the basketball court—she'd drawn her share of fouls over the years—but she had not been raised to be violent.

Instead, she gave Sadie's hand a light shake. "Farren Murakami. How long have you been here, Sadie?"

The girl gave Farren a sly look. "How about you come with me to get cleaned up and I'll answer any questions you have on the way?"

Farren had to smirk. Even for fifteen, Sadie seemed pretty bright. Or, again, maybe she'd been fed these lines. Trained in how to mollify and coddle newcomers.

As much as the idea of taking any sort of comfort from this place appalled Farren, she was filthy, uncomfortable, and hungry; the offer of a shower, clean clothes, and some breakfast was too much to pass up. If she was going to be stuck here—and if she was going to play along until an opportunity to flee presented itself—she might as well try to enjoy herself a bit.

Which was probably how everyone got sucked into a cult, she thought as she accepted the crutches Sadie held out to her.

"What?" Farren asked, settling the crutches under her arms, then remembering to adjust them so her movement looked awkward and unpracticed.

Sadie was staring at her with adoration in her eyes. "You're just so pretty. Are you Japanese? Is that okay for me to ask?"

Farren looked away, feeling her face heat up. She did not do well with compliments. "I'm American."

When she looked back at Sadie, the girl was wearing a look of such mortification that Farren had to laugh again. It didn't escape her that she'd laughed more in the last few minutes, as a prisoner, than she had in the last few months.

Sadie's question was innocent enough, and Farren wasn't sensitive about being asked about her lineage. In fact, she felt proud of her heritage, when she thought about it at all.

"My dad was second-generation American, my grandparents are Japanese," she said. "My mom was half Greek, half mystery meat, and all American."

Sadie grinned at her, either ignoring or not having registered Farren referring to her parents in the past tense. She said, "I bet you get tons of guys asking you out. Probably a lot of creepers too."

They'd started down the path, away from the Sapling Hut and toward a group of cabins. A few kids wandered the grounds, most of them waving good morning to Sadie and giving Farren open looks of curiosity.

"Actually," Farren said, "the foot kind of keeps most of them away. And I'm not always the most approachable person."

Why was she being so open? Already it felt like they were just friends taking a walk together.

"You seem pretty nice to me," Sadie said.

Farren noted that Sadie had ignored the statement about her missing foot keeping boys away, and appreciated it. Most people would have rushed to mollify her with platitudes about how probably nobody noticed it.

"Where are you from?" Farren asked, trying to sound out of breath. "I don't recognize you from Maggie's Knee High."

"Me and my brothers are from Pinedale. This is our

cabin."

She led Farren up three wooden steps to the porch of a large log cabin painted in a shining coat of red.

Farren was surprised by Sadie's answer. Pinedale was fifty miles from Maggie's Knee. She hadn't realized the disappearances were that widespread.

"What is this place, Sadie?"

The girl stopped with her hand on the doorknob of the cabin and turned to face Farren. "We call it the Congo. It's our home and pretty much the coolest place on Earth. You'll see, Jasper's going to take you on a tour after breakfast."

She opened the door and led Farren inside.

"Why the Congo?" Farren asked, stepping through the door.

"You'll have to ask Jasper about that."

Farren had stopped listening. She wasn't sure what she'd expected to see on the other side of the door, but the sprawling great room before her was not it. The place was a palace compared to her quarters from last night. The interior was all polished, natural wood. The ceiling vaulted up some twenty or twenty-five feet and was crossed with gigantic beams of timber. An enormous fireplace, unlit, stood at the far end of the room, its stone hearth almost the size of the Sapling Hut. A couch and a couple of recliners faced a giant, wall-mounted television. An open kitchen was on the far end of the great room; its appliances all looked straight out of the eighties, the only things betraying the age of the place. The cabin was littered with articles of clothing, empty soda bottles, and half-eaten bags of chips.

"This is yours?" Farren nearly gasped.

"Half of it," Sadie said, absently picking a shirt off the floor and tossing it onto one of the recliners. "I share it with my brothers. They're out doing their morning chores."

"Chores," Farren repeated, following Sadie down a hall, where the mess seemed to dry up a bit.

"Uh-huh, we all pitch in," Sadie said. "This is my end of the house. The boys' rooms are at the other end. They don't really come over here much, which is great—I would hate having to share a bathroom with them again. Do you have any brothers or sisters?"

Farren answered that she did not. She'd always wished she had a sibling, younger or older, didn't matter. Someone to confide in. To share her grief over the loss of her parents.

Sadie opened the door to a big bedroom with an ensuite containing both a shower and jacuzzi tub.

"Most of the cabins are like this," she said, seeing the wonder on Farren's face.

Sadie outfitted Farren with a soft towel, a brand-new bar of soap, and bottles of shampoo and conditioner, then slipped out of the bathroom and returned a few minutes later with some clean clothes.

"I know my clothes won't fit you, so I brought you some of my brother's, I hope that's okay," Sadie said as she stepped out of the bathroom again. "They're clean, I do the laundry myself. I don't have any underwear that will fit you but I'll put your clothes in the wash if you toss them out the door."

Farren accepted the clothes. "Thanks for this." She genuinely meant it.

Sadie waved a dismissive hand at her. "I'll wait in the bedroom for you. Take your time."

She pulled the door closed, leaving Farren to bathe and plan a way out.

13

Gordon trudged through knee-high brush along the bank of the river, cursing the tangled mess of dead foliage whenever it tripped him up, which happened every other step. Old Maggie roared off to his right, carrying anything unfortunate enough to get caught in her current toward the spot where the river canted at a deadly, nearly ninety-degree angle before rushing on, away from the town named after the ruinous bend. He'd heard that, back in the late sixteen and seventeen hundreds, savvy travelers on the river would disembark in Maggie's Knee—nothing but forest land then—and portage past the bend, unwilling to risk their lives or their cargo.

He was heading toward that bend when one of Farren's teachers, Peter Hurley, came crashing through the underbrush from the direction of Jessop's Bridge. His bald head gleamed with sweat that dripped down into his eyes and ran into his beard. He lumbered to a stop next to Gordon, panting.

"Found something," he huffed, doubling his massive frame over and planting his hands on his knees, "on the bridge."

Gordon patted him on the back. "Take a knee for a sec. Why didn't they just radio me?"

"Tried," Peter's muffled voice came from between his legs.

Gordon grabbed for the radio on his belt but only wound up smacking himself on the side. He patted all around his waist with both hands. "Shit."

It could have fallen anywhere. The brush was so thick here it was impossible to see anything that wasn't painted DayGlo orange.

Up ahead, Mara Garrow and her intrepid cameraman had stopped and turned their attention to them, which was the last thing Gordon wanted—it was the whole reason he'd taken the rear in this group. Mara made good on her word, they had their cameras rolling at all times. Now they were focused on him.

"What's the word, sheriff?" she called.

He turned his back on her, certain she would be making her way over.

"What did they find at the bridge, Pete?"

"A bag," Peter said. "A backpack."

"Has anyone shown it to Garrett's parents?"

Gordon looked over his shoulder. Mara and her cameraman were indeed heading their way.

Peter put a hand on Gordon's shoulder. "It belongs to Farren."

The words were a sucker punch. Gordon ripped Peter's hand off his shoulder the same way he would handle a drunk who had the balls to come at him and stepped back into a defensive posture, hand involuntarily twitching, just barely, in the direction of his service revolver, a .357 Smith & Wesson Magnum.

"How do you know?" he demanded. "Where exactly did they find it?"

"It's got her name on it," Peter said in a calm voice, probably the same tone he used with an escalating student. "And I recognize it. It's got that death metal band's logo sewn onto it. They found it on the bridge's walking path, leaning against the guardrail."

Gordon reeled. Peter, God bless him, grabbed him with a steadying hand.

He hadn't seen Farren since their argument the day before. She'd stormed off and, he'd presumed, gone to bed. What if she hadn't, though? What if she'd snuck out the back door? It's not as if he would've noticed—the argument had immediately carried on with Melinda.

His wife had infuriated him so much with her selfish heckling Gordon had walked out and taken off in his cruiser, driving around for an hour before feeling calm enough to return home. He was ashamed of himself now for how he'd dealt with things; anger was his go-to reaction for almost everything these days. He tried to remember when it had been different, when he'd been a man of patience and discipline and was heartbroken to realize it was before they'd lost Darya.

The implications of the discovery of Farren's backpack kept adding up to the same thing. He didn't want to believe she would take her own life, didn't even want to acknowledge it as a possibility, but was powerless to stop his cop's brain from computing the problem. The argument, the hurtful words, the fact that her mother died in the water; it was hard to look at those things and not assume Farren had cast herself into

Widow's River, willingly joining the legion of dead who had traveled its current.

And him without his radio.

The news crew was close enough Gordon could hear their footfalls breaking through the brush. Another glance over his shoulder told him they were within twenty feet.

"Peter, I have to get back to the bridge."

The teacher looked over Gordon's shoulder and nodded. "I'll hold them up."

He stepped past Gordon and shouted an enthusiastic greeting at Mara, who did not sound pleased.

For the first time in longer than he would care to admit, Gordon ran.

z

FARREN FOLLOWED Jasper out of the dining hall, loping along on her crutches a bit slower than was comfortable for her. She hoped she wasn't hamming it up too much, but Jasper gave her frequent looks of apologetic sympathy when he realized he was walking ahead of her, and would wait for her to catch up. She soaked everything in on her tour of the Congo, making mental notes of potential hiding places, the easiest paths to run along, and where she might be able to lose pursuers.

Breakfast had been extravagant: eggs, sausage, pancakes, and real Canadian maple syrup. Farren hadn't wanted to seem overeager, but her appetite took over as soon as the irresistible aromas of breakfast reached her nostrils. She'd sat next to Sadie, who yammered on endlessly about all manner of inconsequential things. All around her, kids ate and shouted at one another, and it all felt so natural, so familiar to Farren she forgot to be on edge. She barely even felt self-conscious that she was wearing a strange boy's clothes; loose-fitting jeans, a T-shirt for a video game she'd never heard of, and a navy-blue hoodie. Sadie had pointed out the donor of the clothing, her brother Danny, a handsome kid who looked Sadie's age but was apparently closer to Farren's. He'd been deep in conversation with the guy across from him and hadn't seen Farren looking, which was for the best. It felt awkwardly intimate to be wearing his clothes.

If she'd been at school, she would have kept her head down and focused on her meal. For the most part, this was exactly what she did. But every now and then, she would steal a glance at the other kids in the room. At every table, there was at least one kid looking back at her with mild curiosity. At the head of the room, Jasper and Sasha sat across from each other. A few times, when Farren looked their way, Sasha would already be staring at her with a contemptuous scowl, and Farren would swiftly avert her gaze.

When a few aproned kids bearing bus bins started making the rounds to collect dirty dishes, Jasper sauntered over to their table and asked Farren if she was ready for her tour.

The place was vast. The Congo had no fewer than two dozen buildings and cabins, many of which weren't even in use. The buildings were not only in great shape, they'd been heavily modernized, some in the most juvenile ways imaginable. Jasper seemed most proud of The Shop, which had apparently served as a recreation hall in the Congo's former life. He held the door open for Farren like a Las Vegas doorman, a look of proud anticipation on his face. She understood why as soon as she stepped inside.

The Shop was a large room dedicated to recreation and leisure, mainly in the form of video games. A dozen arcade cabinets, all plugged in and functional, lined the walls. Most of these were ancient, relics from the eighties, but one or two were more modern games. Jasper explained most of the machines had already been here and they'd picked up the newer ones themselves, not going into detail about how they transported such big, heavy machines through the forest— there was no way they pulled them on a sled. Two billiards tables, a foosball table, and a huge TV with an elaborate speaker setup rounded off the room.

"Where do you get all this stuff?" Farren asked as Jasper led her to the next stop in their tour, a much less exciting storage cabin.

"Steal most of it," he said, sounding almost remorseful, as though he hadn't kidnapped her and dozens of other kids. "But you'd be surprised at how much was already here."

The tour wound through the grounds, mostly passing by the numerous cabins the tribe dwelled in. None of the buildings on this leg were anywhere near as impressive as The Shop.

At one point, they passed within sight of a creek that ran along the north end of the grounds.

"What are those buildings used for?" Farren asked, pointing at the two decrepit structures standing on either side of the bridge on the opposite shore.

"The far side of the creek is off-limits," Jasper said without slowing down, or even looking toward them.

Now *that* was interesting.

The only other building of note before their final stop was one that gave Farren chills. It was obviously a church of some kind. Its wooden siding was painted in a faded white, a small steeple sticking out of the center of the roof. The doors were closed and the single window looking inside was dark. Farren thought something flickered past when she glanced up at it but assumed it must have been the reflection of a bird flying behind her.

"You'll get to see the chapel soon enough," Jasper said.

Farren thought that was the least enticing thing anyone here had said to her.

The last part of their tour was the most enlightening, for several reasons. The first and most troublesome revelation for Farren came when a girl who looked perhaps sixteen passed them on the path, waving at them and bidding Jasper a good morning. She had a walkie-talkie handset strapped to her shoulder, as if she was working security somewhere. When she waved at them, Farren noticed the girl wore a gun in a nylon holster on her hip.

"Why does that girl have a gun?" she asked, unable to keep the nervousness from her voice.

"To keep us safe," Jasper said. "Here's our last stop."

He led her toward the large building that stood at the entrance to the Congo. The building with the words that said this place had been called something else quite some time ago.

"What is the Great Forest Outdoor Discovery Center?" she asked, pointing at the words stenciled on the broad window.

The words above the door said *VISITOR'S CENTER*, but she thought that was more self-explanatory.

"That's what this place went by before it was abandoned," Jasper said. "Some billionaire built it in the eighties. He didn't have any permits and kept it super-secret. Had everything flown in to avoid creating roads that could make the place discoverable. There's one dirt track leading away from the north end but it's overgrown and dies out completely about a mile off."

"And what? He just gave up on the place?"

Jasper gave her an exaggerated shrug. "Looks like it. There's no mention of it anywhere online. The guy abandoned it. Maybe it was a non-starter. Or maybe someone caught on to what he was doing and wanted him to file for permits. Either way, it's forgotten and hidden, which is perfect for us."

Farren had the feeling he was only telling her partial truths.

He opened the glass door to the Visitor's Center for her and they stepped inside. The ceiling rose to double the height of Sadie's cabin and boasted the same enormous beams of timber crossing the ceiling, which was gabled and adorned with skylights giving view to the cloudless sky above.

A counter just inside the doors appeared to have once been used to welcome guests. A guy of sixteen or seventeen sat behind it with earbuds in, watching something on a row of monitors that cast a pale glow over his thin face and long, greasy hair. Both his ears were pierced multiple times, each lobe stretched out and filled with wide, black plugs. His lip, eyebrow, and nose were pierced as well. Farren recognized him. He'd gone to her school and had been one of the first kids to disappear from Maggie's Knee. She was pretty sure his name was Wesley.

The kid looked up and gave them a brief nod before looking back down at his screens.

"Wes is our chief of security," Jasper said from behind her

as if this was a perfectly natural title for a kid not yet old enough to have graduated high school.

Farren decided not to acknowledge she knew him, since he hadn't appeared to recognize her.

Jasper led her past the counter and down a hall lined with framed posters, all advertising a different activity at the Great Forest Outdoor Discovery Center. They bore slogans such as *See Nature Up Close!* and *Discover, Learn, Play!* She paused to read each of these, not because she cared what they said, but to give herself more time to think about escape options, though this last stop on their tour was proving to be discouraging. If the screens Wesley was watching were all security monitors, she might not be able to sneak her way out of here.

The hallway opened up into a common area full of tables, chairs, and couches. Many of these were crowded around a big TV with three different gaming systems hooked up to it. Everything was neatly put away, each system's controllers on their own designated shelf.

Jasper waited at the other end of the room for her, next to an open door with a picture of stairs next to it.

"You going to be able to make it up here?" Jasper nodded to the sign with the stairs. "It's only three flights, but ..." He looked down at her foot.

"I'll manage." She sighed, hoping she wasn't playing it up too much.

Farren had become very good at navigating stairs with crutches over the years, but took them slowly and cautiously now, deliberately stumbling a few times. At one point, she took the act too far and nearly fell down the stairs. She stumbled, shrieked, and shot a hand out, only barely snatching the railing on time. Jasper was there in an instant, getting his hands under her armpits. He genuinely seemed concerned with making sure she was okay. She insisted she was and shook him off. He backed off immediately.

At the top of the stairs, he held a steel door open for her and led her outside, onto the flat roof of the Visitor's Center. The peaked glass roof of the lobby rose to their right, its point roughly eye level with her. She could just make out the top of Wesley's head as he stood watch behind his counter.

The day was bright and clear, mild for an early spring morning. Voices echoed from every direction below. A bird sang somewhere nearby. The view itself was amazing. And useful. Farren could see most of the grounds laid out like a map. The steeple of the chapel was barely visible through the trees off to her left. To her right, the plaza, which included the dining hall and The Shop, ran along the dirt road. Far off, beyond the little creek, the forbidden buildings. Left of these, on this side of the creek, was something that made her heart jump a little.

"Is that a baseball diamond?" she asked, pointing.

"You play?"

Instead of answering—she didn't want to give him the satisfaction of getting to know her—she asked, "Why do you call it the Congo?"

He chuckled. "Kind of feels like a Congo, doesn't it?"

Farren wasn't sure about that, wasn't even thinking about it. She was eyeballing the trees beyond the two buildings on the other side of the creek.

14

Farren made a run for it on the way to supper.

She'd spent the time after the tour helping Sadie clean up her cabin, an activity doubtless meant to keep her busy. As they picked up clothing and dusted surfaces, she thought long and hard about her escape plan and realized she had nowhere near enough information to make any sort of move. Jasper's tour had given her the lay of the land, but she'd seen only what he'd allowed her to. They hadn't gone anywhere near the wall surrounding the Congo, for instance. The gate they'd come through was heavily monitored and she had no idea whether or not there were other ways out.

Then there was the girl with the gun. If one person was armed, it stood to reason others would be too. Would they really shoot her if she made a run for it, though?

Farren made up her mind to risk it as they headed to the dining hall from Sadie's cabin. If she waited until she had enough information, she might never get out of here.

She was hobbling behind Sadie, listening to her babble about how annoying it was to live with two messy boys when she realized this was her best opportunity. There was no one else in sight, the rest of the tribe apparently having already made their way to supper.

Glancing around as surreptitiously as possible, trying to appear as if she was just taking in the sights, Farren slowed her pace, dragging out her steps and putting as much distance between herself and Sadie as she could before the girl noticed.

A trio of smaller cabins stood off to her right. She could head for them, go between two of them with enough of a lead to break Sadie's sightline to her, then cut back and go across the bridge over the little creek—trees grew thick just beyond the forbidden buildings.

Her escort stopped talking and turned around when Farren had created about half the length from home plate to first base between them, a little under a fifty-foot head start. Sadie had a sad, knowing look in her eyes.

"You don't have to do this," she said. "It's not going to turn out the way you think you want it to."

Farren wanted to respond, to tell Sadie she was grateful for her kindness and that she wished she had a sister like her. To thank her for her brother's clothes, for the hospitality.

Instead, she gave in to the animal instinct to flee, trusting her body to do what was necessary to survive.

Pivoting on the crutches, Farren launched herself forward, catching herself with her strong right leg. Her arms carried her behind the cabins before Sadie could react.

She risked a look back. Sadie hadn't moved.

Farren used the cabin walls for cover, leaned on them to

conserve strength. She peeked around the cabin, scanning her path to the bridge. Coast was clear. Uneasiness crept over her. She shook it off. No time for jitters.

She powered across the lawn. Made it to the bridge in a few seconds flat. Wished for her blade but had to admit she was doing nicely with what she had.

The bridge was unwalled and constructed of ancient slats and beams spanning the twenty-foot gap across the burbling creek. She took it in a few steps, thanks to the crutches, and stopped dead on the other side.

Something felt off. Everything felt off.

At first, she thought she'd suddenly gone deaf. But she could still hear her own breathing. There was an emptiness to the air over here, a dead calm in the trees. Even the babble of the creek was muted.

A muttering rose in the back of her mind. It sounded like someone speaking unintelligibly on the other end of a distant, antique phone, and holding their receiver at arm's length.

The voice changed tempo; became one word uttered relentlessly, over and over, more of an insistence than a chant. The word seemed familiar, but she didn't recognize it, couldn't even articulate it. She heard it when it was said and then it all but vanished from her mind, leaving behind only its essence and a profound dread. Was she having a stroke?

"Don't move," a new voice said. It was familiar and real and came from behind her.

The voice in her head ceased, but the feeling of emptiness in the air remained. She turned to see Jasper on the other side of the bridge, surrounded by a dozen teenage boys. He held a rifle up to his shoulder, aimed at her.

So they would shoot her after all.

"What is this place?" she called to him. "What's ZIIS?"

The word came to her out of nowhere—she hadn't even known she was going to say it. Now that she recalled it, she could almost hear that relentless muttering again.

"I don't know what you're talking about," Jasper said without lowering the rifle. "Please come back across the bridge. I seriously don't want to use this."

He had to be lying about not knowing what she was talking about, but she believed he was telling the truth about not wanting to shoot her. She was counting on it to save her life.

He lowered the rifle a few degrees and opened his mouth to say something else.

Farren used the opportunity to sprint toward the building on her right, a long hall with pink, peeling paint.

A loud crack from behind her, followed by a sudden, growing pain between her shoulders, stopped her in her tracks. The crutches slipped out from under her arms and she collapsed, smacking her head off the hard-packed dirt path. She tried to push herself up but found she could no longer move. He must have shot her in the spine. Now, instead of an amputee, she was a full-on cripple for the remaining moments of her life. She wanted to be angry but felt consciousness fighting to get away from her.

Somewhere far away, footsteps were stomping on the wooden bridge, coming toward her.

She felt her heartbeat slow. Her eyes closed on their own. The footsteps were on the path now, very close to her.

From far off, Jasper said, "Shit."

Farren wanted to curse him, even if she had been in the middle of having a brain aneurysm when he found her and shooting her had only quickened a slow death. Her treasonous mouth wouldn't make the words. She felt herself slip away and was glad to find it felt a little like deep meditation.

She gave in to it and embraced her death.

## 15

Jasper ignored the knocking for as long as he thought he could get away with it. If he didn't get the door soon, Sasha would use her keys to let herself in anyway. He dreaded every meeting with her now and spent a good deal of energy trying not to draw her attention. But he'd known she'd be coming for him this evening. There was more work to do.

As he pulled himself up from the couch and navigated around a stack of paperbacks, he asked himself—and not for the first time—why he stuck around, never mind he no longer had a choice. He shoved the question from his mind as quickly as it cropped up, terrified Sasha would pick up on it.

She looked furious when he finally opened the door for her. The black clothing, a long-sleeve shirt with leather pants, and heavy, dark makeup didn't help the appearance.

She shoved through the door, nearly knocking him on his ass on the way by. "Time to go, they'll be leaving the McCallister's for dinner in a minute." She saw something in his face. "What?"

He shook his head. "Nothing."

Sasha shot her hand out and grabbed his cock through his pants hard enough to hurt.

Jasper knew better than to make a sound. She was a classic bully in that way—if he reacted, she would only step it up and take longer to grow bored with tormenting him.

"Doesn't look like nothing," she mewled. "Getting sick of me?" She squeezed harder.

He felt his temper rising. Wanted to grab her by the throat and smash her head against the wall over and over until the back of it was bloody mush. He never used to be a violent guy. This place changed him, though. Sasha changed him.

"I'm still getting over bringing Garrett to the Orchid Room this morning," he said. "That shit always makes me sick."

She sneered and laughed in his face, giving his junk a final squeeze before releasing it.

He tried not to show his relief.

"Get over there," she said, stepping back out the door. "The new girl can move much better than she lets on, I don't want you missing her."

"I know, Sash, I got it," Jasper said.

But the door was already closing behind her.

He felt tired, weighed down. It had been such a long day already. Putting on a happy face for his tour with Farren had been exhausting. But he had to admit in his heart of hearts, he had enjoyed spending time with her. He held no false hope anything romantic could ever develop between them—he'd seen the contempt in her eyes when she looked at him. Even if she could look past the fact that he'd been her captor, Sasha would kill them both if she ever suspected something between them.

He opened the closet next to the front door and withdrew a long, hard plastic case. He popped the latches and pulled out a matte-black rifle, loaded it, and hoped things wouldn't come down to having to use it. Slinging the canvas strap over his shoulder, he stepped out of the cabin and tried not to think about what the next few hours would bring.

A dozen steps down the path, he spotted Sadie McCallister stepping out of the cabin she shared with her brothers on the other side of the grounds. Farren came out after her, hobbling along on her crutches.

Jasper ducked behind a giant sycamore and watched the girls come up the path. Farren's helpless cripple act wasn't nearly as good as she probably thought it was. He felt bad for putting her through this, as he did with most new recruits. It was necessary though, an exercise beneficial for them both. He just hoped she made the right choice so things wouldn't have to get unpleasant.

Sasha would have his backup, a small group of volunteers, hidden along the path to the main gate. He would give Farren a lead and follow behind until someone apprehended her, at which point they'd get started with preparations for the Induction.

In an ideal world, Farren would simply follow Sadie to supper. They had a ninety-five percent success rate when a recruit made it through an entire first day without incident. He knew better than to hope for that sort of outcome though; he'd seen her scoping the place out on the tour, was aware of how agreeable she'd been since they'd noticed her missing foot.

It was Sasha who picked up on Farren's behavior right

away. In bed last night, she had brought up Farren's sudden enfeeblement act. It was humiliating how obvious it was once it was pointed out to him; he'd eaten it right up until then.

He was embarrassed about how concerned he'd nevertheless been for Farren when he brought her up to the roof of the Visitor's Center. The rooftop was a standard last stop on the newbie tour, the idea being to show the scope of their operation early on. Sasha called it a confidence deposit, explaining that recruits would be much more willing to invest themselves in their service if they were given the chance to appreciate what they were becoming a part of. Like much about Sasha, it scared him how well-versed in these things she was.

Jasper moved around the tree to follow the girls' progress. Farren was putting distance between herself and Sadie, who was playing her part magnificently, as always. Sadie was their go-to choice for the welcome party when they recruited girls. She had a natural concern for people, which often comforted new arrivals. He'd told her about Farren's missing foot only minutes before she'd gone to welcome her, and she'd berated him for losing the prosthesis. When it came to the well-being of others, Sadie could be a pit bull.

Farren came to a complete stop on the path, effectively ending the other girl's role in their routine.

Sadie said something and, for a second, Jasper thought she may actually have gotten through to Farren. He couldn't quite make out their expressions from here, but it looked like Farren was going to continue following Sadie to the dining hall.

When Farren did run, it didn't surprise him so much as disappoint him, if only because he could have used a peaceful end to the day. What did surprise him was the direction she fled. And how fast. She was like a bio-mechanical cheetah, the way she used those crutches.

Instead of heading toward the gate, she galloped away from his position, toward the trio of storage cabins on the northern end of the camp.

"Why the hell would you go that way?" he muttered as he stepped out from behind the tree.

He jogged up the path, keeping an eye on the cabins. No doubt she would circle around toward the gate, trying to throw any would-be pursuers off her trail.

She proved him wrong again by racing toward the bridge.

Jasper ran out into the middle of the main road and waved in the direction of the gate. After far too long, he spotted a couple of the boys Sasha recruited come out of hiding, stepping out onto the road like cautious deer. He waved them toward the creek then sprinted for the bridge, cocking the rifle, and checking the safety was off.

Only once before had a recruit, an athletic guy named Hugh, crossed the bridge that led to the Museum and the Orchid Room. That had been the last day in the Congo for Hugh.

Jasper slowed to a jog when he spotted Farren on the other side of the bridge, gripping the sides of her head with both hands, crutches braced under her arms. She remained motionless as he crept up behind her. He heard the guys he'd waved into action catching up to him and raised a hand, patting the air and hoping they'd get the message to be quiet.

He stopped just in front of the bridge, not wanting to go across it, not so soon after he'd just been here. He wondered if Garrett's smeared remains still lingered on the ancient floorboards in the Orchid Room. Or had his destroyer, whatever it may have been, already licked them clean?

Footsteps as his backup crowded around him. A couple of the guys whispered to each other, wondering how this would play out. If he was honest with himself, Jasper was just as curious.

He raised the rifle and called, "Don't move."

Across the creek, Farren seemed to come out of a trance. She lowered her hands and turned to look at him. There was a fear in her eyes he knew all too well. She'd experienced some of it, some of what went on here.

"What is this place?" she called to him in a shaky voice. "What's ZIIS?"

The word meant nothing to him, but carried an importance he recognized; it felt and sounded like something from the blackness of the Orchid Room, or the lurking thing that dwelled in the Museum.

Jasper would have to shoot her if he didn't want her to suffer the same fate as Hugh—it was the kind thing to do. Unless he could convince her to return to his side of the creek.

"I don't know what you're talking about. Please come back across the bridge," he pleaded with her. "I seriously don't want to use this."

She looked terrified. Maybe if he could calm her down, she would at least hear him out. She deserved every opportunity she could get. He lowered the rifle and was about to say something to reassure her, he didn't know what exactly, when she bolted.

That was it then.

Farren was remarkably fast, especially for someone

missing a foot, and he had to line up the shot without hesitation. He took a breath and shot her in the back.

She went down right away. When her head hit the dirt, it sounded like a sack of potatoes dropped from ten feet up. Several of the guys behind Jasper groaned at the awfulness of it.

He cursed as he crossed the bridge to retrieve her, hoping she wouldn't have a concussion.

There was a look of dismayed anger on her face that melted into peaceful serenity before she closed her eyes and lost consciousness.

"She okay?" one of the guys called from across the creek.

Jasper threw his hands out to his sides in response.

Kneeling next to her, he put the back of his hand against her neck. Her pulse was easy to detect, though he could feel it slowing. He placed a hand in front of her face and felt short, hot bursts of breath against it. Next, he moved his hand to her back and plucked the dart, full of enough Ketamine to keep her under for a couple of hours, from her back, wrapping it in a rag. He hated to have to use it only twenty-four hours after giving her the knockout cloth, but she hadn't given him much choice. He couldn't let her get to the Orchid Room, for her own sake, never mind that no one was permitted over here, himself and Sasha excluded.

It caused him some difficulty to liberate the crutches from underneath her unconscious body, and he wished at least one of the guys across the bridge were permitted on this side to give him some help. When he'd freed both crutches, he tossed them across the creek to Tyler, a brawny kid of fourteen, then went back for Farren.

She was a slender girl, but he could feel the toned layers of muscle under her borrowed clothes as he lifted her up. He was as delicate as possible in touching her, out of consideration for her and also because Sasha was probably watching; he didn't need to give her anything to use against him, not even an accidental brush of hand against boob.

Once he had Farren across the bridge, he handed her off to two of the guys: Hamji, a sixteen-year-old, hardworking Moroccan kid whom they'd had with them for over a year, and Spencer, who had been recruited along with his twin sister, Lila, only a few months ago.

"She's got a pretty gross bump on her head," Spencer said as he split her weight with Hamji.

"Try to get some ice on it as quick as possible," Jasper said.

"Want me to get Ramses?" Nick, a scrawny little guy of fourteen, said.

Jasper shook his head. "Just let these guys get her to the girls at the lodge. Maybe grab an ice pack and meet them there with it if you want to help."

Nick, always eager to be of assistance, hesitated long enough to give a sharp nod then took off at an awkward jog toward the dining hall.

Jasper's stomach growled at the sight of the building, but he ignored it and walked off in the other direction to his cabin where he would stash the rifle again. He hated walking around with it, despised the look it gave off; he cared nothing for the power associated with wielding a gun, no matter what sort of ammo it carried. He'd had no say in the matter when it came to arming the Congo's security forces.

The word Farren asked him about danced around in the periphery of his consciousness, wanting to be noticed but hiding out of sight when he directed his attention toward it, an elusive bird flitting through a jungle canopy. What the hell did it mean? Why did it feel familiar? Had it been in something he read in his school days?

For the first time in a long time, he deliberately thought back to his life before the Congo and searched his memories of the short stint he had in college as an English major. He rarely permitted himself to linger on these recollections—they brought a bitter remorse to his heart that he wasn't willing to confront, didn't feel strong enough to face.

He had pretty good recall for the things he'd read in school, but nothing so obscure as ZIIS—surely something he would at least have made a passing note of—rang a bell. Instead, he found himself assaulted by the memories of those he'd spent his life with before Sasha, those he'd left behind, hurt, and worse.

This was a dark path he was heading down. Thinking about his old life would only lead to him being too depressed to do anything more than take a bottle to bed. He sent his mind elsewhere, tried to think of something he could do to keep himself busy until the Induction, and attempted to ignore the flickering shadow of that word haunting his outer consciousness.

He'd just come back out of his cabin after having returned the rifle to its place when Sasha came storming up the path.

"What the fuck happened?" she shouted at him before even reaching his front steps.

He came down to meet her. "You didn't see it yourself?"

"I saw her run across the creek."

He shrugged. "Nothing happened per se."

"Per say," she spat. "Don't talk like you're still some

fucking brilliant poser forcing his nose into books about bullshit."

There it was again. Had she known he was just thinking about his past? About the people he'd let—

"Jasper!" Sasha shoved him hard on the shoulder.

"She said something," he said, still coming back from where his thoughts had threatened to take him.

Sasha threw her hands up and opened her mouth in her best *what the fuck is it?* face.

He closed his eyes and cast his inner vision to the shadows he usually tried to pretend weren't there, those that existed in the fringes of his mind, searching for the dark word that now existed among them.

"ZIIS," he said.

When he opened his eyes, Sasha's face had gone a grayish white, like old skim milk. Her mouth still hung open, but now it seemed to be in stupefaction. Drool pooled in the gap between her teeth and her jutting bottom lip.

"Sash?"

She snapped back to reality in a way that was eerily similar to how Farren had come out of her stupor not long ago. What the hell was going on that he didn't know about?

"Where did you hear that word?" Sasha's voice was calm and quiet, which frightened him more than her usual violent cadence and volume.

"It's what she said," Jasper explained, knowing he'd just opened a door that couldn't be closed; he could feel it in his bones. Dimly he thought there must be a German word that described that realization, the sense of being unable to go back.

Sasha slumped to the ground, first crouching, then dropping onto her butt. He'd never seen her so inanimate. His unease grew.

"How can she know it? She can't know it. Only I know it," she murmured.

He knelt in front of her. "You know what it means?"

She looked up at him, a flurry of emotions swirling in her eyes: fear, wrath, jealousy, hatred. He almost fell away from her, afraid the feelings were directed at him.

"It's *his* name," she said in an unsteady whisper.

16

The first thing Farren noticed when she returned from death was the smell, like one of those hippie stores that sold wooden jewelry and CDs of ocean sounds. She opened her eyes to find herself in the middle of a dimly lit room, a haze of incense smoke creating a low, swirling ceiling just above her throbbing head. She reached up to touch the tender spot where she'd hit it. Her arm wouldn't budge. It took another thirty seconds or so of trying to lift it before she realized she was tied to a chair.

Panic was her first instinct. She fought it, knowing it would get her nowhere. Still, she could feel her heart trying to bust out of her chest.

Her head swam with the remnants of whatever it was they'd done to her. She remembered Jasper pointing a rifle at her and then she'd been on the ground. Obviously, it had been a tranquilizer gun. This time.

Looking around, she saw the space she was in wasn't really a room at all, but another damn shed. This one was much bigger than the Sapling Hut and appeared to be a large garden shed converted into a new-age sweat lodge. The chair she was tied to sat atop a large, Mexican-style rug with big, square pillows bordering its edges. Dim lamps and incense holders sat in each corner of the shed. Beyond those accouterments, there was nothing to note except the closed barn doors, no doubt padlocked from the outside.

She tested her ropes and found them to be tied much better than those that had held her when she was being brought to the Congo on the sled; there wasn't the slightest give to these.

The incense was cloying and made it difficult for her to breathe. She would asphyxiate if the smoke wasn't allowed to vent, which could have been the point for all she knew.

How long would they leave her in here? How long had they already?

As if summoned by her thoughts, there was a light knock at the door.

Sadie?

Farren kept her mouth shut, not trusting herself to maintain her composure. Instead of responding, which her visitor seemed to be waiting for her to do, she took a deep breath and attempted to center herself. A miniature tornado of incense smoke descended with the intake of air and shot into her lungs. She hacked and gagged, lungs suddenly on fire.

In the midst of her coughing fit, she vaguely noticed the doors swinging open. Smoke rushed out of the room and she felt immediate gratitude to whoever had let the air in. Electric light streamed in from outside, darkness looming beyond it.

"You're up. Good."

Sasha. Farren's guts froze.

"I want to cut right to the chase," Sasha said as she stepped through the doors, pulling them closed behind her. "Don't worry, I'm not gonna hurt you. *He* won't let me."

"Jasper?" Farren asked, suddenly wondering if he was perhaps in charge after all.

Sasha threw her head back and cackled; an ugly, grating sound—the call of a sick raven. "You know who I mean," Sasha said, laughter evaporating. "You must be important to *him*."

The girl was off her nut.

Farren said, "I swear I have no idea what you're talking about."

Sasha stomped a foot and stuck out her bottom lip in an ugly pout. It was a juvenile gesture Farren may have laughed at if she wasn't tied to a chair, at this psychopath's mercy.

"You told Jasper," Sasha whined. "He'd never heard *his* name before today. Before you dared to utter it."

It became clear then who Sasha was talking about. Farren simply hadn't known it was a *who*. It had felt so enormous, so all-encompassing. An essence more than an entity.

Sasha's eyes lit up. "You do know what I'm talking about. For a second I thought you might be for real, which would have meant Jasper had learned *his* name somewhere else, which would have been something I wasn't prepared to deal with. But *he* asked for you. *He* knows you. It makes sense that you would know *him* too." She came close to Farren, put her face next to hers, and breathed, "ZIIS."

Her breath was foul, rotten. The name came out sounding the same way, dripping with putrescence. It resonated in Farren's head, bouncing off the walls of her skull, skittering into the murk of her sub-conscience, where she could feel it making itself a nest.

Farren jerked her head away.

Sasha stood back from her now, eyes wild and expectant, shrouded with blue makeup so dark it was almost black.

"Well?"

"Well, what?"

Sasha threw out her hands. "How do you know about *him?* Did *he* call you here?"

Tears of panicked frustration threatened at Farren's eyes. Sasha had said she wouldn't hurt her, wasn't allowed to, but how stupid would Farren have to be to trust anything she said? The girl seemed prone to violent outbursts at the slightest provocation.

"I don't know what to say," Farren pleaded, fighting to keep her voice steady. "I don't—" But then she did.

And her Highness must have seen it in her eyes.

"What is it?" Sasha darted forward and grabbed her by the shoulders.

"I saw the name, the one you said, spray painted in an alley in Maggie's Knee."

Sasha stumbled backward as though Farren had puked at her feet. "Don't fucking play with me."

Farren took a slow breath, grateful most of the smoke had been purged from the room.

"I swear to you," she said. "I saw it and then I blacked out or something for a minute. Just the other day, I think. I don't know what day it is anymore."

"Yesterday? Before we recruited you?"

Farren couldn't stop her laughter. "Recruited?"

Sasha stepped close again, murder in her eyes. "Was it the same day we picked you up?"

Farren nodded. It had been a long and memorable day for

all the wrong reasons. Just as the last twenty-four hours had been.

A long silence passed between them.

Sasha walked to the door. "We'll know more after the Induction. Tania will be here to get you prepped in a few. You're going to want to cooperate with her."

She stepped out of the shed and pulled the doors shut. There was a sound of metal sliding on metal as she secured the lock.

Farren burst into tears, releasing a dam she'd been holding up with all her strength ever since regaining consciousness. Tears and snot flowed freely, soaking her in a salty slime. She tried to keep her sobs quiet, but once started, they came out in spite of her best efforts; great, body-shaking heaves of emotion fighting to escape through any available orifice.

The smoke from the four burners had already begun to fill the room again, itching her nose and lungs with every sob. She fought to bring the tears to a stop by regaining control of her breathing. It took a few minutes, but she soon managed to turn the taps off on her eyes and nose. Her throat ached, eyes burned, and her abs felt bruised from the exertion of crying. She didn't get emotional very often and hated the hangover that came after, though she couldn't deny the physical relief crying provided. Normally she would seek release through sports or some kind of physical activity. It made a sort of biological sense she would be more prone to crying if she was unable to do anything else with her body.

There was a quick knock, followed by the sound of someone unlocking the doors.

She wished she had something to wipe her face with. It

would be so obvious she'd been crying, and she still wished to maintain some illusion of self-control.

The doors swung open, once more sucking the incense smoke outside. She was grateful for this at least.

A tall, dark-haired girl with olive skin stepped inside, holding a tray with a tea set on it. She wore black yoga pants and a black, snug-fitting hoodie. She was roughly Farren's age and she was beautiful.

The newcomer looked around with disbelief written on her gorgeous face and shouted, "Holy shit, are you guys kidding me?"

She set the tea tray down on the floor next to Farren and stormed around the room snuffing out the incense sticks in each of the corners. Then she knelt in front of Farren and took her face in her hands.

"Jesus, look at you," she said, full-lipped mouth going into a sympathetic pout. "You allergic?"

"To what?" Farren asked, puzzled.

"Incense. Your eyes are all puffy and your nose is running." The girl went to her tray and plucked a cloth napkin from it. She used it to wipe off Farren's face, then tossed it in the corner. "I told those assholes to light *an* incense for a few minutes just to get the funk out of this place. It was getting musty in here. I'm Tania, by the way."

"What do you want?" Farren asked. She was suddenly tired of people pretending to come to her rescue.

"I'm sorry, I know this sucks." Tania poured a brown, reeking tea from a plain, white pot into a small teacup. "It can be scary before the Induction."

"I don't know what you're talking about. I don't want to be inducted," Farren said.

Tania held the steaming cup up to her. The smell invaded her nostrils and triggered a gag reflex at the back of Farren's throat.

"This'll make you feel better," Tania said.

"What if I don't drink it?"

Tania sighed. "Then I have to inject it, and I hate doing that."

Fear gripped Farren. She'd never done drugs, hadn't even been given anything stronger than Tylenol for her foot, and here was the third time they'd be forced into her system in a little over a day.

"What is it?" she asked.

"An herbal blend," Tania said with a smile that belonged in a magazine. "We've all taken it. Nobody's died from it."

Farren took a shaky breath. What choice did she have? If they were just going to shove a needle in her anyway wouldn't it be better to drink the stuff on her own terms? At least that would reduce the chance of catching something from a dirty syringe.

Tania stared at her with kind, patient eyes.

"Fuck it," Farren said, tilting her head back to drink.

The other girl smiled. "Thanks for not making this a bad experience."

She lifted the bowl and Farren drank.

## 17

Jasper's stuck a hand over his growling stomach, as if to mollify hunger with affection.

"You okay?" Kevin grabbed his arm in a tight grip.

Jasper shook the hand off. "Just hungry."

Kevin Wickerton was the perfect assistant, which was often great and just as often infuriating. Jasper and Sasha had picked him up during their first winter in the Congo. Kevin had been sixteen and working as a shift supervisor at a fast-food restaurant, showing all the signs of being a lifer. Sasha, in her peculiar wisdom, understood they could put his enthusiasm and work ethic to good use.

Now, at eighteen, Kevin was six-three, 225 pounds of muscle, and a complete teddy bear. His concern for Jasper's wellbeing bordered on obsessive and drove Jasper mad. Jasper would sometimes lash out at him, unable to control his frustration at being asked if he was okay or needed anything or could use a hug, or whatever it was at the moment Kevin wanted to do for him. Kevin, in his perfection, never showed it if he was rattled by the outbursts, which made Jasper feel horrible.

Sasha had requested Jasper's presence at the dining hall, which would be empty since dinner had been hours ago and everyone would be doing their part to prepare for the Induction. Jasper would never confess it out loud, but he had asked Kevin to tag along for protection.

Sasha had drifted away like a phantom after their last conversation, having learned of the unsettling word Farren had uttered, a word that belonged to the great and terrible thing they had been serving for two years. He was afraid Sasha's anger may have been kindling since they'd spoken a couple of hours ago and her rage would manifest in violence. He hadn't come right out and asked Kevin to defend him, but he didn't have to. Kevin had stood between them before, acting as a literal human shield. If things got rough, he could easily lift Sasha off Jasper without harming her.

They turned up the short path leading to the dining hall and Kevin jogged ahead to open the door. Jasper slid through without a word, refusing to give Kevin the benefit of being thanked for being so frustratingly efficient. He wasn't the fucking president and Kevin was far from Secret Service, though Jasper could see him taking that professional path if they hadn't picked him up and irrevocably altered his life's direction.

Sasha sat at their usual table, at the far end of the room, watching them. "You didn't have to bring your guard dog," she called as they approached.

Jasper sat down across from her, allowing his eyes to dart toward the shuttered service window leading into the kitchen.

He'd held a slim hope that maybe Kip would have left some supper out for him. His stomach rumbled.

Kevin slid onto the bench, close enough Jasper could feel his body heat even through the denim jacket he wore.

"You missed a good dinner," Sasha said with a sadistic grin.

"What's up, Sash?" Jasper tried not to sound impatient.

She frowned and he thought that was the end of diplomacy already. His adrenaline spiked.

Then she smiled and said, "I'm going to kill her."

"Who?" But he knew full well who she meant.

She scraped her fingernails along the table's surface. "The new bitch."

Jasper was caught off guard by this, but couldn't help feeling a bit grateful her fury wasn't directed at him. Sasha didn't look angry, though. She looked like a bobcat about to pounce on a blind, deaf mouse.

"I thought she was untouchable," he said.

"We'll see how the Induction goes."

"What does that mean?"

She only smiled at him.

"Did you do something?" he asked, fear growing in his gut, not of her but of the one they served. Of the consequences of disobedience.

She raked her fingernails harder on the tabletop. "I'm not going to touch her if she's legit. But if she's an imposter, here to wreck things for us, I'm gonna kill her."

"What the hell makes you think she's anything like that?"

Sasha pounded on the table with closed fists. "How does she know *his* name?"

Next to Jasper, Kevin cleared his throat.

"Kev, maybe go wait by the doors for now," Jasper said without taking his eyes off Sasha.

Kevin hesitated a respectfully concerned second before getting up from the table and heading to the other end of the room. Sasha lunged at him, smacking the table with the palm of her hand.

"Get!" she shouted, the way one might yell at an adolescent dog who just pissed on the floor for the second time in a week.

Kevin, to his credit, didn't flinch. He marched straight back to a seat next to the double doors leading outside, never breaking stride. That was Kevin. Sasha didn't seem to notice or care.

"She said she saw it written on a wall," Sasha said.

"That leads you to believe she's an imposter?"

Sasha leaned in close to him and said, "It makes me think *someone* is an imposter."

"Whoa," Jasper said, sitting back from her, ready to wave Kevin back over. "Tell me you don't think I'm writing that, or anything, on walls. I'd never heard of it before this morning."

Sasha eyed him the way a jackal might stare down an injured calf.

"Relax," she said. "I know it's not you."

They stared at each other for a long couple of seconds before her face crumpled and she stuck out her lower lip, exchanging ferocity for petulance.

"I used to be the only one who got to know his name," she said with a bitter whine in her voice.

"Who do you think did it?"

"Think about it." She stood up from the bench, shoving it

with the backs of her legs so it screeched against the linoleum floor, and headed for the exit.

"That's it?" he said, getting to his feet to follow her out.

She spun around to face him. "What do you want, Jasper?"

Good question. Why was he complaining about having a conversation with her cut short?

Behind her, Kevin stood from where he'd been sitting.

"It's weird you called me down here just to tell me you want to kill the new girl," Jasper said. "Isn't it?"

She looked like she wanted to tear him to pieces but was stuck on the other side of an invisible, impenetrable barrier. What was up with her lately? Ever since they brought Farren here, Sasha had been acting crazier than normal. Jasper was torn between pacifying her and getting to the bottom of what her issue was.

Instead of giving him a chance to do either, she turned on one heel and stalked out of the dining hall. Kevin took a step back as she passed and was probably as surprised as Jasper when she didn't lash out at him again.

"Don't do anything crazy!" Jasper called after her.

He slumped back onto the bench and watched Kevin make his way over.

"She okay?" Kevin asked, sounding genuinely concerned.

Jasper threw his hands in the air, then gestured for Kevin to sit across from him. "Who's been into Maggie's Knee in the last week or two?"

Kevin made a show of thinking it over for a few seconds, even though they both knew he could've answered that question, or a thousand others, immediately and accurately.

Finally, he said, "Just you and Sasha. Last time anyone

other than the two of you went to Maggie's Knee was almost a month ago."

"Who was that?"

"Danny, Hamji, and Melissa," Kevin said right away. "Supply run. It was Ham's first time."

Neither of the three seemed likely suspects for whatever it was Sasha was accusing them of. Vandalism? Treason?

She'd all but come out and said she was jealous. He'd taken it to mean she was bitter Farren knew that word, that *name*, and maybe that he did now as well. But hadn't he noticed Sasha's behavior before this evening? And she'd only just learned in the last few hours Farren knew some of what she did. Which meant ...

"Oh," Jasper said.

Kevin raised his eyebrows at him.

"She's known there's something special about her all along," Jasper said, more to himself, though Kevin nodded thoughtfully. "We both knew it, based on how different this recruitment was. Sasha just knew it more than me. As usual."

Then why was she so shocked when Jasper had repeated that word? Maybe she'd been more upset at the fact he'd heard it from someone other than herself. Her anger hadn't felt directed at him, though, with the exception of a few heated moments.

"All good?" Kevin asked.

Jasper appreciated him then for not being the sort to ask probing questions about things that were clearly none of his business. One of the many good reasons he tolerated Kevin's overbearing nature.

"You ever feel like you're a tarantula and then one day

wake up to the realization you're actually a cricket?" Jasper asked him.

Kevin put on his deep-thought face, brows knit together. "No. But I find it interesting you compare yourself to bugs."

"That's because I know where I stand," Jasper said.

Kevin only stared at him, a very uncharacteristic frown pulling at the corners of his mouth.

Jasper's stomach rumbled.

"Kip will kill me for it but I'm going to raid the kitchen." He stood from the table and patted Kevin on a muscular shoulder. "See you at the Induction."

He shoved through the swinging door into the kitchen and flicked on the lights. There was no sound of Kevin getting up and walking out of the cafeteria, which was strange. Jasper didn't take his assistant to be a very pensive person. On top of that, he was sure he'd only seen Kevin frown the way he had at the table, looking legitimately upset about something, once or twice before, and those occasions had been out of concern for Jasper's wellbeing. When Kevin frowned, he looked like he could tear someone's head off with his bare hands. He'd once confided to Jasper that he used to have anger issues a high school therapist had helped him work through. When he frowned, Jasper was sure he was seeing the Kevin of ago, the one who had nearly been expelled for being involved in literally a dozen fights and sending almost as many kids to the hospital.

The kitchen cupboards had little that appealed to Jasper, so he moved to the fridge and yanked it open. Sitting on the top shelf, covered in plastic wrap, was a thick slice of chocolate cheesecake. Had that been this evening's dessert? All thoughts of Kevin left Jasper's mind as he peeled away the cellophane, licking the whipped cream topping off the underside of the film. He found a fork, sliced off a bite he knew was way too big to chew properly, and crammed the whole thing into his mouth, which salivated around it in a liquid embrace.

He sank to the floor and devoured the cake, forgetting for a few minutes everything that had happened in the last twenty-four hours, lost in the bliss of flavor, texture, and minimal nutritional value.

A few seconds after inhaling the cake, he heard Kevin get up and walk out of the dining hall, his pace heavy and hurried. Eager to get to his next mission, maybe.

Jasper dropped the plate in the sink, intending to leave it there. Then he thought of Kip coming in to prep for breakfast in the morning and finding not only the last slice of cheesecake gone—and if Jasper was honest with himself, it could have been cut into at least two pieces—but also the chocolate-and-cream-cheese-covered evidence left for him to clean up.

"Stay in good favor of the one who prepares your meals," his mother had once said, long ago. She'd been referring to herself, but it was good advice from an okay mom.

He buried the memory and flooded the sink with hot water and soap. There were a few other dishes in there he might as well take care of too. He washed them in soapy water that was almost boiling, then scrubbed down the kitchen counters, stove, hood vent, fryers, and fridges, and swept and mopped the floors. It was a good way to keep his mind off what was to come. Inductions ranked low on the fun meter when they went well, let alone the few times they went very, very bad. And if Sasha was right, this could be one of those minority occasions.

By the time he was finished cleaning, he had half an hour to jog home and shower before the ceremony, which would take place at midnight. As he walked back to his place, he kept his eyes down on the road, acknowledging none of the five or six kids he passed on the way. When he got home, he went straight to the bathroom, where he unenthusiastically scoured himself under hot water like another piece of filthy kitchen equipment.

18

Farren licked her lips, tongue sticking to their dry, chapped skin. Tried to swallow, flexing her esophageal muscles until they hurt. She was glad not to have to worry about the incense anymore but she was so damn thirsty.

How long had it been since Tania left her alone in here? Ten minutes? An hour?

The tea had been disgusting. Tasted like it was made of dirt and weeds. She'd asked what was in it and received nothing more than a smile from Tania.

Now she was so parched she would gladly drink a pint of the stuff. It wasn't doing whatever it was supposed to do anyway.

Sadie stood from where she'd been sitting cross-legged on one of the floor pillows.

When had she come in?

Farren watched as the girl wordlessly stretched, bending back a little at first, and then further than seemed possible. Her back bent a full 180 degrees and beyond. She brought her head up between her legs until she could just raise her eyes to Farren. Then she was standing up straight, though Farren hadn't seen her body weave back through her legs. She looked down on Farren, kid's body appearing much taller from the reduced vantage point on the chair.

Insectile wings, translucent and swirling with color, like the surface of a soap bubble, unfurled from Sadie's back. Just shy of big enough for the cabin, the wingtips folded against the bare wooden walls.

Sadie opened her mouth and something resembling a headless python slipped out of it, spreading her lips wide around the glistening, black flesh. As the thing slid out of her, three feet long, then four feet, then five, it curled in and around on itself, forming a spiral pattern. Farren recognized it for what it was.

They'd studied the insect world in biology this year and there had been a unit on butterflies. Videos her teacher borrowed from YouTube showed the insects feeding on the nectar of flowers by extending a long proboscis—and you can bet the boys in that class were referring to their dicks as their proboscises for the next month—into the flower to suck it out. What came out of Sadie's mouth looked exactly like that.

Farren finally found her voice and screamed, pleading with someone to please let her out, that she'd cooperate. They could induct her or whatever if they just got her away from this Cronenbergian nightmare happening in front of her.

The proboscis shot out and the end of it, which bore a resemblance to a mouth with dark, moist lips, smacked into the floor next to Farren's right foot with a wet slurping sound. It stuck there and sucked at the floor, snapping back into a spiral at Sadie's mouth when it found nothing tasty.

Farren screamed again in startled shock, feeling her control slipping, fear taking hold. She closed her eyes, no longer willing to witness what was about to happen to her.

When there were no further wet, smacking sounds of a sucking appendage not quite hitting the morsel in the chair, she cracked an eye open.

The room was empty.

Even the floor pillows were untouched, nothing disturbed by giant wings unfurling in an enclosed space. No Sadie. No proboscis.

Farren let out a quivering breath and tried to take the next one slowly.

Hallucination. Did she really think, after drinking some gross tea brought to her by cultists, she had been attacked by a mutating bug girl?

Her next breath came out in a harsh laugh. Nothing about this was funny, but the alternative to laughing was falling apart and leaving a sobbing wreck behind.

A knock at the door.

These people's attempts at feigning politeness were getting annoying. Maybe that too was some kind of psychological game. She kept quiet, breathing as shallow as her traumatized lungs would let her.

After three or four minutes with no further sound or disturbance, it became clear the knock was probably another product of the strange tea. How long did the effects last? How was she supposed to tell what was real and what was imagined? It was stupid to have taken the drink so readily. Tania had probably been bluffing about injecting her.

"I saw something!" she called.

Not a sound from outside.

It made a certain kind of sense that perhaps they left her in here to experience some sort of spiritual revelation brought on by hallucinations. And maybe if they thought she'd had her experience, they'd let her out.

One side of the door flew open, coming off its hinges, and floating across the room in slow motion, spinning end over end. A corner of it stuck into the opposite wall.

Tania drifted through the opening in slow, bouncing steps that reminded Farren of astronauts walking on the moon. Another girl bounced in after her; plain brown hair, also around Farren's age, and average height, though being next to Tania made her appear short. When she came in, she was very slightly on the heavy side, but as she moon-hopped toward Farren, she filled out, gaining more weight every second. A beard, the same brown as her hair, sprouted out from her face and grew down over her chest, stopping just above her belly button, which poked through her stretched-out shirt. She resembled a Dwarf from the *Lord of the Rings* movies.

"This girl is gone," Tania said, lightly gripping Farren's face and looking into her eyes.

Tania's own eyes took up Farren's entire field of vision. Shapes swirled within hazel irises, rolling into one another, and resolving into a herd of chestnut mares galloping over fields of wheat. Farren watched, mesmerized, as the lead horse stumbled on something hidden in the tall wheat grass and flipped head over tail. Those behind it followed suit, trampling and falling over the lead horse and then each other until they were a mass of twitching limbs on the plain. Some of them had things hanging off their legs and Farren gasped when she recognized them as bear traps.

Someone had littered the field with the steel-toothed traps and these horses had stumbled into them all at once. They would lay there, bleeding and suffering until they succumbed to their wounds, or until some lucky scavenger happened upon them, or until whoever laid those traps came around to check on them. Perhaps the trapper would be wielding a rifle and would put a swift end to the misery of the poor creatures.

"She's crying," the new girl said. She no longer had a beard and was back to her original size.

"Poor girl," Tania said, standing. "Let's get her to the chapel."

Farren blinked. The horses weren't real. She had to stop blindly accepting every crazy thing that happened. Had to remember the tea.

Tania chuckled. "Oh, I remember the tea."

Had she said that out loud?

The other girl came around from behind the chair and said, "I'm Hannah. It's really nice to meet you. You can get up if you want. Just let us know if you need help."

What was she talking about?

Farren looked down to find she was no longer tied to the chair. She hadn't even felt it when Hannah had freed her.

She lifted a hand and had to stifle a giggle when it seemed to float up on its own. She reminded herself about the tea and tried to reign her hand in before it floated right off her wrist. The more she thought about it, the more frightened she became her hand really would drift away on her. What was even keeping it on? She jammed both of them under her armpits and held them there as tight as she could.

"Can you get up?" Tania held out a hand.

"Where are we going?" Farren countered, trying not to look directly at either girl, in case things started happening again. She noticed the door was back in place.

"The chapel. For your Induction. Before the tea wears off."

"What's in it? How long is this going to last?"

"You'll feel totally normal in the morning," Hannah said in a soothing voice.

Farren withheld a scream.

She had to cooperate, no way around it. She couldn't trust them, but running wouldn't be a great idea with the hallucinations. It didn't take much imagination to see herself jogging straight into the river and drowning because she thought the air was fire.

Trying to distract herself now from the idea of the air being fire, Farren looked down at her feet. Both of them.

Her breath hitched in her chest.

She had her foot back. How it happened didn't matter, only that it was there, on the end of her left ankle. She rotated it and watched it perform a perfectly smooth circle, as if it had never been gone. No more prosthesis. No more itchy ankle. No more looks of pity from everyone she met the second they realized she was missing something they'd always taken for granted. The guilt in their eyes when they looked back into hers, pretending they didn't notice.

She stood. Took a step.

Fell.

Stupid. She had completely believed her foot magically, impossibly reappeared in its old spot. Her chest felt heavy. Her eyes burned.

"Hey," Tania cooed, crouching down to her.

The tears came in a single, coughing sob, accompanied by a blast of snot and saliva. Farren swiped them from her face with the hem of her borrowed hoodie.

"I'm sorry," she said in a tight voice.

"It's the tea. I shouldn't have let you stand on your own, no matter how many feet you have." Tania flashed a mischievous grin at Farren, got an arm under her, and helped her up.

Hannah retrieved Farren's crutches from outside. They were strange to use under the influence of the tea. At first it felt like they wobbled under her arms as if they were made of soft rubber. By the time she could use the crutches normally, they had already walked the short path to the chapel.

The door opened inward as they approached the steps leading up to the small church. An ensconced light shone from just above the doorway, illuminating the stairs. None of its light pierced the darkness beyond the door.

Shapes swirled in the void of the chapel: fangs, claws, leathery wings, and so much more she couldn't process.

"What's in there?" she asked.

No reply. Not that she'd expected one.

Suddenly she didn't want to play the cooperative hostage. There was no way she was going in that place, tea or no tea.

As her escorts took the first stair, Farren jammed both crutches into the ground and pushed backward, away from the stairs. She planted her right foot and crutch and swung herself in an arc, sticking the left crutch in the ground and vaulting away from the chapel.

The tea held off as she broke into a run, putting all the distance she could between herself and the blackness she'd seen through that open door.

Gigantic arms wrapped around her, putting a stop to her

progress. Her foot left the ground, crutches falling out of her grasp and onto the path. She writhed in the gargantuan grip to no effect—whoever held her was so strong and big she was reduced to a kitten in their arms.

The tea. It was a hallucination. Which meant she could fight her way out of this. She's Farren-fucking-Murakami, one-footed scourge of the ball diamond, mangler of ankles with her deadly scythe of a blade foot, which she again wished for with all her heart.

She took a deep breath and twisted to the left, digging her elbow into her captor's ribs, kicking off his knee with her right foot. Or that's what she meant to do. What happened was nothing at all. The hallucination was holding up and she was trapped in the grip of a behemoth.

"Good job, Guppy. Bring her in," a guy said from behind them.

Her perspective swung around so sharply she felt her stomach racing to catch up. One second she was facing a dirt path leading who knew where, and the next, she was facing that short white chapel again. She hadn't made it anywhere near as far as she'd thought. The one who held her (Guppy? She must have heard that wrong) was up the stairs in a few long strides.

A wheelchair sat outside the chapel, leather straps with buckles on the ends hanging off its arms and front axle.

"No!" Farren screamed, wrenching her body back and forth.

Of all the things they'd done to her, all the means of confinement and mind games, putting her in a wheelchair was the worst of it. When finally her stump—her vestigial limb, Anika insisted on calling it—had healed enough for Farren to start using a prosthesis, she'd sworn she would never again be reduced to using a wheelchair. And here she was, helplessly being carried toward one resembling a horror movie prop.

Her handler practically threw her into the seat, hard enough to hurt. Tania and Hannah fastened the crude straps over her arms and legs.

Farren looked up, no longer possessing the strength to struggle. The tea was still doing its thing. A giant looked down on her from an impossible height. His face was huge and infantile. Brown eyes the size of baseballs gazed down at her, an amused goo-goo smile on thick, pink lips. Black hair was cropped close to his head in what looked like a mirrorless do-it-yourself haircut.

She stared up at the smiling, baby-faced giant as he wheeled her around and through the door, which he had to duck under on an angle. His face disappeared in the shadows. Everything disappeared in them. Except the shapes. They flitted and soared around what must have been a high, vaulted ceiling, just slightly blacker than the total darkness they dwelled in.

Jasper's voice floated out of the dark. "Let's begin."

19

Voices. Chanting in a sort of call and answer. It had been going on for some time but Farren couldn't understand a word of it. As the chant went on, those shapes darted and drifted through the inky gloom above her.

Dimly, Farren felt something drilling its way into her mind.

How long had she been in the chapel, in the dark, bound to the wheelchair? How long had the unlit ceremony been going on? The voices were muffled, like she was hearing them from under a pile of thick blankets.

That sensation of her mind being invaded grew stronger, more painful. She wanted to scream, was going to scream, when the voice spoke.

*Be still.*

At least, it felt like a voice. More likely it was a ventricle in her gray matter popping loose, spraying gunk all over the inside of her head.

*Guess again.*

She felt the voice more than she heard it, vibrating through her skull, orbital sockets, cheekbones, and teeth. Buzzing in her head like a billion flies clambering to break free. It could hear her thoughts.

Another hallucination then.

*Let me show you something.*

She didn't want to be shown anything, dreaded what that could even mean coming from something that sounded and felt like this. It was unnerving something this frightening could exist even in the murkiest corners of her subconscious.

*You did not dream me up. I will show you things that make you believe. You will choose to stay.*

"I'm not staying here," she said, surprised by the clarity of her own voice in the dark.

The muffled chanting droned on around her.

*I can give you what you seek.*

"No one can give me that."

There was a pressure all at once, deep in the back of her head. Something was shoving at a door in her mind she hadn't even known was there. She was reminded of Bonzo—anytime she wanted to close a door when he was around, he'd shove against it relentlessly until he either slipped through or she managed to snick the door shut without catching any of him in it.

Whatever it was trying to get in was waiting for permission. It was being pushy, shoving hard, but could only go so far. No idea how she knew, but it felt like a certainty, which was enough.

No fucking way was she letting it in.

As if the thought convinced it, the pressure stopped. Whatever had been shoving at the door was gone. She only just started to feel relieved when she felt something else there; that sense of someone being at the door even though they haven't knocked yet. And this new presence felt different. Whatever had been there before was infinitely monstrous, full of darkness, brimming with power.

This new presence, however, was much smaller. And felt familiar.

"Kaeru."

The voice destroyed her. She slumped in the wheelchair, squeezed her eyes shut, told herself she hadn't heard it. What she'd thought she heard was an echo from long ago, flashing through her brain.

"Farren," the new voice said.

A smell came to her now, one that would stay with her if she lived two hundred years, and forever be a bittersweet reminder. It was the scent of her dad's—her *real* dad's—cologne mixed with the ginger shampoo he used. It was a bizarre combination of aromas that couldn't have worked on anyone else. As a little girl, if she'd found one of her dad's shirts or sweaters lying around, she'd be unable to resist shoving her face into it and breathing deeply, taking in his scent with all the space in her lungs. She hadn't smelled it in years, since they'd gotten rid of the last of his things.

"Dad?" she said, voice breaking so it came out in half a dozen syllables.

A shape came toward her from the gloom, the familiar silhouette of her dad, Junichi Murakami, known to everyone except his parents as John. The shadows parted around him and she found herself face to face with her dad for the first time in seven years. Since the last time she'd walked on two feet.

He knelt before her, looking the same way he did on his last day alive; in his old leather jacket, faded dad jeans, and white sneakers, capped off with the same old Osaka Kintetsu Buffaloes hat he'd worn every day of her life. He took her cheeks in his hands and beamed at her with a smile that took up his entire face, scrunching his eyes almost completely shut.

She pressed her face into his palms and whispered, "I miss you so much."

His lips, always so thin and dry, pressed against her forehead. "I miss you too, Kaeru," he said, using his old nickname for her, Japanese for frog.

He'd started calling her that when she was four because, for almost an entire summer, she'd hopped everywhere she went. It was an affectation that had driven her mother crazy, but her dad had found endlessly amusing.

"I'm scared," she said.

He lifted her face so she'd look at him, his dark brown eyes full of love. "Don't be."

Right here, in this moment, it was easy to take comfort in those words, to find protection in his embrace, even while she was still strapped to the wheelchair. But even through all that was going on, all she was feeling, she knew this couldn't last. She'd have to face what was happening to her in the real world soon enough.

"What do I do, Dad?"

He put his forehead against hers and said, "Be strong. This is where you belong."

She jerked back from him, already hating herself for the hurt in his face. "Why would you say that?"

His eyes searched her, took in her close-cropped hair, the

lack of a foot on her left leg. His gaze lingered on her ankle for so long she thought he may have fallen asleep.

"You've been hurt so much," he said, sorrow weighing down his words. "You deserve to have a real family around you."

Angry tears prickled her eyes. "I had a real family," she said, voice wavering. "You all left me."

"I know."

"So what? You think I should stay with these freaks now? Just forget what they did to me?"

Her dad smiled patiently, lovingly. "They may just be the freaks you need. They'll look out for you, care for you, love you. I know how much you suffer at home, without your mom or I there."

Farren heard the implication in his voice; the unspoken acknowledgment of the wreckage of her parental situation. Not only was she stripped of her birthright, to be raised by the parents she was born to, she'd also been stuck with some of the worst replacements possible. Granted, Gordon had been a good enough stand-in for her dad at one time, but he'd brought Melinda into their house to take her mom's place. For that, she could not forgive him.

"They kidnapped me," she said.

"Their recruitment tactics are a bit rough around the edges," her dad conceded. "Maybe they could use your help with that. You're a smart girl, you'll be appreciated here. Community is important—you should belong to one."

It was an insane suggestion. But why would he tell her to do anything that wasn't safe? He was her dad. Even if this was an intense hallucination, which it must be, why would her own subconscious tell her to stay if she didn't think there was something to it?

"They shot me with a tranquilizer dart," she said. "They're keeping me prisoner. At least at home I'm ..." she trailed off.

Her dad looked so sad.

"I saw you on the bridge, Kaeru," he said, letting those words sink in for a moment. "You will be free to go when we're done here. They'll tell you that in the morning."

"Then why tie me up and imprison me?"

"They had to get you here to talk to me. To show you what can be, what is possible with a little faith. I never wanted any harm to come to you, but between some rough treatment—which I know you can take—and not having you here at all, it was worth the discomfort." He stood, pushing himself up with his hands on his thighs, and smiled down at her. "I have to go. Give them a chance, at least. See what it's like to live with a family who appreciates you again. Who will love you. Someone who wants you around."

Farren shook her head, tears flowing freely. "This was just a stupid hallucination. A mind game they're trying on me."

Her dad chuckled and kissed her on the head. "My stubborn, bright Kaeru. You'll see."

He turned and walked away at the carefree amble she remembered him for. She knew then, as she'd been told countless times by those who'd known her, she got all of her intensity from her mother.

Her dad, or the dream of him, or whatever this had been, opened up a hole in her heart that swiftly filled with the thick muck of grief. It had been a long time since she'd dwelled on his memory. She thought often of her mom, probably because there were more reminders of her around the house, at least until Melinda had her way with the place.

An idea came to Farren then and she conjured an image of her mother in her mind, remembering her brilliant smile, her thick, raven-black hair, always allowed to hang freely and proudly around her shoulders. She focused on the dark in front of her, where her dad had appeared, and barely noticed the dark shapes were no longer flying around above her. She poured all her willpower into making her mom appear the same way her dad had, staring so hard her eyes began to ache.

Instead of her mom appearing, she felt her consciousness waning. Her eyes felt heavy, unable to focus. At the same time, her body seemed to become lighter. Just as she noticed the straps were gone from her arms and legs, she felt herself lift up from the wheelchair, floating into the air. Weightless.

It was still completely dark in the chapel so she couldn't see how far she was rising. The room below was silent. Had everyone left?

Air whisked past her cheeks, fluttered her hair as she flew upward, faster now. Straight for the ceiling.

She raised her arms above her head, for whatever good it would do; she was flying at least as fast as she could bike, speeding up with every second. How hadn't she hit the ceiling yet?

Up and up she flew, no longer afraid of crashing into the roof, knowing she'd passed right through it and was now floating up into space. But shouldn't there be lights below her somewhere? She couldn't see anything in any direction. All she knew was the swift flight that brought her ever upward, toward more black nothingness. She flew so long she began to question whether she was actually going up.

All at once, her motion ceased.

She caught a whiff of ginger shampoo and her heart fluttered.

A gentle voice spoke to her in a whisper, *Will you stay?*

She hovered in empty space, sensing immense patience from whoever or whatever had asked the question; it didn't quite sound like her dad. She considered what he'd told her. He was right about a lot of things, though she still didn't feel she could trust anyone who treated her the way she had been. Except there had been kindness here too, hadn't there? And if she was free to go, what was the harm in at least giving the Congo a shot?

With that thought, she fell. Her stomach knotted; her gorge rose. She dropped for what felt like an age. And then, when she was beginning to think she may be trapped in an eternal plummet through space, she hit soft ground.

Her arms and legs spasmed. Her body bounced.

Panting, she opened her eyes to bright sunlight streaming through a window to her left, spilling over the plush white covers of the bed she was in, the one she'd been having night-mares in.

What the hell?

The bed was huge and so damn comfortable. It sat in the middle of an equally enormous bedroom with hardwood floors and a vaulted ceiling. She sat up slowly. How had she gotten here?

She stuck her legs over the side of the bed, her right foot sinking into a thick sheepskin rug on the floor. Her eyes drifted to a large wooden dresser across the room and what rested on top of it.

Impossible.

She stood, barely conscious of balancing on one foot, and hopped across the room in three big leaps.

*Kaeru.*

She leaned on the dresser and snatched up what had caught her eye, the thing that could not possibly be there. She held it by its red brim, darkened by decades of her dad's dirty fingers pulling it off and putting it on his head, making countless little adjustments to it throughout the day, ensuring it sat perfectly—she'd never met anyone more finicky with their hat than her dad. The front of the hat, which had once been white behind the blue buffalo logo, was stained to a brownish-gray from decades of sweat and wear.

She turned it over, the pinwheel pattern of white and red with spokes of blue around the interior bringing back memories of her childhood. She'd always loved looking at the pattern on the inside of her dad's hat; he would spin it on his fingertip, making the pattern swirl in a kaleidoscope of color in front of her eyes for the few seconds he could balance it. She flipped down the hat's liner and took a shuddering breath.

His name was written there in faded black ink. *John Murakami.*

It was impossible. She had to still be feeling the effects of the tea. But even as she thought this, she knew it to be untrue. She'd woken up sober and clear-minded, if a little disoriented from the falling dream. The memories of the previous night, as long ago as it already seemed, had clearly been hallucinations.

Yet here she held her dad's lucky Osaka Kintetsu Buffaloes hat, given to him by his grandfather. He prided himself on having worn no other baseball hat in his adult life, though he did don a knit cap in the colder weather. You couldn't even get Osaka Kintetsu Buffaloes hats anymore unless you went to a collector or got lucky enough to find one secondhand; the team had been merged with another Japanese ball team, the Orix BlueWave, to form the Orix Buffaloes, a merger her dad never quite recovered from and ranted about often.

She would know this hat anywhere. It was her dad's. Which still made this impossible. He'd been buried in it.

"Okay, Dad," she said to the empty room, her throat aching with emotion. "I'll give them a shot."

## 20

Gordon slurped at the piping hot coffee that had only seconds ago finished brewing. He winced at the searing hot liquid spraying over his tongue, while simultaneously relishing the day's first contact with the magical brew. As it moved through him, scorching his insides, he felt his higher mental functions warming up, the gears and pistons of a complex machine coming alive. How could anyone not drink coffee? Melinda hated the stuff, or thought it was trendy to hate it. Instead, she opted to drink expensive herbal teas; absurd concoctions like dandelion fluff and birch bark—things that had no business being steeped.

He stood next to the coffee machine for a beat, taking in the activity around the office. There was more staff in today than had ever been to work at once in the Maggie's Knee Sheriff's Office; it was all hands on deck. Four deputies, three of whom accounted for over half his full-time staff, sat at desks with phones to their ears, typing furiously on the fancy new desktops council had sprung for last year—their most recent technological update in well over a decade. Even Tim Henchek, a part-time deputy in his early thirties who was usually impossible to get to take on any extra shifts, had come in on his day off to work the phones. Only Freddie Nancarrow, his overnight deputy, and Charlene Anders, who had just gone on maternity leave, weren't here. And all it took was the sheriff's stepdaughter going missing. Gordon wanted to be optimistic about finding Farren, but a nagging dread had stalked him ever since the discovery of her backpack.

Finding the bag hadn't been all bad. Yes, its abandonment on Jessop's Bridge did point to the possibility Farren had fallen —or jumped—into Widow's River. But the contents of the backpack didn't indicate suicidal intention. She'd stuffed it with a sweater, a few pairs of socks, cash, snacks, and a water bottle. Her phone was there too, stashed in one of the smaller zipper compartments on the side. These things all pointed to someone who had planned on living for at least a little while. It was the luggage of a runaway. That it was abandoned, to Gordon, could only mean Farren had been taken against her will. Surely, if she'd fallen, they would have found her body during their search for Garrett Mews yesterday—a search which had quickly shifted focus once Farren's backpack had been found. Normally such a discovery wouldn't prompt a search effort so quickly but Gordon didn't want to waste any time.

In an hour or so, Gordon and his full-time deputies would hit the streets to interview friends, potential eyewitnesses, and, of course, family. It was only a matter of time before Gordon would have to disclose there had been a fair amount of arguing in their house the last little while. When that happened, he could be sure the investigation would be taken out of his hands.

Until then, he would do everything he could to locate Farren.

A hand on his elbow startled him, causing him to slop coffee over the front of his tan uniform shirt.

He was suddenly glad to have refused the office petition to change their uniform shirt colors to white. That whole ordeal last summer had been the most drama the office had ever seen under his leadership. Most of his deputies didn't talk to him for a week or more after he'd refused their signed document demanding he bend to their demands. He didn't consider himself a harsh leader and had no aspirations to be, but there were times when he needed to put a solid foot down and say no. Never mind that he preferred not to wear white—case just proven—the decision was out of his hands to begin with. Council had decided on the uniform color ages ago and he would be damned if he'd go before them and slog through their bureaucratic bullshit just to give in to a fashion whim.

Marco Alejo, the deputy he'd be hitting the streets with today, still wasn't the same around him since Gordon had put a stern end to the discussion. He was courteous, but there was a dispassion behind it, a flame that died out over a simple matter of what color shirt he wore to work.

Barb clasped her other hand on Gordon's arm, shaking him from his thoughts. "I've got a good feeling we'll find her alive and well," she said with a quiver to her voice that betrayed the lie.

She didn't seem to have noticed she'd caused him to spill coffee all over himself. Why bother telling her?

"Thanks, Barb," he muttered.

After waiting for her to fix her own coffee with an obscene amount of cream and sugar, Gordon refilled his mug, sipping from it immediately, once more relishing the punishing heat on his mouth.

Back in his office, he flopped into the chair behind his desk and shook the computer mouse to quit the screensaver. Four photos took up the monitor, one in each corner. The one on the top left was a shot of Old Maggie from the middle of Jessop's Bridge, the river disappearing into the dense forest surrounding the town. Next to that was one of Farren's backpack leaning up against the sidewall of the bridge, as though she'd placed it there carefully before doing whatever she did next. The third picture was of some tire tracks on the bridge his gut told him had nothing to do with anything.

The fourth photo was the one he found himself staring at most often. It had been enhanced slightly, using the free software that came with his computer, to make some of the edges stand out and to brighten things up a bit.

Paul Obasi, an ex-football player in his late twenties, and Gordon's youngest full-time deputy, made the discovery and had the presence of mind to take a picture before anyone could tromp through and muck it up. That kid was going places.

Regardless of age, Gordon was lucky to have him. Paul had come from a poor Nigerian family who had moved to the United States when he was two. He worked hard all his life, got straight As and honors in school, and received a full football scholarship, which he used to study law and criminology. Then he quit football and applied to be a cop. He'd never admit to it, but the rumor around the office was that he would have been an early pick for an NFL team and could have been living the dream. He'd given it up to serve and protect.

The photo Paul had taken showed twin tracks, just straight lines, going through a wet patch of mud next to the river. The tracks were only about three meters long, but it was enough to tell they likely belonged to a sled. The first thing that came to mind was a hunter bagged a deer and hauled it back to his car. Hunting wasn't allowed in that part of the woods, but that didn't mean it never happened.

Still.

Across the river had been a shabby lean-to, likely where one of the guys who hung out at the Mission was living. Gordon made a mental note to ask around about who lived in that tent; it had been searched thoroughly and there was no sign of Farren or of a struggle, which she would certainly have put up. The hope was whoever lived there had been home when whatever made those tracks had come through.

He printed half a dozen copies of each of the photos to pass out to his deputies. They were going out in teams of two and he wanted every officer to have their own copies to show around. He and Marco would be heading downtown to chat with anyone who may have seen Farren on the day she disappeared, while Paul and Trina Kostecki, his second-most senior deputies, would call on Farren's friends and teammates. He knew she didn't have many close friends, but she played on a lot of sports teams and had to talk to some of the girls she played with. At least he hoped that was the case.

He'd once caught her hanging out with a guy in his forties out in front of the Mission. The guy had been wearing a pleated skirt over tight black leggings and a white blouse that would have made him look like a pirate if it wasn't for the blinding purple lipstick and bright yellow eyeshadow he'd been wearing. The guy had hugged Farren as if they were old girlfriends. Gordon didn't get the idea the guy—Stacey, Farren had said his name was—had any sexual interest in Farren, but Gordon also wasn't confident he was the best influence on her. He forbade her from going back to the Mission, which meant there was a good possibility she'd been there recently. It was as good a place to start as any.

## 21

An hour or so later, Gordon pulled his cruiser into one of the municipal parking spots next to the Mission. He surveyed the crowd of maybe fifteen men and women as they milled about on the sidewalk in front of the three-story building. His office received no end of complaints about the place; from folks being accosted on their way to dinner at one of the upscale restaurants in the neighborhood, to the number of cigarette butts and trash people staying at the Mission dumped onto the street every day. They were legitimate complaints, but he had very little way of addressing them.

For one, he needed to catch the offenders in the act, and they always seemed to see police coming from a mile away. And they only had two small holding cells at the station. On top of all that, they simply didn't possess the manpower to dedicate to the constant check-ins required to keep the relative peace. He'd tried to enlist help from the people who worked at the Mission, and had been all but laughed out. Not only did they not have the resources, they faced enormous liability if they ever laid hands on one of their residents, which meant all they could do was speak sternly to any rule-breakers and call the police.

The existence of the Maggie's Knee Mission wasn't the issue; no one could deny they did good work there and legitimately aided in keeping homeless addicts and alcoholics off the streets, even guiding a small percentage of them into complete rehabilitation. The problem was the location, smack dab in the middle of Main Street. It had been established long before KnowMe arrived and turned the humble town into a bustling day trip destination.

When the social media giant moved in, they brought a lot of wealth along with them, and the town had seen a dramatic turnaround. Not many of the locals were happy about it initially, but no one could deny their town had been decaying around them and that KnowMe had, for better or worse, brought them back from the brink of oblivion. With the wealth came trendy people and savvy entrepreneurs who swiftly turned Main Street from a scene in *The Walking Dead* to a hot spot for foodies and boutique shoppers.

"No sign of Stacey," Gordon said.

Deputy Marco Alejo, sitting shotgun, slurped from his travel mug, a stainless-steel job with vivacious curves bearing what Gordon thought of as the Logo of the Beast, that creepy siren mermaid, smirking out a him from under the deputy's thumb. Marco stashed the mug in one of the cupholders. It was too tall to fit with Gordon's computer mount in the way, so he had to jam it in on an angle.

"Been a couple days since I've seen him around. They kicked him out again. Might be for good this time."

"Great," Gordon muttered. "Let's see if anyone knows where he might be."

"Or where *Farren* might be," Marco added.

Instead of responding—he didn't want to tempt fate by getting his hopes up—Gordon pushed out of the car, securing his hat as he stood. He made a show of looking around, as if he wasn't sure why he was here, then honed in on the Mission, scanning the crowd. A few of those out front were staring his way, but most either hadn't noticed him or were pretending he wasn't there.

A woman who looked old enough to be his great-grandmother sat on the front steps, holding a cigarette between tanned, leathery fingers. She watched him with watery eyes and no perceivable emotion. Her hand shook as she raised the cigarette to her lips to take a long drag. Smoke oozed from her nostrils as if her only form of respiration was one slow, steady exhale.

Scotty Smith, who'd had a few run-ins with the Sheriff's Office, jitterbugged back and forth on the sidewalk in front of the old woman. Scotty was a tweaker prone to removing his pants and taking a dump on the sidewalk or in the street. He'd once snuck onto the patio of the little Italian place across the street, but the owner had tackled him and dragged him back across the street before he could drop his pants.

Marco marched ahead and went straight to Scotty, taking him gently by the elbow and leading him off the sidewalk to chat in the parking lot. Scotty looked nervous, but that was nothing new.

Gordon looked around, trying to ignore the old woman's gaze, and spotted a stovepipe hat in the back of a circle of four guys smoking cigarettes. He recognized all the guys in the circle but didn't know their names offhand. One of them was a rough-looking kid of twenty or so with a shaved head, prison tattoos, and a hard glint in eyes that watched Gordon's every move. Gordon smiled at him, a move he knew threw off most people who saw him as just another big cop. The kid looked at the ground and pulled on his smoke.

"'Scuse me," Gordon called to the group.

They all looked up and he pointed a finger directly at the guy in the silly hat, holding him with his eyes so he knew he was being spoken to directly.

"Got a minute?"

The guy in the hat looked at the others in the circle, who suddenly all found the ground as interesting as their skinhead friend did. Stovepipe Hat shrugged and stepped through the circle to where Gordon stood, a few feet away.

"I've got nothing on me," the guy said before Gordon could speak. He was forty or fifty, with about a week's worth of rough stubble.

"That's good news." Gordon gave the guy his disarming smile, in case he didn't see it the first time. "I need your help. What's your name?"

The guy shuffled from foot to foot. "Pietro."

"Pietro. I'm Sheriff Gordon Noble. We haven't met formally, have we?" Gordon held out his hand.

At first, Pietro only looked at it. After a few seconds, he gripped it in weak fingers and gave it a light bounce.

"You need my help?" he said, taking a last drag of his cigarette and pitching it into the street.

As soon as the cigarette landed, Pietro shot a look up to Gordon, panicked guilt in his eyes. He bent to retrieve the butt and was stopped by Gordon grabbing him gently on the arm.

"Not worth diving into traffic for," Gordon said, releasing Pietro before he could assume any violent intent. "Just use the butt bin next time. You know a guy named Stacey?"

Pietro's look went from worried to wary. "What's he said?"

With each word the bitter tang of alcohol mixed with pungent cigarette smoke wafted from his mouth, mingling with the odiferous sweat and filth from his body and clothes. It was a smell Gordon was used to, but one that still turned his guts. Took some effort not to recoil from the guy.

Gordon held up a reassuring hand. "Nothing, I only need to speak with him."

"Haven't seen him in a while," Pietro said. "I haven't been around."

"You don't stay here?"

Pietro shook his head. "I camp ... I stay somewhere else."

"You camp?" Gordon tried to keep his voice even. "By the river?"

Pietro danced on the spot again, clearly torn between lying to Gordon and risking losing his home.

"It's okay," Gordon said. "I'm not going to make you move. You have the blue tarp? North of the bridge?"

"I keep it clean, I promise. And I don't do nothing I shouldn't. Drink a bit, that's all. I don't even do drugs," Pietro pleaded.

"Have you seen anything down there? Anything out of the ordinary?"

It didn't take a cop to catch the change in Pietro's demeanor. He went from wary to downright scared, eyes darting back and forth as if he thought they were being spied on.

"What did you see?" Gordon pressed. This could be the break he needed.

"Shadow people," Pietro muttered.

"Shadow people? What are they?"

"They take the kids."

"You know who took the missing kids?" Gordon asked, unable to keep his cop voice from coming through.

Pietro shook his head, wide-eyed.

"Who took them?"

"The shadow people come at night and take them and eat them."

Gordon grabbed the guy in the stupid hat before he even realized he was doing it. He dragged Pietro down the sidewalk, into the parking lot, to his cruiser. Shoved him against the car. The stupid hat went flying and landed somewhere behind them. In his peripheral vision, he registered Marco stalking across the parking lot toward them.

"You saw them do that?" Gordon shouted, unable to stop himself. "You saw them eat someone?"

Pedestrians were stopping to watch what was going on. A twenty-something sitting by herself on a cafe patio across the street was holding up her phone, no doubt recording this.

Pietro held his hands up and cowered against the car.

Marco reached them, scooped up Pietro's hat, and put a hand on Gordon's arm, subtly, so no one watching would see.

"Sheriff, you all right over here?" He stared Gordon hard in the eyes.

Gordon forced out a breath. "All good. Thanks, deputy."

"What's going on?"

"Pietro here says he knows who took the missing kids."

Marco's eyes widened. "Took them?"

"Tell him," Gordon said to Pietro. "Tell him about your shadow people."

"They take them and they eat them," Pietro repeated.

Marco handed the hat back to him. "How do you know this?"

"I just know," Pietro said, placing his hat back on his head.

Marco turned his back on Pietro and once more took Gordon by the arm, a little less subtly this time, and led him away from the car. "You sure you want to entertain this guy's drug trip fantasies?" he said in a low voice.

"He denied doing drugs."

Marco's incredulous look told Gordon what he thought about that statement.

"You stop to think you might be too close to this?"

Gordon squared off with Marco, standing close, so the deputy would have to look up at him. "What if his fantasies are tangled up in reality?"

Marco held his ground. "We have tangible leads to follow. Don't you think we would have found something if we had cannibals eating people out in the woods? Especially if they're careless enough this guy can spy on them?"

"What about the tracks?"

As soon as Gordon said it, he knew he sounded desperate, as legitimate as his interest in them may be.

"We'll follow the river then, see if we can pick them up again. Let's do some real police work instead of having this guy tell us fairy tales," Marco was pleading, talking to Gordon at the level they'd been used to before the whole uniform fiasco dented their working relationship.

Marco was right; Gordon had latched onto the first crazy

thing he heard from the first person he interviewed—the guy in the ridiculous hat.

He looked away, embarrassed. "You're right. I'm sorry. I'm worried, I guess."

"No shit," Marco said. "Let's get out of here before we give the influencers anything else to record." He nodded toward a fashionable young couple with their phones out and pointed their way.

Had Gordon been loud enough for the phone mics to pick up? Either way, he'd no doubt be hearing from Byron about this.

Gordon dismissed Pietro and got in the car with Marco. He was lucky to have a guy like him by his side during what just happened. If Deputy Alejo had been any sort of hothead, things could have gone an entirely different way, one that could have cost them their jobs or worse.

The moment Gordon pulled the car onto Main Street, the sky turned gray as slate and the temperature dropped by ten degrees. Marco rolled up his window and Gordon followed suit.

"Didn't you say clear skies all day?" Marco asked, looking up at the sky through his window.

"That's what the weather app showed," Gordon said. "Wasn't a cloud in the sky a minute ago."

The first raindrop that hit the windshield must have been the size of a tennis ball; it splattered across the glass, startling both officers and exploding in an enormous puddle. There was a full five-second delay between that and the next drop. The following billion or so came down one second after.

The cruiser's wipers slashed at the rain, which threatened to drown the car. Gordon had never in his life seen this much rain coming down at once. It was as if they'd driven under a waterfall. Melinda had made him go on vacation with her to the Dominican Republic last year during storm season, when the resorts were all at their cheapest. It only rained once during their stay, but it had been a doozy. They'd been at the poolside bar when the sky darkened and a torrential downpour started, rain hitting the tiled pool deck hard enough to soak both of their legs, though they'd been sitting under an awning. The rain only lasted a few minutes but it had been the hardest rainfall Gordon had ever seen. That downpour didn't even come close to this.

Gordon started his lights flashing and put the car in park along the side of Main Street. Nobody was going anywhere in this.

He realized Marco was saying something next to him.

"What?" Gordon shouted, marveling at how much the noise of the rain drowned out his voice.

"I said, there go our tracks!"

He was right. This sort of rain wouldn't just wash the tracks away, Gordon wouldn't be surprised to find whole chunks of the riverbank broken off and washed down Old Maggie from the force of it. All evidence of Farren's disappearance gone in seconds.

Almost like something didn't want him finding her.

He sat back and watched the deluge.

Jasper stopped at the bottom of the library steps to tie his shoe. Cold November wind blew across the parking lot and froze his fingertips. He really should have tied the errant lace inside the library—he'd noticed it was undone while sitting in his favorite chair, reading this week's selection for his Modern Classics class; Hemingway's *To Have and Have Not.* Jasper consumed most of the book in the few hours he'd been sitting there, looking up every few minutes to watch the darkly sexy girl browsing the stacks. She must have crossed his field of view five or six times, lingering at the shelves directly in front of where he sat, looking for some book or another. She was a bit shorter than him and very skinny, but she wore her weight well in tight black jeans and a faux fur-lined winter coat that hugged her frame. A black wool hat covered her straight-cut, blonde hair. She wore dark makeup; just enough to be considered heavy, but not so much that it didn't work for her. Her features were severe, all harsh angles, but she had a mysterious, mischievous look to her. She wasn't exactly pretty, but she oozed sex appeal. Jasper couldn't stop thinking about her.

Following the exploits of Hemingway's tragic Harry Morgan had made Jasper thirsty. As much as he wanted to convince himself he could ever work up the courage to talk to the brooding girl in the library, he was itching for a cold drink. Something with rum.

Shoe tied, he ambled up the sidewalk to where he'd parked his mom's car, thinking about where he wanted to stop on the way home. Without any of Hemingway's rowdy Cuban bars to drop into, he settled on Rusty's, a pub he'd been frequenting since starting his college journey in September.

The pub was convenient, being roughly halfway between home and campus. And it was quiet, which Jasper enjoyed, particularly when he had schoolwork to do. At nineteen, he was underage, but nobody at Rusty's ever asked him for ID. He had a fake one, just in case, but it was nice to not have to lie. They must have assumed no kid under twenty-one would come into the place on his own. Or maybe they left him alone because he kept to himself, limited himself to one or two drinks, and behaved better than most of the regulars. Regardless, it was the perfect place to kill some time before heading home.

Jasper loved not having to pay rent, live on campus, or buy his own groceries, but living at home had plenty of drawbacks.

He couldn't bring girls home, not that they were crawling over each other for a date with him. His parents never went to sleep and his older sister, Fiona, had moved back home and was living in the basement after breaking up with her boyfriend of ten years. She did not love unexpected visitors in her space. Jasper was basically confined to his room unless he wanted his parents hovering around him; Mom asking if he'd met any nice girls yet and did he think he might be gay, and Dad talking his ear off about how much he'd made in commission that day and how the vast majority of English majors weren't pulling in half of what he was with his "experience" in business.

So living at home sucked. But he was saving a ton of money that he would be able to put to use getting him far away from home the very second he graduated. He'd picked up some freelance work writing articles for a couple of blogs. Writing was something that came naturally to him, though he lacked the imagination for fiction and couldn't tell a story to save his life. Articles, though, were a cinch. Jasper was frequently praised by his clients for his ability to suit his writing to the tone of their website, blog, or whatever he was working on.

Neither of his parents ever seemed to accept it was a skill with any merit, so he'd learned his value relatively late in life. He started writing the articles in his last year of high school, at the encouragement of his Creative Writing teacher, Mrs. Redding. She'd seen the passion Jasper possessed for the written word and hadn't wanted him to feel discouraged when he couldn't produce a coherent, entertaining, or even slightly readable story. She'd called up a friend, showed them an example of Jasper's writing from an assignment in which the class had to create their own advertisements, and landed him his very first gig writing one article a month for an outdoor living company.

They sent him all the information he needed, plus a bunch of links for reference, and he put it together into something they could stick on their blog. He received high praise for his first piece, and one article a month swiftly turned to almost one a week for half a dozen different websites. Not only was he getting paid for his writing, he was learning about things he never thought to educate himself in; camping, survival, fishing, computer technology, psychology, and bitcoin were just a few of the subjects he was becoming at least conversationally proficient in just by writing about them.

He never told his parents about the job. Thought Mrs. Redding might let it slip in one of his reports. If she did, his parents never mentioned it to him, which was okay since they'd never thought much of his passion to begin with. He'd opened his own bank account upon turning eighteen and built up a respectable little fortune with his writing.

In the library parking lot, Jasper slid into his mom's car, a blue BMW sedan. He'd started it remotely from the library doors so it was already warming up by the time he got in and tossed his backpack in the back seat. Holding his hands up to the vent, he was thankful he'd found a parking spot relatively close to the doors—he'd had to park on the street several blocks away on more than one occasion.

The passenger door opened just before he put the car in gear, and the girl from the library lowered herself into the passenger seat. She closed the door and looked up at him, a grin spreading on her sharply defined face.

"Hi, Jasper." She held a hand out to him, all dainty as if she was royalty. "I'm Sasha."

He took her hand, still unsure of what to say. Her skin was soft, delicate fingers ice cold in his warmed-up palm. She closed her hand over his and lowered it, maintaining her grip so they held hands over the center console.

Finally, he managed to say, "What are you doing in my car? How'd you know my name?"

Not as if he minded. Minutes ago he was fantasizing about this very thing happening exactly this way. He'd had girlfriends in the past, but had never really picked any of them up, so to speak; they'd all been friends who had evolved into something more.

The girl, Sasha, slipped her hand from his and gripped his thigh, sliding her hand up toward his stiffening organ, just the way he imagined. Put her lips against his ear, sending jolts of excitement from it, through his neck, and into his lower regions where it powered the hardening process, causing his pants to feel a size too small. Grabbed his bulge, squeezing with more strength than he imagined those fingers could possess.

He came immediately, helplessly bucking his hips and groaning despite how caught off guard he'd been—or maybe because of it. She held him firm until everything stored up in him had evacuated, leaving a cooling, sticky mess in his jeans.

With her mouth still against his ear, she said, "We're going to be friends."

# PART 2

## 22

Farren held a hand up to call for time-out. She stuck the end of her bat in the dirt, leaned on it like a cane, pulled the Osaka Kintetsu Buffaloes hat from her head, and armed sweat from her brow. Even in the relative coolness of the forest, it had been a scorching summer and August seemed eager to offer up the hottest days yet. She was grateful for the shade provided by the countless trees populating the Congo. Not only did it provide some relief during the ballgame, it made the lack of air conditioning much more bearable.

The grounds had limited electricity provided by a ten large generators, two of which were designated exclusively to power the arcade cabinets and televisions in the Shop. To save fuel, none of the generators powered any sort of climate control. Farren would have much preferred to have air conditioning in at least one building but accepted part of living in a community run by kids was accepting their priorities may not always be the most practical. And besides, she enjoyed the amenities of the Shop as much as the rest of the tribe.

Farren had already been present for two periods of gas rationing when the only buildings allowed to keep their power on were the dining hall and the Visitor's Center, where the Congo's security hub was located. Naturally, the Shop was the first place to give up its share of fuel when rations were implemented. Since the generators were too big to move, some lucky kid would be chosen to siphon the gas from the Shop's generators for use in the priority buildings. The rationing typically didn't last for more than a day or two, the tribe had tremendous luck tracking down and obtaining supplies with little or no resistance.

The fuel bringers went out once a week, pulling huge gasoline cans on the sled, and always returned with them full. From what Farren understood, they mainly siphoned from parked vehicles, but also managed to steal from gas station pumps undetected when they were desperate. Farren had asked Jasper how they managed to get away with stealing so much so often and he'd given her a puzzled look.

"We're taken care of. Protected and provided for." As if that should be obvious.

Farren didn't understand what he meant, or if he was speaking figuratively, but it certainly felt like *something* was looking out for them. At first she wondered if it was her dad, who had convinced her to stay here in the first place. But the more she thought about it, the more ridiculous it seemed he would spend his afterlife babysitting a bunch of kids in the woods.

"No batter!" Danny McCallister called from first base.

It pulled her from her thoughts. He was giving her his big

shit-eating grin, which she couldn't help but laugh at.

"No batter!" Guppy bellowed from behind her.

She cast a glance back at the youngest McCallister and found herself marveling again at the size of him. The first time she saw him after her Induction, she'd almost curled into a ball and hid, certain she was experiencing some sort of flashback from the tea. Then Sadie led him by the hand to where Farren had been standing, stopping a few feet away from her, and introduced him. None of what Farren had seen in him on the night of her Induction had been a hallucination. The boy—he was only twelve—stood what had to be almost ten feet tall and must weigh close to five hundred pounds.

"Farren," the giant's spritely sister had said, "this is Guppy, my little brother."

"Hi," Farren managed to squeak.

Guppy's baby face had lit up in an enormous smile.

"Hi!" he'd shouted at her, his voice a thunderous basso.

Then he'd run at her. Farren had shrieked and stumbled backward, tripping over her crutches and spilling herself on her ass. Next thing she knew, he was picking her up as if she weighed nothing at all. He held her upright with one surprisingly delicate hand and retrieved her crutches with the other, gently sticking them under her arms like she was an action figure.

That had been how she'd officially met the twelve-year-old behemoth playing catcher in their third official Congo baseball game.

Farren insisted on getting together as many people as were interested for a game after she'd come around—a term the tribe, now *her* tribe, used for recruits who decided to remain in the Congo. She'd discovered the shed full of baseball equipment, most of it untouched since the place had first been established. Their first game, organized entirely by Farren, took place on a Sunday afternoon in the middle of June.

Deciding to remain in the Congo hadn't been an easy decision, even after seeing her dad in the chapel (imagined or not, he'd made a compelling argument) but baseball helped her cope immensely. Until conceiving of the idea to organize a ballgame, she'd felt ill at ease in the Congo, though the tribe did their best to make her comfortable. Sleep hadn't come easy if at all most nights. She'd stare up at the ceiling in the dark of her room, trying not to think of the name of the thing she'd been told dwelled in the Museum. And then, turning her dad's hat over in her hands one afternoon, the answer to her malady fell on her with a suddenness impossible to ignore. Sports had been how she coped in her previous life, so why not try the same thing here? And with that, the Congo Baseball League was born.

Farren winked at Guppy and hoisted the bat in both hands, finding her grip and settling into her stance. Without her blade, the curved prosthesis she wore for sports, she wasn't as fast as she wanted to be, but she'd grown accustomed to the replacement made for her by Nick, the Congo's resident handyman.

Turned out Nick, who was all of fourteen years old, was insanely gifted at making things as well as fixing them. He'd approached her out of nowhere a couple of weeks after her Induction and handed the replacement to her without preamble.

"It's to help you walk," he'd said, seeing the puzzlement on her face. "You'll probably have to let me resize it but I think I got it pretty close."

Farren had broken down in tears and hugged the blushing boy fiercely before trying it on.

It was little more than a peg leg, a rod of aluminum Nick had turned into a working prosthesis. He had affixed a small disc to the end of it, attached on a balljoint to give some flexibility to her steps. The part that attached to her leg was made of tough, soft rubber. He also provided her with interchangeable, washable cloths made of wicking material to sit between her stump and the attachment. It fastened on with a strap he'd fashioned with supple leather. The whole thing was more comfortable than it had any right to be and needed no size adjustment at all. Nick was apparently also some sort of savant when it came to eyeballing measurements.

Now Farren dug her new prosthesis, which she had dubbed the "Piston", into the dirt behind her. From the pitching mound, Hamji gave a nod to Guppy, as if the catcher had been throwing signs. Farren adjusted her grip on the bat. Hamji had a fair arm and had struck her out in two games.

The pitch came in low and away. For a millionth of a second, she thought she might let it go. Her instinct knew better, however, and demanded she swing. She gave in to the urge, barely reaching for the ball and knowing it would be a good one when it curved slightly into the strike zone, framing itself on the sweet spot of her bat. She leaned into it and grinned when she felt that perfect impact and heard the sweet crack of ash on horsehide. She followed through and watched the ball sail high and deep, past the fence bordering the field, and into the thick bushes beyond.

Her bench cheered, rattling the dugout fence, and shouting her name. The opposing team booed from the field and their dugout, but the tone was friendly and she blew them a playful kiss as she jogged around first. It wasn't her first home run of the Congo's inaugural baseball season, but it was the first she'd hit out of the park. It was a good feeling, something she'd been having a lot of these days.

The elation of the homer faded a bit when she noticed who was standing just outside her team's dugout. Sasha leaned against the fencepost and clapped awkwardly like it was the first time she'd ever performed that sort of movement with her hands. In spite of the heat, she was dressed in a black, long-sleeve Korn shirt, black skinny jeans, and her stupid purple Doc Martens—the absolute worst footwear for life in a forest.

Farren high-fived a fifteen-year-old kid named Marcus, waiting for her at home plate.

"Nice slap, Murakami."

"Nice slap yourself."

Marcus hit before her and had driven the ball straight at Tania, who was playing short stop. Tania had wisely leapt out of the way, allowing for Marcus to make it all the way to third before the ball was thrown in.

Farren patted Marcus on the shoulder and made her way toward Sasha. Might as well get this over with.

Sasha looked her up and down as she approached, apparently wanting Farren to know she was being appraised.

"Nice hit," Sasha said. "Maybe I should start playing."

Farren ignored the remark.

There was no love lost between the two of them; Sasha had made it clear she didn't trust Farren and thought she was here to destroy their home. All Farren could figure was that she was jealous of one of two fallacies: Either Jasper was interested in her, or she was somehow favored by the thing they served, the thing she tried her level best not to think about throughout the day, but was helpless to keep from her dreams. Sasha and whatever that thing might be were the only two very dark spots on her otherwise complete happiness in the Congo. And still, they were easier to deal with than Melinda.

Sasha had apparently been upset that Farren learned the thing's name, though Farren hadn't had a clue what the word meant until Sasha told her on the day of her Induction; the day before she'd woken up to discover her dad's hat on the dresser of her new room.

"What's up?" Farren asked, eager to have Sasha gone.

"This." Sasha waved her hands between them.

"I don't know what *this* you mean. If there's something you want to say, say it."

"Easy, tiger. I mean us. We got off on the wrong foot, no offense." Sasha shot a look down at the Piston.

"Pretty sure you said you want to kill me," Farren said.

"I said I would *if* you were here to betray us."

"You also said you thought I was here to betray you."

Sasha shrugged. "Like I said, wrong foot."

"Stop with that."

"I want to make it up to you."

Farren waited, keeping her face as still as possible, trying not to let Sasha see she wanted to knock her teeth in. Sasha was trying to talk all sweet, but it just made her come across as whiney. There had to be some other agenda.

"I want to get your prosthesis back," Sasha said, folding her hands in front of her as though pleading with Farren for the privilege.

"What are you talking about?" Farren's suspicion grew, a storm siren working up to full blare.

Sasha took one of Farren's hands in her own. Farren pulled

it back, not hard, but forcefully enough to make her point.

"I was just thinking, you've come a long way since we brought you here. People already look up to you. You started a baseball league." Sasha gestured around them as if to indicate Farren had built the whole diamond. "I think the Congo will be a better place if the two of us are on the same side. Or at least if we get along. I thought I could make you a peace offering."

Farren tried not to let any hope creep into her voice, "We've looked for it. These guys have spent enough of their time crawling around out there in the mud trying to find my foot. It probably fell in the river, like I've said, which means it's gone."

Four parties had gone out looking for her missing prosthesis, with her along for only two of the trips. This had been after an especially wet second half of spring, starting with the insane storm the day after her Induction.

Sasha shook her head. "The other one."

"My blade?" Farren laughed. "That's at my house, man. The sheriff's house?"

"We've got it covered."

She seemed sincere, which threw Farren off balance. Sasha had been nothing but cold and mean toward her since she got here, especially since Farren opened her stupid mouth and told them what she'd heard in her head. She was glad they told her what the word meant, but just knowing it caused her nothing but trouble.

And she was terrified of it. Of what it might belong to, of what or who it might be the name of. Just thinking the word conjured an almost physical presence in her mind, her own mental *Beetlejuice*. But Michael Keaton's character resembled a birthday clown compared to the presence she'd felt in the chapel and on the other side of Eagle Creek. She was willing to stay here—and had so far enjoyed herself—but she refused to drink the tainted Kool-Aid being offered.

"I'll go too," Farren said, looking into Sasha's gray-blue eyes.

Sasha shook her head. "Sorry, babe. Party's already made up. We're going tonight. Can't afford to have you seen around there. Too many questions will come up."

"So why tell me?" Farren demanded. "Why not just go?"

"I need the door code."

"How'd you know we have a code lock?"

"We've already checked the place out, to make sure we can pull this off," Sasha said. "You can see the keypad on the front door from the street."

Gordon had installed keyless locks on their place back when Farren's mom was alive. Her mom was notorious for losing her keys and had locked herself out on more than one occasion; it was one of her few flaws. Gordon changed the code a couple of times a year. The current combination got Farren's blood simmering every time she had to use it.

"It's Melinda's birthday—one, zero, two, four," Farren said.

Sasha snickered.

"That's *if* Gordon didn't change it," Farren added. "He switches it up twice a year."

"When?"

Farren shrugged, enjoying the frustrated pout that appeared on Sasha's face.

"We're taking the field!" Hannah called from the bench.

Farren turned to follow her team to the outfield but Sasha grabbed her arm.

"He'd keep the code the same for you, wouldn't he?" Sasha demanded. "In case you came back?"

Farren shrugged. "Before Melinda, I would've said yeah. I honestly wouldn't be surprised if she made him change it to keep me out, though."

She pulled her arm from Sasha's grip and headed to the bench for her glove.

Jogging out to right field, Farren let herself hope for a brief moment they would be successful and make it back with her foot. She couldn't even imagine what would go down if they were caught in her house.

Farren came to the decision without having given it any thought until that second. She would follow them. No idea how she would pull it off, but she needed to see how this went. It was her foot after all. And if the house really was empty, she may even pop in to grab some things.

If she was caught though ...

That bridge, if it existed, could be crossed when she got to it. It's not like they were prisoners, she was free to leave if she wanted. To abandon the tribe would mean exile, but she wouldn't be leaving in that sense. This was a mission just like any other scavenging or recruiting trip.

Sasha had been right about one thing, though; Farren couldn't be seen anywhere in Maggie's Knee or the search parties would start again and the tribe would be at risk of being discovered. Nobody could legally drag her back, of course, she was eighteen—if she wanted to take off, she had every right to. But there were a lot of much younger kids here who didn't fit that criteria and who she could now be legally held accountable for.

So she would be careful. She wouldn't let anyone in

Maggie's Knee spot her and would get back to the Congo well ahead of the party.

It would be worth the risk. She wanted to see Bonzo, if only for a minute. Give the big old goof a kiss on his silly nose. She suddenly missed him fiercely, which solidified her decision.

At her place in right field she turned to face home. Sasha was already out of sight. Good. Being around her was akin to being in the presence of a housebroken jungle cat; the risk far outweighed any benefit. Sasha was apt to explode at any second, without cause. Farren had witnessed her share of freak-outs.

It wasn't Sasha she was really afraid of, though. They weren't allowed to talk about the thing in the Museum, the thing whose name had infected her mind. Farren still wasn't allowed on that side of the bridge, and wouldn't have chosen to go over there even if she was. But she had a feeling whatever was in the Museum played a bigger role here than anyone realized. For the majority of the tribe, "the one they served" was an idea more than an actual entity they paid allegiance to. It was hardly discussed outside of Inductions. But she had felt something on the other side of Eagle Creek, and Sasha knew exactly what it was. Jasper seemed to have only a vague understanding of what it might be. Farren feared it had more of a hold on them than anyone realized or wanted to admit.

She squinted at the sun and guessed it was around three in the afternoon. They were in the top of the ninth now. She'd have plenty of time to think of these things after the game. She squatted, stretched her legs, shook out her arms, and shoved all thoughts of the evening to come from her mind.

This was time for baseball.

23

J asper crouched behind the hedgerow lining the driveway that had once belonged to the Murakami family and which now led to the Noble household. The house, a ranch-style bungalow, was set back from the road and surrounded by mature trees and tall hedges. The sconce over the front door was the only light on. A full moon hung in the clear sky overhead, bathing the property in cold, white light, and illuminating fleeting clouds of Jasper's breath. They would need to use flashlights inside, which always made him nervous, but their intel was good and they knew both Nobles would be out all night; the sheriff taking his turn on the night shift, and Melinda out at a friend's birthday party, where she would be spending the night.

Morgan, their resident IT sorceress, had made hacking Melinda Noble's email account seem easy. Once in, she'd been able to access Melinda's personal calendar. She kept records of both hers and Gordon's schedules, every little thing they did, right down to what they would have for supper each night. If plans changed, Melinda made the necessary adjustments in her phone calendar, which synced across all of her dozens of web accounts. As a result, they knew her every move, and most of the sheriff's. Still, they would have to be quick and quiet.

Farren had told Sasha everything they needed to know about the house; the door code, where to find the prosthesis, which floorboards were squeaky, that sort of thing. They could be in and out in a few minutes.

Which made Jasper wonder why Sasha insisted on bringing Guppy along. She said it was for protection and that it would give the giant some experience in case they ever needed him to go out with a scavenging party. But Guppy was the absolute last person he would ever consider bringing on a scavenging mission, let alone breaking into a house, one belonging to the sheriff, no less. The youngest McCallister stood out like Bigfoot in a grocery store. Not only that but the kid was much simpler than most twelve-year-olds; he was all brawn. Jasper couldn't see the benefit in having him along, other than to maybe act as a pack mule. But Sasha had insisted and stuck out her bottom lip almost to its limit, so he figured it was best to just roll with it and hope the streets stayed clear.

Guppy sat on his butt between Sasha and the last member of their party, Gabe Tulli, one of their regular scavengers. Gabe was sixteen and had spent a couple of years in Cadet Corps before he'd been recruited. He was a tall kid with a farmer's lean build and the tan to match. He wore a black Pirates cap over his short, sandy hair. Sitting there, he reminded Jasper of Jason Bourne. It was no wonder the girls, and some of the guys, found him so appealing. He was a real-life action hero.

"What's the plan?" Jasper asked, keeping his voice low, though he was sure there was no one around to hear them.

"Looks empty," Gabe said. "I'll go first and get the door open. The rest of you follow as soon as you see me open it unless I wave you off. Get right inside and get the door closed. In case anyone does show up, we don't want to tip them off that we're here."

"Take Guppy," Sasha said, butting her smoke out in the grass.

"What for?" Jasper hissed.

Gabe shook his head. "Bad idea. No offense, Guppy."

"No offense," Guppy repeated. He was hunched between Jasper and Sasha, his enormous head sticking up over the hedgerow.

Sasha raised her hands to silence them. "Not up for debate. Let him punch in the code and go first."

"What the hell is wrong with you?" Jasper hissed, fighting to keep his voice down. "Why risk anything going wrong?"

"What's going to go wrong?" she snapped. "Gabe will be right there. Guppy could use some more responsibility. He's twelve. He can open a frigging door."

There was nothing to say to convince her when she became adamant about something. She was jutting her bottom lip at him like a challenge. Whatever her reasons for wanting Guppy to go with Gabe, she wasn't about to budge.

Gabe shrugged. "Sounds fair. Guppy, you want to push some buttons?"

"Yeah!" The giant's eyes lit up.

Jasper watched over the hedge as Gabe led Guppy up the driveway. It would have been funny to see had the stakes not been so high. Gabe crept along the asphalt, keeping low in a half-crouch while towering just behind him, Guppy strolled along as though he was still in the Congo. Jasper wasn't even sure he'd be able to fit through the door.

"What's going on?" he said to Sasha without looking over at her. "Why have Guppy open the door?"

He felt her shrug. Tore his gaze from the two approaching the door and stole a glance at her. She was sitting on the grass, staring out into the night, the ghost of a smirk on her face. He didn't like it.

Jasper jogged along the hedgerow, stealing glances over the bushes to keep tabs on what he thought of as his breach team. The boys were standing in front of the door now, bathed in the halogen glow of the overhead light so they resembled actors about to be abducted in a cheesy sci-fi movie. Gabe was explaining something to Guppy and appeared to be looking for understanding from him. Jasper couldn't hear them but he could see Gabe snapping his fingers in front of Guppy's face.

This was going nowhere. Jasper sprinted to the end of the hedges, across the driveway, and up the porch steps. Gabe saw him approach and gave him an exasperated look.

"What's wrong?" Jasper asked, looking between the two who should have had the door open and been inside by now.

"He wanted to go first," Gabe said in a whisper, throwing up his hands. "Up the stairs, I mean. I was leading the way so, naturally, I went up the stairs first and now he's sulking. How was I supposed to know?"

Guppy was frowning and looking at his enormous feet, clad in the cloth boots Nick made for him—it was impossible to find size thirty-five shoes. He had to hunch under the patio ceiling, which made him look even more sullen. Big, fat tears welled up in his eyes.

Jasper touched his arm gently at the elbow because he couldn't reach his shoulder. "Hey, Guppy. Did you want to go up the stairs first?"

The giant nodded, the top of his head scraping the patio ceiling.

"Did you tell Gabe that?"

Slow shake of the head.

"You know people can't read your mind, right?" Jasper spoke gently, the way he would talk to a four-year-old. "If you say what you want, you're more likely to get it, okay?"

"Okay," Guppy muttered.

"Want to open the door? Remember the code?" Jasper asked, pointing at the keypad built into the doorknob.

Guppy nodded and knelt in front of the door, which made his head just barely clear the height of the doorway. He stuck out an enormous finger and for a second Jasper feared it might be too big to push the buttons with any accuracy. Slowly and carefully, Guppy pressed the digits for the code, each button push punctuated by a beep that sounded loud enough to reach the street.

After the fourth beep, the whirring of motors in the door lock told them Guppy had successfully entered the code. He beamed down at Jasper.

"Did it!" he shouted and shoved the door open.

Guppy was getting to his feet when Jasper heard the bark.

Why hadn't they known about the dog? And why had it been quiet until now?

A clicking of nails on stone tile told him the animal was coming for the door from not too deep in the house. It was impossible to see any more than a few feet inside, especially around Guppy's mass. He tried to shove the giant out of the way, but Guppy was rooted in place. Jasper imagined the look on his face was what tornado victims wore just before a twister touched down on their house.

Something in the back of Jasper's mind was telling him he knew what was wrong. Even as the clicking of the nails grew louder, he zoned out, searching his memory for relevant information that was just out of reach.

Then it hit him.

It was a conversation he had with Danny months ago. They'd been on dinner clean up together and were washing dishes when Jasper mentioned he'd wanted to convince Sasha to let him get a dog or two for the Congo, more as pets than for any measure of security. He used to have a dog, Panzerotti, a shih tzu his father had brought home for his mother and that she neglected from the start. The dog had become Jasper's responsibility until it died of old age the year before he graduated high school.

Danny had dropped the plate he'd been scrubbing. Looked Jasper in the eye, pleading with his stare. "Please promise me you won't ever let dogs in here."

When Jasper asked him why he was so against dogs, Danny had at first refused to get into it. His face had paled, which Jasper felt bad for, but which also made him all the more curious about what had happened in Danny's past.

"It's not me," Danny had said, finally. "It's Guppy. He's not just afraid of dogs, he hates them. *Hates* them."

Jasper had pestered Danny for the rest of the evening but Danny refused to go into any details about his brother's attitude toward dogs. The look on the eldest McCallister's face, though, was enough to convince Jasper that maybe a couple of cats would be a better idea.

So that had done it for dogs. Until now.

The beast shot out of the house, teeth gnashing.

Jasper made himself move—couldn't let it get to Guppy.

He shoved himself into the small space between the giant and the doorframe, heaving back on Guppy in hopes he'd get out of the way. And he did, taking a big step back. Jasper reached for the doorknob, but it was too late. The dog lunged at him, rearing up on two legs to grab at him and bring him to the ground.

It planted its paws on Jasper's neck and licked his cheek with a long, drool-covered tongue. It was a big dog, some kind of mix that almost certainly contained German shepherd, and maybe lab given how friendly it turned out to be. The dog woofed and smiled at him.

"Well, hey—" Jasper began to say.

Something yanked him backward. He slammed into the porch banister and the wind was knocked out of him.

Guppy loomed in the doorway once more. Jasper couldn't see what he was doing but the giant's body shook back and forth while the dog growled and barked, suddenly alert. And afraid. Guppy jerked to one side and the dog let out a final, pained yelp before going silent.

"No!" Jasper tried to shout. But he was still winded and all that came out was a wheezing gasp.

Guppy ducked into the house and tossed a dark mass out the door. It flew across the porch, over the stairs, and hit Gabe square in the chest, knocking him to the ground. The scream that came out of him froze Jasper's blood.

Using the banister to pull himself up, Jasper got to his feet and stared in horror at the mass of bloody fur Gabe was scrabbling out from underneath. Gabe's screams turned to a wet gagging sound and then he was turning his head to the side and puking.

Sasha came running up to them now, hissing for Gabe to shut his mouth.

Jasper turned his attention from the pile of gore that had once been the dog back to the house. No sign of Guppy.

What a mess.

He turned around to see Sasha grab Gabe by the shoulders and haul him up to his feet. Gabe looked pale, weak. Nothing at all like the tough guy Jasper had been admiring only minutes ago.

"What the fuck was that?" he demanded when Sasha came up the porch stairs.

"Please elaborate."

"Don't play games, Sash."

"We needed to get rid of a dog. Guppy was perfect for the job."

"You knew about it?" he shouted, heedless of the danger.

She slapped a hand over his mouth. "Keep it down, idiot."

He pulled his face back. "It was a nice dog. It was licking me. You had him kill a perfectly gentle dog. And who even knows what this just did to poor Guppy." He felt emotion tighten his throat and swallowed against it.

"We didn't know it was a nice dog until we got here," Sasha said.

"This is messed up," Jasper said, stomping across the porch to the door, deliberately making more noise than he should.

He slipped inside and felt Sasha following close behind.

24

Melinda sipped her vodka gimlet and widened her eyes at Pamela Furrman, who was telling the absolute, most boring story of the evening about the vacation she and her husband—whom she insisted on referring to in conversation as Dr. Isaac Furrman—had taken to the Cayman Islands where they had done nothing except eat and drink. All of her stories were about their meals.

The night had already been significantly less than Melinda had hoped for. When Irene Sandler sent her an invitation to her forty-fifth birthday party at her chalet in the Alleghenies, Melinda was certain the commercial investor had come around in her thinking regarding the business proposal Melinda pitched to her over cocktails three weeks ago. It was plenty of time to consider it and the only reason Melinda could fathom for taking so long to get back to her was because Irene planned on speaking to her in person at the party.

Melinda had arrived in good spirits and apologized profusely for forgetting her present at home. She hadn't bought anything for Irene, because what do you buy for the woman who has it all? Her plan was to send an email later to apologize and explain that she'd bought Irene a gift identical to one she'd already received and it only made sense to just bring it back. It was Gordon's money, after all.

Melinda had also practiced what she would say when Irene made her an investment offer.

*Oh, Irene, I'm so thrilled for this amazing opportunity to work together*, she'd say. *I want you to know you've been my preferred partner ever since I conceived of Café Meli.*

Upon arriving, she'd hugged Irene and gone through her routine of realizing she'd forgotten the present but dropped the pretense when the birthday girl reminded her the invitations had requested donations to the Humane Society in place of gifts.

Melinda dropped the topic of presents and asked Irene if she'd had a chance to consider her proposal for the cafe.

Irene had laughed. "That was a serious business proposal? I thought we were shooting the shit."

"Oh," Melinda had said, face growing hot. "Well, would you consider it now?"

More laughter. "Absolutely not. I'm sorry, Mel, but you can't just talk about how you want to open a coffee shop on Main Street—"

"A *cafe*," Melinda had interrupted, growing angry.

"Whatever. Talk is cheap. There are already half a dozen *coffee shops* on Main. And you have a new business idea every month. What happened to those protein shakes you were selling?"

Melinda had lifted her chin. "I think a wiser business person would call me innovative."

"Then innovate," Irene had said, turning on one Gucci-clad heel and walking away. "Thanks for coming."

The shakes Irene was referring to had been a bust.

Melinda had been messaged on Instagram by an influencer who wanted her to be a brand ambassador. She'd been so excited for the opportunity she'd invested five thousand dollars in inventory that included shake mix in three gourmet flavors, special shaker cups that maximized your nutrient intake, and diet programs and books. She and Gordon had argued when they came home one afternoon from lunch at the country club to find over two dozen boxes bearing the company's obnoxious logo piled up on their porch.

The shakes themselves tasted terrible. Worse than terrible. Strawberry Sundae tasted like cheese, Chocolate Mousse was what she imagined battery acid must taste like, and Vanilla Latte made her gag before she'd been able to swallow it. That hadn't stopped her from trying to peddle it to her friends, who all thought Melinda was playing a cruel joke on them after tasting the shakes.

Weeks after she'd received her product, Melinda received a notice that the company had been shut down and was under investigation for exhibiting unsavory health and safety practices, including drying out and grinding up insects that had likely been found in the wild, according to investigators, for use as ingredients in their shake mixes, which were found to contain almost as many toxins as supplements. But none of that had been Melinda's fault. She'd made an unwise investment and paid for it. It happened to everyone.

Now, three gimlets later, Melinda had about had her fill of pretentious, upper-class bitches and their successful husbands and their charities and funds and Caribbean vacations. The only reason she'd been invited, she knew deep down, was because her husband was sheriff of Maggie's Knee and had a modicum of political clout, even if he wielded it as a feather duster instead of the hammer it was meant to be.

And Pamela was *still* rambling about the Caymans.

"The conch stew was exquisite, especially when paired with the chardonnay we had flown in from our vineyard. Dr. Isaac Furrman has his own winery. Can you believe it?"

Melinda put her empty glass down on a nearby minimalist Scandinavian end table and said, "Pam, nobody cares."

The timing was either perfect or horrible, depending on the desired outcome. She'd said it between songs in the tacky, all-crooners playlist that had been playing through hidden speakers, and during a lull in the general conversation. Two dozen freshly salon-ed, perfectly made up faces turned toward her with two dozen mouths full of glistening white teeth open in perfect Os of dismay.

"I care, Pam," Sheila LeFleur, wife of town councilor Antoine LeFleur, called from across the room.

"Me too, Pam," said Jennifer Naysmith-Davis, president of Maggie's Knee Business Association and owner of two beauty boutiques, both on Main Street—so tacky.

Twenty-two other voices chimed in with "Me too" and "I care" and "We love you, Pam."

"Maybe it would be best if you left, Melinda," Irene said from where she reclined on a suede sectional.

The room was silent. Someone had stopped the music for this.

"Just wait and see if Gordon looks the other way next time he sees you or your husbands speeding," Melinda said in as dignified a tone as she could muster, though there was no keeping the tremor out of it.

There were a couple of gasps of surprise at that but then Irene started to laugh and the next woman closest to her took up the call and then the entire party was laughing Melinda out of the chalet. She searched for something to say back to them all, some way to get to them, but knew she'd already failed in her bluff about Gordon.

She hoped he didn't find out what she'd said. He never spoke to her about work or who he caught doing what. Probably because he knew she'd be powerless to resist telling whoever she next had cocktails with. It was his fault she was in this position. Knowledge is power and if he would share what he knew with her, she wouldn't be watching the women she used to think of as her friends laugh at her, some of them even filming her with their phones.

The nerve of these entitled bitches!

Melinda knew when retreat was the best option. She turned and ran out the door while the laughter of the room grew to hysterics. Cursed herself for making such a cowardly exit.

Back in her Camry—not the newest or most expensive car in the driveway by a long shot—Melinda allowed herself to cry for just a second. She'd save the bulk of her tears for when Gordon was around. Make him help get her reputation back.

She started the engine, shoved her car into gear, and rolled out of the driveway while flipping through her phone for a suitable album to sing along to on the hour-long drive home. She settled on *Jagged Little Pill*.

At least she no longer had that hobbling, moody brat to deal with when she got home. Maybe she'd drink some wine, eat Chinese, and watch a crime documentary tonight. Something about disappearances.

Z

MELINDA PULLED up to the house in just under an hour with her spirits slightly lifted from singing along to Alanis Morissette. Her good mood, however, was promptly shattered the moment she pulled into the driveway.

The front door stood wide open. Which meant the dog had probably escaped.

"Shit," she spat.

Who had left last? Melinda was pretty sure it had been her. But she was equally certain she'd locked the door behind her. Maybe Gordon had popped in on a break.

She parked in her usual spot and was walking toward the door when someone said something from inside the house. She stopped and held her breath. The voice had been indistinct, but she was sure it had belonged to a young guy.

The TV?

No. She was absolutely, positively certain she hadn't had it on before leaving earlier this evening.

Trespassers then. Robbers.

She backpedaled to the car and pulled her phone from her back pocket. She tapped Gordon's number and put the phone to her ear. He answered in one ring.

"How's the party?" he already sounded tired and still had over six hours left in his shift.

"There's someone in the house," Melinda whispered into the phone.

His voice took on an edge. "What makes you say that? Aren't you at Irene's?"

"I came home. The door was open and—oh my God."

"What?" he shouted, his voice jumpy, like he was running.

She'd at first thought what she was looking at was one of Gordon's jackets that Bonzo must have dragged outside. Then, as her eyes adjusted to the moonlight, she assumed it was the carcass of an animal the dog must have found in the trees. Now she noticed the thick leather collar sticking out of the mess.

Melinda let out a sob.

Then the night took another bad turn.

Farren jogged toward her from out of the dark. She'd lost weight, her hair had grown out a bit, and she wore a peg leg instead of the prosthesis that had cost so damn much, but it was definitely her.

"Farren?"

"What? Melinda!" Gordon shouted. "Is Farren there?"

Farren snatched the phone from her hand and ended the call. "Was that my stepdad?"

She must have some nerve, to come back to this house and then have the audacity to touch Melinda's property.

"You don't get to call him that anymore," Melinda said.

She shot her hand out to snatch the phone back. Farren easily lifted it out of her reach, as if she was playing keep-away with a toddler.

"Are they still in there?" Farren asked.

Clarity dawned on Melinda. "You killed him, didn't you, you little psycho?"

Farren's jaw dropped. Busted.

"K—kill who?" she stammered, trying a little too late to sound innocent. "Is Gordon okay?"

"And here we thought the dog was the only one you didn't hate in this house," Melinda said.

Farren pretended to appear gutted and then looked around, as though she didn't know exactly where Bonzo's corpse lay. She pretended to spot it and ran to the mess, falling all over it in an act worthy of short applause in a community theatre production. Even conjured real tears.

Gordon would be here soon. Time to exert the authority of the sheriff's wife.

Feeling much more confident, Melinda strode toward her house, pausing to scoop up her phone, which lay forgotten on the ground.

She stepped over Farren, leaving her to continue or give up the performance, and up the stairs to *her* patio, leading into *her* house. Stormed through *her* hallway, toward *her* living room, where she was certain Farren's thieving friends would be carrying *her* UHD TV out the sliding back door.

It turned out she was right about where they were, but entirely wrong about what they were up to.

25

Gordon risked a glance at his phone as he jogged across the parking lot to his cruiser. Either someone had broken into the house or Farren had come home. Or both, which was what he truly feared. He supposed it was also possible that someone who looked identical to Farren had broken in.

Phone to his ear, trying to reach Melinda back, he ripped the driver's door open and dropped into the seat, rocking the car on its suspension. He gunned the engine and peeled out of the parking lot, lights flashing, though the roads were empty.

Break-ins were rare in Maggie's Knee. The last there'd been was a string of robberies committed by a drifter who'd been camping out in the woods. He robbed four houses before they caught him and recovered everything he'd stolen, which he'd buried around his campsite. That had been almost five years ago.

The fact that someone had broken into the sheriff's house, if indeed it was a break-in, told him, if it wasn't Farren, it had to be someone from out of town. All of Maggie's Knee knew where he lived. The only person who enjoyed less privacy was Mayor Hatfield.

He flew down Main Street, giving a short blip of his siren in case anyone thought to stumble into the street right at that moment. It was a Wednesday night, though—just barely Thursday morning in fact—and he had the streets to himself. Even the Mission was quiet.

The drive home took him seven minutes.

Gordon turned on the car's spotlight and pointed it straight ahead as he pulled into the driveway. The spot illuminated his front porch and the bloody pile of fur at the foot of its steps.

"Oh, Bonzo," Gordon said as he ground to a stop a few feet from the porch. He'd genuinely loved that dog.

He adjusted the spot so it shone through the open front door, illuminating the hall and blinding any potential intruders. Grabbed his radio handset from its mount and gave Tim, the deputy on duty with him, the rundown of what he was looking at, telling him to stand by in case he was needed. Got out of the car and stepped around the corpse of what used to be Farren's dog.

As he mounted the porch steps, he heard a distinct, "Ssh."

"Sorry," whined a second, incredibly deep voice.

Gordon's left hand pulled the Maglite from his belt while his right unbuttoned the strap securing his firearm in its holster.

"Maggie's Knee Sheriff's Department," he bellowed, "and the owner of this house. Call out if you hear me, I don't want any surprises."

Silence. Or almost that. From deeper in the house came a faint slurping, gurgling sound, almost like a backed-up pipe.

Gordon moved down the hall, flashlight pointed in front of him, despite the spotlight illuminating the hall. He checked the doorknob to his study as he passed; locked, just as he'd left it. Next, he shone his light into the open door of the bathroom across the hall. Stepped in and peeked behind the door. Empty. On to the kitchen, off the end of the hall on the right. The bedroom hall ran off to the left. Between the hall and kitchen was the short staircase leading to the sunken living room.

His flashlight picked up the blood on the living room floor. Tracked it to its source.

Melinda lay in a pool of her own blood, throat slashed, doubtless the source of the gurgling sound, which had stopped.

Gordon took the four stairs down into the living room slowly, unable to believe what he was seeing, still keenly aware whoever did this was likely still in the house.

Movement across the room. He drew his .357.

Three distinct shadows crept along the wall, toward the open sliding back door.

Gordon took aim. Fired. Pulled his finger off the trigger when his Maglite lit up Farren's shocked, tear-streaked face. She was looking down, covered in blood.

Gordon's hands shook, causing the shadows around his stepdaughter to dance, making her appear to flicker. He forced himself to lower the light to see where he'd hit her and at first thought he must have gone into shock; she was covered in blood but didn't appear to have been hit. Someone else's blood, then. Melinda's?

The edge of the flashlight's beam caught something on the floor and he directed the light at it. A kid, maybe fifteen or sixteen, lay on the floor clutching his stomach, which shot a gout of blood between his fingers. A long-haired guy in his twenties knelt over the younger kid, pressing his hands to the bleeding hole. Both were dressed in black, as was his step-daughter.

Farren dashed past the boys and out the door before Gordon could react. He started after her.

Two more shadows emerged from the gloom. He pointed his light at them and screamed in surprise.

The first was a skinny, strung-out-looking, goth girl, also in her twenties. She slipped out while Gordon's mind tried to process her accomplice, who appeared to tower as high as the elevated living room ceiling. Gordon moved his light up the vast length of the giant's leg, up its barn-door-sized chest, and into its face, which the giant immediately covered with an enormous hand. Gordon only caught a glimpse of it, but he was certain the giant had a child's face, blown up to enormous proportions. Its eyes—Gordon had a hard time thinking of the creature as human in the limited light and considering the situation—were the size of Gordon's fist. The giant looked like it could fit Gordon's entire head in its mouth.

The goth stuck her head back in the door. "Guppy," she said, pointing at Gordon, "make him go to sleep."

The sheriff's hands shook as the giant took a foundation-shaking step toward him. He knew he should fire, or at least shout a warning, but his dismay at the incredible size of the creature stalking toward him, coupled with the shocks he'd just been subjected to—Melinda bleeding out on the floor, Bonzo dead on the lawn, almost shooting Farren, and shooting a kid close to her age—froze his motor functions.

"S—stop," he managed to say before the beast swung a basketball-sized fist at his head.

There was an explosion of pain and then it, along with everything else, was gone.

26

Farren wished she could run faster. It wasn't her foot slowing her down either; the Piston wasn't ideal but she could move pretty well in it. If she ran as fast as she wanted to she would outpace the rest of the group, and she needed to follow them back to wherever they'd parked the van they'd stolen. She wanted answers about Bonzo and Melinda.

Part of her wanted to leave them behind, to strike out on her own and make a new living. She would never be able to go through with it though; they were a family and she could at least wait for an explanation for poor Bonzo's death. Her heart ached thinking about his poor body, bent and twisted at cruel angles.

That they had killed a person was extremely troubling. The fact that it was Gordon's wife added nothing to the wrongness of it, though Farren couldn't help feeling a hint of pity for Melinda; nobody deserved to die like that.

What Farren did care about, what made it impossible for her to survive on her own, was that she would be the one accused of killing her stepdad's wife. Gordon had seen her there, fucking *shot at her*—she'd thought he hit her when she looked down and saw the blood on herself, but quickly realized it belonged to Bonzo—and would jump to the obvious conclusion that she came back to exact revenge on Melinda for ruining her life.

Another reason she couldn't leave the others behind was she felt at least partially responsible for the way things had gone down. If she'd stayed in the Congo, Melinda might still be alive. What the hell had she been doing there anyway? She was supposed to have been at a party all night. Maybe it ended early?

But then wouldn't Melinda have gone into the house anyway?

At the very least, if Farren had stayed in the Congo, she wouldn't have been seen in the house, with blood on her, even if it was poor Bonzo's.

She should have gone back when she'd lost the party at the carpool lot. Would have if she hadn't happened across the bicycle.

There hadn't been any trouble getting out of the Congo. Becca, the girl she'd first seen rocking the gun on her hip during her tour, was on the overnight shift in the Visitor's Center. She had opened the gate without question when Farren told her she was meant to be in the party going to her place.

After following the group for a short while, which was easy enough since they'd decided to bring Guppy along, Farren realized they weren't headed to Maggie's Knee by the usual route. By her best guess, they had been headed in the opposite direction. The reason for this became clear after following them up a steep hill that took Farren forever to climb—the ground on the incline was loose and the Piston kept getting stuck between rocks and in the soft earth.

The trees at the top of the slope went on for a few feet before opening up to a manufactured clearing next to a gravel parking lot; a rest stop at the side of Route 12, complete with a couple of picnic tables and a small patch of grass for travelers to stretch their legs or let their dog crap on. She'd just reached the summit in time to see Sasha, Jasper, and—hilariously—Guppy pile into a dark-colored van.

Guppy had to almost fold himself in half to squeeze his bulk through the sliding door of the vehicle and when he got in, the suspension creaked as the van canted to one side. The vehicle's interior light revealed Gabe behind the wheel; he'd apparently gone ahead to steal the van.

Fast in, fast out.

It was a better idea than escaping on foot and risking being followed. They may be kept hidden but that didn't make them invisible; someone smart and persistent enough could find them if they knew how and where to look.

Farren had waited in the shadows of the trees as Gabe piloted the car onto Route 12, toward Maggie's Knee. She cursed and shouted at the top of her lungs when they were out of sight. She wasn't even sure she could have found her way back to the Congo from there if she'd tried. More likely she'd have become lost in the endless woods and fallen prey to the environment or wild animals.

Instead of going back through the forest, she decided to walk back up Route 12 to Jessop's Bridge, where she could more easily find her way back to the Congo.

She hadn't gone half a mile when she noticed the bicycle.

It was as if it had been left there for her. A blue mountain bike —nothing fancy; the kind they sold at Walmart—leaned against a speed limit sign posted at the side of the road. The bike was in mint condition, the tires firm. Even better, the pedals were oversized, which would make pushing them with the Piston a lot easier.

Farren got to the house seconds behind Melinda. If she'd been half a minute earlier, Melinda would have run her over, whether she'd seen her or not, in all likelihood.

She'd hit the brakes when she spotted Melinda's car pulling into their driveway. Stashed the bike at the end of the hedgerow close to the road.

After hiding along the hedges and watching Melinda retreat from the house and pull out her phone, Farren had decided it was best to confront her before she did anything rash. She'd been too late by seconds. Melinda had called Gordon.

Even with her stepfather on the way, Farren had felt entirely in control of the situation until Melinda drew her attention to Bonzo's broken body. It had shattered something within her, some last, pathetic vestige of hope for things to just be all right. She felt gray.

Nothing else mattered in that moment except what she'd let happen to her dog. It had been a mistake letting them come back for the blade, something she didn't really need.

She should have at least stayed outside with Bonzo. Then, when Gordon arrived, he would see her crying over her dead dog, covered in the poor thing's blood, and understand she'd been a victim too.

But she couldn't have known they were going to kill Melinda, even after seeing what they'd done to Bonzo.

She'd spotted Gordon's lights flashing from the road through the trees, a flicker of red and blue she would have missed if she hadn't been looking at just the right second. She'd kissed Bonzo on the only spot she could find that wasn't covered in blood, near his hindquarters, and had slipped inside.

Melinda had been standing in the middle of the living room, surrounded by four shadowed figures, one of them a giant. She'd heard Farren come in and turned toward her, eyes narrowing.

"Tell your friends to get the hell out," Melinda had commanded. "You heard me on the phone, Gordon will be here any minute."

"He's here now," Farren said to the group.

Jasper cursed and, as if it was a signal to attack, Sasha had pounced from the shadows behind Melinda. She wrapped an arm around the woman's head then plunged a kitchen knife into her throat, flinging the blade outward, and slicing a ragged gouge in the flesh there. A fountain of blood followed the knife out.

Melinda's lips moved but all that came out was, "Urk."

She collapsed to the floor, hands clutching the gushing hole in her throat.

Farren had watched in stunned horror as her stepdad's wife twitched and gargled on the floor, life draining from her by the second. Melinda's eyes had wandered across the ceiling, as if she was looking for an escape route she knew was up there, if only she could focus on the right spot. She'd looked at Farren for a brief second but there was no recognition in her eyes.

"We need to go," Sasha had said, taking off her jacket and wrapping the knife in it.

She was wearing tight, black gloves. Had she been planning on killing Melinda? How could they have known she would come home early? Something about the whole situation stank, but Farren was too overwhelmed to give it any thought at the moment.

The hallway leading into the kitchen had suddenly been illuminated in bright, white light. In the lower level of the living room, they were spared being lit up by the direct beam.

Gordon followed the light in seconds later.

Then everything had gone even further to hell. Gordon had seen Melinda's body and opened fire on them. Not something Farren, or any of them, had been prepared for. He'd shot Gabe in the stomach, but she couldn't tell if anyone else had been hit.

She'd fled then, darting out the open back door and into the night.

Now Farren slowed down a bit to fall in step with the rest of the group, shooting glances toward the house, unsure if Gordon would be more bent on pursuing them or attending to Melinda. She was pretty sure he'd choose Melinda, as he always had.

When they reached the property line, Farren was relieved to see Guppy emerge from the sliding door with Gabe in his massive arms.

"What are you doing here?" Sasha demanded between breaths.

"I thought you could use my help," Farren said, in spite of the incredulity she felt at Sasha having the nerve to question her after the violence she'd just wrought.

The stolen van was straight ahead, parked innocuously along the curb on a stretch between lights.

"Well now you're wanted for murder," Sasha said.

"Who killed my dog?"

The answer became clear right away. Guppy, who had caught up to them in spite of his burden, turned to look at her with a childish expression of guilt on his face. It almost summoned enough pity in her to outweigh the anger she felt. Almost.

She slowed to a stop. "You, Guppy? Why?"

Jasper grasped her arm and tugged her along. "We have to hurry. He didn't mean to. I'll explain later."

All at once, Farren was certain her dog's death was somehow Sasha's fault. That she'd goaded Guppy into killing Bonzo.

The group piled into the van; Jasper behind the wheel, Sasha in shotgun, Farren in the very back, and Guppy taking up the entire middle section, still cradling Gabe in his arms.

Farren felt herself go numb as Jasper pulled the van away from the curb and off into the night.

z

THEY DROPPED Sasha off in Fissing, forty-five minutes west of Maggie's Knee, so that she could steal another van. After leaving her in a shopping center plaza parking lot, Jasper drove them to an abandoned quarry far on the outskirts of town. Gabe died on the way.

Farren hadn't known him all that well and was more upset about Bonzo than any of the human casualties. Jasper seemed more concerned with driving, so Gabe only had Guppy to mourn him. The enormous boy cried all the way to the quarry.

Jasper had Guppy push the van, with Gabe's body inside, into the black water, close to a hundred feet below. The van hit the water with a splash Farren felt was much too conspicuous, even as far outside of town as they were, but Jasper seemed unconcerned.

Sasha pulled up half a minute later in a van that looked nearly identical to the one they'd just sunk, as if the whole routine had been perfectly synchronized.

The drive back was solemn and wordless. Guppy huffed and sniffed but generally recovered himself by the time Sasha dropped them off at the carpool lot before taking off again to ditch the van and return by a different route.

Their walk through the forest to the Congo was as silent as their drive. Jasper led the way, using a high-powered flashlight to illuminate the path that wasn't quite a path. Farren followed close behind him, lost in her thoughts. Guppy trailed from a dozen yards back, seemingly too ashamed to walk with them.

## 27

"She knew he'd kill Bonzo!" Farren slammed a hand on the kitchen island but it wasn't enough.

She wanted to tear Sasha apart.

Hours after they'd returned to the Congo, Farren found Jasper wandering the grounds, looking dazed. He'd agreed to meet with her in private, but they had to be discreet; if word got back to Sasha they were discussing something in secret, she'd make their lives hell. So they'd agreed to meet in the dining hall kitchen.

Farren questioned Jasper on every aspect of the trip to get her blade. According to him, he'd been kept in the dark about any plans of violence and was shocked, but not entirely surprised, at what Sasha had done to Melinda and had tricked Guppy into doing to Bonzo. He'd explained about Guppy's fear and agreed it looked a lot like Sasha had set things up to have Guppy kill Farren's dog.

"Why would she want Bonzo dead?" Farren asked, throat tightening again at the thought of him lying there on her lawn.

Jasper only stared at her, open-mouthed, as if he thought a response would float out on its own.

"Just to upset me?" Farren went on. "I wasn't even supposed to be there. Unless she knew I was going to follow you guys, but I didn't tell anyone what I was planning, just Becca on the way out and I don't even think she was paying attention. She's not the best security guard."

At that, Jasper's face paled several shades and his eyes widened in a way that reminded Farren of Johnny Depp's character in *Pirates of the Caribbean*. She may have laughed in other circumstances, but the look told her she'd said something that scared him.

"What?" she said. "Something about Becca?"

Jasper shook his head. "What you said about Sasha knowing you were planning on following us ..." he trailed off.

Farren wanted to shake him. "And?"

His eyes went distant, like he was puzzling something out.

"It doesn't make sense," he said.

"What doesn't?" she almost screamed.

"Nothing," he said, waving it away. "Wouldn't she have killed Gordon if she'd wanted to upset you? Or just your dog? Why Melinda?"

Something about the way he'd dismissed her question told Farren he was hiding something from her about all this. About Sasha?

It was suddenly obvious to Farren. "She wants to frame me for killing Melinda. The whole thing was set up to make it look like I came home, killed my dog and my stepdad's wife, and made off with my prosthesis. But I'd never hurt Bonzo."

Jasper sat heavily on one of the stools around the island.

He obviously thought there was something to Farren's theory. She sat down across from him.

"They'll blame it on drugs," he said. "Easy explanation for your dog. They'll tell people you stole the prosthesis to sell for drug money."

"But then why wouldn't I take more? Or something else? Something a little easier to hock than a custom-fit, carbon fiber foot," Farren said. "Unless Sasha did. Take more, I mean."

"That's the beauty of drugs," Jasper said. "It doesn't have to make sense." He seemed to be about to say something else, then snapped his mouth shut.

"What is it?" Farren pressed.

"I don't know," he said distractedly. "I was thinking she could have planted evidence, but I'm not sure what she would have left. Is there something you have that she would want? Or something Gordon or Melinda might have had there?"

"No idea. What are you getting at?"

"Wish I knew. She was wandering around the house a lot before you arrived. I thought she was just snooping but the more I think about it, the more I think she was looking for something."

Farren couldn't fathom what they might have in the house that Sasha could possibly want. Or why Sasha wanted to ruin her life so badly. Why recruit Farren in the first place if Sasha hated her so much?

But Farren had known early on the decision to bring her to the Congo hadn't belonged to Sasha. She took orders from something higher up, something that lived in those buildings across the creek.

Something that had asked for Farren to be here.

She hadn't allowed herself to dwell on that knowledge until now. What she'd felt across the creek had been frightening in enormity and presence and she'd caught only a glimpse of it, barely brushed up against it.

Yet it wanted her here. And had used her dad, or her memory of him, to convince her to stay. The more she thought about it, the more certain she was the thing she'd spoken with in the chapel had no more been her dad than Jasper was. But she so desperately wanted to believe it she'd been willing to put her doubts aside, to ignore all evidence suggesting this was not just one big, happy, teenaged commune.

In wanting to get rid of her, was Sasha acting against the will of whatever it was that ruled this place? Farren had the feeling Sasha was behaving like a little girl jealous of the new baby born to her parents.

"What's in the buildings across the creek?" Farren asked, locking eyes with Jasper, pleading silently with him to open up to her.

He breathed a heavy sigh and stood. Farren watched him shuffle to the walk-in cooler, heave the giant door open, and disappear inside. The sound of boxes being shifted came from deep within and was followed by glass clinking against glass. A few seconds later, Jasper emerged holding two frosty bottles of beer in each hand.

He sat down, set two of the bottles in front of Farren, placed one on the counter in front of himself, cracked the other, and drained two-thirds of it before setting it down next to its mate. He belched loudly.

"It's barely after lunch," Farren said. She'd never been much of a drinker.

"You're gonna need one if you want to hear what I know, which isn't much—not compared to Sash," he said.

He reached across the counter and slid one of Farren's beers next to his.

Then he told her his story, the parts that mattered.

Jasper woke with a start. Had there been a noise? Or was it part of the nightmare he'd been having?

He sat up in bed and shivered, pulling the sheets up around him. It was a chilly morning and he only ever wore boxers to bed. The first day of spring had been last week, which meant his dad had done the same thing he did every year and shut off the furnace. Didn't matter how bad the weather was, the heat always went off on the morning of the equinox.

When Jasper was ten, he'd caught pneumonia and had been experiencing the worst of his symptoms when his dad put the furnace into its reverse hibernation. It got so cold his mother had taken Jasper and his sister to live with her parents until the weather warmed up and Jasper recovered. His mom never brought it up again. In fact, no one talked about it except his grandparents, who refused to speak to his dad after that spring.

It was still dark outside but it was even darker in his first-floor bedroom. Enough ambient streetlight seeped into his back yard that he could make out a dark, thin figure standing at the edge of the property. Only one person it could be.

The figure wound up like a pitcher on the mound and threw something that cracked off the brick wall inches from his window.

What the hell was she doing?

Sasha cast about on the ground and came up clutching something in her hand.

She took aim and wound up.

Jasper ducked down onto his bed and had the presence of mind to pull the comforter over his head a second before the window exploded inward. Glass flew into his room, showering his back and the bed.

A maniacal cackling he'd come to know and grow fond of these last three months spilled in through the broken window. As much as he adored it, he also feared that laughter. It rarely meant anything good.

He'd spent a few nights a week with Sasha ever since she slipped into his car in the parking lot of the library. Would have seen more of her if he'd had his way but she frequently disappeared for days at a time, which was part of the mystique he so enjoyed about her.

What had started off as intense infatuation blossomed and deepened more with each moment spent together. They shared an almost tangible bond. At times it was as if she knew exactly what he was thinking, especially in bed. Desires and urges he'd barely known he possessed had been rooted out, satisfied, and utterly exhausted. When they made love, she seemed to sense everything he wanted her to do to him in exactly the way he wanted her to do it.

She was the wildest person he'd ever met, uninhibited, operating on sheer instinct and desire. It was a seductive way to live. At the same time, she possessed insight and cunning that continually surprised him. He could never be sure whether she deliberately hid those things under a mask of jubilant insanity or if it was a natural part of the package.

The influence she held over him was obvious, as his family and the few friends he had frequently let him know.

He'd done things these last few months he'd never dreamed of getting involved in. They'd broken into homes, stealing and destroying all manner of property in the process, often just for the thrill of it, making love in every house they burglarized.

Two weeks ago, they'd breached another level of madness —a point of no return for Jasper that haunted his dreams every night since.

He and Sasha broke into the house of someone who was still home and awake. Jasper knew it was reckless but by then the thrill had become an addiction worse than any drug and he was already becoming desensitized to it.

The homeowner, a successful mystery writer they later found out, had been upstairs in his office with music playing—an old rock band Jasper couldn't place—and could be heard hammering on his keyboard, pounding out whatever it was that paid for the very nice roof over his head. They'd prowled through the main level and basement, shoving anything of value into their backpacks. When they'd gone through the lower levels, Sasha grabbed Jasper and shoved him onto the floor of the living room. She'd straddled him and ground her hips into him while he craned his neck to watch for any sign of the homeowner.

She was just opening his zipper when Jasper spotted the reflection of movement in the living room window. He tried to shove her hand away but she'd gripped him tightly, painfully, and refused to let go.

"Is somebody here?" Mr. Writer had called from up the hall.

Jasper tried to wriggle out from under Sasha but she'd held him firm between legs that were surprisingly strong, obviously enjoying the power she had over him. He hadn't thought of her as a dominatrix until that point but, lying under her in that writer's living room, Jasper wondered how he could have been so blind to the fact.

There wasn't much time to dwell on the epiphany before Mr. Writer stepped out of the hallway and into the living room. He was a heavy, fifty-ish guy in a thin blue bathrobe, gray sweats, and a Flyers T-shirt. He came straight toward them, holding one arm out in front of him.

"Stay right the fuck there, you sick freaks," he'd growled.

Jasper saw the man had a gun in his outstretched arm, pointed at Sasha.

And still she didn't look up. Just kept her gaze trained on Jasper.

"There's so much more than this," she'd said and then leaned down to kiss him.

Jasper had kept his eyes trained on Mr. Writer and shouted a muted warning into Sasha's open mouth when the man stepped closer, holding the barrel of his gun three inches from her head.

She nipped Jasper's tongue in the way that drove him wild.

"I said," Mr. Writer began. But those, probably to the writer's chagrin, were the last words he ever uttered.

Sasha moved like Scarlett Johansson. She slapped at the gun and it flew from the man's grip. Before he could react, Sasha leaped to her feet and delivered a solid kick to his groin with one of her square-toed Doc Martins. The guy fell to his knees, holding his balls in both hands, wheezing. Sasha left him there and sauntered to where the gun fell.

She'd hefted it in one hand, testing its weight, then cocked it expertly.

"Sash," Jasper had said, getting to his feet and pulling up his zipper, "let's just get out of here."

Sasha pointed the gun at Mr. Writer's head, looked Jasper in the eye, and said, "This means nothing."

The gun went off. Mr. Writer's brains appeared on the sofa in a spray of blood, and he collapsed with a heavy, wet thud.

Next, Sasha turned the gun on herself, holding it under her chin.

"You have a decision to make, Jasper," she'd said, cocking the gun again. "A sacrifice needs to be made or a member of the tribe recruited. And since I'm the only member so far, I'm going to have to be the sacrifice."

It was a hell of a melodramatic proposal and Jasper managed to stammer out as much, unable to keep his eyes off the gun.

"I'm not talking about marriage," she'd said. "This is so much bigger than that. Bigger than us. But we do get to be the first. Together."

"Okay, yes," Jasper had shouted, wanting to agree to whatever it took to get her to stop this insanity. He couldn't tear his eyes from the ruined skull of the man on the floor. "I'll join your tribe."

"Not mine," she said, lowering the gun.

"Whose?"

A cunning smile was her only response.

Leaving the house, she told him not to worry about getting caught for any of what they'd done, that they would be protected, especially now that he was part of the tribe.

She said she had something big in store for him.

He'd seen her a few times since then but she'd been spending more time away than usual.

News had blown up about a prolific paperback mystery writer being killed execution-style in his home, with his own gun, which had not been found. The running theory was that a fan, or hater, of his work had committed the crime. Apparently dusting for fingerprints was out of the question because the writer had hosted a large party at his place the night before and the house was littered with evidential refuse.

As if Jasper and Sasha really had been protected.

But he knew better. Sasha knew there had been a party there the night before. She must have staked the place out before they broke in and pretended to choose a house at random when she'd returned with him. Because he definitely wouldn't have wanted to break in if he'd known it belonged to a semi-famous writer Sasha planned on murdering.

Once he was confident they were in the clear, it almost became easy to push the whole thing to the back of his mind. But he would never forget it entirely. His nightmares would forever be plagued by the sudden hole appearing in the writer's head, directly above an eyebrow that had been raised in horrific realization, or the ejection of blood and brains that sprayed out behind him, covering the soft leather couch and its calfskin pillows with a pulpy, red lacquer.

Now the girl who had destroyed the brain responsible for over two dozen bestsellers was smashing windows on Jasper's house and all he could worry about was one or both of his parents coming downstairs to find out what all the noise was about.

When no further rocks came through the window, Jasper peeled the blanket off himself, trying unsuccessfully to keep the shards of glass wrapped up in it. He bundled it as safely and quickly as he could, unable to stop a piece of glass the size of a dinner plate from crashing to the floor, then peered out the window.

Sasha popped her head up, inches from the glassless window pane, just as he looked up. It frightened him so badly he fell backward, off his bed and into his dresser. His hip slammed into it and he cried out in pain, his whole left side going numb.

From the window Sasha said. "That looked like it hurt."

He could only gasp in response. It was sheer luck he hadn't sliced his feet open on the glass covering his floor.

"Get your ass out here. Bring your wallet."

Jasper pulled himself up using the same dresser he'd fallen on for support. He found a pair of jeans on the floor and tugged them on, then did the same with a plain black T-shirt and hoodie. He heard his dad clomping down the stairs as he pulled his sneakers on.

His dad's fist on the door shook it in its frame.

"Great," Jasper said, rolling his eyes at Sasha.

She reached her arms through the window. "Just come through here. Let me deal with him."

Jasper snatched his wallet off the dresser and climbed out the window. "All yours."

The door burst open just as he stumbled through the window. His father stood in the doorway, panting from his jog down the stairs. He was a stocky man with ruddy features and a bald head circled by a corona of dark hair, a dozen strands of which were combed over his shiny dome.

"What the hell is this mess, Jasper?" he shouted, searching the room for his son. He spied Sasha through the glassless window. "I told you I don't want that whore around my house."

Sasha pulled something out of her pocket.

"I'm not a whore, sir," she said. "But if you want a go with me, I'm sure Jasper wouldn't mind."

Jasper bristled at that but said nothing, hoping she was bluffing, not that he thought his old man would ever take her up on such an offer.

His dad gave into her goading and charged at her, apparently forgetting he'd have to climb through the window before mauling her.

She raised the thing from her pocket as he mounted the bed, only losing a fraction of his momentum in doing so. A stream of something shot out from her hand and hit Jasper's dad directly in the eye. She moved her hand in circles so the pepper spray hit his other eye and mouth.

Jasper's own eyes began to sting and water, his nostrils burned. He backed up, not wanting to catch any back-spray.

His dad roared, clawing at his eyes, and falling out of sight. There was a crash, a wet *thwock*, and then silence.

Jasper peered through the window and gasped. His dad lay in a swiftly growing puddle of blood, which poured from somewhere on his head. The corner of the same dresser Jasper had fallen into now had a bloody mound of flesh stuck to it, several dark hairs protruding from the mess.

"Dad?"

Sasha grabbed Jasper by the arm and pulled him away, toward the side of the house.

"We should call someone," he said.

Sasha hustled him up the street. "He's gone. We need to be too. Did you bring your wallet?"

Z

TEN HOURS LATER, Jasper piloted a stolen Corolla down the long, empty stretch of highway that led into Maggie's Knee, a pretty town nestled in dense, hilly forest in the southern end of the Pennsylvania Alleghenies, and home to the KnowMe base of operations.

Sasha said very little about where it was they were going, only that it would blow his mind. Also that they had a new home now, which was just as well since they were likely wanted for murder.

But there was also a chance they wouldn't be wanted at all; or at least that Jasper himself wouldn't.

His mother had seen him at home, in his bed late last night. His window had been busted from the outside and he was missing. For all anyone knew, his dad had been trying to fend someone off; someone who wanted to take his son away. Assuming no one had seen them.

"Slow down," Sasha said, bringing Jasper back to the present.

He did and she pointed to a gravel carpool lot ahead and to the left. A couple of picnic tables sat in the grass to one side of it. There was no traffic, so he drifted into the oncoming lane for a few hundred feet before turning into the lot.

"What's this?" he asked, switching off the ignition.

"Home."

Jasper didn't question it. Just followed her out of the car, into the crisp, spring afternoon. Evergreens, he had no idea what kind, towered over them as far as the eye could see. The air was rich with the scent of the early spring thaw; damp earth mingled with pine sap. The road bent out of sight, toward Maggie's Knee.

When he looked down from marveling at the trees, Sasha was standing at the edge of the lot, stepping off the gravel and into the forest. She disappeared from view as if she'd stepped off a cliff.

"Sash!" he called, jogging toward her.

He reached the tree line, afraid to see what happened to her, ready to scream her name again. For a moment, when he reached the edge of the lot, his breath was taken away and he forgot about Sasha, injured or not. The slope went down about fifty feet before leveling off again on the forest floor. Jasper had thought the trees gigantic before he'd known they were rooted so much lower than the road. The size of them was awe-inspiring. The majority had to be around a hundred feet tall.

He spotted Sasha. She was descending the steep embankment in a controlled slide, about a third of the way down.

"What are you doing?" he shouted.

She said nothing, only slid the rest of the way down the hill. When she hit level ground, she walked purposefully into a sea of densely packed trees.

Jasper looked around the lot, at the stolen car. He had nothing. Only his wallet and the clothes on his back. And she wanted him to follow her into what was very likely unmapped woodland?

He sighed and pushed the doubts to the back of his mind. Too late to go back now.

Z

"IT WAS ONCE an educational outdoor getaway camp for families," Sasha said in the tone of a practiced tour guide. "Started up by a billionaire named Stuart Brierton. He invested millions, spared no expense, everything is state of the art."

An hour after leaving the carpool lot, and after navigating a labyrinth of colossal trees and dense brush, they stood in the middle of what struck Jasper as a woodland resort more than any kind of learning camp. Luxury cabins had been built around the perimeter with overgrown dirt paths going from them to the many outbuildings populating the grounds. Prehistoric trees were scattered throughout. There was a basketball court, a cafeteria, and a creek running through the far end of the grounds, with a couple of bigger buildings on the other side of it, reachable by a small footbridge. A building near the entrance even housed a bunch of old arcade cabinets. A great, log fence surrounded the park, presumably to keep wildlife out. Here and there, Jasper noticed modern updates; things like gigantic generators behind several of the buildings and HD security cameras mounted around the grounds. Had Sasha done all of that?

"This has just been sitting here for forty years?" Jasper asked, unable to believe it. There was no way a place like this could simply be forgotten.

Sasha only looked at him.

"How?" he asked.

She took his hand and walked him toward the far end of the park, in the direction of the creek.

"They were all set to open for business," she said as they strolled along what barely resembled a path anymore, weeds brushing at their pants. "To celebrate the opening they held a complimentary, full-service friends and family weekend. They were keeping it top secret though, to make sure they'd worked out all the kinks—nobody was allowed to tell anyone where they were going that weekend. Everyone in attendance was flown in by chopper because Brierton didn't want roads leading here before he was ready for it to be seen by the public. It was all investors, builders, contractors, bankers, lawyers—people who had a stake in the place. They weren't going to blab and spoil what they'd built together.

"They were at half capacity for that weekend, the maximum was somewhere around a hundred and fifty guests. Still, lots of people. Somewhere around two dozen staff were flown in to attend to them. Everyone who RSVP'd was checked in on that Friday afternoon. Then they disappeared."

Jasper stopped, putting a hand on her arm and pulling her to a halt as well. Her face flickered in a scowl that looked purely demonic; eyes narrowed, teeth bared, bottom lip jutting out, something he'd found cute about her at first. The look threw him off so much he almost forgot what they were talking about.

"How can you know all this?" he said, recovering slightly.

"It was shown to me," she said, matter of fact.

"By who?"

She kept walking, pulling him along.

"What happened to them all?" he asked.

"Like I said, they disappeared. Everybody involved and their families, including Brierton and his wife and their two sons. They were all on the grounds that night. The next morning, none of them were. There was no one to remember this place."

"That's impossible."

"Well, that's what happened," Sasha snapped.

He'd seen her worked up before, but she'd never directed her wrath at him. It was frightening.

They walked in silence for a few steps before he said, "Isn't it weird nobody else has found this place?"

She gave him an impatient look.

"I just mean we only really hiked an hour or so. Aren't there professionals who come out to survey these places? How did you find it?"

She turned to him, with a smile on her face he wasn't sure he liked much more than her frown. Not in the present circumstances anyway.

"I was called here," she said. "One year ago today."

He couldn't stop his eyes from widening. "What does that mean? Is this where you've been disappearing to?"

"Ever hear a voice in your head that's not your own?" she asked, pulling him along again. They were approaching the short bridge leading across the creek.

"Nope."

She chuckled, a laugh that suddenly reminded him of small stones being ground together.

"Have you?" he asked when she didn't elaborate.

She came to a stop in front of the bridge and put an arm out to keep him from going any further. The creek trickled past, on its way to wherever it disappeared into the earth or fed into something bigger. A woodpecker hammered away at a nearby tree, digging for an early supper.

"A little over a year ago, I started hearing something in my head," Sasha said, staring out across the bridge. "It felt like something living in there, touching my brain. It stayed there and every now and then, it would talk to me but I couldn't ever understand it.

"Then I started having these super intense dreams about this place; about meeting somebody here, but I could never remember who. Soon the dreams showed me the way here, the whole time that voice talking to me like it was trying to give me directions to go with the visuals." She stared across the little creek with a far-off look in her eyes. "When I arrived, I met the presence from my dreams, the voice in my head. *He* was the one who called Brierton here, and the one who did away with him and everyone involved in building this place. Because it wasn't yet *his* time." She turned to Jasper, took his hands in hers, and looked him in the eyes. "Six months ago, *he* showed me you."

Jasper tried to step away from her, to pull his hands back, but she maintained a firm hold on them.

"You're saying something told you to come get me?" he said, feeling his voice rising.

"I'll introduce you," she said, pulling him toward the bridge.

He dug his feet in. "Wait. If this is what you say it is, that means you what? You've been grooming me for this? Is that why you killed the writer?"

She tightened her grip on his hands, digging her thumbnails into his wrists hard enough to draw blood.

"This is bigger than your hurt feelings," she said through clenched teeth. "There's no turning back."

"I can't turn back if I was never on board to begin with!"

She pushed his hands away. "You swore an oath."

"What oath?"

"To keep me from being sacrificed," she said in a sulking voice.

"I thought you were talking about us. And you had a gun to your head," Jasper tried to keep his voice calm but couldn't stop the tremor in it.

"Is that what it takes?" She reached into her shoulder bag and withdrew a revolver not much different from Mr. Writer's.

"Sash, don't."

But she was already putting the gun to her head.

"Safety's off," she said bluntly. "I have to be sacrificed by sundown if you're not going to cross that bridge."

"Okay. Whatever you want," he pleaded. "No more guns."

She jerked her head toward the bridge, gun never leaving her temple.

He stepped around her and onto the bridge. The creek babbled pleasantly underneath his feet, oblivious to what was going on.

As soon as Jasper's foot hit the grass on the other side, he knew there was something to what she'd been saying. The sound of the creek was immediately muted; not gone entirely, but sounding as if it was behind a thick wall or deep under-ground—separated. The birds too, he noticed right away, had gone silent. He turned to face Sasha and she nodded at the question in his eyes.

It was dead over here.

He spun around, suddenly certain something monstrous was looming, just behind his back.

Nothing.

But he felt *something*. A presence on this side of the creek, a heaviness in the air. And that absence of life.

Something grabbed him and he screamed, darting away from it. He turned to face whatever touched him.

Sasha.

He expected her to smirk at him, to poke fun at his skittishness, but her face remained solemn. He'd never seen her like this.

She gestured to the building on their left, a large structure built out of enormous beams of timber, and started toward it. Jasper fell in step with her, not wanting to be on his own on this side of the creek.

The scary side.

She'd been coming here by herself for a year? He would never have returned here on his own after crossing that bridge for the first time. If there'd been no crazy girlfriend—or whatever she was supposed to be to him—holding a gun to her own head, he'd have been back across that creek in a heartbeat. Of course, if it wasn't for her, he'd be writing his finals right about now.

For the first time since meeting Sasha, he wondered if perhaps he'd fucked up gigantically. If maybe he'd let her feed on his angst toward his parents; something he could have dealt with by moving out. He'd had enough money.

They came around the front of the building. Over the double-doored entrance were the words *Great Forest Museum*.

Something emanated from the building, like heat waves

without temperature, or silent sound waves—a disruption in the atmosphere, or maybe in reality itself.

"This is where *he* dwells," Sasha murmured in his ear.

"Who?"

"The one we serve."

She led him up stairs made of stone slabs, and through the doors.

28

Gordon swam toward consciousness as if he was deep underwater and it was open air. He pushed up to the real world and to steadily increasing pain. His entire body hurt, but his head was in its own special kind of torment. The more aware he became of the throbbing, pulsating ache, the less motivated he was to swim toward the world of the wakeful.

Slowly, he became aware of another pain.

Melinda.

If he was swimming in some vast sea of unconsciousness then this new hurt was a harpoon from an unseen ship, ripping through his chest, piercing his heart, and yanking upward, dragging him toward the surface by his flesh.

He opened his eyes and his skull erupted with pain, the agony of it forcing his eyes shut again. Must have suffered one hell of a concussion.

Gordon cracked his eyelids again. Even the tiny amount of light that seeped in was like needles in his eyes.

He was in a hospital room, this much was apparent by sound alone. Monitoring devices beeped nearby, in the hall a low voice said something in an authoritative manner, and a muffled PA announcement seeped through the thin wall, though he couldn't make out exactly what was being said.

A door opened and footsteps came toward him. Gordon opened his eyes just enough to make out the blurry outline of someone with dark skin wearing what he presumed to be a white smock coming into the room. He blinked his eyes open the rest of the way and thanked a God he hadn't spoken to in years when his pain didn't worsen.

"Sheriff, it is good to see you awake," his visitor said with a lively Indian accent.

"Doctor Bakshi," Gordon muttered. Each syllable he spoke was a jackhammer through his skull.

Viraj Bakshi had accepted the position of chief of medicine at Maggie's Knee General last year. The doctor dragged his family from New York to take the position and Gordon had done what he could to help them settle in. He'd invited the Bakshi family over to dinner, which had gone swimmingly, save for the awkwardness between Farren and Bakshi's daughter, Priya. By then Farren had been pretty fresh into her dark days, which Gordon had been internally referring to them as, and hadn't been up for making new friends. She'd left the table as soon as she'd finished eating and locked herself in her room for the rest of the night, leaving Priya to endure the adult conversation.

"You remember my name," Dr. Bakshi said. "That is very good news. I imagine you have a terrible headache right now. A nurse will be here shortly with acetaminophen for that. You have suffered a nasty concussion and will need to take it very easy for a few days." As he spoke, he fiddled with the saline drip plugged into Gordon's arm, adjusted the IV hose, and typed something on one of the monitors.

"I can't take it easy," Gordon tried to say, but the pain was too great and he only managed every other syllable.

Dr. Bakshi put a hand on his arm. "I am sorry about Melinda."

Gordon pulled his arm back and looked away from the doctor, fighting the emotion threatening to bubble up.

Dr. Bakshi stared at him over rectangular glasses that sat low on his long nose. He was a slight, balding man in his late-forties and smiled incessantly.

"What?" Gordon said, seeing the doctor wanted to ask him something.

"There are some very upsetting rumors about what happened at your house."

"And?"

"Was Farren involved?" Dr. Bakshi's voice shook in what Gordon was surprised to realize was anger. His smile became a grimace. "Has she had something to do with the kidnappings?"

Gordon moved to sit up but fresh pain forced him back down. Dr. Bakshi pulled a remote from beside the bed and pressed a red, arrow-shaped button on it. The bed rose, sitting Gordon upright.

"Thank you," Gordon said, speaking slowly and breathing through the sickening throb in his head. "I don't know where these rumors started but Farren had nothing to do with any sort of kidnapping."

He did in fact have a pretty good idea of where the rumor started, Tim Henchek had been in the office when Gordon received the call from Melinda. The deputy overheard Gordon mention Farren's name and had been shouting questions at him as Gordon gathered his things and ran out of the office to his cruiser. He'd told the deputy to stay put and keep his mouth shut but the order obviously hadn't stuck. Tim also must have been next on the scene, showing up to check on Gordon when he couldn't reach him.

"But Farren *was* at your house," Dr. Bakshi said, accusing.

"Yes. But you have to keep that to yourself, doc."

Not that keeping a lid on it would do any good now. If Viraj Bakshi knew about it, odds were most of the town did already as well.

Dr. Bakshi looked at his feet and said, "She played basketball with my Priya."

"So what?" Gordon said, suddenly furious. "She's not a kidnapper or anything of the sort, she's a confused teenager who apparently fell in with the wrong crowd. Farren lost both of her parents, tragically, not to mention her foot. Not only is she then stuck with me but I go and marry the exact opposite of who her mother was, not because I resented Darya or who she was, but because I could never be with someone who reminded me of her even a little bit. And all Farren sees is a guy who seems bent on erasing any and all memories of her mother. No wonder she hates me."

Both men were silent for a time.

Gordon hadn't meant for any of that to come out, hadn't even known he had it in the chamber. Apparently it was something that needed to be said out loud, but why now? Why so soon after the violent death of his wife? Had he been feeling guilt over it all this time?

He didn't need to be thinking of these things right now. *Shouldn't* be.

But that was what he always did. Avoided thinking about distressing personal issues; sealed them up in a great pit until they grew into winged, venomous monsters and broke free. And when they escaped, they no longer resembled what they were when he banished them—they emerged as senseless, enraged things manifesting as angry words and aggressive behavior. It was something he'd been trying to work on.

The doctor looked up and met Gordon's gaze. He seemed to come to some sort of decision and his face softened, the usual smile already creeping back into it. He sighed.

"I know Farren is a good girl deep down. I worry about everything now," Dr. Bakshi said. "Kashvi caught Priya sneaking out the same night Garrett Mews went missing. Now I worry about everything she does."

"I get that," said Gordon, glad to be talking about something other than what he'd been thinking of. "I feel the same way about Farren. Which is why I need to get out of here."

"I'm afraid you can't do that."

"What now?" Gordon felt his temper rise again, and he tried to reign it in, to cast a net over another escaped demon.

"Two reasons. I would like to order a CT scan to make sure there is no serious damage up here." The doctor pointed to Gordon's head. "To be rendered unconscious for," he checked his watch, "approximately fifteen hours by such an injury can be a sign of serious brain damage."

"No time," Gordon said. "Next."

Dr. Bakshi sighed as if he expected this response from Gordon. "There are two men from the state police here to speak with you. They asked to be notified the moment you regained consciousness."

Gordon swore. "They're going to tie me up with so much

reporting and legal BS I'll lose any chance of finding Farren. I might even be a suspect in …" his voice hitched. He coughed, cleared his throat. "Did you tell them I'm awake?"

"I will tell them, once the nurse has brought the acetaminophen I ordered for you."

"How long until she gets here with it?"

"I can't guess. These nurses think they run the place. I ask for a thing and they tell me one hundred other things they need to do first. But of course, I cannot live without them."

"You probably have things to do now, right?" Gordon asked, holding the doctor's eyes with his own.

He could see Dr. Bakshi mulling it over, what he was asking him to do, while not actually asking anything of him at all.

The doctor flipped through his chart. "I think perhaps you've suffered a more serious head injury than I at first thought; I'll send the nurse back to fetch something stronger. You don't seem to be in your right mind at the moment, so I will inform the men who wish to speak with you that I recommend you be allowed to rest a bit longer to let the pain medication work." He stepped out of the room, pulling the door closed behind him.

"Thank you," Gordon whispered, already pulling the IV from his arm and sliding his legs out of bed.

He hadn't known he was going to look for Farren on his own until he said it to the doctor, but there was no choice in the matter. He'd let the search for her, for all of the missing kids, slip for the last three months. With no leads and what little evidence they had washed away by the spring monsoon, there was nowhere to direct their efforts. But now, after everything that had happened in the last twenty-four hours, he knew he had to track Farren down.

He owed it to Melinda to find out what happened. Owed it to Farren as her adoptive father; he still considered himself her guardian, even if she was eighteen. And he owed it to Darya. He'd promised her at the altar he would cherish and protect both her and Farren, and "'til death do us part" did not mean his commitment to Farren was broken.

So he needed a plan. Home was out of the question, there would be law enforcement crawling all over the place for days. Which only left him with one option for somewhere to go; a place he was glad he'd kept secret for all these years. But he'd need some things and there was no way he could afford to risk showing his face anywhere in Maggie's Knee right now.

He got to his feet and swayed for a moment as a fresh wave of pain crashed against the inside of his skull. When the intensity of the headache—probably his brain's way of telling him it was far too early to be standing, let alone performing solo rescue missions—died down a bit, he shambled across the room to the shallow closet where his clothes hung.

His gun and uniform shirt had been taken, which he'd been expecting. They'd left the rest of his things alone though, including his phone. Miraculously, the only sign of violence on his undershirt was a small splash of blood on the hem. He refused to let himself wonder whether or not the blood belonged to Melinda.

Sneaking out of the hospital was a breeze, though he felt like a criminal on the verge of being caught the entire time he was making his escape. Taking the elevator down to the main floor, he'd been certain the doors would open to chiseled cops with aviators and mustaches ready to take him down. But there had been nothing to worry about.

He allowed himself to breathe a little when he made it to the street, but still felt exposed. Needed to get into hiding or, at the very least, change out of his partial uniform.

Up the street a few blocks was Tanner Park, which was little more than a patch of grass surrounded by trees, but would give him the modicum of privacy he needed. He walked to the park and sat down at the lone picnic table, glad to have the place to himself. Pulling out his phone, he found the number he needed, and froze with his thumb over the call button.

Was he really about to persuade someone else to be an accomplice to his escape? Technically he had nothing to worry about. Even if he was a suspect in Melinda's murder, there was no physical evidence linking him to it. He would have questions to answer when he was finished whatever it was he thought he planned on doing, though, especially since he'd discharged his weapon at the scene.

*And shot a kid.*

The thought rose up out of nowhere, the image of the boy lying on the floor, bleeding out. He felt guilty about shooting a teenager, but considering what the kid and his friends had done to Melinda, he at least felt justified. Not that justification made it any better.

In his mind's eye, the image of the gut-shot kid was blocked out by the silhouette of the giant that had put him out for over twelve hours with a single blow. This vision quickly shifted to his memory of Melinda lying on the floor in a pool of her blood.

Gordon rubbed his eyes and tried to put the thoughts out of his head.

He looked back at the phone screen without a clue as to what he planned on doing. He had no idea where to start.

Despite what he'd said to Dr. Bakshi, he had a feeling that, as much as he didn't want to admit it, whatever was going on with Farren had everything to do with the missing kids. He didn't think she was directly involved in the disappearances but he had a feeling the kids she was with were. The kids who had brought a literal giant with them to invade his house. He had to have imagined the size of the thing that bashed his brains in, but the pain in his skull told him there was at least some truth to his recollection.

He hit send on his phone and held it to his ear. It barely ran twice before being answered.

"Sheriff?" Barb said from the other line.

He almost hung up, suddenly stricken with guilt for even thinking of dragging her into his problems. She could lose her job helping him evade the state police. If she decided to help him.

She said, "Sheriff, you need my help with something?" And then in a lower register, "Staties are sniffing around the office, talking about an inquest. Everyone's pretty nervous."

"What deputies are in today?" Gordon asked, deciding in that instant he needed the help of someone he could trust, and of all those he had left in the world, nobody could be trusted more than Barb. "I'm still out of it from the hospital."

"You're out of the hospital?" she asked, incredulity raising her voice several octaves. She had the presence of mind at least to keep the volume down.

"I'm not exactly supposed to be so keep it between you and

me. Now who's in? I need someone to run an errand for me, if there's anyone there I can count on to do so."

*Anyone there I can trust* is what he wanted to say.

"I could use some fresh air," Barb said. "Is it something I can take care of for you?"

Thank God for Barb. He'd been hoping she'd volunteer and wasn't at all surprised she did. Gordon promised himself to fight for a significant pay increase for her at the next budget meeting—if he still had a job at that point.

A couple of teenagers wandered into the park, no doubt looking to make out or smoke. They spotted him sitting at the only bench and their faces blanched. Seeming to remember they were supposed to be somewhere else, they wandered right back out of the park.

"Okay, you may need to write some stuff down, so grab a pen," Gordon said into the phone.

"Got one already, sheriff."

He smiled and told her everything he needed.

Z

GORDON SHOVED the door to the cottage open but found himself unable to step inside. Memories flooded back to him—mostly good ones, but some, one in particular, that fueled his nightmares.

Barb squeezed past him, carrying an overflowing cardboard box in her arms.

"Anywhere you want me to put this stuff?" she asked, already through the hall and into the cozy living room. "Well, this place is just darling. You still come here?"

He didn't answer. Couldn't have if he wanted to.

The photo hung on the wall next to the door. He'd completely forgotten about it.

In the picture, Darya and a fourteen-year-old Farren sat next to each other in camp chairs by the blazing fire pit, both of them wearing their thick, black hair down past their shoulders, almost blending into the summer night beyond the light of the fire. In the photo, mother and daughter each held one of those double-pronged metal roasting sticks. Both of their sticks were loaded with marshmallows, all of which were on fire. They were smiling at each other, mid-laugh, in a way that broke his heart. Farren had just grown used to having him around and had seemed to actually enjoy his company. He remembered how good it felt taking that picture, not guessing for a moment the grief that was soon to follow.

Barb was suddenly next to him, putting a gentle hand on his arm.

"She was so beautiful," she said.

He nodded, cleared his throat. "She really was."

There was an awkward silence, not something Gordon was used to around Barb. He guessed she was debating whether or not to say something about Melinda. He should say something, he knew; acknowledge his second wife's passing in some way. But the moment slipped past.

"Need anything else from me?"

"That should do it for now," Gordon said, conjuring a smile for her. "I really appreciate everything."

She shuffled back to her car and said, "There's a thermos of coffee and a couple of sandwiches in that box for you. Make sure you eat."

Her car door slammed shut before he could thank her again. She smiled out her window, gave him a wave, and took off up the long, private road, likely headed back to complete her day at the office.

Gordon's stomach growled at him, telling him not to forget about the sandwiches. It was as good a reason as any to give up his boycott of this place.

He took a breath and stepped into what had once been John Murakami's summer home for the first time since he'd let Darya die here.

29

Stacey paced along the bank of the river, kicking anything in his path loose enough to be kicked.

Pietro, that fucking wino, was supposed to have met him here hours ago. Stacey had trusted him with literally all of his money. He had a bit socked away for food and cigarettes, sure, but no more junk money. And no junk!

He hadn't fixed in far too long and could feel his grip on things starting to slip.

Stacey tugged at his leggings, pulling them down at the crotch, briefly liberating his balls, and stormed back toward Pietro's tent, where he'd already spent half the day waiting for his so-called friend to return with the heroin Stacey had been stupid enough to trust him to buy. Pietro said he had a guy but the dealer was shy and didn't trust new people. How the hell did he expect to get any new business?

And Stacey was qualified to give business advice; before he'd gotten himself perilously hooked on junk, he'd been in proprietorship of a pretty successful boutique art supply store in Pittsburgh with his best friend and occasional lover, Atticus Sherman. Attie was a talented artist and had the body of a Caribbean lifeguard to boot. Their partnership—and friendship—ended when the monkey on Stacey's back started taking money from the cash register and then selling inventory online at severely discounted prices, simultaneously robbing and undercutting the business they built together. Attie had been more heartbroken than angry and moved back to Toronto to live with his mother after the store went into receivership.

Stacey thrust the flap of the tent aside and was about to step inside, fully intending on snooping around in Pietro's belongings for something to take the edge off—Pietro didn't fix but he smoked weed occasionally and Stacey was hoping he kept a stash on hand—but stopped with one foot through the flap.

Something, he couldn't be sure what exactly, had caught his eye. Movement.

At first, all Stacey could discern was the vague impression of something moving through the trees.

Pietro?

He was about to call out when he realized Pietro wouldn't be walking *into* the woods, on the opposite side of the river.

A deer then.

Except the closer this thing got, the more it seemed to move and act like a person. Two people in fact. They were obviously trying not to be seen, walking well away from the edge of the river locals called Old Maggie, winding between trees and picking their way through thick snares of brush dotting the forest floor. They must not have spotted Stacey standing there.

He ducked behind the tent and watched the pair trudge

past. They were maybe fifty yards away, a guy and a girl, both looking like soft-core goths, all in black but no makeup. They looked like Stacey's kind of people. And maybe they had stuff with them. Stuff Stacey might be able to stick directly into his bloodstream or even his nose. He'd even settle for a can of Coke right now.

He stepped out of hiding, ready to call out to them. Fuck Pietro.

Then he noticed the way the guy held both arms behind his back. Handcuffed?

The guy used one hand to brush hair out of his eyes as if he was demonstrating to Stacey that his hands were not bound, so sorry, guess again.

Pulling something then. In fact, his posture reminded Stacey of Kieran, the older brother he had not allowed himself to think of for maybe five years now. Kieran used to pull Stacey around on a sled in the wintertime. Back then, Stacey had gone by Alexander, his father's name—and there was someone else Stacey had managed not to think of for a very long time, he was on a roll. Kieran, pulling Stacey through the snow, had walked with both hands behind his back, fingers hooked through the rope affixed to the sled. Even now Stacey could vividly conjure the image of Kieran's back, shoulders jostling as he bore his younger brother off to school or the park or the only hill in town that didn't lead directly into street traffic.

Sure enough, the guy hit a bit of a clearing and Stacey could see he was dragging a sled in the same fashion. Difference was this was the middle of summer. What the hell was he doing with it?

Maybe they intended to hunt? Or had been hunting

unsuccessfully? A fair enough guess, but then where were their guns?

Something like a flint being struck went off in Stacey's mind.

The sled.

Dark clothes.

From the forest.

*Shadow people.*

Dear fucking fuck, Pietro had been right. They were real fucking shadow people. There was still plenty of daylight right now but already the two were hard to spot, even given the girl's blonde hair. They would absolutely look like shadows at night, especially to Pietro who was perpetually drunk.

Had they taken Farren?

For the first time in years, Stacey was not even peripherally thinking about getting his next fix. It was as though he'd been struck with divine inspiration. He wouldn't have been surprised to see a white dove descend in a beam of golden light in front of him. Stacey's heart bristled with purpose. He felt energized and sharpened, ready to do serious damage.

Farren was alive and he needed to help her.

## 30

The Congo was surprisingly quiet at night, especially for a place full of minors. Lights were out in most of the cabins by midnight and the pathways were empty. The only regular sign of activity came from the Visitor's Center, where whoever was on security shift for the night sat monitoring the cameras and likely playing a lot of video games. There wasn't any explicit rule about being out at night; nobody did it was all. Until recently Farren had been one of those to never step foot outside her cabin after nine or ten. She hadn't even thought about it until her chat with Jasper in the dining hall kitchen two days ago.

His story sounded like something out of a Tarantino movie. Or maybe if Tarantino teamed up with John Carpenter.

He'd told her what it was like inside the Museum, dark and full of scary things. Home to *it*.

She'd trained herself not to think of its name. When she did, she could feel it worming its way into her mind. She'd even stopped thinking of it as a *he*, not wanting to give it the power of persona.

Jasper had been pretty open about the Museum, about how he and Sasha would go there to receive instructions on who to recruit next. They always went together but only Sasha ever received the summons. Jasper described the way *it* spoke to him; a scratching in his head, the same thing she'd experienced.

He'd flat out refused to discuss the Orchid Room, except to say that especially difficult recruits would sometimes be sent there.

They'd recruited again on the evening after the slaughter at Farren's house. Jasper had left his meeting with Farren to discover Sasha was looking for him. Farren had watched from a distance as Sasha appeared to accost Jasper ambling down the path to his cabin. They'd spoken for a moment, Sasha throwing her arms around in wild gesticulation, before leading him up the path to the Museum. The following morning there had been someone crying in the Sapling Hut.

The girl they'd recruited was inconsolable from the moment she woke, locked in the hut. She screamed at the top of her lungs for hours on end, weeping in great, wailing cries. The only time she stopped was when Sasha went in to speak with her. The silence only lasted a few seconds and soon the girl could be heard screaming at Sasha from behind the closed door of the hut. Sasha had stormed out of there, red-faced, with her stupid bottom lip leading the way.

It didn't take long for whispers of the Orchid Room to start circulating. Farren had played dumb and asked a few people to explain it to her, but no one seemed to know much more than she did, only that the new girl would be brought there and would either take it down a notch or be turned loose soon after. Nobody knew of anyone joining the tribe after being sent to the Orchid Room, though.

Farren wondered about that. Would they let the girl go if the Orchid Room therapy didn't do the trick? What were they going to do to her in there? She needed to find out.

Word had come this afternoon at lunch. Sadie had plopped down next to Farren and asked if she'd heard about the new girl.

"They're sending her to the Orchid Room tonight," Sadie told her when Farren had pleaded her ignorance.

"When do they do it?" Farren had asked.

Sadie had shrugged and said, "After I'm in bed."

Now Farren crouched in the shadows of the same trio of cabins she'd hid behind during her escape attempt in the spring. What would happen the next time she crossed the bridge spanning Eagle Creek? She'd spent an hour in meditation before coming out here tonight, trying to focus her thoughts and steel her mind against the thing in the Museum, not that she thought it would help.

The new recruit had stopped screaming about fifteen minutes ago, which Farren assumed meant she'd fallen asleep.

A soft grinding noise accompanied by footsteps came from up the path and Farren made herself small, staying out of the glow of security lights dotting the grounds. Jasper passed within five feet of her, pushing a wheelchair up the path, its tires crunching softly on the hard-packed dirt. It was hard to see in the dark but Farren was confident it was the newest recruit in the chair. Jasper must have drugged her the same way he'd drugged Farren when she was recruited.

A flare of anger surged up in her and, for a split second,

Farren thought she would be unable to help herself from creeping up behind him and bashing him over the head. See how he liked being rendered unconscious.

But she needed to see what was going to happen. Needed to know what uncooperative recruits were subjected to. And if she was going to attack anyone in the Congo, it would be Sasha.

Jasper's story hadn't exactly endeared him to Farren but she at least understood where he was coming from. He'd made some really stupid decisions and had caused a lot of misery, but she could tell he was allowing himself to be dragged along now. It made him a coward in her eyes, but at least he had some excuse for his involvement.

She watched him push the chair to the bridge and pause at the edge of it. Jasper pulled something from his pocket, unscrewed its top, and tilted it up to his mouth. He held it there for some time before screwing the cap back on, bending down, and placing it upright on the ground.

He pushed the wheelchair across the bridge at a fast walk and made a right, never breaking stride. He wheeled the girl around the corner of the Orchid Room and then they were out of sight.

Farren debated waiting for him to come back before crossing the bridge herself but decided if she passed out or anything due to mind invasion, at least he would be likely to come across her and bring her back to safety. She hoped so anyway.

She sprinted through the night, relishing the extra spring provided by her newly re-acquired blade. It would never beat the real thing, but she loved running with it.

The glass of the whiskey bottle Jasper had placed on the

ground glistened in the light of the moon. He'd pick it up on his way back, Farren was sure. She'd never seen a piece of litter in the Congo. Another weird thing for a place full of kids.

It was only when she reached the fork in the path on the other side of the bridge that she realized nothing was happening in her head. Was the mind-invader busy with Jasper and the new recruit?

Or had it been imagined after all? Could have all been part of some chemical imbalance in her brain, or the echoes of an injury from her accident, as she'd first thought.

It *was* different over here, though, as if the world was muffled. The crickets and tree frogs that had been singing seconds ago were now a dim chorus of far-off static. The creek sounded like someone had tossed a heavy blanket over it.

There was something otherworldly, for lack of a better term, going on in the Congo. Hallucination or not, seeing her dad and then finding his hat had solidified it for her. They couldn't fake something like that, could they? He'd been buried with that hat. Would they have dug him up just to get to it? Just to convince her? It wasn't a far stretch of the imagination now that she thought about it. She could picture Guppy in six feet of earth with a shovel in his hand, Sasha standing over him.

But they couldn't have known what she'd seen in the chapel. Couldn't have known how much the Buffaloes hat meant to her, how representative of her dad it was. She pushed the useless speculation from her mind.

A presence seemed to coalesce around her as she approached the long hut with the peeling pink paint. More than one presence, in fact. The strongest came from behind her, in the direction of the Museum. What she felt coming from the Orchid Room was less *present* but just as powerful, as if only partially there.

She crept around the back of the building to the far side, hoping to take advantage of the cover. It was black as pitch on that side, away from the distant glow of security lights, and the moon obscured by the longhouse. She paused halfway along the side of the Orchid Room and listened.

The silence around her was eerie. Made her feel vulnerable, exposed. Gave her the sense that something might be prowling nearby, following her progress.

Silence from out front as well. Jasper must have already carried the girl inside.

Farren crept the rest of the way to the front of the building. That sense of there being a wild presence behind the closed door of the Orchid Room intensified.

The door flew open.

Farren lunged back into the shadows at the side of the building. Had she been heard? Seen?

She peeked her head around the corner in time to see Jasper pull the door closed then shove the empty wheelchair back down the stairs. He was pale and wide-eyed. Frightened. Of something in the Orchid Room?

Did she really want to do this? Was it worth potentially confronting whatever it was that had terrified Jasper? Might save someone's life. She didn't know exactly what went on in there but she was certain this girl wouldn't be joining the tribe or going back to the life she knew before Sasha and Jasper had intervened.

Farren crept out of hiding and was relieved to see Jasper bearing the wheelchair across the short bridge. He stooped to snatch up the bottle he'd left behind, as she'd known he would.

The door of the Orchid Room simultaneously beckoned to and repelled her. Only a few broad steps leading up to them, but it looked to Farren like the climb was miles long—a trek to some great temple in the mountains.

Something spoke in her mind. A single word.

*Yes.*

Referring to her thought of the Orchid Room as a temple? Yes. But also something much different, much *more*. Temple was the closest thing to it her mind could grasp. And instead of being on a mountain, it was in its own universe, its own reality. These doors didn't lead into the Orchid Room, but to somewhere else entirely. She knew this as much as she knew her own name.

Her throat was suddenly bone dry. Swallowing was like trying to choke down a tissue. There was a jug of ice-cold water in the fridge back at her cabin. That sounded good right about now.

She started back toward the bridge.

"No," she said, stopping on the path.

Speaking the word aloud helped her recover herself.

What the hell had that just been? Had she really been about to bail because she was a little thirsty?

Something clicked.

The quiet nights. The general orderliness of the Congo. The well-behaved kids. Her own complacency, which, visions of her father aside, was way out of character for her.

She saw clearly then.

These kids had all been mollified by something hidden in plain sight. It was the only thing that made sense. They were brought here against their will, locked in a shed, drugged, and put through some pretty traumatizing shit, and then they all, herself included, just woke up and said, *Okey-dokey, let's live in the Congo!*

Feeling her resolve flex itself like a second spine, she climbed the stairs up to the double doors before she could change her mind again.

She grasped the door handles, heart jackhammering.

Someone grabbed her from behind, yanking her back from the doors, and jamming a cloth over her face. A familiar scent invaded her nostrils and filled her lungs.

*No-no-no-no-no!*

She thrashed against the arm locked around her but her world was already going black.

Z

THE TRAIN DREAM AGAIN.

*She knows it's a nightmare but, unlike what she's read online about lucid dreaming, is powerless to change anything.*

*Her bare feet—both of them—slap against the smooth, rounded stones laid into the ground. Walking next to the same set of tracks.*

*In the distance, a train howls.*

*She walks faster, opens up her stride.*

Dad wants me to keep moving.

*The thought startles her.*

*In her dreams, her father always wants her to keep moving. So why, when she'd seen him in the chapel, had he told her to stay in the Congo?*

*There is untenable conviction behind the thought, the* knowledge, *that her dad, her real dad, wants her to move. To go.*

*To escape.*

*The train shrieks again.*

*Louder.*

*Closer.*

*She breaks into a run, pumping her arms. Tracks blur past in the corner of her vision.*

*Another shriek.*

*She casts a glance over her shoulder. Screams.*

*It isn't a train.*

*The thing behind her races along the tracks on colossal, spider-like limbs, gripping the rails in talons the size of windmill blades. Its greater mass, an amorphous bulk of dark, glistening flesh, takes up most of her field of vision. Even at its unfathomable height, she sees its countless baleful eyes staring into her. They probe her being, scrape the insides of her skin, dig into every corner of her body, into the tips of her fingers and toes, wriggling along the inside of her belly, finally coalescing in her head, unfurling within it like a sea anemone, suckling at her gray matter with snaking tendrils.*

*She feels all of this and knows it is happening to her real self as well. Something is looking at her. Some immense, abominable thing. Something she'd felt the edges of before but that she now sees in its unmasked form. Or at least a version of that form.*

*Throughout all of this, she continues to run and it maintains its pursuit.*

*It appears bound to the tracks. But so is she. In these dreams, try as she might, she can never leave their side.*

*A shadow falls upon her as the thing closes the distance between them.*

*She looks up and shrieks.*

*It looms directly over her now, one claw like a strip off a* ship's hull clinging to the track just behind her. It keeps perfect pace with her so they may as well both be standing still.

The thing lowers itself over her, as if squatting, and for an absurd second, she thinks it's going to take a dump.

Instead, it brings what passes as its chest, geographically at least, closer to Farren.

It's as if the sky is collapsing on her. Vertigo makes her unsteady on her feet as a being the size of a small planet lowers itself to within a few dozen feet of her.

Her dad's face sticks out of the thing's abdomen. He appears caught in some great avalanche of glistening, swampy green flesh; only his face and hands stick out of the thing. His skin sags like old glass.

He opens his eyes.

Farren wants to call to him but terror steals her voice. She needs to wake up.

Her dad opens his mouth and screams. A scream of fear and torment. Worse, a scream without hope. One of defeat and suffering. The scream of the damned.

Sobbing, she runs harder. It's her *dream*, she should be faster.

She begins to pull ahead of the thing with her father inside it. The voice in her head makes an outraged sound, a million angry hornets buzzing. That encourages her. She usually keeps it reigned in but she can be a sore winner. Hearing her opponents groan when the girl with one foot crushes a fastball out of the park or steals a base is bliss.

"Eat shit!" she calls and pours on some more steam.

The thing's shadow falls away, disappears from view entirely.

She chances a look over her shoulder. The monster has

*fallen behind. Only after a few seconds does she realize it's wait-ing, watching her, an expectant glint in those infinite empty eyes.*

*It's too late by the time she looks ahead. She's going too fast.*

*The ground gives out in front of her. Not just a pit or even a crevasse, the whole world ceases to exist. And she can't stop. She digs her heels in. Stumbles. Trips. Hits the ground hard.*

*Her momentum takes over.*

*She tumbles over the edge of the earth.*

Z

FARREN WOKE WITH A JOLT, recalling the nightmare in its entirety, and wishing she could erase it from her memory. She couldn't get the image of her father—and the thing he'd been trapped within—out of her head, even as she took in her new surroundings. Or tried to.

It was almost completely dark wherever she was. For a brief moment she thought she'd been locked in the chapel, but had the sense of being in a much bigger space rife with the stale smell of age and neglect.

She was surprised to find she was unrestrained, sprawled on a rough blanket. Her muscles felt stiff. Must have been there for at least an hour.

Had they locked her in the Orchid Room? The notion momentarily panicked her but she quickly dismissed it. She'd know if she was in there.

*I have him.*

That voice. Almost familiar.

She tried to stand and fell to her knees, only then realizing that her blade had been taken. Fear was the only thing that kept her from screaming in outrage. It was gone now and she couldn't help that. She'd deal with whoever took it once she got herself out of here, wherever here was.

Barely visible silver light, likely from the moon, hinted at its presence through what she assumed were windows painted black. To keep light out or to keep people from seeing inside?

Something passed through her vision; a dark blur whose size it was impossible to guess at. She fell back onto her hands and scooted backward, putting as much space as possible between herself and whoever or whatever was in here with her.

She kept still. Breathed steadily, quietly. Listened.

An unidentifiable squelching, sucking sound came from behind her and she screamed. Scrabbled back to her blanket and pulled it around her, reverting to juvenile methods of self-preservation. She trembled and sobbed, holding the fabric over her face to muffle the sound.

After a minute, maybe five, she made herself to stop crying. Silence.

Taking a long, deep breath, she threw the blanket off and got back to her knees. Made herself look around and couldn't help gasping when something enormous scuttled past in the dark, chitinous appendages clicking like iron picks on the tiled floor.

*You smell good when you're frightened.*

The voice filled her head.

It occurred to her she could still be unconscious but this felt like no dream. And she always had two feet in her dreams.

This thing wanted her scared. Was messing with her to frighten her, she was suddenly positive of this. It had pretty well said as much itself.

She knew who—*what*—the voice belonged to and realized where she was.

They'd locked her in the Museum.

A putrid, humid wind blew into her face, accompanied by the sound a whale made through its blowhole. Farren steeled herself against it, willed herself not to be afraid of the monstrous thing breathing in her face.

She remembered her dream and how frustrated the thing chasing her had been when she'd outrun it, ignoring the fact it had responded by literally ending the world in her own dream. She wanted to piss it off.

Hot breath poured over her, bathing her in a slimy, putrescent sweat while overhead a leathery flapping came from somewhere in the dark, the sound of heavy ship's sails being whipped about in the wind. Whatever it was flew around in widening circles that went impossibly far, given that she was indoors; the Museum wasn't all that big.

Farren focused on her breathing, the way Anika had taught her to. She breathed deep, ignoring the foul stench of the damp exhalations falling on her like a cloud. Focused so that all there was in her world was her breath. In and out.

In.

Something like an enormous slug coiled itself around her waist.

Out.

A rough, warm hand the size of a couch cushion closed on her shoulder.

It was impossible to ignore the things touching her, so she searched for some aspect of them to focus on that wasn't terrifying.

The thing wrapped around her was gross, she held onto

that. Disgusting. Like a worm. Like the worms Devin Hughson had put on her back in fourth grade. Farren had been chatting with Esther Freely and Jess McKinnley when Devin said her name from behind her. Both her friends' eyes widened and Farren had spun around to see what gross Devin Hughson wanted. She barely registered his grin and then he was holding a yellow plastic bucket over her head and upending it. She looked up, expecting water.

But it was worms.

At least fifty of them. They rained down on her, falling across her face. Landed in her eyes, her hair, her mouth. She'd gagged on half a dozen of them and vomited violently for thirty minutes, unable to stop herself from retching every time she thought of the twitching, writhing things in the back of her throat, tickling her gag reflex. Even now, focusing on that memory, Farren could feel her throat constricting against the idea of worms in her mouth. But revulsion was much easier to deal with than fear.

The thing around her waist was gone. The hand on her shoulder too. She'd been so deep in that revolting memory she'd forgotten to be afraid of what was happening to her now.

A low chuckle bubbled up from the gloom. Or had it been in her head?

*You are tenacious.*

She cringed away from the voice, though there was no escaping it—she needed to have a physical reaction to it or she'd lose her mind. It had come from everywhere. Not only was it deep in her thoughts, it resonated from everything in the room. As if she was inside the being itself.

*You are not far from the truth, at least to the degree you are capable of knowing it.*

Farren knelt on shaking legs, as tall as she could make herself. She would not fear this thing. Wouldn't give it anything to find delectable about her.

That low chuckling again.

*You have work to do, girl. Atonement.*

"Fuck you," Farren said, adrenaline spiking at her own audacity.

*Kaeru.*

Hearing her dad's pet name for her was a gut punch.

"Only my dad gets to call me that," she said in a small, breathless voice.

*I told you I have him.*

Was it trying to make her angry?

"Why? What do you want from him? What do you want from me?"

*I will show you.*

She had the sense of some immense thing rising before her, as though it had been coiled right in front of her the whole time; a mountain of shadow invisible in the dark. It rose to an incredible height, keeping its attention on her all the while. Not the thing from her dream, thank God, but they were certainly related, if not parts of the same whole. It reached out to her, she sensed this as clearly as if she'd been seeing it, which she was glad she couldn't. She wanted to retreat from the thing but her entire body was frozen in place.

As soon as it touched her, the world fell out from underneath her. She found herself suspended alone in empty space.

Cold panic gripped her. How long would she be trapped in this void? She shivered both because she was suddenly freezing and because she was scared shitless.

Just when she thought her mind might actually snap, a red

light exploded around her. It enveloped everything, including her own body. She watched her hands disappear into crimson rays, a bath of red light. Her world was flooded with it.

She felt herself move along the light, traveling it the way marine life rode ocean currents or the way a blood cell moved along arteries. All she could see was the red light, so she only had the sense of movement but no way of orienting herself or charting her progress. Hours passed and still, she drifted.

Eventually, a day had gone by. Or what she was reasonably sure had been a day. Or had it been more than that?

A week passed. It was strange to think about it too hard but she seemed to be traveling for a long time without taking a long time to do it. She had the sense of weeks and then months passing but they went by in a moment.

Years passed and she wondered if she would float forever.

And then she was slowing, moving to the edge of the light like merging off a highway.

*See.*

This voice was different from the one she'd heard in the dark of the Museum, so long ago. It was deep and somehow benevolent. Speaking secretively. Confiding in her.

The light was gone in an instant and she found herself in the dark of night, hovering a couple dozen feet over the roof of a familiar house.

She plummeted toward it but didn't worry about injury since she seemed to no longer have a body. For now, she was simply an invisible, intangible consciousness. This didn't bother her the way she thought it maybe should.

She sunk through the roof until she hovered over a bed. Two figures slept within it. The figure on the right had long, dark hair that covered most of her pillow. The one on the left had shorter, dark hair. It was impossible to make out the rest of their features in the dim light.

A digital alarm clock sat on the end table next to the figure on the left. The green glow of its digits illuminated something sitting on the corner of the table. A hat with a familiar logo.

Farren gasped.

She was looking at the sleeping forms of her parents.

## JOHN

### 8 YEARS AGO

Junichi "John" Murakami sat up in bed and cocked his head in a manner similar to Bonzo, their new lab-shepherd puppy. The little beast was adorable but John couldn't wait for it to grow up enough to stop messing all over their new house.

He'd brought the dog home for Farren two months ago as a sort of apology and appreciation gift. What he'd done to his family wasn't fair; accepting a lucrative job with the burgeoning social media giant KnowMe under the condition he relocated to their new tech park in Maggie's Knee, PA, three thousand miles across the country from their former home in downtown Seattle. Farren had been unreasonably good about the whole thing, especially for a ten-year-old, which made him feel worse about the move. He didn't deserve that kid or her mother. And so, the puppy.

Which was what he assumed had roused him. He didn't hear anything now, which probably meant the little monster had gone back to sleep. Good. He didn't want to get out of bed.

He dropped back onto his pillow, turning onto his side and spooning into Darya. Stuck his face in her mane of thick, black hair and inhaled. It smelled faintly of patchouli with heavy undertones of the spices she'd used in dinner, which had been penne and meatballs, one of his favorites. But then, he loved anything she made. He wrapped an arm around her firm stomach and allowed it to creep up until it brushed against the swell of her breast. Debated waking her up.

A scraping, scratching sound came from somewhere in the house. Sounded like one of the kitchen chairs being dragged across the floor. Bonzo? He was locked up. At least, he was supposed to be.

John rolled out of bed, clad only in his Street Fighter comfy pants, and padded out of the room. He crossed the hall and poked his head into Farren's room. In the pink glow of her My Little Pony nightlight he could see the spill of her dark hair, so much like her mother's, spread over her pillow. He watched the shallow rise and fall of her chest as she slept. His heart swelled and he had to take a second to consider his daughter was already in the double digits. She'd be a teenager in no time at all. Would she still like baseball when she was in high school? Would she still like him?

He forced himself away from her door, down the hall, toward the kitchen and living room. Already he'd decided what he'd heard would turn out to be nothing at all, only the extra space getting to him. They'd lived in a two-bedroom condo in Seattle and were used to being within a dozen feet of one another at any given time of day. Here they had multiple bedrooms, a big sunken living room, and a basement! He'd never had a basement before.

At the end of the hall, he peered around the corner,

suddenly sure he would see a raccoon or maybe a coyote in his living room. They were living among the pines of Pennsylvania now—he assumed wildlife intrusions must be common.

The living room was clear, as was the kitchen. The dinner table, which sat in the dining room connected to the kitchen, had not been moved.

Flipping on the light, he descended the stairs into the living room, then took the adjoining staircase into the basement. Bonzo's cage sat at the far end of the den, a space John had unsuccessfully tried to turn into his man cave.

"You can have a man cave when Farren moves out for college," Darya had said when he'd announced his intention. "If she moves out at all." She'd given him one of her mischievous grins then, the kind she knew drove him wild.

Now he shoved Farren's semi-completed Lego Hogwarts Castle aside with one foot as he crossed the floor of the den to Bonzo's cage. The dog had indeed been asleep but woke up when John moved the Lego set. He yapped, high-pitched and far too loud in the silence of the house.

"Ssh," John said, knowing it would only incite more noise from the dog.

He flicked off the basement light and Bonzo cried from behind him, giving a few yaps before settling into a steady whine. When the dog had quieted, he went back up the stairs, having half forgotten about the noise that woke him in the first place. It was entirely possible it had been part of a dream.

John reached the top of the stairs and stopped. Stared across the room at the sliding glass door that led outdoors from their living room, at first mistaking what he was seeing for a runic design of unknown origin.

Written on the glass in a thick, dark substance was a single word.

ZIIS.

The S on the end of the word was jagged, so it looked like a backward Z.

Something about the way it was written, or about the strange word itself, gave him such a strong sense of vertigo he had to grab the wall to steady himself. Weird as it made him feel, he was unable to look away from the word. It had a sickening pull, the way he found it almost impossible to stop picking at a scab once started.

All at once he needed to know more about this new word. At the same, time something told him he would be enlightened before long. Not tonight. Soon.

Along with this realization came the sudden imperative to make sure neither Darya nor Farren saw this. They didn't even need to know about it.

He crept back down the basement stairs, ignoring Bonzo's renewed yaps, and slipped into the laundry room to fetch some cleaning supplies.

Z

JOHN STEPPED out of what was laughably referred to as his office and into the warm June sunlight spilling over the grounds of the tech park. His team's building, which often felt like an extremely well-funded fraternity house more than a workspace, fronted a lush green lawn spotted with massive trees that perpetually had someone sitting underneath them eating lunch, reading a book, or just taking it all in. The tech park itself resembled a ski resort, nestled as it was in the hills and trees on the outskirts of Maggie's Knee. The KnowMe

Technological Park, a far too ordinary name for such an extraordinary place, was pedestrian traffic only, with the exception of the company's own transportation system.

P.E.T.S., or Personal Electric Transportation System, was part rideshare program, part shuttle service. Folks who wished to walk as little as possible—and there were a fair number of those in this industry—could summon a PET to their parking spot, or anywhere in the park, via an app developed exclusively for KnowMe. Within minutes of using the app, one of the park employees, whom John and his co-workers referred to as drones, would arrive in one of their beefed-up golf carts and hand deliver an electric scooter. Or, if it was raining, the drones could be summoned to chauffeur you from place to place. Their golf carts were enclosed and sported better technology than any vehicle John had owned until recently. In the winter months, the scooters and golf carts were stored and the drones shuttled employees in electric SUVs equipped with four-wheel drive.

Any hesitation John had about taking the position of systems and network architect had been washed away when he had been given the tour of KnowMe's new center of operations. The park was a world-class, self-sustained technological wonder of efficiency, comfort, and quality of life and work conditions. It even had its own Starbucks and five-star steakhouse.

Enjoying the sunlight on his face, John crossed the grass at a lazy stroll. He preferred to walk when he had the time, which was most days; KnowMe prided itself on its strict no-schedule policy. Theoretically, he could walk in late to a meeting with Jeremy Hrongar, founder, president, and CEO of KnowMe, and not have it held against him in any way.

He bumped into Faizel Hussein, one of his engineers, in line to get a latte on the way to his car. They chatted briefly about the update they would be releasing next week, which both men were excited about. This was a relatively minor update compared with the big one they were working toward releasing the following spring. The imminent update was merely a slat in the bridge they had to build to get to the big one—the update they'd dubbed "the Kraken"—and was part of the necessary series of updates they'd be releasing throughout the year.

Most of the updates would be relatively unnoticeable to the majority of their two billion users and would be announced on only the most obscure of KnowMe's web pages in the vaguest jargon their lead content writer, Enzo, could muster. The Kraken itself would completely change the way social media was used. There were rumors that secret contracts from several governments were funding it and, though John hadn't heard anything firsthand about it, he had no hard time imagining that being the case. And if that was the case, it wouldn't just be social media they were changing forever, but the world they lived in.

After leaving Faizel, John took his time walking back to the parking lot, sipping his latte and relishing the piping hot coffee burning its way to the pit of his stomach.

Back at his car, John stuck his travel mug—KnowMe was almost entirely paper-free—on the roof while he slid his backpack off and tossed it on the passenger seat. He heard the voice the second his bag landed. At first, he thought it was the sibilant slide of his backpack on the seat material he'd heard. Then it came again, a swarm of bugs in his head.

*Junichi.*

Somehow he knew what he was hearing had something to do with the word written on his back door a couple of months ago. He'd cleaned what had turned out to be foul-smelling muck off the door easily enough and all but forgot about it by morning. Within a couple of days, it had entirely escaped his mind.

Now it was back. A voice to go with the word.

*My name.*

John shuddered. His mind couldn't even grasp at what the word might be the name of, what the voice in his mind might belong to.

Thinking of the name—ZIIS—tweaked something in his brain and he winced against the sensation of having his thoughts invaded by something much bigger and stronger than himself.

*Come.*

Powerless to disobey, he got into the driver's seat, abandoning his travel mug on the roof, and started the car. No idea where he was going, only that he needed to be moving. He pulled out of his spot without looking and narrowly avoided colliding with a PET. The drone driving remained expressionless; they weren't allowed to lash out at KnowMe employees for any reason. John gave a half-hearted wave of apology and sped toward the exit.

Z

IT WAS about an hour before sunset by the time he reached his destination. For several minutes all he could do was stand in awe of the wall of giant logs towering before him. He wasn't sure what he'd expected to see when he ducked into the naturally occurring tunnel of twisted branches and vines he'd just fought his way through, but this had certainly not been it.

The voice hadn't spoken since he'd left work; he'd been following an insistent pull on his psyche, a mental leash tugging him along. At the carpool lot on the other side of town, he hadn't given a second thought to getting out of his car and hiking through the woods for miles on his own without any supplies, save for his half-full bottle of water.

After an hour, he came across a dense thicket too overgrown to navigate and felt his attention drawn toward a narrow, shadowy passage he barely fit through. Navigating the tight arteries through the nearly impenetrable foliage had felt almost like the work of instinct but he couldn't deny the sensation of being led.

Built into the enormous wall was a door overgrown with vines. Something was written above it in big block letters, obscured by the vines. A sign. But for what? What sort of place could this possibly be? His first guess was a military installation or research facility. Whatever it was, the place was abandoned.

John cleared the vines away easily enough and was only slightly surprised when the door opened for him without fuss. Beyond the door was a short archway leading through the wall. He stepped inside.

Sudden, blaring music made him jump. He whipped his head around in a panic, searching for the source of the noise. When he calmed down enough to recognize the song, he laughed. It was the Beastie Boys singing "Fight for Your Right" —his ringtone for Darya. John ignored the call. He'd call her back soon.

Through the archway, he stepped into another world.

With the exception of the overgrown vegetation, he was standing in a perfectly preserved resort. To his left was a gabled building with a glass facade. Above the door was a large sign that said: *WELCOME TO THE GREAT FOREST OUTDOOR DISCOVERY CENTER!* And on the door itself, *VISITOR'S CENTER.*

To his right, running along a dirt road overgrown with weeds, were half a dozen buildings set up like a strip mall. Most of their signs were overgrown and tough to make out, but he could read the one for the third building easily enough, it read: *GREAT FOREST DINING HALL.* The road opened up beyond these buildings, branching off into various directions and leading to a staggering number of structures, many of which appeared to be luxury cabins.

It was basically a small village in the middle of the seemingly endless forest. How the hell could it be here without anyone knowing about it? There had to be a road leading in from one of the other directions.

His nerd brain was in overdrive and wanted to methodically search each of these buildings as if he was a character in a post-apocalyptic video game. He had a feeling he would get his opportunity before long, but for now, he felt himself drawn to the far end of the Great Forest Outdoor Discovery Center, to a pair of buildings on the other side of what appeared to be a small river or stream. Whatever he was here for was in one of those buildings. The same pull that led him here was magnified a hundred times, beckoning him closer. He walked toward the buildings as if in a dream, barely feeling his feet touching the ground. The rest of the world faded into the background, only dimly perceptible in his peripheral vision.

He crossed the bridge and soon found himself standing at

the foot of a short flight of stone stairs leading up to a building primarily constructed of wooden beams, possibly harvested from the surrounding forest.

The words over the door read: *GREAT FOREST MUSEUM.*

Z

ENTERING the Great Forest Museum was like going back in time. The place had a distinct eighties feel to it the moment John stepped inside. The air was stale. Dead.

How long ago had someone last opened the doors or cracked a window?

The foyer was decked out in faded banners and signage welcoming guests to the Great Forest Family and Friends Weekend. The walls were covered in framed photos, plaques, and displays, all celebrating the discovery center itself. A framed photo on the wall next to him portrayed a burly, grinning man, roughly in his sixties, wearing a tuxedo. He had a full head of gray hair and a thick, gray beard to match. One broad arm was held around the shoulders of a beautiful, smiling woman who looked ten years the man's junior. She wore her lush, blonde hair in a complex updo and was dressed in a collared jumpsuit the same deep green as the needles of the evergreens also in the photo. The couple posed outside the wall, in front of the same door John had come through. In the picture, the wall was clear of vegetation and the sign for the discovery center could very clearly be seen. A caption was engraved on a brass plaque below the photo: *Stuart and Cheryl Brierton - August 1987.*

John whistled to himself. The sound fell flat in the room.

A twitch in his head. Time to keep going.

He shoved through double doors leading down a long hall decorated on one side with plaques and posters giving a historical overview of the pioneers who'd settled in the area. A truly cringeworthy mural of an Iroquois tribe welcoming a wagonload of Pilgrims was painted on the other wall.

At the end of the hall was another set of steel double doors. Something radiated from them, a growing pressure. The presence in his mind, ZIIS, grew more active the closer he came. It seemed excited.

He pushed one of the doors open and peeked into the room beyond. Let himself breathe when nothing jumped out at him.

The room was enormous and full of exhibits from tree cuttings to wildlife specimens. A stuffed gray wolf and black bear stood side by side in a far corner, eternally baring their teeth while a spotted wildcat swiped down at them from a shelf several feet over the bear's head.

The middle of the room was dominated by what John supposed was a tribute to the settlers who had come to Pennsylvania in the late seventeenth century. It featured a rocky terrain bordered on one side by a blue plastic strip representing a river. Impossible to tell if it was supposed to be Widow's River. Some realistic-looking plants and trees were arranged around the display. All of this surrounded the diorama's centerpiece: the mannequin of a boy of perhaps twelve, dressed in Pilgrim's garb, complete with the buckled flat-topped hat. It stood with one foot on a foam boulder, looking positively triumphant with its fists on its hips and lifeless eyes gazing over land so successfully taken over.

John wondered what had possessed Stuart Brierton to

make such an exhibit the center of this beautiful room. Especially when he had a trio of fearsome predators stuck in the corner. Different times, he supposed. Didn't matter. The display was apparently what he had come for.

An energy thrummed out of the diorama, originating from the Pilgrim boy at its center. John found himself unable to peel his eyes from it. The longer he stared, the more substance the boy took on. The distant, painted-on, blue eyes of the Pilgrim boy seemed to gaze into his own.

Outside windows set high into the walls, the sun cast its last orange-red glow into the Museum and finally dipped below the horizon, taking the light with it.

The air changed the moment the sunlight left the room, as if a vacuum was created by its absence and a powerful energy was rushing in to fill it.

And still, he stared into the eyes of the mannequin.

Even when the light left the room completely, he could see the eyes of the Pilgrim child.

A voice came from the direction of its mouth.

It said, *Welcome.*

Z

JOHN STOMPED the snow off his boots and stepped into the warmth of his house. The day had been frigid and the night even colder, especially wading through the knee-high snow blanketing the forest. He'd carved a path through the powder to the discovery center, but a fresh snowfall this morning had filled it in entirely.

After the first snow of the year, he had been afraid to return to the discovery center for fear that someone might follow his footsteps and stumble upon his secret, but his fears were quickly assuaged by his despot. ZIIS had shown him—it never spoke outright anymore—the discovery center, and all evidence of it, was kept hidden, as if a veil was drawn across the three or four miles surrounding it; one only John could penetrate.

For eight months now he'd been returning to the discovery center three or four times a week. His excuse to Darya was, with all the preparation for the Kraken update, he had to spend significantly more time at the office. She never questioned him.

He had no recollection of what occurred in the Great Forest Museum after hearing the voice he was pretty sure had come from the mannequin. He'd woken up in his own bed the following morning, with seemingly nothing amiss. The only thing different was the imperative, constantly present in his mind, to prepare the discovery center. Who or what he was preparing it for, he didn't know and never questioned. His assignments bubbled up as desires from the deepest corners of his heart.

His first job had been to black out all the windows in the Museum, the effect of which was instantaneous. As soon as he'd painted over the last clear inch of glass, eliminating the last beam of daylight, the room took on a new feeling, as if he was in a different place entirely. ZIIS thrived in the dark.

After darkening the Museum, he'd set to work clearing weeds and vines from the various buildings and cabins on the grounds. That finished, he set to work on the technological infrastructure, which was practically non-existent. The place had been built in the eighties and was equipped with eighties tech. So John had gone shopping.

The first thing he'd taken care of was to outfit as many buildings as possible with gas generators. He had to rent a moving van to get them to the carpool lot and used the biggest wagon he could find to lug the first one to the discovery center before adopting the use of a sled for the rest of them. Even well before the snow fell, the sled was a lifesaver. Pulling the generators through miles of dense woodland on his own was long, back-breaking work, but he never faltered or even considered giving up on the job.

Next he outfitted the discovery center with a full commercial security system and intranet, turning the Visitor's Center into a security hub. By the time he was done, he had closed-circuit cameras watching nearly every angle of the grounds as well as half a dozen outside the wall, watching the perimeter.

One of the buildings in the strip near the entrance was a recreation hall equipped with an impressive selection of arcade cabinets, all of which were in immaculate condition. John cleaned each one inside and out before starting them up. For an entire night, he took a trip down memory lane vis-a-vis video games from his youth. *Pac-Man*, *Donkey Kong*, *Frogger*, *Paperboy*, and *Joust* received the bulk of his attention—this last more than any other. He used to play *Joust* for hours on end with Gavin Walsh, his best bud through elementary and high school. They'd had their fair share of physical fights because of those dueling ostriches.

His latest project had been to clean up the cabins. They were beautiful, especially for an educational getaway. He was about two-thirds of the way through them when he'd called it a night for this evening.

Now exhausted, wet, and freezing, he stepped into the foyer of his family's home and braced himself for the predictable assault of love from Bonzo, who was growing to be a large and loyal companion, especially to Farren. But the dog didn't come. No one did.

"Ladies?" he called into the house, the hint of alarm tickling the back of his neck. It was strange not to have anyone greet him at the door when he got in.

"Kitchen," came Darya's voice from down the hall, quiet and subdued.

Uh-oh.

He kicked off his boots and shed his coat, taking his time so he could mentally prepare himself for whatever was to come. The signs didn't point to anything good: no dog or daughter to greet him at the door, quiet house, Darya waiting for him in the kitchen.

He found her sitting at the table in her fluffy, powder blue bathrobe, her insanely thick, black hair falling loose around her shoulders. She was nursing a cup of tea, staring into her mug, absently swirling the bag around by the string.

"You okay?" he said before anything else. "Is Farren okay?"

Darya nodded, eyes never leaving the tea. Something was definitely up.

"Farren's reading in her room with Bonzo," she said quietly.

"The dog reads?" John said, immediately regretting trying to make a joke in the face of what appeared to be the start of a serious conversation, though he was still oblivious as to what it could be about.

As passionate as he was about his little project in the woods, thoughts of it all but disappeared from his conscious thinking as soon as he left the discovery center. It wasn't that he forgot about it; more like it moved to the back of his mind, hiding in the shadows until it was time for him to clock in, the way he never gave any thought to his bladder until he had to pee. In spite of how often he'd been going to the discovery center, he never knew when he would be summoned. No matter what project he was in the middle of, he never went back until he was called—always by the tugging in his mind. So it caught him entirely off guard when that turned out to be what was up.

"Where were you?" Darya asked.

"Working."

Technically it wasn't a lie. Still, he was being dishonest.

She looked up at him then. Her eyes were bloodshot, the flesh around them red and puffy.

John pulled out the chair next to her and sat down, noting the way she drew her legs away from him, tucking them safely under her own chair.

"Dar?"

She pinned him with her stare, dark eyes boring into him, rooting him in place. "Were you working at the office?"

He almost said he was, even though he knew she must have some idea about where he'd been. For a split second, he was ready to defend his lie to the grave or the end of their marriage, whichever came first. But he hesitated, considered it. Looked deep into Darya's eyes; those brown eyes—so dark they were almost black—that had loved him unconditionally for the last fifteen years, thirteen of them under the sanctity of marriage.

"Let me save you some trouble," she said, voice icy like he'd never heard it before. "I know you've been going to that carpool lot at least a couple of times a week. Beyond that, I can only guess." She waved off the question that formed on his lips.

"I just happened to be driving past it a few weeks ago, on my way to Kilnsburg to pick up that drafting table I found online. The lady who was selling it lives out that way, so Farren and I took a road trip to get it together.

"We went out for dinner at the burger place she likes on Route 12, Juno's. It was snowing and dark by the time we were headed back and I wouldn't have even noticed the Mercedes if it hadn't been for Farren. She was the one to spot her father's car parked on the side of the road, slowly being covered in snow. I assumed you met someone there, so I followed you out the next time you went.

"Don't look so surprised—you've had your head in the clouds for months. I thought it was because of work." She coughed out a bitter laugh and shook her head. "I pulled along the side of the road a ways back and I almost hoped you'd see me, maybe call off the whole thing. But you didn't get in someone else's car like I expected. Instead, I watched my husband get out of his car and disappear into the woods like some kind of mad man. What the hell is going on, John? Are you in trouble? *Are* you having an affair? Please be honest. For once."

When she was finished, he was the first to pull his gaze away, shame suddenly making his head heavy.

All at once it was as if he'd been living in the dark these past eight months and the sun had just risen. For the first time since that afternoon in June, he questioned what exactly the hell it was he'd been doing this whole time. Wandering into the woods and restoring an old, abandoned, and, evidently, haunted summer camp? At night? Behind his wife's back? With their money?

How much of their savings had he spent on this insane

project? And how could he think of it as simply a project? He'd been listening to a voice in his head, and not even so much as that after the first day. Apparently, it didn't take much to make him dance like a marionette.

John confessed everything. It came out in a babbling torrent and Darya had to make him go over parts of it multiple times. Her mood shifted from anger to incredulity, then confusion to real concern. He assumed she would think he was losing his mind.

But after it was all said, and once she had her questions answered, Darya, his rock for this very reason, held his face in her hands and said, "We'll get you out of this."

The shame he felt at not having confided in her before was an anvil on his heart. He took little solace in the fact that he hadn't been entirely with it while he was working for the thing in the Museum in the woods.

He refused to even think its name anymore. Didn't tell it to Darya, didn't even tell her he knew it; couldn't chance it being let in somehow. Seeing the name seemed to be how he had fallen prey to it. His wife was strong though, stronger than him. John had a feeling she would have resisted the summons right away. And knowing her, she would have flipped it off as well, just to make sure it got the point.

They agreed he wouldn't go back to the Great Forest Outdoor Discovery Center. He was going to give Darya his agenda every day—no-schedule policy be damned—and update her immediately with a call or a text if things changed. If he wasn't home when he said he'd be, she would assume he'd gone back and she would go after him.

It worked. For a while.

Z

JOHN ARRIVED at the office soaking wet but energized. The weather all day had been darkened by charcoal clouds and steady rain. It was the week before the Kraken update was to launch and they were way ahead of schedule. Could launch today if they wanted to. It was a good feeling.

Instead of getting ahead of themselves though, they decided to take the extra time to go over everything once more to make sure they hadn't missed anything. There were some complaints of it being a make-work project but most of the team agreed it couldn't hurt to check things again. It was, after all, a revolutionary leap in social media technology, one that would make waves in the industry for some time. KnowMe would lose users over it, true, but the loss would be a small percentage, and even then most of those would eventually return. They wouldn't be able to help it after a while.

Once he'd checked in with his team leaders, John fixed himself an espresso and shut himself in his office. He fell into the gaming chair behind his desk and tapped the keyboard to wake up the three-monitor display in front of him. Sipping at his espresso, he opened the folder containing their master copy of the Kraken update, slipped a thumb drive into computer, and was in the process of copying the update over when he stopped himself.

What the hell had he been about to do? If he'd been caught copying the file to an sexternal drive, he could not only be fired but sued into oblivion.

For the first time in months, he thought about the thing in the Museum out in the woods. Had he just been under its influence?

He shot up from his seat and strode out of the office, dialing Darya and sticking his phone to his ear.

"Hey, babe," she said from the other line. "I'm at the grocery store. Anything you can think of?"

He ignored her. "I think it's happening again."

There was a long pause while he walked past his confused and concerned-looking co-workers and out into the rain.

"I'll meet you at home," Darya finally said.

Z

JOHN PULLED into his driveway twenty minutes later and was just stepping through the front door of the house when Darya's car pulled in next to his.

Inside, she put the tea kettle on while he told her what he'd been about to do in his office.

"And you didn't feel it coming on at all?" she asked when he'd finished talking.

He shook his head. "I sat down at my desk and started to copy the update as if that's what I'd been planning to do when I got to work."

"Why would it want you to do that?"

Darya knew he was excited about the update and that it was a big deal, but he hadn't discussed any of the details of it with her. He took his non-disclosure contract seriously and, even though he knew she would never break his confidence, he kept most details about his work to himself. It wasn't a big challenge, Darya had zero interest in the finer points of any of the work he did, which he loved about her.

He said, "The update integrates government identification with users' KnowMe accounts. Once the update goes live and a user installs it, they'll be prompted to upload all government identification, even library cards, to our servers. It also matches users with their friends and family, automatically connecting their accounts to everyone they know based on their communications, and everything their devices pick up through listening technology. If all goes well, next year we'll be rolling out banking and credit connectivity."

"How is that possible?" Darya asked.

"Anyone with a KnowMe account has already signed off on these permissions, whether they know it or not," he said. "We've been building a foundational database for years. They'll have to agree to it again when they install the update but ninety-nine point nine percent of users don't even skim those agreements."

"So what does that thing want with it?"

John threw his hands up. "The same thing any hacker or terrorist might want with it, I guess. Information. Access. Friends?"

"That's scary, John."

"I know," he said. "I also think I know what I have to do."

He told her his plan while she poured their tea.

Z

THE TECH PARK was a ghost town on a Wednesday at midnight. The rain had died down to a light drizzle, which John was thankful for as he jogged across the lawn to his office.

He hadn't run into anyone on his way in; security was mostly automated with personnel on hand in a lounge near the front gate. They piloted camera-equipped remote-controlled vehicles around campus, keeping an eye on things from a distance. Apparently they got lazy at night when no one was keeping tabs on them; John hadn't seen a single bot.

It only took an hour to collect the hard drives and master copies of the Kraken update; most of it was kept in John's own office, on his computers. Even Jeremy Hrongar hadn't wanted access to it—more out of a sense of self-preservation than anything, John thought. The CEO couldn't be bought or blackmailed if he didn't have access to such sensitive material.

John was securing the last hard drive in his backpack when the voice, the same one he'd first heard almost a year ago in the parking lot, spoke to him like a whisper from his subconscious.

*I know what you're doing.*

John zipped his backpack up and slung it over his shoulders.

*You will atone for this*, the voice said. *Your family will atone. Your wife. Your daughter.*

That made John pause for a moment. Was what he was doing putting his family at greater risk? He would have eventually lost his wife and daughter if he'd kept up his work in the forest, he knew that now, but was risking their lives a better alternative?

He and Darya decided on this course of action together, though. Who knew what damage the entity he'd been working for could cause with something like the Kraken update in its possession? And as far as the risk to his family went, all evidence suggested the thing in the Museum couldn't even clean up its own home without a human servant, let alone lash out at those with whom it had a vendetta to settle. John felt certain once he was done, the spirit or entity or whatever it was would leave him and his family alone. Maybe it would find someone else at KnowMe to be its janitor and thief—but there would be no update to steal.

Back outside, he was grateful to find the rain had stopped. Things were going his way.

Z

TWO HOURS LATER, John stood at the edge of a roaring fire he'd built up in the pit behind what he and Darya referred to as their summerhouse. They'd bought the place outright soon after moving to Maggie's Knee, as a nearby family vacation spot. John knew he wouldn't have much time for extended vacations for his first few years with KnowMe, so they'd decided a cottage close to home was their best bet to be able to get away as a family.

It was a beautiful place; two full bedrooms with an ensuite attached to the master, a full kitchen, a big living room, a loft where Farren loved to read on rainy days, and a long back yard that sloped into Piper Lake. It even had an artificial pond in the garden, though John still hadn't gotten around to filling it up with water, let alone the requisite koi.

The cottage was only an hour out of town so he could easily make jaunts back to the office if necessary. They liked the place so much they'd taken to spending the entirety of July and August there. If John had a busy week, he stayed at their house, collected the mail, mowed the grass, and was usually back at the summerhouse before supper on Friday.

Now he stood over the fire pit where they'd already spent many nights together laughing and roasting marshmallows or watching fireworks over the lake—there was always someone setting them off on weekends between the Fourth of July and

Labor Day. He watched as the last of the black hard drive casings melted into the glowing embers of the blaze.

He'd incinerated all but the master copy of the Kraken update. There wasn't a reason he could think of to resurrect it, but he could never bring himself to throw out the last copy of anything. He had dozens of hard drives with files dating back to the late nineties and about five hundred floppy disks going back even earlier. Even his grade school report cards were living in a banker's box in the climate-controlled storage unit he rented out.

The master copy of the Kraken was hidden somewhere else though, under the lining of the koi pond, where no one would think of looking. He would make a point of filling the pond when they opened the cottage for the summer, just in case. Unless the majority of the programmers and coders had kept notes or personal backups of their work—which was prohibited and punishable by immediate termination and indictment; they were strictly monitored—there was no way to salvage the program or the data they'd been uploading to it for the last five years, since the Kraken update was first planned.

Z

DAWN WAS BREAKING when John pulled into the driveway at home. Darya met him at the door and wrapped him in a hug when he stepped inside, planting kisses all over his face and neck. She barely let him get his shoes off before dragging him to their bedroom where they made love.

Afterward, John lay awake while Darya snored softly next to him. He stroked her hair absently while he thought about everything he'd just done.

He would, of course, be fired. They had discussed as much before he'd stolen all the update material and decided together John would go freelance once the impact of what he'd done settled down a bit. There was also a good chance he'd go to jail. They'd talked about this too. Enough was stashed away and invested to make sure Darya and Farren would be all right if it came to that, but John would fight like hell to stay with them. Already he was thinking of a plea of insanity.

He dozed off with the morning light warming his face.

Z

JOHN WOKE JUST before noon and found Farren in the living room, curled up on the couch with her battered copy of *Harry Potter and the Goblet of Fire*, by far her favorite of the series. She'd read them all more than once, but John was pretty sure this was her fifth or sixth time through this one. He was fiercely proud of her love of reading, especially for an eleven-year-old, but sometimes wished she would branch out a bit. He'd tried getting her to read *The Lord of the Rings* books and had so far only succeeded in convincing her to read *The Hobbit*. She wouldn't even look at *Ender's Game*, even when he insisted it was basically Harry Potter in space.

He kissed Farren on the top of her head, sneaking a fatherly sniff of her thick, black hair—so much like her mother's and nothing like his own, which had always been thin and limp and mostly kept hidden under his Osaka Kintetsu Buffaloes hat.

His grandfather had given him the hat when John was in his early twenties, attending Berkeley. John was third-generation American and had, to his shame, never been to Japan, his grandparents' country of birth. He was as American as they came, even if he had to put up with the occasional ignorant asshole who wanted him to know how much they hated Chinese people. He never bothered to correct them.

John and his grandfather had watched the Osaka Kintetsu Buffaloes—and, grudgingly, the Orix Buffaloes after their 2005 merger—together since he was a kid. John's own father wasn't much into baseball, Japanese or otherwise, and always seemed to resent the bond John and his grandfather shared over the game.

John had gone back to visit his grandparents in San Francisco during a break from school and his grandfather gave the Buffaloes hat to him as they sat down in front of the television to watch their first Nippon Professional Baseball game together in years. That had also turned out to be their last baseball game together. John had rarely taken the hat off since.

He squeezed his daughter's shoulders. Hoped he'd get to watch just as many baseball games with her. Maybe he could get her into Japanese ball, it had been ages since he'd watched the Buffaloes play.

"Wanna go into town? Get breakfast at that coffee shop you like?" he asked.

Farren dropped her book in her lap. "Can I get a latte?"

"Decaf, but I'll throw in a scone."

"Muffin."

"Both."

"Deal." Farren tossed her book on the coffee table and leaped off the couch, sprinting to the front door and pulling on her shoes.

An hour later, they were on their way home, full of coffee

and pastry. They'd picked up a croissant and a cappuccino for Darya, both of which Farren kept safe on a tray in her lap.

John was swiping through the music app on his phone, trying to find Foreigner's "Cold as Ice", a favorite tune for him and Farren to rock out to together.

"Dad!" Farren screamed.

He looked up and slammed on the brakes, the Mercedes' technology taking over and stopping the car almost instantaneously. A painted turtle was in the middle of the lane, a dozen feet in front of their car, probably frozen in terror at the giant, metal machine bearing down on it. John glanced in his rearview, grateful there had been no one behind them.

Without a second's hesitation, Farren hopped out of the car and ran to the turtle. John's heart melted as she picked it up by the sides of its shell and carried it to safety, far off the shoulder in the direction it had been headed. Pride blossomed in him as she delicately set the turtle down and gave it an encouraging pat on the back.

He'd wanted a boy before they had Farren, he and Darya both had. Of course, they'd fallen head over heels in love with their daughter as soon as she was born. And now he was glad they'd had a girl—boys could be nurturing as well, but if he'd had a son anything like his brothers or some of their friends, the turtle would more likely find itself being punted further into traffic rather than carried to grassy safety.

Farren got back in the passenger's seat and looked up at him.

"What?" she said, fastening her seatbelt.

He ruffled her hair, which made her cringe. "I love you, my little Kaeru. That's all."

She smiled at him. "Love you too, Dad."

They were halfway through their second time playing "Cold as Ice" when they came up on the rail crossing. With the dense tree lines on either side of the road, it was impossible to see down the tracks in either direction. The lights were off and the arm was up, so John didn't give a thought to crossing.

At some point during their drive, a minivan had come up behind them. John caught a glimpse of the driver and passengers in his rearview mirror; a middle-aged woman in a golf cap and sunglasses was chauffeur to four or five kids, all leaping about in the back of the van like spider monkeys. Seeing them made John glad he and Darya had stuck to one kid.

Ahead of the Mercedes, a dark green pickup with a cap over the bed was crossing the tracks.

Foreigner was wrapping up their encore of what John had long ago told Farren was their ode to ice cream. He never intended to correct her on that, though he suspected she'd already figured it out herself.

"One more time?" he asked, grabbing his phone from the cupholder where he always tossed it instead of installing and using the dash mount Darya had bought him.

He fiddled with the music app.

"Stop!" Farren shouted.

He almost asked her if she'd seen another turtle. Then he looked up.

They were crossing the tracks. On the tracks. And the pickup had stopped in front of him. John jammed his foot on the brakes, laying on the horn at the same time. He hit the truck, just a light bump, but contact all the same, and cursed. Last thing he needed was a collision with some redneck, no matter whose fault it was.

The truck didn't move. John considered getting out but the

last sound he wanted to hear in that moment rooted him in place.

*DANG-DANG-DANG-DANG-DANG-DANG-DANG-DANG!*

The clanging of the crossing bell sent an icicle into his heart.

He hammered on the horn. The truck's brake lights were on.

Farren was saying, "Dad?" over and over again and it bled into the clanging of the bell, making John's head swim.

When the jolt came, he was sure the train already arrived. They both screamed and then he realized they were still sitting on the tracks in one piece. He looked in his rearview.

The lady in the van was gritting her teeth and leaning into the steering wheel, pushing John's car with her own. Smoke billowed out from her spinning tires, the van no match for the Mercedes and the big truck in front of it. The children in the back were freaking out. One of them stuck her head between the seats, mouth open in a scream. The woman's fist came up in a way that would have been funny in a nineties comedy, but which horrified John when it connected with the little girl's face. Blood splattered on the headrests in the front seat and the girl fell back, disappearing from sight. John looked away.

He gunned the engine. Jerked the wheel from side to side, trying to wiggle the car free. It felt impossible.

The truck's reverse lights came on.

"Hey!" John screamed.

"Dad!" Farren grabbed his chin, forced him to turn his head, to look out his own window.

He'd been watching Farren's window for the train. Why? There was no reason to suspect it would come from one direction over the other. So why hadn't he been watching both ways?

The voice spoke at the same moment he saw the enormous engine charging toward them from around the bend, maybe half a mile away.

*Atonement*, it bellowed inside his head.

"No," John said.

How could the thing in the museum have orchestrated this?

He twisted, unbuckled Farren's seatbelt, leaned across her, got caught in his own seatbelt, fought with it. Stuck. How?

The train screamed.

John fumbled with Farren's door. Shoved it open. Pushed her out.

She pulled on his arm, cried his name.

"Move, Farren!" he shouted over the clanging and the infernal scream of the train's whistle.

His daughter's face collapsed in sorrow as she made what he knew was an impossible decision.

"Go," he said.

She moved back from the car. Not fast enough.

He risked a glance over his shoulder.

The train, a bright red and black steel behemoth, was right on top of them.

He twisted back. Caught a glimpse of Farren's back as she ran for her life.

John wanted to call out. Tell her he loved her. Opened his mouth to do so.

Then the train, which had not been able to significantly reduce its speed—added his life to its cargo.

# PART 3

31

It had been a rough week for Jasper. Certainly, there were people who had it much worse, and by his own hand, but he was going to allow himself to wallow in self-sympathy.

The ordeal at Farren's house had been a test of his commitment to everything they'd built so far. Sasha would correct him, tell him he meant everything *she* built. He was starting to grow old of what he'd once found to be a tolerable flaw.

Sasha had orchestrated the murder of Farren's dog and possibly—no, probably—the sheriff's wife as well. They'd killed before but this was the first time Sasha tricked him into being part of an innocent person's death since she'd blown that writer's brains out.

What could he do about it though? There was no contest for her leadership.

He could leave.

Right. And be hunted by the tribe. Live on the run or be tracked down and slaughtered, just like Melinda Noble. And the writer. And his dad. He'd learned, after his third month in the Congo, that his father had succumbed to his injuries and that Jasper himself was considered dead or missing, with the probability heavily resting on the former. There were no televised pleas from his mother, no social media campaigns launched. Fiona had posted on her KnowMe page saying, *Where r u little bro?* accompanied by a crying emoji but had neglected to tag him or even fully spell out her query.

He'd burned every last bridge he had available to him. Even let his writing fall to the wayside. He stopped responding to client requests at about the same time he dropped out of school, not long before Sasha—and, indirectly, he—killed his dad. Jasper wished he could feel something about that other than fear of being caught. Remorse, perhaps. Sadness about losing his dad, maybe? What he really wished was that he'd had a father worth missing; someone who showed any interest in him whatsoever.

Jasper flopped onto his living room couch and tried to lose himself in the pages of one of a couple of dozen paperbacks the scavengers picked up a few months ago. Gabe had been on that run.

He read from where his bookmark indicated he'd left off but couldn't remember a thing that was happening. Was this the one about vampires or had that been the last book he read? He feathered the pages back to beginning of the chapter. Still nothing recognizable. He read anyway because he dreaded what was coming in the real world.

Any minute now his doorbell would ring or there would come a knocking or Sasha would just barge right in, which was the most likely scenario when he thought about it.

Then he'd have to go back *there* and get *her* from inside and he had a pretty good idea what came next.

He hated himself for not doing something about it. Told himself he intended to set her free or whisk her away, but knew in the end, he would subject Farren to the same fate he'd sentenced so many others to. Difference was, he'd never gotten to know and like the others.

And he had to admit to himself, even if he could admit it to nobody else, that he did have feelings for Farren. He hated himself for that too. Not because of their age difference, which was only about four years, but because it was stupid to even entertain the notion she might reciprocate his feelings. He'd fucking kidnapped her. Sure, she had come around and joined them willingly, but how do you come back from drugging someone with a rag? Twice.

A small, wretched fist hammering on the front door freed him from thinking about Farren.

He opened the door to find Sasha standing on the doorstep, looking exuberant. Of course she'd be happy about this. It meant the end of her perceived competition.

"Ready?" she asked, stepping from foot to foot, back and forth, that stupid, open-mouthed grin weighing her face down. She had a black, long-sleeve shirt on over black, leather pants.

Jasper walked past her and down the front steps of his cabin, onto the path.

"What's your problem?" Sasha demanded, stalking after him.

He ignored her and tried not to curse when he heard her running to catch up to him.

She grabbed him by the arm. "I'm talking to you."

Once more he found himself having to resist throwing his arm back and decking her.

"It's just been a long week," he said, knowing that wouldn't do it.

"And? You don't think the rest of us have had a hard time?"

"You don't take these people to that pink hell house. You haven't had to step foot in there since we first opened its doors."

Sasha scowled at him. "I have *much* bigger things going on."

He turned his back on her, taking some satisfaction from the gesture, knowing it was one of the things she hated most, and continued along the path to the Museum. Might as well get this over with.

Mercifully, she didn't chase him down this time. Which worried him. Sasha never missed the opportunity to get a dig in and did not tolerate being ignored. But he had no time to worry about that, not if he wanted this whole business to be finished.

It was time to sentence Farren to her death.

$$32$$

Gordon shoved the last bite of an enormous roast beef and horseradish sandwich into his mouth and soaked it with a generous sip of coffee. He plucked the last, very stale, donut from the box Barb had dropped off with him days ago, and took half of it off with one bite. He would need to beg her to do a grocery run for him if he was going to be here for much longer. It had already been three days. He was becoming stir-crazy.

With no leads and no police authority to back up his investigation, his search for Farren had come to a swift halt. He didn't even have a car to get him back into town.

He spent most of his first day at the summerhouse going about the opening procedures. Even though he'd neglected the place for two years, the bills had been paid and the cottage had been maintained by a seasonal caretaker—all part of Darya's will. The summerhouse, as she'd insisted on calling it, would go to Farren when she turned twenty-one. For this reason, and probably for some more personal reasons he wasn't ready or willing to admit, he'd kept the cottage a secret from Melinda. Even now he didn't feel guilty about that. It was not hard to be honest with himself about what sort of person his second wife had been. If she'd learned of the cottage, she would have made it her own until Farren came of age. And he had a feeling Farren wouldn't want anything to do with the place after Melinda had taken over and sterilized it of every trace of her parents and childhood.

He felt guilty for thinking so disparagingly of Melinda, but there it was. Probably had to do with being amid so many reminders of Darya, the touches of her flair, the ghost of her fragrance. What would she say if she'd met her replacement?

Gordon realized he hadn't really mourned Melinda yet. Didn't really have to wonder what that meant.

To distract himself from where his thoughts were taking him, he set up the personal hotspot on his phone and cracked open his laptop, one of the many things he'd had Barb bring with her when she picked him up in the park following his hospital escape. He logged into the Maggie's Knee Sheriff's Department server and brought up the photos taken from along the side of the river when they'd been looking for Garrett Mews. This was his third or fourth time logging onto the server; he'd stopped worrying someone might trace the activity when no one came for him after the first occasion. If anyone had noticed him logging in and had any concerns about it, they would have restricted his access by now. Odds were nobody was paying any attention to the server's login activity at all. Not yet anyway.

He clicked on the photo of the tracks next to the river and stared at it for a long time, willing something new to jump out at him.

When his eyes began to water, he sighed and went to log out again. A second before he signed off, he noticed there was a new note attached to the file. Dated that morning. He clicked to open it.

The note was actually a document attached to the file; an incident report filed by one Stacey Medallion, the guy Farren used to hang around outside the Mission. Gordon's heartbeat quickened.

In the report, Mr. Medallion mentioned seeing some people "creeping around" close to Jessop's Bridge. He reported having seen them trekking into the forest along Widow's River, pulling a large sled.

"Didn't I say sled tracks?" Gordon muttered to his computer screen, trying to reign in his growing excitement.

Medallion went on to state he'd followed the people, who were dressed in black, into the forest. He said they were easy to follow because they moved slowly, weighed down by the sled.

At that point, Medallion was asked by the interviewer, Freddie Nancarrow, what the sled had been weighed down with. Medallion responded by saying it was girl of seventeen or eighteen.

When asked if he could tell if the girl was alive, Medallion had said no, he couldn't tell.

Nancarrow asked Medallion if he recognized the girl.

No.

Was it Farren Murakami?

Gordon hesitated before reading the next answer. But he knew. Medallion would have recognized Farren. He took a breath and read the response.

Medallion: *No, it wasn't Farren. I know Farren. But I think they took her too. My friend Pietro already spoke to the sheriff but no one listens to him. Probably because he calls them shadow people. But, sweetie, that's what they are.*

When asked how he lost them if they were so easy to track, Medallion became cagey. Nancarrow was a good, patient cop and had pressed lightly, though there was probably a bit more said than what was written down in the report. Medallion stated he was afraid Nancarrow would think he was some crazy junkie looking for attention. Nancarrow assured him, and urged him to go on.

Medallion's response said: *They left the edge of the river after a while but it looked like they were just wandering through the forest. I was scared they knew I was following them. Then they walked into this really dense area and, I shit you not, the trees closed in around them. I tried to follow them through but it was literally impossible. I almost didn't find my way back.*

Gordon signed off, closed the laptop, and drummed his fingers on the casing. He needed to speak to Stacey Medallion. Today. But he couldn't ask Barb to risk getting fired by driving him.

There was only one person who might be as motivated as he was to track these shadow people down. He still had the number he needed in his phone and dialed it before he could convince himself not to. At first, he thought he wouldn't get an answer. He would have understood if his call had gone ignored. But then the ringing stopped and the line clicked on, though no one spoke.

"Franklin?" Gordon said into the phone.

"What do you want?"

Gordon was momentarily stunned into silence. This

sounded nothing like the man he'd known before Garrett Mews had gone missing. This person sounded deflated, on the verge of giving up living altogether. When was the last time he'd seen or spoken to either of the Mewses? During the search for Garrett. Gordon had been frustrated with Franklin for bringing the press in. Combine that with the fact that Farren's disappearance overshadowed Garrett's, and Gordon could see how the banker might hold a grudge against him.

Gordon blurted, "Franklin, don't hang up. I know you hate me but I need your help. I have a lead on where the missing kids could be, or at least who might be responsible. I can't promise anything, but this is the closest I've come to a lead in any of the cases."

There was another painfully long silence and then, almost too low to hear, "Why would you need my help with this?"

Gordon decided to go all in and bring Franklin completely up to speed. He told him about the call from Melinda, coming home to find her dead, and her killers—just kids—still in the house. He confessed Farren was with them but glossed over seeing a giant. Only said one of the kids snuck up on him and hit him over the head. He told Franklin about his escape from the hospital and holing up at the cottage for the last three days. When he was done talking, he had to ask Franklin if he was still there. When the response came, it was unexpectedly spirited. Energized.

"Let's find out what that character at the Mission knows," Franklin said. He sounded short-breathed, like he was struggling with something. "I'm pulling my pants on now. I'll be there to pick you up in an hour or so."

The line went dead and Gordon sat with the silent phone pressed to his ear for a moment. Then he went to the kitchen and poured himself a new cup of coffee to celebrate the fact that every now and then things went his way.

Z

A LITTLE OVER two hours later, with Gordon riding shotgun, Franklin Mews pulled his Acura into the parking lot next to the Maggie's Knee Mission.

"Which one is he?" Franklin asked, a little too eagerly.

Gordon was scanning the sidewalk in front of the Mission but couldn't spot Stacey Medallion anywhere. He said as much to Franklin.

"Where else would he be?"

"I'm going to try to find out," Gordon said, opening the passenger door. "Be right back."

It felt great to be able to stretch his legs—even with the seat pushed all the way back, the car was a tight fit for him. Most were. His cruiser had been one of the exceptions to that rule, but something told him he wouldn't be getting the keys back when all this was over.

When he was halfway to the small crowd gathered in front of the Mission, he realized he was in the civilian clothing he'd had Barb drop off for him, jeans and a flannel button-up—he always kept a couple of changes of clothes at the office. He also hadn't had a shave in three or four days, which was a long time for someone used to shaving every morning. None of the people gathered in front of the Mission seemed to recognize or even notice him beyond potentially being someone who has money or cigarettes to spare.

Could be to his advantage. Nobody was running scared. Only the old woman sitting in the same place on the front steps looked at him the same way she did when he'd last been here, in uniform, months ago.

He approached the first group he came to; two men, one scrawny guy in his sixties with long white hair and a beard to match, and the other maybe half the old man's age and ten times his weight. Standing between them a heavyset woman in track pants that sagged low enough to show she wasn't wearing underwear. They all smoked cigarettes and drank out of paper cups.

The big guy spotted Gordon first and said to him, "Sir, do you have a dollar or two so I can get something to eat?" He wore an open denim vest over some kind of heavy metal band T-shirt, the band's name illegibly spelled out in what appeared to be ancient Celtic runes.

Gordon stood across from him in their circle. "I've got ten dollars for you if you can tell me where to find Stacey Medallion."

"I'll tell you anything you want for ten bucks," the big guy said, grinning as if he'd just said the wittiest thing any of them ever heard.

"What do you want Stacey for?" the woman asked, lighting a fresh cigarette with her old one and flicking the butt into the street.

Gordon smiled at her, trying to appear as unthreatening as possible. "I think he knows where a friend of mine is. She might be in trouble."

The woman squinted up at the roof of the bistro across the street and took a long pull of her cigarette, seeming to think long and hard about what to say to him. Finally, she looked him in the eye, blew smoke into his face, and held out her hand.

Gordon handed over a five. "You can have the rest once I hear what you've got to say." He waved a second bill in the air, then folded it into his pocket.

She spat. "Stacey got banned a while back. You can't bring drugs inside if you wanna sleep here. He's been staying at Pietro's a lot."

"Pietro's the guy with the hat?" Gordon said, holding his hand high over his head.

She nodded.

The old guy had been staring at Gordon and now he pointed two fingers holding a cigarette at him.

"Ain't you the sheriff?" the guy said in a gravelly voice, smoke spilling out of his mouth and nostrils, mingling with his beard and hair.

The woman and the big guy looked up at Gordon, eyes narrowed.

"You're supposed to tell us if you're police," the woman snapped.

"Apologies," he said, raising his hands in innocence. "It's not official business. I'm looking for my stepdaughter."

They'd all turned their backs to him though. He'd lost their trust and they wouldn't tell him anything else. But at least he had a place to look for Medallion.

Turning to head back to Franklin's car, he almost plowed into the little old woman who had been watching him from the steps. He tried to sidestep her but she grabbed his arm with a gnarled hand and pulled him close.

"Farren is your stepdaughter," she said. Not a question.

"She is," Gordon said, pulse quickening. He stooped to make it a bit easier for her to talk to him. "Have you seen her?"

The woman closed her eyes and slowly shook her head. "She has been dwelling among the Proud One's children."

"What does that mean?"

She looked up at him. "Her life is at stake. Not just her existence, but her ideals, her soul."

Gordon grasped the woman by her slender shoulders, reminding himself to be gentle. "Where is she?"

"He hides them from us," she said. "He needs to be heard but we cannot bear to listen to him for long. But they can. The children. And when he has enough, his power will grow and the rest of us will have no choice. We will have to listen. And it will destroy us."

He wanted to shake her. "I don't know what any of that means."

The woman reached up and took his face in her hands. "You are marked by him too."

She pulled him closer and he relented, more out of surprise than anything else. Her leathery palms gripped his face, milky gray eyes looking into every corner of his own. Ten thousand wrinkles around her eyes expanded and contracted as she searched his face for something she seemed desperate to find while dreading it at the same time. Like someone looking for a live bomb.

"He is closer to his time than we thought. It's too late." Her fingers dug into his temples. "They'll take it from you. The key to his victory."

He pulled her hands from his face, firmly but gently, and forced his way past her. She screamed something after him but it sounded like more of the same.

Gordon stormed toward the parking lot, using every ounce of willpower not to break into a run. What the hell had that been all about? He was used to homeless people acting a little nuts, but that woman had genuinely freaked him out.

When Franklin asked what the fuss with the old woman was about, Gordon responded by telling him she was crazy. Told him where the woman without underpants said to find Stacey.

"I remember the tent," Franklin said, already backing out of their spot. "From the search last spring."

Gordon shifted in his seat. After a long silence, he said, "I'm sorry Garrett got pushed to the back burner when we found out about Farren. There's no denying that's what happened, but I want you to know it wasn't deliberate. The public excitement of something happening to the sheriff's kid, combined with my obvious personal concern for her just made it too easy to forget everything else going on. And I'm sorry for that, as the sheriff and as a friend."

Franklin stared straight out the windshield, both hands on the wheel, twisting it like a throttle. Gordon didn't need a response and didn't expect one. If their positions had been reversed, he would not be in the forgiving frame of mind.

"I appreciate that," Franklin said in a tight voice, surprising Gordon. "I know it wasn't deliberate. Rose told me as much more times than I can count."

They made the rest of the drive to Jessop's Bridge in a more comfortable silence.

Z

"WELL, SHIT," Franklin said, panting and wiping sweat from his face with the collar of his polo shirt.

Gordon armed sweat off his own forehead and nodded, regarding the wall of green that loomed before them.

The tent where they were told they could find Stacey had been a bust. All they'd found was a ripped grocery bag containing a stick of bright pink lipstick, a fishnet tank top, and a shit-stained thong, which all could have belonged to anyone. The only other things in the tent were an old, smelly sleeping bag, and a pair of winter boots, soles worn completely smooth.

Not wanting to give up the search, the men followed the river deeper into the woods. They'd spent almost an hour trudging through the trees only to be faced with what must have been the thicket Stacey referred to in his statement to the police.

Trees here grew so close together that many of them had entwined with one another, creating an impassible wall of trunk and branch. The few spaces between trees were block-aded by fallen trees and brush grown so thick Gordon could hardly even stick an arm into it.

The two of them had split up, walking along the perimeter of the thicket in opposite directions, each searching for a gap they might be able to pass through. They'd met back where they started, baffled by the growth.

"Even if we could get in somehow," Gordon said through heavy breaths, "there's no way we'd be able to find our way around. I didn't bring a compass and I doubt the sun would do us much good in there."

"What are you suggesting?"

What Gordon wanted to suggest was that they return with gasoline and matches and burn the whole thing down. It almost seemed like a reasonable course of action to find their missing kids. It was frustrating to be this powerless. And clueless. What small lead they'd been given had evaporated at the wall of vegetation.

Gordon sighed. "I think regrouping is our best bet. Think this through. I can get some maps of the area, whatever the Department of Conservation and Natural Resources' Bureau of Forestry has on the area. Maybe we can find a way around it or another way in. Might also be smart to have some supplies with us, water especially, if we're going to return." He didn't bother mentioning that he'd also feel much better having a gun with him.

"You really think they might be in there?" Franklin asked.

Gordon picked up on the unspoken part of the question, whether or not he thought they were alive. He was pretty certain Farren was alive, though he was less sure they'd find her in the woods. Garrett was another story. He had no idea what these kids, and whoever else was with them, were about. Only that they'd killed someone he loved, two someones counting Bonzo. They'd effectively taken away his entire family.

After a long pause, he said, "We'll find them, Franklin."

Instead of responding, the banker turned and trudged off in the direction they'd come from. After a few seconds, Gordon followed.

33

Consciousness returned to Farren like smoke filling a bottle, first trickling in, then erupting in clouds. She sat with her head bent forward, chin tucked to her chest. When she tried to look up, her neck cried out for mercy, stiff from being in a terrible position for however long she'd been out.

She wanted to rub her neck, but her hands were tied behind her back. It was almost funny how many times she'd woken up restrained in the Congo. So kinky.

Her first thought upon opening her eyes was she was still in the Museum. She waited for her vision to adjust to the gloom but the darkness was complete.

It was hard to put her finger on, but this place felt different. Someone else, some*thing* else, lived here. Different from what lived in the Museum.

*ZIIS.*

This thought wasn't her own. Wasn't that of the thing in the Museum either. Whatever had spoken to her was undoubtedly a different entity. And just like that, she knew where she was.

"The Orchid Room," she whispered to herself, voice shaking.

They just kept scaling up the horror of the places they locked her up in. Of course, if she really was in the Orchid Room, this would be her last stop. It was almost a relief.

Farren went through her breathing exercises, willing herself not to panic. She felt surprisingly serene and wondered if she might be in shock.

"Hello!" she called.

She hadn't expected a response but, seconds after she shouted, a door opened directly in front of her. Moonlight, blinding compared to the dark, spilled inside.

A figure filled the doorway, its shadow falling long on the floor ahead of it.

"About time," Jasper said.

"Untie me. Please," Farren begged.

Jasper didn't move.

*He is afraid. They are all afraid.*

The words resonated deep in the back of her head, like a subwoofer strapped to the base of her neck. This voice, different from that of the thing in the Museum—

*ZIIS. Do not fear him.*

—came from outside her mind. Nothing close to the invasive, insectile feeling she got from the other one. It wasn't necessarily a kind voice, but it lacked the malice of the Museum dweller.

Jasper leaned against the door, watching her.

*Do not fear the boy either.*

"I don't want to be doing this," Jasper said.

"Doing what? Why won't you come any closer?" Farren asked.

Jasper took a step inside, casting glances all around him as if he expected to be attacked from any direction at any moment.

"We have rules, you know," he said.

"Like what?" Farren said. "Stand aside and let you kill our dogs and family members?"

"I told you; I didn't know Bonzo would get hurt," Jasper said. "Or Melinda. But you never gave a shit about her, so I don't know what you're crying about."

So this was the real Jasper. The way he told the stories, he seemed so innocent, a victim of Sasha's wile and enticement. But he'd have to be at least a little bit off to disappear into the woods with the girl who had made him an unwilling accomplice to two murders, one of which was his own father. Even the way he'd told the story, there didn't seem to be a whole lot in the way of remorse from him, she now realized.

"What do you want?"

He glanced behind him, took another step inside, and muttered something unintelligible.

She didn't ask him to repeat it, didn't want to know.

"This place scares the shit out of me," Jasper said, louder. "I really am sorry we have to do this to you." He repeated what he'd said before, but he was still speaking too low.

"What are you saying?" Farren asked, feeling stupid for some reason. It had sounded like he'd said *bite thumb*, but what sense did that make?

With the moonlight to his back, it was impossible to see Jasper's face in the dark, but the way he straightened made it seem as if he was trying to keep someone from hearing them. The voice?

Jasper took another small step closer to her, obviously terrified.

"Right thumb," he said more clearly, and then, voice raised, "It was good to know you."

He turned and stepped out into the moonlight, pulling the door closed behind him, and once more steeping her in the vast lightlessness.

"Jasper!" Farren screamed. "Hey!"

Instead of echoing off the walls, as it should have, her voice kept going, carried off into space with nothing to bounce off of until it evaporated.

Farren shook in the chair, strained against the ropes, but they were tied too tight. She leaned her head back, wincing at the stiffness in her neck.

Nothing to look at. Nothing to hear or smell.

Her arms and legs had gone numb enough it was easy to imagine herself as nothing more than a head floating through empty space. Similar to how she'd felt floating on that current of red light.

That thought brought her back to the dream or vision or whatever it had been that she'd woken from only moments ago. How much time had passed between then and now? Minutes? Hours? Days?

Seeing her father again had been bittersweet in the extreme. Following him around during his time under the spell of the thing in the Museum woke strange new feelings in her. She couldn't help feeling angry at him—a feeling she'd never held toward her late father, not since his death anyway. How could he have allowed himself to be duped so easily by the thing in the Museum?

He hadn't had a choice, though, as she'd seen herself. She'd witnessed displays of the thing's power. Many had fallen under its spell. So how had she managed to escape its influence? *Had she* escaped it?

Watching the accident, experiencing it from her father's perspective, shook her. The vestigial limb on her left leg throbbed with the memory of the loss of her foot. There'd been no pain at the time of the accident. She'd failed to get completely clear of the car and when the train struck it, she'd been hit by the Mercedes' bumper, which sent her sprawling while neatly severing the foot from her left leg. She'd been knocked out cold and most of her memory leading up to the accident had been foggy until now. No idea what had become of the driver of the truck or the woman in the van; certainly, they weren't held to blame. Someone else must have seen the accident and tended to Farren immediately or she would have bled out.

On the one hand, it was easy to assign blame to her dad, to be angry with him for falling prey to the malicious, manipulative being in the Museum. But she'd been privy to her dad's thoughts and feelings and knew he couldn't have helped himself any more than she could help breathing. That he'd broken free of it, with the help of her mom, was what she held onto.

She'd also felt his love for her. There had never been any doubt her dad had loved her but now she knew exactly how that love felt. It had been overwhelming. The memory of it threatened to bring her to tears.

So now she knew what exactly had happened on the day of her accident. And so what?

*You saw what you needed to.*

That other voice again.

"Who are you?" Farren shouted into the dark.

*You can stop them. Stop him.*

"What does that mean? My dad?"

No response. Was she losing her mind?

All at once the darkness around her was lifted and she was standing on the sidewalk along Main Street in Maggie's Knee. In broad daylight. She tried to turn her face up to the sun but found she wasn't in control of her body. Through her own eyes, she watched as she waved goodbye to Stacey and walked up the street, plugging in her ear buds. Heavy metal filled her ears and her head bobbed to the rhythm as she walked. She knew where this was going.

Her gaze shifted from the sidewalk ahead of her to an alley coming up on her right.

ZIIS was painted on the wall in black.

And then the whole scene disappeared and Farren was so suddenly cast into the dark it felt like a physical punch.

"You showed me that?" she asked. "Why?"

*To connect you.*

"To that thing in the Museum? To bring me here?"

Silence.

"Why not show me your name?"

*You cannot know my name.*

"Bullshit. You could've tried something else, something other than sticking me with this cult."

*You can save them.*

"Save them yourself."

*I can only interfere so much.*

She laughed. "Who are you, God?"

*No. Though I work for Him from time to time.*

It was hard to know what to say to that.

"What do you want?"

*Finish your father's work.*

"What work? Programming?"

*Destroy it.*

Farren thrashed in the chair. "Destroy what? How? I'm tied up and you can only interfere so much."

*Your friend gave you what you need.*

"I don't have any friends."

*The boy.*

"Jasper?" She threw her head back and mock-laughed. "He's not exactly the helpful sort of friend. More like the kidnaps-you-and-absorbs-you-into-a-cult sort of friend."

*Be swift. The portals are shifting.*

Her put-on grin faltered. "What's that supposed to mean?"

Silence.

"Hello?"

But she could already tell the thing that had been speaking to her was gone. What had it meant about portals shifting? And that Jasper had given her what she needed? All he'd done was lock her up and act as if he was sorry about it.

And mumble at her.

Right thumb. As she thought about it, she twisted her right thumb and found there was the slightest amount of give in the rope around it. She jiggled it again and a loop around it seemed to loosen. Was that what he'd meant? Couldn't be a coincidence.

Why the whispering though? Unless Sasha had been nearby. Listening at the door?

Farren worked her thumb in growing circles until she was able to rotate it fully.

As the rope loosened, the air she breathed grew thick. Humid. A stench wafted from out of the dark behind her, fetid and sickening.

She was just wedging her thumb under the loosened rope when a noise in the gloom froze her movements; a heavy double-slap followed by a sliding noise like a giant sandbag being dragged across the floor. The stench grew stronger, invading her nostrils and making her want to gag.

*Slap-slap. Slide.*

Impossible to tell what was behind her. Sounded immense. A bullfrog the size of a house. Slapping the ground with webbed front feet—*slap-slap*—its bulbous throat dragging on the floor—*slide*—as it pulled itself closer.

*Slap-slap. Slide.*

Farren shook all over. Got her thumb under the loosened rope. Wiggled her index finger free.

*Slap-slap. Slide.*

The rope tightened around her wrist again. A frustrated sob escaped her.

She was panicking and working against herself. Told herself to breathe. Made herself inhale slowly, ignoring the rancid taste the air had taken on. When she let the breath out, her hand easily slipped free of the rope.

A breeze whipped past her face. Something large and wet hit the floor behind her. A slurping sound as it oozed past her on the ground a few feet away. The gargantuan frog fishing for her in the dark with its long, elastic tongue, patiently casting it out and reeling it in.

Something smacked into one of the chair legs. Wet, spongy flesh pressed against her stump.

Revolted, terrified, Farren screamed.

The thing yanked the chair legs from under her and she crashed painfully to the floor. The chair was tugged in jerky fits, one or two feet at a time, the tongue pulling her toward the frog-thing's mouth.

Fighting panic, she twisted her shoulder and yanked her right arm free.

A hot wind rushed over her, reeking like a swamp full of the dead.

Farren retched. Pulled the rope over her head, unwinding it from around herself, shaking with the effort it took not to move too fast. Last thing she wanted to do was tighten the rope again.

The chair rose into the air. Her lower half went with it. Hot, stinking breath fell over her in quick bursts, like the thing was panting in hungry anticipation. She was about to be eaten.

She worked the ropes around her legs. Freed herself.

Farren hit the floor from a few feet up and immediately crawled away from the thing, cursing whoever had taken her prosthesis. There was a wet crunch of the chair breaking, followed by a smacking, chewing sound.

Had to keep moving. Needed to be away from what nobody would be able to convince her wasn't a giant frog. Even if it didn't exactly resemble a frog, she knew in her bones it behaved like one in the ways that mattered to her survival.

She hit a wall hard, smashing her face on it. Felt blood explode from her nose and pour into her mouth. Almost collapsed. She put a hand against the wall and pulled herself to standing. It took her swimming brain a moment to realize she was holding onto a doorknob.

*Slap-slap. Slide.*

Faster now. Apparently pissed it had mistaken a chair for its dinner.

Farren twisted the knob and fell into the moonlight as something smacked against the floor behind her.

34

Farren lay in the grass outside the Orchid Room for longer than she should have. The need to catch her breath from the nightmare she'd just been through outweighed all practical reasoning. What she should be doing, instead of staring up at the stars and sobbing, was getting her ass back to the other side of the creek.

Then she would run, commission from the strange voice be damned. She wanted to snicker at the word, terrified as she still was. But that was what it had been, wasn't it? A commission. To somehow stop the thing in the Museum and save—who? The tribe? Right.

All she could think of now was getting out of the Congo.

Her legs were numb, likely from all the being tied up and drugged. Took fifteen minutes of vigorous massaging to convince her blood to flow to her lower half again. The actual hop down the path to the creek took no time at all.

She didn't bother looking around to see if anyone was

watching. Felt as if it might be two or three in the morning, way past the tribe's bed time.

The bubbling of the creek grew louder as she thumped across the bridge. It took an immense amount of willpower to keep herself from collapsing in relief when her foot hit the path on the other side.

The Congo slept, still and peaceful.

She'd taken only two or three hops from the bridge when a dark figure sprung from the shadows and grabbed her from behind, putting a strong hand over her mouth. For an instant, Farren could swear she smelled the rancid stench of whatever it was they'd drugged her with multiple times.

Using the strength of the arm holding her for support, she swung her left elbow into the stomach of her attacker. A muffled wheeze and the grip on her loosened. She twisted away and crouched, fingertips on the dirt path in a sprinter's starting position.

Jasper was doubled over in front of her, one hand on his stomach and the other held out in defense. His breath wheezed slightly. Farren almost felt bad.

Through gasping breaths, he said, "I'm sorry. I want to help."

Farren let herself relax on hands and knees. "You could've whistled or something."

"Didn't want to startle you," he said.

Farren laughed. It was louder than was wise but she wanted to rattle him, she owed him that much at least.

He must have known he deserved it because he didn't bother to shush her.

"I have your crutches." He dashed behind a tree, presumably the one he'd been hiding behind, and came back with them held them out to her. "Let's go to my cabin. It's the only place we're sure to have to ourselves."

Farren considered for only a second. Not much choice but to trust him. If he'd planned on dragging her back to the Orchid Room, he no doubt would have drugged her again, since he seemed to love doing it so much. And he had helped her escape that hall of horrors in his own bumbling, passive way.

She got to her feet, accepting the crutches and settling them under her arms. "Lead the way then."

35

Farren was surprised by how neat Jasper kept his cabin. And by how many books he owned. Every wall bore at least one shelf crammed with literature. The books he didn't have shelf space for were arranged throughout the cabin in intricately aesthetic configurations. There were spiraling towers of fantasy, cabins of classics, walls of horror—he'd made a place for every book he owned.

"You weren't kidding about having been an English major," she said after a quick look around.

"More of a bibliophile than an academic," he said, shoving his hands into the pockets of his jeans. "Most English majors would cringe at my collection."

Farren plucked a paperback off a nearby stack. The cover featured a sort of cat person baring her fangs.

"You mean *Night-Shriek* isn't considered high-brow literature?"

Jasper raised his eyebrows at her in mock-innocence. "I wrote a paper on that book."

Farren groaned.

They went to the living room, Jasper awkwardly standing with a beer in each hand while he waited for Farren to find a seat. To avoid giving him the opportunity to sit next to her on the couch, she took a plush recliner but had to get up almost immediately.

"I think I've had enough of chairs for at least the next couple of days," she said, avoiding his eyes and hopping over to the couch.

He seemed to get the message that she didn't want to get cozy. He handed her one of the frosty bottles and dropped into the recliner. They clinked bottle necks and drank.

For the first time in her life, Farren experienced the therapeutic effects of a much-needed drink. It was just regular Budweiser but she drank it fast and had no idea when she'd last eaten. Her head pleasantly buzzing, she leaned back into the couch and closed her eyes. When her world started to spin in a way that was far too recently familiar, she opened her eyes again and sat up straight. Jasper watched her from his chair, a pensive look furrowing his brow.

"Why did you put me in there? Why chance it if you wanted to help me?" Farren asked, wanting to feel angry but ultimately giving in to the calmness of the buzz she had going.

There were other, more practical things she should know, but she needed him to tell her why such a deception was necessary. Especially one that left her at the mercy of indescribable horrors.

Jasper drained his beer and pulled himself out of the chair with a sigh. He walked to the kitchen, holding his empty bottle up in the air.

"Another?"

"Just water for now," Farren said. "Do you have anything to eat?"

She couldn't believe she was thinking about eating so soon after what she'd been through, but the combined extra-dimensional experiences had left her drained and famished. The only reason she didn't accept a second beer was because she wasn't positive she could trust herself around Jasper under the influence of alcohol. He wasn't what she'd call her type but he had a dark appeal, like a nineties vampire; Lestat or Angel.

Jasper came back from the kitchen and placed a glass container of leftover lasagna on the coffee table in front of the couch, setting a glass of water and a fork next to it.

Farren pounced on the food. It was not only the best lasagna, it was the best meal she'd ever had. Didn't matter that it was cold—lasagna was the king of leftovers, good hot or cold days after it was made. In fact, she preferred it leftover to fresh, something that had always horrified her mom. She devoured the entire dish, two big pieces, in minutes, gulped down most of the water, and belched.

Jasper gave her a gentle applause then said, "Sasha was standing right outside the doors. Even if she hadn't been, I think sometimes she can read my mind."

Farren didn't know if he was being literal and didn't care. "Then she'll know you're helping me."

He nodded and she noticed how worn out he looked, like he'd aged ten years in the few months she'd known him. His skin, already fair, was the pale grayish-beige color of old, water stained paper.

"Why did you put me in there?" she asked. "Why do you put anyone in there? Why not just kill them?"

Jasper actually looked shocked. "I don't want to kill anyone."

"Same difference."

He dropped his gaze. "I know. I tell myself there's honor in not committing the actual act but you're right, it's the same as plunging the blade in myself."

He spoke differently when it was the two of them, she noticed. Or was it whenever Sasha wasn't around?

Farren said, "Please don't make me ask why again. Especially if you-know-who lives in the Museum."

Jasper guzzled his beer and cracked a third. "We didn't even open the doors of the Orchid Room at first. It was just a nameless, spooky building." He took a long swig from his new beer and set the bottle down on a small table next to the recliner. "All I knew was it gave me the creeps and Sasha told me not to go near it. For a long time, her word on anything was good enough for me and I was happy to have an excuse not to bother with the place.

"Winter came along and by then we'd been recruiting for a bit already but hadn't had to lock anyone up in the Sapling Hut yet. Then we brought in this kid, Leopold. He was eighteen and an aspiring poet. He wore capes and wide-brimmed hats and shit to school and had the shit kicked out of him dozens of times. But from what we could tell, the beatings just encouraged him to lean into the image he built for himself. Anyway, we thought it meant he was resilient. We were so wrong.

"From the moment he woke up here, he was like a terrified cat, flailing his arms and legs so no one could get near him, screaming at the top of his lungs. Never ran out of energy. Even pissed and shit himself."

Farren said, "I don't know how you guys can do that to someone."

Jasper spread his hands. "No excuse. And I will forever regret a lot of things I've done in this place and since I've known Sasha, including locking Leopold in the Orchid Room. But I swear he was putting on an act, trying to wear us down.

"I think we'd been dealing with him nonstop for around thirty hours when Sasha suggested we throw him in the Orchid Room. I was surprised she didn't want to kill him and I honestly can't say I would have tried to stop her if she had. She said she'd received instructions to bring those who won't be accepted into the tribe after twenty-four hours to the Orchid Room. Another twenty-four hours in there and then, if they're still with us, they can go free."

"How many have been allowed to go free?"

Jasper only looked at the floor.

"What is the Orchid Room?" Farren asked.

"I'm getting to that." He took another big gulp of his beer, belched into his hand, and excused himself. "We had to tie Leopold up after a couple of hours because he was tearing the place apart. So by the time Sasha told me the plan, he was already bound to a chair with duct tape. I put him on the sled, chair and all. He screamed the whole way to the Orchid Room, even louder than he'd been screaming before, as if he knew what was coming.

"When I locked him up, it was just the same as it was when you were in there; empty, dark, spooky. When I went back to get him, twenty-four hours later ..." Jasper emptied his beer in one swallow and stared at the bottle, turning it in his hands. "I knew something was wrong as soon as I opened the doors. Like, wrong with the world, or at least how I believed it worked. The air coming from inside was hot and damp and stunk like death. Right away I could see Leopold was gone. The chair wasn't empty, but it was obvious, in what little light there was, nobody was sitting in it. I turned on my flashlight and stepped inside.

"The floor was soft and wet and the light glistened off it. I'm not going to come right out and say I was standing in a mouth, but that's exactly what it made me think of. I couldn't see teeth or anything but my light didn't carry very far. There was a hot wind that would blow past me for almost a minute and then it would switch directions and cool down, blowing that way for another minute or so before it would switch again. Like breathing; hot breath going out and cool air coming in.

"I couldn't leave Leopold in there, Sasha would never let me live it down, so I ran over to the chair to see if there was any sign of him. *Something* was still duct taped to the chair and I think it had once been Leopold. It looked like the skin had been peeled from his body. Whoever did it peeled around the duct tape so that he stayed fastened to the chair. I have no idea if they skinned any other part of him because the torso was all that was left behind; the flesh where his head, arms, and legs had once been was ragged. He'd been ripped apart. I just hope it was before they peeled his skin off. I left him there after all, chair and everything."

"That's brutal," Farren said after a long silence. "But that still doesn't tell me anything about what that place is."

"I have a rough guess. I brought Sasha back there, after a ridiculous amount of convincing, to show her what I'd seen. I don't know why I expected the room to be the same or

Leopold's body to still be there. When I opened the doors to show her, the place had shifted back to normal. Dark, empty, no Leopold, no chair.

"I think the Orchid Room, the inside of it at least, is sort of like an elevator that goes between dimensions. Strange to say but I can't think of a more reasonable explanation, especially after what you told me about your frog monster."

Farren only barely heard anything after Jasper said the place had shifted back to normal.

"The portals are shifting," she mumbled.

"What was that?" Jasper asked, getting up and trudging to the kitchen.

The sound of the fridge door opening was followed by the hiss and pop of a beer bottle being cracked.

"There was something else in the Orchid Room with me before the frog thing came," Farren said. She tried to recall her conversation with the mystery voice before she was attacked.

Jasper wandered out of the kitchen with a beer bottle raised to his lips. "Another monster?"

Farren shook her head. "I think it wanted to help me. Or wanted me to help it. Said I could help the tribe. It told me I could stop it—the thing in the Museum. Told me not to fear it. I got the feeling the voice was ridiculing it, talking down about it."

Jasper stood in front of the coffee table, eyebrows raised in obvious incredulity.

"Forget any of that though," Farren said. "It said something about the portals shifting, just before it stopped talking to me and the frog thing showed up."

"Portals? Plural?"

Farren nodded gravely. "Exactly. Maybe the Orchid Room is a cosmic roulette wheel that opens on more than one place. I have no theories on why it switches or what makes the portals shift or whatever. But I think the thing I spoke to is a regular in there and Z is afraid of it."

"You won't say *his* name," Jasper observed.

"I don't like how it makes me feel. Neither will you, for the record."

Jasper shrugged.

There was a long, not uncomfortable silence between them.

"What are you going to do?" Jasper asked, voice having taken on a gentle slur.

"About what?"

He gestured around them. "This. Us. Z."

Farren drained the rest of her water and plunked the glass back on the table. "Nothing."

He looked surprised. "You're just going to ignore your calling?"

She grabbed her crutches and stood. "For all I know, I imagined that voice. I'm not staying here any longer than I have to."

Jasper gave a slow nod. "I get it. Where would you even get started? Doesn't sound like that thing gave you much direction."

It was hard to tell if he was being sarcastic.

Jasper stood, swayed, and stuck his hands out as if he was on a tightrope. "I think I'm just buzzed enough to help you now. If I'm caught, she'll kill me. Or have me killed. She'd probably make Kevin do it."

"Thanks," Farren said. "Almost makes up for drugging and kidnapping me."

Jasper looked as if he was going to retort then seemed to think better of it. Instead he held up a finger and walked out of the living room, down the hall leading to what Farren assumed were the bedrooms and bathroom, catching himself with one hand an instant before smashing into a wall.

Farren sat on the coffee table and read the titles of the various formations of books around the room. When Jasper finally emerged from the hallway, she was admiring a stack of David Eddings novels, a spiraling tower of the books making up *The Belgariad* and *The Malloreon*, which happened to be two of her favorite fantasy series ever since she'd grown tired of re-reading the Harry Potter books.

Jasper leaned against the entry wall of the living room, both hands behind his back.

"A going away present?" Farren asked, allowing a bit of mockery to creep into her voice.

He shrugged and brought his hands into view, unceremoniously holding out what he'd been hiding.

Her prosthetic foot.

She snatched it from him, turned it over in her hands. It was hers all right, sneaker and all. The shoe on her prosthesis didn't match the one she was wearing now, a hiker she'd found in the clothing cabin, but she was too happy to care about fashion sense; it wouldn't make much practical difference. She brought it back to the couch and immediately set about fastening the prosthesis to her ankle.

"You found it?" she asked as she attached it.

"Danny, actually," Jasper said. "Just this morning. He couldn't find you, obviously, so he left it with me."

Farren felt her throat tighten. She didn't want to feel gratitude toward Jasper after all he'd done, to her and everyone else he'd brought here, but in that moment she couldn't help it. Foot attached, she sprung from the couch and wrapped him in a hug. He returned the gesture, respectably keeping his arms at her shoulder level.

Without giving herself time to think about it, Farren wrapped one hand around the back of his head and pulled herself the half-inch it took for her lips to reach his. At first, he stiffened, almost pulling back from her. Half a second later, though, his arms slid down to her lower back and he kissed her back, parting his lips slightly. His hair was like cornsilk around her fingers. Her other hand traced his arm, his shoulder, his back. He was surprisingly firm; well-toned muscles barely giving under her touch. Their kissing grew heated. She pressed herself against him and felt him react.

Suddenly she wanted him. All of him.

She backed toward the couch, pulling him with her. Their tongues touched and danced in each other's mouths, their breathing devolved into animalistic panting. Beads of sweat prickled on her back. Her body had taken over. She grabbed the back of his jeans and ground herself into him hard enough to hurt.

And then his hands were on her shoulders. He pulled his mouth from hers. She leaned into him but he held her back.

They stared at each other for a handful of seconds that passed like hours.

Jasper broke eye contact first, looking up at the ceiling.

"We need to get you out of here," he said, turning his back to her and striding to the door before she could reply. He held it open for her, catching her eyes briefly with his own.

In any other situation like this, Farren would have been mortified. Would have taken it as rejection. But she'd seen the regret in his eyes when he pulled away from her. She would have given herself to him, any way he wanted it. And he knew it.

She smiled and walked through the door.

Z

GETTING out of the Congo was almost too easy. Becca was working the overnight shift and was typically apathetic to who left at any given time. Security's focus appeared to be primarily about keeping unwanted people out.

Still wouldn't do for Farren to be seen leaving the Congo, so Jasper went into the Visitor's Center and distracted Becca long enough that he could buzz Farren through the gate. It must have been easy because Farren had only just stepped up to the exit when the door buzzed, allowing her to slip through.

Nobody tried to stop her as she jogged through the hollow leading away from the Congo and out of the dense thicket. The indigo glow of predawn lit her path, August air already warm and humid. Her prosthesis felt good, she was walking normally for the first time in months. Nick's invention—the Piston—had been a decent substitute but was still effectively a peg leg.

Farren's plan was rudimentary but it was at least something to go on. She would stick to the woods and head to Huggy's Roadhouse, just outside town. It was one of the last truly blue-collar establishments left in Maggie's Knee and guys who were too wasted to drive often left their cars in the big gravel parking lot. She remembered Garrett and Patrick talking about boosting cars from the lot and figured that was her best bet for finding a ride. With no idea how to hot-wire a car, she was hoping a patron of the bar had been drunk enough to leave his or her keys in their vehicle.

Once she had a car, the plan was to head to her parents' old summerhouse and lay low.

## 36

Gordon carried a pair of steaming coffee mugs into the living room of the cottage just as a knock came from the front door. Franklin, who had been sitting on the couch with his face in his hands jerked his head up.

"That'll be Barb," Gordon said, setting the mugs down on the coffee table in front of Franklin.

The men had spent the night at the summerhouse, though neither managed to get much sleep. Gordon spent much of the previous evening doing fruitless research on his laptop while Franklin paced behind him, occasionally looking over his shoulder and asking if he'd found anything. Around midnight, Gordon finally suggested Franklin try to get some sleep in Farren's old room, which, thankfully, the banker did.

Gordon had contacted the Bureau of Forestry and spoken to a less-than-helpful woman named Joy, who informed him any maps he may be looking for could be found online. He'd searched in the places she told him to and had called her back to inform her he could not locate a map for the area he was interested in. Instead of searching on her end, as he requested, she insisted if the map wasn't on the website, it didn't exist in their system.

"There must be some old survey maps or something laying around that haven't been uploaded yet," Gordon had pleaded with her.

Joy answered glibly, "Contrary to popular belief, sir, not everything in creation has been mapped."

For some reason those words sent a chill down his spine.

After that call, Gordon spent another few hours performing vague web searches for missing kids, forest communes, and shadow people. This last turned up results with some of the most ludicrous theories and speculations Gordon had ever come across, none of which appeared to have anything to do with what was going on in Maggie's Knee. But he'd still scoured the results as thoroughly as his weary eyes would let him.

Shortly after sending Franklin to bed, Gordon had collapsed on the couch and closed his eyes, which were exhausted and dried out from hours of staring at the computer screen.

Instead of sleep taking him, as he'd hoped it would, an unsettling melancholy descended on him. He felt weighed down, all energy—physical, emotional, and spiritual—having bled out of him. His eyes had felt like heavy stones rested on them, but sleep would not come.

An anxious fear crept at the edges of his consciousness, not for Farren, but, strangely, for himself. Lying on that couch with his feet hanging over the arm, the edge of it digging painfully into his ankles, Gordon felt as if a vast, malevolent force was watching him with black, predatory eyes. He wanted to chalk it up to all of the ridiculous articles on shadow people he'd been reading, but it went deeper than that.

He felt doomed.

The word had popped into his head unexpectedly but it perfectly described the sensation he'd been feeling—and still felt even now, in the light of day. Like a war general with his forces depleted, watching an enemy hundreds of thousands strong march toward his camp. It was an odd thing to be feeling, especially since they were just looking for a couple of lost kids. No one would be coming for him except the police. And if they did, he'd be in a bit of trouble, but he still wasn't guilty of any major felony. He'd simply evaded questioning, which he thought was perfectly excusable after having watched his second wife bleed to death.

But lying there in the living room, eyes closed against the coming dawn, he'd known it wasn't the police he was afraid of.

"The shadow people," he'd mumbled to himself.

Was Farren a part of their gang, or whatever they called themselves? Or was she with them against her will?

Farren never did anything she didn't want to.

The thought hammered home the notion that she might have been involved in Melinda's murder. Did Farren really hate her enough to kill her, though? He thought back to the phone call Melinda made to him before she'd been killed. She'd said Farren's name, as if she'd been right in front of her, and then the line had gone dead. Pretty incriminating. If it had been anyone else, he wouldn't hesitate to go after them with everything at his disposal. But whether she truly hated his late second wife or not, he just couldn't see Farren being a part of something so violent.

Which begged the question, why had she been at the house in the first place? Why had any of them?

With those thoughts on his mind, he'd finally drifted into a restless semi-sleep just as the sky was beginning to lighten for the day.

He slept that way for maybe a couple of hours before Franklin had started banging around in the kitchen, looking for a coffee maker. Gordon, feeling no more rested than when he'd shut his eyes, had slid off the couch and taken over coffee making duties.

Now he opened the front door to reveal a smiling Barb standing on the stoop, a bright purple gym bag slung over one shoulder. She held a white box in her hands with a tray of steaming coffee cups balanced on top of it.

"I brought fresh croissants and muffins," she said. "And I assumed no one would say no to coffee."

"You, my lady, are an angel sent from above," Gordon said.

He took the box from her with one hand and held the other out for her bag, which she slid off her shoulder with a grunt. He took it and nearly spilled the tray of coffee in surprise at the weight of the thing.

"Geez, Barb. You bring every pair of shoes you own?" he said, carrying the bag and the breakfast to the living room.

Franklin's eyes widened when he saw the box. "That looks like a box from Bean There."

"Only the best for my two vigilantes," Barb said.

Franklin ripped open the lid of the box and the room was filled with the mouth-watering aroma of fresh, buttery croissants. In spite of his exhaustion and the malaise he'd been feeling, Gordon's mouth filled with saliva. He plucked a pillow-soft croissant from the box and bit half of it off with a single chomp, groaning with satisfaction as it melted on his tongue.

"So what's in the bag, Barb?" he asked with his mouth full.

She gave him a coy smile. "Toys."

## 37

Becca talked forever.

Jasper scolded himself for not remembering this about her. It was the reason they'd put her on the night shift to begin with; nobody else around to distract or be distracted by—all it took to sidetrack her was an ear to listen. Apparently sticking her on graveyard shift meant everything she wanted to say was bottled up, shaken, and sprayed all over the first person she came across.

He'd walked into the Visitor's Center well over an hour ago, to aid Farren in escaping the Congo undetected. He wanted to tell himself his intentions were completely noble, but he'd done it as much for himself as for Farren; if Becca raised an alarm, there would be no convincing Sasha of his innocence. Now he wondered if he would have been better off at Sasha's mercy.

"I told him he wouldn't even have to worry about social media anymore since we aren't allowed to use internet-enabled devices anyway," Becca was saying. "And he was all worried about his followers still being there and I had to kind of wake him up, mentally I mean, and tell him, 'Look man, you're not ever gonna see those people again. There's no situation where you go back to normal life from this.' And I wasn't trying to scare him, I mean, maybe scare a little common sense into him, but he got all weird and it took like three days for him to get over it. But after that, he found me again and he was like, 'Becca, man, you were fucking spot on and it's okay and I'm okay and I love this place.' And I help people like that all the time, man. And I think if you and Sasha let me be part of the welcome wagon or whatever you call it, or even the Induction team or whatever, I think I could be a really valuable part of that. Like maybe an intake coach or something along those lines. It doesn't have to be called an intake coach."

Jasper jumped at the opportunity to say something. "That might be a good idea," he said, already backing up to the door. "Let me talk to Sasha about it and maybe we can have a meeting to discuss."

Becca started to say something else but he was already through the door and pulling it shut behind him.

"What were you doing in there?"

He startled, heart leaping up to his Adam's apple.

Sasha stood at the bottom of the short stairway in the glow of a reddish morning sunbeam, arms crossed, bottom lip at full protrusion.

"You scared the shit out of me," he said, laughing a bit to cover up the sudden anxiety he felt.

"You going to answer my question?" Sasha demanded.

He forced himself to smile, trying to act as though he was still shaken from being surprised by her.

"Looking for something to read," he said, heading down the stairs toward her.

She made a show of looking at his hands. "What'd you decide on?"

"Nothing I felt like reading in there."

"You said you've read everything in the Visitor's Center," she said, stepping in front of him as he made it to the bottom of the stairs. "The other day, when you were talking to Kevin about how you wanted to add books to the next scavenging list."

"I'm obsessed," he said, trying to sound just the right level of casual. He could almost feel her probing around in his mind. "If you come across anything good, send it my way."

"Always do." Sasha stood aside to let him by.

He walked past her without another word, trying to look casual but suddenly unable to remember how he normally walked. Did he always swing his arms this much?

"Oh, hey," she called after him.

He froze.

She said, "I almost forgot to mention it. Big meeting this morning, right after breakfast. All hands. Action immediately following."

He turned to face her. "What kind of action?"

"Nothing you have to worry about right now. Just go find that next great book."

She waved him on, using both hands as if she was shooing children out of the house.

Not wanting to draw out the conversation any longer, Jasper headed back down the dirt road to his place, no longer concerned with how he was walking. He checked his watch;

breakfast would be in just a couple of hours. He had until then to dread whatever it was Sasha had planned.

Z

THE LIGHTS in the dining hall went out half an hour into breakfast. A couple of girls shrieked then laughed and more than one guy shouted "Penis!" which got the rest of them laughing.

"Okay everyone, calm the hell down," Sasha shouted from the front of the room. She had her hair tucked up under a black ball cap and wore an unusually modest amount of makeup. Her black cargo pants and army jacket gave her the appearance of a rogue military leader. She pointed to the back of the room and whoever had turned the lights off flicked them back on.

Seeing their leader standing at the front of the hall, everyone immediately shut up. Even Kip poked his head out the kitchen door to hear what Sasha had to say.

She hadn't invited Jasper up to join her. When she'd gotten up from her seat to go to the front, he made to do the same but she raised a hand to still him and had signaled him to sit back down. It was an obvious play to belittle him in front of the tribe, to show them he no longer mattered as much as he once had.

The desperate urge to run stole over Jasper. Hair stood up on the back of his neck and his stomach clenched. He dug his fingernails into his thighs and forced himself to give Sasha his attention; to keep up appearances for the time being. He could feel the eyes of the tribe on his back, wondering what had happened between their two leaders.

Sasha looked at him and smiled.

"I know most of you want to know why I'm up here without Jasper," she said. "I'll get to that. I'm about to drop some big bombs on you guys so smoke 'em if you got 'em."

To demonstrate she was being literal, she pulled out a cigarette and lit up. Smoking wasn't exactly prohibited indoors anywhere, they just never really did it in the dining hall. Now several kids around the room sparked up a cigarette while many more pulled out their vapes and spewed sweet-smelling clouds of vapor to combat the cigarette smoke. Kip went around the room opening windows and turned the ceiling fans on high.

"Some of you have an idea of who we serve," Sasha said.

The room fell dead silent. They never discussed this stuff openly.

She said, "A long time ago, when I was just a teenager, like most of you, I was a little rich bitch in a big house with a hundred-millionaire dad I rarely saw and a mom who treated me like a tumor that had fallen out of her—one she had to keep happy or it might eat her face off."

Several of the kids in the room nodded in understanding; it was a familiar story for many of them. Not for the first time, Jasper wondered why it was that many of their tribe came from ridiculously wealthy families. He understood the kids who came from broken families; they were looking for a place to belong, for real family. Then again, just because a family is together, it doesn't mean they aren't broken. His own family was a good example of that.

What really captured Jasper was that he'd never heard any of this from Sasha before. He'd asked her about her background, where she came from, where she went to school, yada

yada. She'd always been flippant about it, giving only the vaguest hints to what had apparently been a lie anyway. If asked before this morning, Jasper would have sworn Sasha had grown up in poverty with an abusive dad as her sole caretaker.

"Anyway," she said, "one day I started hearing this voice in my head, only the voice is more like a feeling than something you hear. It's like that game where one person draws on another person's back and the person whose back it is has to guess what was drawn.

"At first it only seemed to want attention. Like it would say my name and then just wait and watch how I react. I could feel it curled up in the corner of my mind, watching my reactions, and I knew I was being tested. So after a while I asked it what it wanted and I could tell that made it happy.

"It led me to Maggie's Knee and showed me this place, our home. When I arrived, I discovered someone had prepared the Congo for me. Everything was cleaned and up to date, even though the place was built and abandoned before I was born. I knew that *he* had arranged it all for me. For us. Turned out it was Farren's dad who did all the work."

Heads turned this way and that as the tribe looked around for Farren. A murmur bubbled up amongst them when they realized she was absent.

"She's not here," Sasha snapped.

At once, all eyes were back on her, every mouth closed except to smoke or vape.

"The one who brought me here told me this place was for me to grow my own family, a real family. A tribe. *He* said we'd have everything we need. And we do, don't we?"

A couple of kids whooped.

She gave them a warm smile Jasper would never have thought her face capable of making.

"But he needs something in return," she said. "Our allegiance. Our service. You know this already. You can all feel the pull toward something greater."

Many heads nodded. Jasper felt completely out of the loop.

Sasha turned around and picked an open can of paint off the floor, the handle of a brush sticking out of it. Without a word, she swished the brush around in the can and painted a thick black line high up on the plain white wall at the back of the room. After a few seconds, during which the only sounds were the whisper of the paintbrush being dragged against the wall, she stood back and admired her work.

She turned toward the room, gestured at what she'd painted.

The word ZIIS glared back at the room, black droplets oozing down from each letter.

Seeing the name written down made Jasper feel worse than when he'd heard it. The letters looked so wrong in that sequence, especially written so the S resembled a backward Z, making a simple ambigram of the word. The sight of it repelled him more than any violent or appalling image. The blackness of the letters seemed to deepen, to grow darker, so that it appeared as if they were carved into the wall, exposing the bleakest depths of space beyond.

Jasper looked away from it, up at Sasha, and felt a change in the room's atmosphere.

She looked him in the eyes but it was as if she was no longer there—something else was staring out at him. It moved her gaze to the tribe.

Jasper surveyed the kids gathered in the hall; the same thing was reflected in all of their eyes.

"We have work to do," Sasha said in a voice slightly deeper than her normal tone. "Go and gather what's needed."

The tribe sprang into action. Everyone got out of their seat at the same time and marched to the exit, not a word uttered between them. The silent action was eerie to watch.

Jasper got up and went to Sasha. "I thought you said I'd find out what you have planned."

She looked up at him with a blank expression, a strange stillness to her normally expressive bottom lip.

"You didn't hear?" she said.

Before he could respond, a pair of enormous, rock-solid arms wrapped around him. A second later, his feet were no longer on the ground. Jasper didn't have to look behind him to know it was Guppy holding him in a grip that could liquefy his guts in a second. Would the giant really hurt him though? He didn't want to chance finding out.

"Guppy, put me down. Please." He gasped, struggling to fill his lungs.

"Sasha say no," Guppy's voice boomed in his ears, loud enough to make them ring.

"Why not?" Jasper was asking Guppy but implored Sasha with his eyes.

"Too old," Guppy said.

"Sasha's older than me."

"Sasha special."

At those words, Sasha's mouth curved up in an impish grin. She shrugged and said, "You've fulfilled your duties, Jasper. You did well. Enjoy your rest." She looked up at Guppy and said, "Make sure you tie him tight. Danny, I'm leaving it to you to make sure someone is watching the doors at all times—everyone in the tribe is now welcome to cross the bridge."

Jasper hadn't realized Danny stayed behind as well. Didn't care right at that second; he was too focused on what Sasha was implying.

"Wait," he said, heart going from a gallop to Mach 4 in an instant. "Don't put me in there. Please. Just kill me if you want me gone."

He felt Guppy straighten. He hoped that meant the giant didn't want to hurt him.

"Danny, please!" Jasper shouted.

"Take him to the bridge," Danny said, presumably to Guppy. "I'll grab some stuff to tie him and meet you there."

"Go with you," Guppy said anxiously.

"You move too slow," Danny said. "I'll still beat you to the bridge."

"Race?" Guppy asked, suddenly happy again.

"Sure, big guy."

There was the sound of footsteps and then the door to the dining hall opened and shut. Guppy turned to follow Danny out but was stopped by Sasha's voice.

"Hold on, Guppy."

"Sasha, please don't do this," Jasper begged.

And now he did struggle, because he'd rather have Guppy tear him limb from limb than be bound and locked up in the Orchid Room. His efforts didn't faze Guppy—the giant didn't even seem to notice it; his arms stayed locked immovably around Jasper.

There was the sound of rummaging behind them and then a cloth was being held over Jasper's nose and mouth, the acrid odor of the knockout compound they used burning in his eyes and lungs.

"You've always said you wanted to know what this stuff feels like," Sasha said. "Now you can …"

Her voice faded out along with the rest of the world. His last thought was he hoped it was possible to overdose on this stuff and that Sasha had given him too much.

38

Sasha watched Guppy carry Jasper's limp body out of the dining hall, effortlessly shifting him under one arm to open the door. She had expected much more of a fight from her former lover and partner in crime. Definitely hadn't expected him to allow Guppy to sneak up on him so easily. Hadn't he seen what was happening? Or was he that removed from what was going on?

It was easy to forget how it felt not to have ZIIS co-existing within you, as every member of the tribe now did. Almost every member. She wished Jasper could join them but she'd known before she even brought him here that this—or something like it—was how his role in all this would end.

She ran a hand over the letters she'd painted, smearing them a bit. So long she'd been carrying this name around with her, all to herself. She'd loved the exclusivity; being the only one *he* had chosen to hold *his* name, to build and lead *his* tribe. It sucked having to share the knowledge, but she was still in charge, still the favorite.

Soon it would be more than just the tribe who shared her privilege. Their army, *his* army would be an overwhelming, globe-spanning force. And she would lead it.

First there were things that needed to be taken care of, the way Jasper had needed to be taken care of. In less than an hour, they would be launching the first critical phase of their plan.

Things were speeding up now. If all went well, ZIIS would have his army built by this evening and she would be the most important human being in the world.

Still standing at the head of the room, she turned in a slow circle. This would be the last time she stood here. And good riddance. The Congo had been convenient for their purposes but she was ready to take ownership of the finest residence Beverly Hills had to offer. Or maybe she'd have a castle built for herself and reign as true royalty.

Because that is what she would be. A queen.

Z

LESS THAN AN HOUR LATER, every member of the tribe stood before the dining hall, each of them well armed.

Most of the kids held handguns and rifles, easy stuff to get without raising any eyebrows. They probably could have laid their hands on some automatic weapons without much trouble but it hadn't been worth the risk.

Those who didn't have a gun were armed with knives and blunt weapons like baseball bats and tree branches. A few kids wielded tools; Tyler held a pickaxe over one muscular shoulder and wore a tool belt containing a hammer and a hand axe, Ramses had a crowbar in one hand and what appeared to be a

Molotov cocktail in the other, and Hamji brandished a gardening machete, as well as a Smith & Wesson .45 tucked into the front of his pants.

Wesley showed up last, looking like he'd stepped out of an eighties action movie. He had a Sig Sauer P227 in a holster on each hip, a Marlin 336 lever-action rifle strapped to his back, and three hand grenades dangling from his belt on a carabiner. In his left hand he held a sheathed katana that Sasha thought looked authentic, though she had no idea where he'd obtained it. Completing the look was a red bandana tied around his head, holding back his long, dark hair.

"Don't blow us up, John Wick," Danny said, taking a few steps away from their security chief.

There were a few chuckles at that; the mood in general was almost merry. The tribe's spirits were so light Sasha almost doubted they knew what was going on. But they had all gone and gathered what they'd been told, mainly weapons, and there was a cold hardness to each of their faces, the coming violence recognized and reflected in them.

Sasha stood before them, arms once more held behind her back in a very deliberate general's pose. She stared across the crowd of kids gathered in front of her and, almost as one, they shut up and gave her their full attention. It felt great.

"You're all very brave," she said. It wasn't like her to say such things but she was no longer entirely herself. *He* had stepped forward. "You're about to change the world forever. Some of you will die, but your names will live on eternally as those who prepared the way. There is no higher honor."

There were a few cheers at this.

"Danny," she called.

"Here," Danny said, stepping to the front of the crowd.

"Who's watching Jasper?"

"Nick is there now," he said. "Sadie will take over tonight."

"You think your sister will be all right if he manages to get out?" Sasha asked.

Danny smiled. "He won't get out of the knots I tied. And Sadie's well armed. I've been working with her at the range, she's a pretty good shot."

It wasn't ideal but it would have to be enough. Sasha needed as strong a force as possible for their mission. Made sense to leave Nick and Sadie, arguably two of their weakest, here to guard Jasper, who was absolutely not going to escape the Orchid Room anyway.

"Then let's move out."

Everyone cheered. A few of the guys even gave an "Oorah!"

They marched out as one, falling into a somber silence as soon as they were all through the gates of the Congo. Danny, knowing the plan, and having stumbled into what was swiftly beginning to look like the role of Sasha's lieutenant, was in the lead, walking several paces in front of Becca, the next person behind him. The rest of the tribe kept a uniform two paces apart as if they'd rehearsed the formation ahead of time. Sasha brought up the rear, almost a dozen feet from Tyler, who was the last person ahead of her.

When they reached the carpool lot, Sasha was relieved to see the school bus already waiting for them, engine idling. She'd sent Tania, who, no shit, had experience stealing buses, ahead of them last night to secure the ride. Sasha had simply scrawled ZIIS on a sheet of paper and held it up for Tania to see. The girl's eyes had darkened and she'd left without Sasha having to utter a word.

The tribe filed onto the bus without a second's hesitation, filling it up, two to a seat, from the back forward. A single empty seat was left for Sasha, as if this had all been ordained from the start. It was easy to wonder how much any of this had really been her own doing. Not that it mattered, as long as she got what was promised to her when the time came. Still, it was daunting to learn she was nowhere near as in control as she once believed herself to be.

She took her seat at the front of the bus. Without a word, Tania pulled the door closed, put the bus in gear, and pulled out of the carpool lot, bearing the tribe off to their first destination.

39

Gordon munched on the last muffin—poppyseed—and mulled over their plan. It was half-assed at best, though he had to admit he couldn't come up with anything better and he was tired of sitting on his hands in the increasingly cramped quarters of the summerhouse.

Barb had once more exceeded his expectations, not just packing weapons for each of them—Gordon had a hard time picturing Barb even holding, let alone shooting a firearm—but also canteens of water, trail rations, flares, and a first aid kit. Gordon had gone through the gym bag feeling foolish for not thinking of any of these things himself. Humble as ever, Barb had waved off the praise he and Franklin lavished on her.

The idea was for the three of them to breach the thicket where Gordon and Franklin were confounded the day before. There was a pretty sharp machete in the summerhouse's garden shed and Gordon thought they'd be able to clear a fair amount of the brush with it. They'd toyed with the idea of bringing a chainsaw but the problems it would pose far outweighed any benefit. The trees in the thicket grew close together and Gordon didn't think there would be room to fall if they did manage to cut one down. So they would go around the trees and cut their way through the brush until they found the spot the kids were using as a camp or until they ran out of daylight. Basically the same thing the two men had done the day before, only with a little more planning and preparedness.

"Barb, are you sure you're up for this?" Gordon asked, checking the magazine of the Beretta M9 he'd selected from the gym bag of goodies. He secured the gun in a shoulder holster he'd strapped on.

Barb gave him a hard stare, a look he had to struggle not to find adorable.

"I go hunting with my brother twice a year," she said. "I'm not the most physically fit but I'm an okay shot with my Remington—it's in the car—and I'm used to trudging through rough terrain."

"Surprises never stop with you," Gordon said.

Franklin was turning a Glock 19 over in his hands, looking at it as if he didn't know which end to hold onto. Gordon had taken the clip out of it before handing it over for inspection. Watching Franklin now, he decided he would hang onto the magazine until it was needed.

"Only thing left to do is—"

An explosion from outside stopped Gordon's sentence and rocked the cottage's foundation, knocking frames from the walls and books from the shelves.

"What the hell was that?" Franklin shouted, turning in circles as if he expected to find the answer written on one of the walls.

Gordon ran to the front door and didn't have to pull the

curtain back to see one of the cars in the driveway was on fire. He yanked the front door open. Barb's SUV was ablaze, the two tires Gordon could see already melting to the gravel drive- way. Beyond the inferno was a surreal vision.

A bright yellow school bus shimmered beyond the heat waves rising from Barb's burning car. It sat a couple dozen feet back from the blaze. Looked empty.

Movement drew Gordon's gaze to the right. Someone darting through the trees bordering the property.

He threw the front door closed, twisted the deadbolt, and ran to the back of the house.

"What was that?" Franklin demanded.

Without responding, Gordon pulled back the blinds drawn over the sliding back door. Only the screen was closed, letting in a cool breeze from the lake.

None of the dozen or so youth standing in the back yard were present on the night of Melinda's death, but they had to be part of the same twisted group. Every one of them was armed, guns aimed at the cottage.

Flashes of movement in his peripheral vision. The house was being surrounded.

"Sorry, sheriff! Didn't know you'd be here. Kinda works out better, though," a girl's voice called. It carried easily through the screen.

At first he couldn't tell who had spoken, then someone he recognized stepped into view from behind the shed. The older girl who'd been at his house the night Melinda was killed. She was dressed for guerrilla warfare and carried a huge handgun, what looked to Gordon like a Desert Eagle, though he couldn't be sure. Hadn't seen one in years. Something in his heart told him this girl was directly responsible for Melinda's death.

Was she the ringleader of these kids? There were so many of them. A dozen questions flew through Gordon's mind in an instant.

"What do you want?" he called.

She gestured at the cottage with her gun. "Just here to pick something up."

All at once a voice drifted out of the fog of Gordon's memory. The old woman saying, *"You'll let them take it. The key to his victory. You have no choice."*

What the hell was going on? Why did he feel like this was bigger than just a bunch of kids acting out to the extreme?

That sense of doom washed over him again.

Doom. The word was the strike of a bass drum in his heart. *Doom. Doom. Doom.*

"I'm not about to let you take anything from here," he said.

The girl chuckled, like they were chatting about the Pirates' chance of making it to the World Series. "We all know that, sheriff."

She turned to the kids lined up behind her and gave a signal with her hands Gordon couldn't see. Didn't matter. He knew what it meant.

Training took over. He leapt for the couch. Shoved Barb down behind it.

Franklin stood in the middle of the room dumbfounded.

"Franklin!" Gordon shouted. "Get down!"

The world erupted in gunfire.

z

GORDON LAY SPRAWLED over top of Barb, hands laced over his head. Half a dozen different calibers ripped through the walls and windows, tearing the summerhouse to pieces.

After an eternity, the cacophony stopped. Over the ringing in his ears and the crashing of glass and wood falling to the floor, Gordon heard the clicks and clinks of dozens of firearms being reloaded.

Barb stared up and through him, eyes wide.

"Franklin?" Gordon called without lifting his head.

He thought he heard a grunt and what could be the shuffling sounds of the banker trying to get to his feet.

Gordon rolled off Barb. Helped her to her hands and knees.

"Keep your head down and try to crawl to the master bedroom," he said in a low voice.

Barb nodded and scurried across the floor on all fours.

Gordon pulled the M9 from his shoulder holster and flicked off the safety. Not enough ammo to take out all the kids —was he really considering shooting more children?—but maybe he could scare them off.

As he was about to break cover, Barb let out a shriek from across the room.

"Barb?"

"It's Franklin," she sobbed. "He's—they got him."

Gordon closed his eyes and tried to push aside the guilt that immediately followed. It was his fault they were here. He'd allowed the search for Garrett to end prematurely, gone rogue, and dragged Franklin into his illegal investigation without giving a thought to the man's wellbeing. He was to blame for Rose Mews having her entire family ripped away from her.

Gordon stood from cover and squeezed three shots into the back yard, aiming over the heads of the kids who once more directed their weapons at the cottage. Mercifully, the majority of them dove to the side or crouched in place. Gave him time to move.

He sprinted from the couch toward where Franklin lay. Blood soaked the floor. The man was definitely dead. At least two rounds had pierced his abdomen and, more telling, a third shot, likely from one of the bigger rifles, had blown away a significant portion of his head above his left eye. His mouth was frozen in a grimace of fear. Brains leaked from Franklin's skull into the pool of blood. The mess resembled a cauliflower tomato stew Melinda had made just two weeks before and Gordon turned away in grief-struck revulsion.

He sprinted for the short hallway and crashed into the master bedroom.

"What the fuck is happening?" Barb shrieked as soon as Gordon slammed the door behind him.

He'd never heard her cuss before.

Barb's skin had gone pale gray and her eyes bulged, ready to pop from her head at any second. She rubbed her hands up and down her cargo pants and took loud, deep breaths through her nose.

Without answering, Gordon dragged a mahogany dresser in front of the door.

"Where did they get so many guns?" she demanded. "I should've grabbed Franklin's gun. Oh, that poor man. Why did I leave the Remington in the car? Where's your gun?"

Gordon held it up for her to see. His one firearm with a pitiful eleven rounds in the mag and one waiting in the chamber. If he'd spent any amount of time up here, there would almost certainly have been a shotgun in the closet.

"We'll get through this," he said, feeling stupid as soon as the words were out of his mouth. It was a platitude without conviction.

He crept to the window on the far wall and peaked through it. A single round had pierced the glass and, for now, the rest of the window remained intact around the spiderwebbed hole. Their besiegers had obviously concentrated fire on the rooms they'd known were inhabited. He could see no movement out the window but stepped away from it anyway.

"How did they blow up my car?" Barb asked in a small voice.

Good question.

"Could've started a fire."

"Wouldn't that have taken a while? Wouldn't we have seen something?" Barb's eyes grew clearer with each question. She benefited from analyzing a situation.

Gordon nodded. "There's a good chance they have explosives. I didn't want to say that. Sorry."

Barb arched a shrewd eyebrow at him and opened her mouth, no doubt to offer some witty retort about being able to handle the truth. Whatever it had been, Gordon didn't get a chance to hear. The window he'd just left exploded in a spray of glass and something blew through Barb's neck, exiting on the other side, and lodging itself in the wall. Barb's throat erupted in a gout of blood and she fell to the floor in a choking, twitching heap before Gordon could register what had happened.

Horrified, he stumbled back from her. For a nightmarish second, it was Melinda on the floor. Twitching, bleeding, dying.

The rest of the assault ripped through the now-glassless

window and occasionally through the door over the top of the dresser, which still held fast.

They were inside.

Barb became still. Her eyes glassed over. The blood pumping through the ragged hole in her neck slowed to an ooze.

The door to the bedroom rattled. Gordon raised his weapon at it and backed deeper into the room. He reached the walk-in closet. Took cover within.

From beyond the door, someone shouted, "Guppy!"

Something shook the floor in the hallway hard enough to vibrate through to where Gordon stood on the other side of the room, back to the rear wall of the closet. Sounded like they were rolling a cannon through the cottage.

The mahogany dresser blew into the room. It collided with the bed, flipped over the mattress, and slammed into the wall, leaving a hole big enough for Gordon to climb through. The door followed, exploding into kindling against the wall.

The giant, the one from the night of Melinda's death, squeezed through the door, cracking the frame on both sides. He looked around and stopped when he saw Barb on the floor.

"Lady hurt," he called in a booming voice that shook the walls.

He was gigantic, at least eight feet tall, Gordon thought. It was hard to tell because the brute had to duck his head to avoid hitting it on the ceiling.

*The eight-and-a-half-foot ceilings*, Gordon thought.

The giant looked to be solid muscle protected by a modest layer of fat. His face was like that of a toddler, from the thick lips on his large mouth to the cowlick of black hair curled over his forehead. His eyes were big and dark.

"Get the man, Guppy," a young guy called from the hall. "Get the man and bash him! Just like a dog!"

The giant, Guppy, looked up and locked eyes with Gordon. The grin that formed on the behemoth's face was terrifying.

Gordon made himself step out of the closet and stare up at the giant. "You killed my dog?"

Guppy growled, a low rumble from deep in his massive chest.

Gordon raised his weapon and the giant flew across the room with terrifying speed. Gordon got a single shot off but had no idea if it hit, enormous as his target was.

The giant wrapped his enormous palm around both Gordon's hand and the gun. Squeezed. Gordon's bones crumbled like potato chips. He screamed.

Guppy yanked him upward and Gordon's shoulder left its socket with a wet pain. The giant tossed him and he flew across the room, crashed head-first into the wall, and collapsed in a heap of bruises and broken bones.

Gordon flipped himself onto his back. His head swam. Body cried out from a hundred different agonies.

Guppy faced him and Gordon could see the giant had been hit after all. A growing red patch on his shirt over his right shoulder revealed where Gordon's shot had landed. The brute didn't seem to have noticed.

Using his left hand, Gordon grabbed the gun from the destroyed fingers of his right. Took aim at the approaching beast.

He opened fire just as the giant flew across the room at him, cinderblock fists raised over his head, ready to bash.

40

Farren glanced in the rearview mirror at the state police cruiser that had just passed in the opposite lane. As far as she could tell, the officer driving hadn't so much as glanced her way. Still, she watched it in the mirror until the cruiser disappeared around a bend, obscured by the wall of pines lining the highway. She tightened her grip on the wheel and gave the car a bit more gas.

Stealing a car had not been the quick and simple errand she'd assumed it would be. The actual driving was fine; she had her license, had obtained her learner's on the morning of her sixteenth birthday, and completed her sixty-five hours of in-car training as fast as possible so she had been one of the only kids in Maggie's Knee to have her full license before seventeen. Farren had assumed a lot more freedom would come with the license but quickly learned that, without her own car, all she'd done is make herself eligible as an errand girl for Melinda. She'd swiftly lost interest in driving.

There was a lot more to actually *stealing* the car than she'd been led to believe. For one thing, she had to find one—there were no cars parked at Huggy's, which meant she had to quest about closer to town.

After several hours of wandering around the outskirts of Maggie's Knee, she came across an old, wood-paneled station wagon parked at the end of the driveway of a ramshackle house on Mountain Road, which led out of town and into its titular territory. The door had been left unlocked and the keys were under the floor mat. While she was grateful for the good fortune, Farren wondered whether it was laziness or something else that prompted people to leave their keys inside the car. Maybe some people were much more trusting than she could ever be; a notion that made her feel horrible for breaking someone's faith in humanity. She'd made a silent promise to the car's owner that she would return the station wagon if at all possible, with a full tank of gas.

Now, almost an hour later, she bombed down the lonely country roads leading to the summerhouse, where she had some of her best and one of her worst memories.

She swallowed a hard, painful lump in her throat.

It had been years since any of them had been back to the summerhouse and she wondered what sort of condition it would be in when she arrived. No doubt there would be some cleaning and airing out to do.

The sky had darkened in the last hour, slate-gray clouds hiding the sun and cooling the air with the promise of significant rain.

Even against the gray of the clouds, she spotted the thin trail of black smoke rising above the trees long before she reached the driveway of the summerhouse. At first she thought it must be one of the other cottages nearby but then remembered they owned the road; a private, nameless gravel strip that ran the mile from the single-lane roadway that had taken her up here from Route 12.

What would she do if there were squatters in the cottage? Maybe if she sat outside and honked, they would assume the owners, which, technically she was, had returned and would sneak out the back.

As soon as she rounded the bend that brought the summerhouse into view, she forgot entirely about politely shoeing hippies out.

The blackened, smoldering wreck of what appeared to have been an SUV sat a dozen or so feet back from the cottage. Just beyond it was a silver Acura, untouched by whatever had destroyed the SUV. She eased the stolen station wagon to a stop a safe distance back from the wreck.

Something, beyond the obvious fact of the burning car in the driveway, felt off about the situation. She tried to convince herself it had nothing to do with her or the Congo.

She turned off the car and sat with one hand on the door handle and the other still holding the key in the ignition

The property looked quiet, though she could barely see the house beyond the smoke rising from the charred SUV. If it hadn't been for the fact that she was probably wanted by the police, she would get the hell out of here right now. But she had nowhere to go.

To return to the Congo was suicide. She couldn't go home; Gordon would cuff her and drag her to the station himself. He probably thought Farren was responsible for Melinda's death, that the whole thing had been her idea. And she had no friends to speak of. No other family. The only living relatives she had were her father's parents who lived in Seattle and who she hadn't seen in over a year. They'd always tried to be kind to her but she could tell, the last time she'd seen them, that they didn't approve of who she'd grown to be, a bitter cripple.

So there was only the summerhouse.

She honked the horn three times, holding it down on the last beep, hoping to drive out whoever might be in the cottage. Nothing stirred.

What if someone, like the guys from school, stole the SUV, took it for a joyride, and set it on fire way out here in the middle of nowhere? They would have had another car and, after the initial explosion and a couple of bro shouts and high fives, would have taken off for fear of the police blocking them in—there was only the one road out of here. But then what was the Acura here for? Did they plan on coming back to blow it up too?

Whatever the explanation, she couldn't stay in the car all day. It was either leave now or suck it up and investigate the cottage. If someone was here, they almost certainly would have come out when she honked.

Mind made up, she stepped out onto the gravel driveway, wrinkling her nose at the acrid smell of burned oil, rubber, and fiberglass.

She gave the burning wreck a wide berth, feeling the heat wafting off it, and stopped as she came to the other side of it.

The summerhouse was in ruins, a crystalline outline of glass surrounding it. The windows were all smashed, the wood-paneled walls shredded, several basketball-sized holes blown out of them. How could a car explosion do that to a cottage?

Something clinked underfoot and only then did she notice the metallic glint blanketing the property. If the sun had been out, she likely would have noticed the bits of brass much sooner, maybe before she'd even gotten out of the car.

The ground was covered in bullet casings of all shapes and sizes. Some were no bigger than the tip of her finger, while others were as big as a disposable lighter. They rolled under her feet as she walked over them, bumping into each other with dull clinks. The ambience of a war zone.

The front door hung open on one hinge, as though a bomb had gone off inside.

She thought about turning around and getting back in the car but forced herself to move toward the house, one slow step at a time. It was obvious whatever had gone on here was over now.

Who had done the shooting? And who had they been shooting at?

She eased the door open. It dropped off its remaining hinge, hitting the floor with a *thunk* that rattled the walls. She held her breath, half-expecting someone to come running out of the shadows at her, knife held high over their head.

Silence.

She leaned the door against the wall and crept into the gloom of the summerhouse. It looked like something really had exploded in here—the walls just inside the door were blackened, chunks of them blown away. Along with the bigger holes were small, ragged punctures where bullets had ripped through the walls.

"Anyone here?" she called.

Her voice fell flat in the destruction. The place was empty.

She shuffled through the chaos. Books were ripped from the shelves, the old tube television had been smashed on its face, glass from the screen littering the handmade rug her mom had bought in Mexico. The kitchen was ransacked, plates and glassware smashed to bits.

The glass of the sliding back door covered the floor in shards. Through it, she could see the dry bed of the koi pond. The black plastic lining had been ripped out and lay in the garden.

Something about the sight tripped an alarm in her mind. With vicious clarity, she recalled the memory, or whatever it had been, of her dad's that she'd lived out.

He'd hidden the Kraken update under the koi pond.

The memory was never meant for her at all. She'd simply been the conduit for the thing in the Museum to spy on her dad in the past. Was that why it had wanted her there so badly?

There was no longer any doubt in her mind that the tribe was responsible for this.

She picked her way through the destruction of the cottage toward the back door. She had to see it. Had to know if they'd really come here just for an old social media file.

Stepping out into the back yard, her eyes rose to the sloping lawn leading to their private little beach on Piper Lake. The lake was placid in the stillness before the coming summer storm, which Farren could smell in the air, the water gunmetal gray under the darkened sky.

She was cast back in time against her will, memories surging forward and washing out the present.

z

FARREN SWATS *a mosquito poised to take a drink from her thigh. It leaves a brown smear on her leg and she swipes it off with the edge of the paperback she's reading,* Magician's Gambit *by David Eddings, the third book in what she has grudgingly accepted as her new favorite fantasy series. Up until six months ago, when she read the first in the series,* Pawn of Prophecy, *she'd been convinced no literature would be able to hold her attention the way the Harry Potter series had. Now she is hooked.*

*She lets her eyes drift up to the lake before her, where her mom floats in a dingy so bright yellow it makes her skin look jaundiced. Farren's mom wears oversized, dark sunglasses and a hat with a brim almost as wide as the dingy. She also has a book open in front of her, the latest Dan Brown. Farren and her mom share a passion for reading but their tastes are pretty far apart. Farren prefers entirely made-up worlds, creatures, and races. Her mother is more into spy thrillers, historical fiction, and whatever shows up on Oprah's reading list.*

*Farren watches her mom for a few minutes and can't help feeling a twinge of envy. She knows deep down that she inherited at least some of her mom's exotic beauty, augmented by her dad's Japanese lineage, but her mom has both feet and wields her sculpted legs like a couple of deadly weapons. Farren's own legs are just as long and toned, but one of them ends in a garish stump.*

*She puts the book down and closes her eyes.*

*Somewhere behind her, Gordon is singing a CCR song at the top of his lungs while he grills up some burgers for their lunch. Seventy-five percent of the meals they eat at the summerhouse consist of burgers or hotdogs. Every meal includes some form of grilled meat. All part of cottage living.*

*Leaning back in her lounger and taking sips from a lukewarm iced tea, Farren lifts her book to her eyes, which are growing heavy under the midday summer sun. She can feel sleep creeping up on her and does nothing to resist it. This is what summer is all about; reading and snoozing under the sun, skin cancer be damned.*

*She lets the book drop onto her chest and gives in to the drowsiness.*

*A scream snaps her awake. She sits up and leans on an elbow, searching for the source of the sound.*

*Apparently, she'd fallen asleep for a while, though it doesn't feel like her eyes have been shut for more than a couple of minutes. Her mother is in from the lake, probably inside getting fresh with Gordon. Gross. Farren has caught them smooching and touching a few times. At first, it was weird, seeing her mom be affectionate with someone other than her dad. But Gordon has been good to them and Farren has accepted him as a part of their life—has even come to love him. But it's still gross seeing them make out.*

*She shoves herself into an upright position and chugs the rest of her iced tea. As she lowers her glass, something floating in the middle of the small lake catches her eye.*

*A yellow dingy. A giant sunhat.*

*Why would her mom leave them? It's a relatively tiny lake and there is only one cottage on the other side, home to a reclusive but friendly seventy-something-year-old painter, but it still seems irresponsible to just leave stuff floating in the lake. Especially the hat.*

*Something breaks the surface of the water and at first, Farren thinks it's a bass jumping for a fly. Takes another second to realize she's seeing an arm. A thrashing arm.*

*"Mom?" she calls.*

*Her mom is an excellent swimmer, it can't be her out there.*

*But the hat.*

*Her mother's head erupts from the surface of the lake next, dark hair plastered over her face so she resembles a water monster from a low-budget horror movie. A faint shriek, much quieter than the one that had woken Farren, echoes across the lake.*

*"Mom!" Farren screams. "Gordon!"*

*She leaps from her chair, meaning to race to the water's edge and swim out to her mom, but instead stumbles and falls face-first into the sand. A harsh reminder of her missing limb.*

*Farren drags herself to the water. Without the flippers she wears for swimming she won't be much use to her mom, but she has to try. If she can just get to the dingy, it will hold them both afloat.*

*She's just made it into the water when a heavy thumping comes from behind her and a herculean mass of flesh soars over her and lands in the water with an enormous splash. Gordon.*

*Her stepdad speeds through the water, massive arms pulling him forward swiftly.*

*Farren waits in the shallow water on her hands and knees, frozen in terror, gaze shifting between Gordon doing his frantic front stroke and the place she last saw her mom's head pop up.*

*Gordon reaches the dingy and treads water, looking around, as if for a clue. He disappears underwater for much too long. When he comes up, he is alone. He jerks his head back and forth and dives again.*

*The effort is repeated twice more before he emerges with something dark wrapped in one arm. He struggles the shape onto the dingy, wraps an arm around it, and backstrokes toward the shore.*

*Her mom's face is a pallid, blue-gray color as Gordon drags her up onto the sand. Farren crawls toward them, still on her hands and knees, and cradles her mom's head while Gordon starts furious compressions.*

*Sand and twigs are tangled up in her mom's mane of black hair from being dragged up the beach and Farren absently picks it clean while she whispers her mother's name, waiting for the breath that will definitely come, just like in the movies. Any second now, her mom will cough up a lungful of water, look up at her, smile, and deliver a cheesy quip that will make them all laugh with tears of relief in their eyes.*

*But there is no such moment. Instead, she watches her mom's lifeless face jiggle with each compression her stepdad makes.*

*"Call nine-one-one," Gordon grunts as he pumps.*

*Farren scrambles back to her chair, fumbles in its mesh pocket for her phone, and curses when it refuses to respond to the touch of her wet, sandy fingers.*

*Gordon performs CPR for over thirty minutes, which is how long it takes the ambulance to make it all the way out to them. They both know it's too late long before but neither of them can bear to accept it.*

*As the paramedics proclaim her mother dead, Farren lets Gordon hold her. Even through her sobs, she can feel the muscles of his arms quivering from the exertion of trying to save her mom's life.*

*She watches from Gordon's arms as a thin white sheet is pulled over her mom's face.*

## 41

Farren let out a shaking breath and turned away from the lake. She hadn't allowed herself to think about that day for a long time. Years. She'd forgotten how hard Gordon worked to save her mom—had deliberately refused to acknowledge it since the day he told her about Melinda. She swiped at tears that had apparently been falling for some time now.

The bed of the koi pond was nothing more than a muddy hole with the plastic lining removed. A few worms slithered through the muck, thick chunks of soil adhering to their repulsive, glistening bodies.

Had the tribe come here just for the hard drive? What possible use could they have for something like that? Blackmail?

Not her problem anymore.

With no other place to go, the only thing to do was to clean and patch up the cottage. She kicked herself when she realized she hadn't brought any supplies with her; no food, clothes, nothing. And it wasn't as if she could order a pizza out here—even if she wasn't an hour away from the closest delivery place, she did not have a good explanation for the smoldering wreckage out front or the bullet holes in the walls.

She'd have to risk going into town for some supplies. Not Maggie's Knee, she'd drive out to Fissing or Pinedale.

First she would have to find some cash; the only money she had was in her backpack, which was almost certainly either in police custody or the trunk of Gordon's cruiser, which both amounted to the same thing. There had to be some stashed away in the summerhouse.

She made her way back inside and was trudging through the mess to the master bedroom, where the likelihood of there being cash was the highest, when she noticed the body.

It had been easy to miss on her path from the front door to the back, hidden as it was on the floor on the other side of the couch and under a pile of debris. All she saw at first was a foot sticking out from under a torn throw pillow. She moved toward it and was about to call out to whoever it might be when the head came into view.

Farren screamed.

She didn't recognize the obliterated face, there was too much blood from where the poor man's head had been half blown off.

The room spun around her. She steadied herself on the nearby couch. Her hand landed on a rough fabric draped over the cushions and, more to avert her gaze from the body than anything, she looked down to see what she was touching.

A tan shirt with the Maggie's Knee Sheriff's Department crest. Her blood froze.

Gordon was here. Or had been here. Had he been

involved in the shootout? She dared not hold onto the hope he'd taken some or all of the tribe into custody, but she could at least entertain the possibility. Gordon could have received reports that the tribe was headed here, then rallied the troops and taken them by surprise. That would explain the obscene amount of shell casings scattered around the place. She could see it in her mind; the tribe holed up in the cottage, maybe with the mystery man on the floor as a hostage, then Gordon and the rest of the department show up and there's an epic showdown. It would explain the car wreckage and the destruction of the cottage. What other explanation could there be?

Staying at the summerhouse was suddenly out of the question. Even if she did manage to repair the damage, she couldn't stay here with a dead body and she sure as hell wasn't about to try to dispose of it. And now it occurred to her the police might return to go over the crime scene. She had to hurry.

Giving the body a wide berth, she made for the bedroom hallway. She would give herself five minutes to pack up anything useful, then head out. To where, she no longer had any idea. Her best bet was to find enough money to get some food and maybe a motel room for the night. She could figure out the rest of the plan once she was far away from all this.

Looking inside her old room gave her pause. It had been ransacked, same as the rest of the cottage, but it still filled her with a sense of nostalgia. The single bed she slept in was tucked in the corner with the circus glass pendant light hanging over it, unbroken. She'd read by the orange-red glow of that lamp for more hours than she could count. Next to the bed, her bookshelf was facedown on the floor, paperbacks scattered around it, many of them with pages and covers torn out.

She left the room, sickened.

Crossing the hall, it first appeared as if the door to the master bedroom was standing open. Then she noticed the cracked plaster in the doorframe. Standing in the doorway, she saw the hole in the opposite wall, just beyond the bed. Shards of the door were scattered over the comforter. Like the door had been blown off its hinges by a bomb.

The master was a fairly large bedroom so it took her until she'd fully stepped inside to spot the gigantic set of feet, clad in custom-made shoes she recognized all too well. They'd been cobbled by Nick, who had also put together the impromptu prosthesis she'd used for most of her time in the Congo.

"Guppy?" she whispered.

A rank odor of sewage mixed with heavy copper hit her. There was blood everywhere.

She made herself take another step into the room, and spotted Gordon.

42

He looked small. Reduced.

Gordon was crumpled on the floor as if he'd been thrown there. A huge dent in the wall above him suggested that was exactly what happened.

He was a mess of gore. Blood pooled around him but she couldn't tell where the majority of it came from. One of his legs was bent at a sickening angle, something jagged poking into his pants where the bend occurred, what was likely a broken bone protruding through his skin. His body was covered in blood from a dozen injuries. One shoulder was dislocated, the arm hanging as if it had been tied in place with an old shoelace. The hand on that arm was crushed almost beyond recognition, fingers bent, broken, and bloody in a way that gave it the appearance of an absurd sea creature. The index finger looked chewed off.

Gordon's face was almost unrecognizable. His jaw was canted at a severe angle, one eye no more than a bloody pit, and there was a visible dent in the top of his head, where it appeared a lot of the blood came from.

Farren managed to turn her head to the side just before the vomit sprayed from her lips and all over one of Guppy's feet. She hadn't eaten much in the last twenty-four hours and most of what came out was a thin, yellow fluid, though she did recognize bits of leftover lasagna in the mess.

Guppy was facedown on the floor, one arm over his head as if he'd fallen asleep there. Farren watched his back for any sign of breathing but he was still and lay in his own lake of blood.

Next to Guppy was another familiar body, this one with a hole through her neck. Farren didn't think her heart could break anymore, but the sadness she felt seeing poor Barb's body lying there almost matched what she felt for Gordon. She'd known Barb almost as long as she'd known him. The woman was always patient with her, always kind. Farren got a birthday card from her every year, accompanied by a home-baked treat. This year, for Farren's eighteenth birthday, Barb had made her a red velvet cupcake so big Farren had to eat it over the course of two days.

A wheeze startled her so badly she screamed and ducked, covering her head with her hands.

Gordon's chest rose and fell almost imperceptibly. She fell to her knees at his side and waved her hands over his body, looking for an uninjured place to touch. She found his left hand and held it softly in her own.

"Fair?" he gasped, almost too quiet to hear. Every breath of his was accompanied by a rattling sound from within his chest, similar to the sound of a playing card flicking against the spokes of a bike tire.

Tears spilled from her eyes. "Yeah, it's me, Gordon. I'm gonna call for help."

She couldn't tell if the next sound he made was another wheeze or a laugh.

"No," he whispered. "Too late. They'll arrest you." Through his broken jaw, the words came out garbled and barely understandable.

"You need a hospital."

He coughed, winced. "They took something."

"Who?"

But she knew who. And she knew what.

"Girl who killed Melinda," he breathed.

"Doesn't matter," Farren said, starting to stand. "We need to get you help. It doesn't matter if they arrest me."

She almost made it to her feet before he stopped her. It must have hurt for him to do it but he pulled her closer to him with the hand she held.

"You have to stop her. Stop *him*."

She wanted to play stupid. To ask what he meant. But she'd been told already, just didn't want to accept it.

Could she have prevented what happened to Gordon? Gotten ahead of the tribe and claimed the hard drive, or at least got him out of here?

No, even if she'd made it here sooner, she couldn't stand up to the firepower the tribe brought with them, and there was no reasoning with Sasha.

"I'm sorry," Farren said.

Gordon moved his broken hand toward her as if to comfort her. She took it gently with her free hand and cradled it in her lap, trying not to think of all the shattered bones she could feel moving under the skin, trying not to imagine what Guppy had done to him before Gordon fired enough bullets to fell the simple giant.

"I'm sorry I blamed you for so long," she said, suddenly sobbing. "Sorry I made you suffer for wanting companionship. My mom needed the same thing after my dad died and she found it in you. I should have known you needed someone. Should have tried harder to be as good to you as you always were to me, even when I was a total bitch.

"When you started dating Melinda, I let myself forget how close we all were and blamed you for my mom's death, told myself you never loved her. But you did everything for us. You tried so hard to save her. And you loved her so much. Loved both of us."

Gordon removed his shattered hand from her own, lifted it to her face, and dragged one useless finger down her cheek before letting the hand drop. A slow breath came out of him, and he was still.

Farren sat for a long time with his hand in her lap, wishing, regretting. All he'd ever done was love and care for her, even after her mom was no longer in the picture, and all Farren had done is try to drive him away.

A chill came over her and a rushing sound like white noise filled her ears. At first, she assumed it was shock or sorrow or both that caused the sensation, but when she finally looked up from Gordon's ruined body, she saw the clouds had let go and a windless rain was showering the cottage.

Gordon and the mystery voice in the Orchid Room both said she needed to stop Z or Sasha or both. Yet neither of them could give her an idea of how or where to start. But she had been shown already, hadn't she? When she'd had her vision of the past, of her dad's last months alive, she'd heard a voice that did not belong to Z. A voice that sounded a lot like the one in the Orchid Room. It had told her to *see*.

It was suddenly obvious where the tribe was headed.

She pulled the comforter off the bed, shook the shards of glass and plaster from it, and draped it over Gordon. Next, she took the top sheet and covered Barb.

Farren refused to cover Guppy. He could be sweet and the violence he'd inflicted had either been because he was afraid or had been manipulated into it, but she couldn't forgive him for killing Gordon. Or Bonzo.

She planted a final kiss on the top of Gordon's head, through the comforter already becoming saturated with his blood, and left the room.

The rain drenched her the instant she stepped out of the cottage. She stood for a minute and let it wash over her, rinsing the tears from her face and Gordon's blood from her hands. Closed her eyes and took a deep breath through her nose, focusing on how the moist air felt as it filled her lungs, then releasing it through her mouth in a whoosh.

Soaking wet, she dropped into the station wagon, turned it around, and left the summerhouse behind for good.

43

Stacey crouched next to the bridge abutment, watching the violence unfold and praying he was hidden well enough. He couldn't believe what he was seeing.

But he'd known something was going to happen, hadn't he?

It had been a weird week.

From the moment he'd seen those two kids pulling the sled —everyone under thirty was a kid to Stacey—he felt like a storm was brewing. And sure, there were absolutely threatening clouds gathering overhead, but it wasn't precipitation Stacey had been fearing. This felt like something much bigger.

After losing the kids he'd been following through the woods, something had stirred in Stacey; an unshakeable need to be somewhere and do something to help Farren.

Even as he'd walked into the sheriff's office, he'd known it was not what he was meant to do. What else could he hope to accomplish, though? He hadn't been able to track the kids worth a damn, and hadn't seen any sign of them since. But he'd had to perform some kind of action to feel like he was satisfying the imperative that tickled at the back of his mind like a particularly strong urge to fix.

And that was another weird thing. Stacey hadn't felt the desire to shoot, snort, or smoke much more than a cigarette since seeing those kids and feeling what he was starting to think of as a Calling come over him, capital C and all. He couldn't remember the last time he'd been completely sober. Years ago, at least. He'd even thought he might have avoided any form of withdrawal, until just before dawn this morning when he'd woken up shaking in a puddle of his own vomit.

And now this.

From the moment he woke, he felt compelled to sit exactly where he cowered now. He'd hardly taken the time to brush the puke from the nylon unitard he wore before scaling the sharp slope leading from underneath Jessop's Bridge, where he slept last night, to the spot he now occupied, next to its abutment.

So he'd been present and accounted for when the explosive crunch of vehicle-on-vehicle resounded from the bridge. Stacey had looked over the short wall in time to see a school bus full of teenagers backing up from the wreckage of a minivan. Through the van's windshield, Pietro could see a woman with her head resting on the steering wheel. There was fresh blood splashed against the interior of the glass.

The bus had reversed and turned so that it blocked the entire road crossing the bridge, and did so too fast to give the sedan behind it time to move. The bus easily caved in the front end of the car while simultaneously driving it backward, into the car behind it. An instant later, a final, smaller car had added itself to the wreckage, plowing into the vehicle in the rear.

Stacey had been ready to run out into the chaos swiftly building on the bridge's narrow road to offer help. Now he was beyond relieved he'd hesitated.

Seconds after the bus came to a halt, the doors opened, and its occupants flooded out, streaming to the vehicles in teams of five or six. Everyone on the bus was in their teens, some of them barely even looked old enough for high school. They ran whooping and hollering with all manner of weapons raised, garden implements and tools mostly, though one kid had an actual ninja sword. A lot of them were armed with guns, though all but a few remained holstered.

Two of the kids went straight to the van, tore the driver's door open, and dragged the woman from her seat. She regained consciousness as they did so and immediately began to thrash and scream at the top of her lungs. The two guys who had pulled her out of the van held her down while a blonde girl of maybe fifteen strode toward them, a pitchfork in her hands. Before Stacey could look away, she raised it and plunged the tines into the woman's throat. Her screams turned to a ragged gagging sound and her thrashing quickly slowed to stillness. The two guys dragged her lifeless body to the railing, forcing Stacey to duck down further, though it was impossible to conceal himself any more.

They didn't seem to notice him as they dumped the woman's body over the railing. Stacey watched it topple and plummet the fifty feet into the roiling river. The water was moving fast today and the current swept the body away in an instant.

Holding both hands over his mouth to stifle the sobs,

Stacey forced himself to take another look at what was happening on the bridge. The guys who had dumped the woman's body were back at the van and were now pulling a screaming girl of eleven or twelve from the back seat. They held her still in the same way they'd held the woman who had presumably been her mother. An older girl, maybe in her twenties, dressed all in black, strode toward them. It took Stacey a second to realize this was one of the two he'd tried to follow through the woods. Only his hands clasped over his own mouth kept him from gasping at the realization.

The girl in black held something in her hand that Stacey couldn't see from where he hid.

"No, no, please no," Stacey muttered to himself.

Kneeling in front of the sobbing youth, the girl in black held the thing in her hand up. The instant the crying girl looked at it, her sobs stopped. Stacey could see the change in her demeanor as her tears dried up. The boys helped her to her feet and led her back to the bus. She seemed to be going willingly and Stacey could swear she was smiling now.

"What the shit," he whispered.

"Becca, Hamji," the girl in black shouted.

A slender girl with a backward ball cap and a dark-skinned dude holding a machete jogged over to her. Both wore guns on their hips. The girl in charge said something to them and they both nodded their apparent agreement. Then she put her hands to the sides of her mouth and hollered, "Back on the bus!"

The chaos came to an immediate halt. Only now did Stacey see that the occupants of the cars piled up behind the bus were dealt with in the same way as the woman in the van. Only the woman's daughter, it seemed, had been spared.

The kids filed back onto the bus. Relief washed over Stacey as he watched them climb back aboard. Within minutes, the bridge was empty again.

Except that wasn't right. The two who had been called over—Becca and Hamji—remained on the bridge. As soon as the bus was gone, the two left behind set about moving the vehicles. It didn't take Stacey long to realize they were barricading the bridge. But why?

He slumped to the ground, back against the bridge. Had to assume he was safe from discovery.

Because somehow he knew his job here wasn't finished.

## 44

Something was happening in Maggie's Knee. Farren had seen signs of it on the road leading into town but hadn't known what they meant at the time. Even now, she could only guess at what was going on.

She'd barely registered the first car in the ditch; an old, rusted pickup that could have been sitting there for ages for all she knew. The next one was a newer sedan and was off the road, nose pointed into the ditch, same as the truck. Only since this car was newer, it was more obvious that something had forced it off the road—the driver's door was dented in and there was a scrape of yellow paint running from bumper to bumper. There didn't appear to be anyone inside.

Jessop's Bridge, on the only road leading into town from the west, was barricaded with abandoned vehicles. It looked like a roadblock out of a post-apocalyptic movie, especially under the gray sky, and with the rain coming down as it was. Farren stopped the station wagon in front of the bridge and got out. The only sounds were the roar of the river and the drumming of rain on the hoods of the cars and the bridge's tin roof.

She spotted the first body at almost the same instant she stepped onto the bridge; a guy who had maybe been in his fifties was hanging half out of the passenger door of one of the cars blocking the road, held in the vehicle by the shoulder strap of his seatbelt. He stared up at the sky, eyes wide and mouth agape, as if in fear of the rain. His throat was cut from ear to ear. The violence didn't disturb Farren as much as the word carved into the guy's forehead. ZIIS was spelled out in his skin, the rain having washed the blood away so Farren could see parts of the man's skull under the separated flesh.

Was the tribe taking over the town? Slaughtering everyone in it? Where were the police?

Farren continued past the guy hanging out of his car. She felt like she should do something for him, pull him out of the car and cover him with something or, at the very least, brush his eyes closed the way they did in movies. But she had to keep moving. No idea what Sasha and the tribe were up to, but she needed to put a stop to it if she could.

Was Jasper with them? Had he participated in the violence at the summerhouse and on the bridge? She couldn't picture him doing so, not after all he'd told her and what they'd been through together. She was sensible enough to admit to herself he was, after all, one of the leaders of the Congo, and had subjected an unknown number of kids to nightmarish deaths. Just because she and him kissed didn't mean he was suddenly a good guy. But she sensed goodness in him. Or, at the very least, the desire to be good, which had to count for something.

A noise from behind a minivan pushed up to the bridge rails disturbed her from her thoughts. A survivor?

"Hello?" she called, realizing it was exactly what she would be screaming at the TV screen for, had she witnessed some hapless slasher movie bimbo doing the same thing. But she had to check. Couldn't leave anyone to die out here. After all, someone had saved her back when that train had ripped away so much of what she loved and took for granted.

A whimper from behind the same minivan. Someone was definitely hurt.

She jogged to the wreckage, casting her eyes left and right to keep an eye out for danger.

The second she came around the side of the van, something slammed into her stomach, knocking the wind from her, and sending her stumbling backward. She doubled over, clutching her stomach, mind racing to determine what had stolen her breath.

A feminine figure stepped toward her, shaking her hand as if she'd punched Farren in the face instead of the soft flesh of her stomach.

For a brief second, Farren was sure it was Sasha. Then her brain caught up to her eyes and she recognized Becca, the night guard from the Congo; the first tribe member she'd seen armed with a handgun. That same gun was holstered tightly to her hip. Farren had the presence of mind to be thankful the girl hadn't just shot her from hiding.

"Man, she was right," Becca said with a chuckle.

"Who?" Farren gasped, already knowing.

"Sasha said you'd be coming this way. I don't know how she knew. Wait." Becca raised her hands to her head as if to keep it from exploding. "Did Jasper let you out? He did, didn't he? That's why she sent him there."

Farren's heart skipped a beat. "She sent him to the Orchid Room?"

Becca stage-laughed, throwing her head back and holding her belly. Then, an instant later, the laughter died and her face went serious. Something dark flickered in her eyes. She reached for her gun.

Farren had been focusing on her breathing, trying to get her wind back. Her lungs still weren't operating at full power, but she had no more time to wait. It was move now or be shot where she stood.

She sprung at Becca. With her left hand, she batted the other girl's hand away from the still-holstered gun. Drove her right fist into Becca's face, connecting just below her eye. The night guard's head snapped back and she stumbled away from Farren, though she kept her footing. Becca spit a red wad of phlegm onto the road. Ran at Farren.

Her strength caught Farren off-guard. She looked like a scrawny stoner but fought like a cage match champion. She slammed an elbow into Farren's temple, took hold of her around the throat, swept her legs out from under her. Farren landed hard on the asphalt, just managing to keep her head from slamming into it.

"Hey!" a guy shouted from off to their left.

Farren turned to see Hamji approaching them, gun raised in both hands, aimed at her. There was a sword or something hanging from his belt. He inched toward them, obviously gearing himself up to shoot Farren, the girl he'd been playing baseball with for the last few months.

Becca was straddled over top of Farren and leaned back so she sat on her kneecaps, giving Hamji a clear shot.

Movement behind Hamji caught Farren's eye; a blur of hot pink. Becca was looking down at her, arms crossed over her chest, so she didn't see what Farren had.

Hamji stopped and assumed a shooter's stance, feet shoulder-width apart, both hands on his gun.

And then the pink was there again and Farren couldn't help smiling.

Stacey, clad in a bright pink sleeveless unitard, stepped up behind Hamji. He held an enormous stick, more like a log, in both hands, and swung it around, connecting with Hamji's head and sending him crumbling to the ground.

"Hey, bitch," Stacey said, blowing Farren a kiss.

Becca was too stunned to move at first. Farren bucked, trying to shake her off, which only served to remind Becca she was there. Before Farren could get out from under her, the other girl leaned forward and threw punches into her face.

The blows didn't last long. Farren only barely got her hands up when the weight on her disappeared. Stacey had yanked Becca off Farren and now held her in a chokehold, his face turning red from the exertion of strangling her. Becca writhed and slapped at Stacey's hands but her efforts quickly slowed. Her eyes rolled up into her head and her own face went the same shade of red as Stacey's before darkening to a deep purple. Her arms went limp, entire body slumping forward.

Stacey held on for another thirty seconds or so, shaking from the effort. When he realized he was strangling a corpse, he let out a disgusted, throaty sound, and released Becca, letting her drop to the asphalt. He turned to Farren and gave her a reassuring smile that was half terrified grimace.

Farren was about to say something, probably thanks. She forgot what it was the instant the machete buried itself in Stacey's neck.

Stacey stumbled toward her as Hamji pulled the blade from his throat. A fountain of blood followed. Stacey put a hand to the gash in the side of his neck. Opened his mouth and blood bubbled from it.

Farren screamed.

She got to her feet but Hamji shoved her back on her ass. He pointed the machete, still dripping Stacey's blood, at her. One of his eyes was swollen shut where Stacey had clubbed him.

Farren's world was white noise. She couldn't hear herself scream. Couldn't hear Stacey's dying gurgles.

Hamji pushed her again. Seemed to be herding her to the railing of the bridge. Maybe his plan was to send her into the river. Without much choice in the matter, she backed away obediently.

She'd just made it to the railing when thunder crashed and Hamji shuddered and fell to the ground in a heap, his machete clattering onto the road. Blood gushed from a hole in the back of his head. Just beyond him, Stacey lay propped up on one arm, soaked in gore, Becca's gun in his free hand. He caught Farren's eye and winked.

Then he collapsed.

## 45

It took Farren twenty minutes to reach downtown on foot. The day was warm in spite of the rain but she still felt chilled to the bone, soaked as she was. Throughout her journey, she spotted more cars run off the road, many with the telltale yellow paint scraped onto them.

She'd spent more time than was probably wise crying over Stacey's body. He'd been dead when Farren crawled over to him on her hands and knees, tears and snot falling from her face. She held his head in her hands and kissed his forehead, his cheeks, his lips. Thanked him over and over for saving her. Why he'd been at the bridge was a question she would puzzle over later. Right now a grief-filled gratitude left her numb to speculation over anything aside from how she was going to stop the tribe. And even then, she had nothing to go on. All she was certain of was where to find them.

So she marched on, through the rain, trying not to think of her friend's corpse still laying on Jessop's Bridge, now covered with the only thing Farren could find; a tattered blanket from the wreckage of the minivan.

Every house she passed had windows smashed or the front door ajar, often both. ZIIS was spray painted on each house in stark, black letters—most often on the garage or front door. She could tell she was catching up to the tribe when she came across dripping, washed-out depictions of the name, obviously spray painted onto the houses as the rain fell.

As she passed what must have been the twentieth house with ZIIS painted on it, she realized something had changed. Before coming to the Congo, she'd seen the name spray painted on an alley wall and it had messed with her so much she'd almost been run over. It used to be that she couldn't even think the name without feeling as if bugs were crawling around in her head. No more. As though it lost its grip on her, even as it seemed to have strengthened its hold over the tribe.

And its grip on them had almost certainly increased. She couldn't imagine the majority of the tribe taking part in something like this otherwise. Most of the kids were decent enough people—rebellious, sure, but not *evil*.

The word came to her unbidden and unexpected. But it fit. Her mother had taken her to church a couple of times a month when she was alive, so Farren had an idea what the word was supposed to mean, but she'd never really considered the reality of such a concept. Evil as an objectively bad, purposeful force was a hard thing to conceive of. But to see the work of the kids she'd played baseball with as recently as a week ago, the notion was hard to deny. What was happening here was inarguably evil.

Main Street was in ruins. Every storefront, facade, and display window smashed and trashed. Several of the businesses were on fire, the flames contained within the buildings thanks only to the heavy rain. Cars were pushed off the road up onto the sidewalk. The insides of many of the shops had been strewn about onto the street and sidewalk; food, furniture, books, even money littered the ground.

Bodies everywhere. Most were fallen on the street or sidewalk, unceremoniously left where they'd died. A few were still strapped into the seats of their cars. Three bodies were stacked one on top of the other atop a bistro table in front of Bred n' Stu, Farren's favorite restaurant. A couple of bodies were draped over the frames of broken display windows like casualties in a spaghetti western shootout. More lay in heaps in the doorways of businesses.

ZIIS was spray painted on every available surface so the whole street paid homage to the presence in the Museum.

It occurred to Farren she hadn't seen any bodies of children or teenagers. Had kids been fortunate enough to stay out of the way or were they being spared?

She turned the corner off Main Street, went east onto Kessler Street, and immediately saw why the police weren't anywhere to be found. Even in the rain, the sheriff's office blazed, flames licking out of the shattered windows, smoke billowing out of the building and blending into the gray cloud cover.

It took her a moment to spot Byron Hatfield among the ruins of the sheriff's office. The late mayor's body hung by the neck from the flagpole out front, the actual flag nowhere in sight. Had he been alive when they put him up there? Probably. Farren had never liked the man but her heart ached at the way he'd been killed. Nobody deserved that. A strong breeze caused the body to sway, making the flagpole creek. She had to look away from it then.

Thunder rumbled in the distance, echoing off the mountains. A minute later, lightning flickered in the sky to the west. As if it had been waiting for its cue, a strong wind blew in, raising gooseflesh on Farren's soaked arms and neck.

The flames lashed out of the windows of the sheriff's office in response to the wind, hungrily lapping at the extra oxygen.

Farren pressed on, trying not to think about how many people had been in the building when it was set ablaze. She knew almost everyone in the department, being the sheriff's stepdaughter. She thought of Barb, dead in the summerhouse with her throat blown open.

Anger overlapped the fear she'd been feeling up until now, anger at the tribe but also with herself. They'd destroyed everything she loved, her home, her family, and her only real friend. But she'd cast most of that from her life years ago, out of a selfish sense of bitterness. She had a lot to be miserable about but she'd blamed those who tried to help her and had pushed away any and all attempts at love and comfort. Was it because it felt better to be angry or because she didn't want to risk losing more people she loved? Might never know for sure.

Kessler Street turned into Pine Valley Road, which ran southward out of town before terminating at the KnowMe Technological Park, nestled in the low valley of evergreen-covered hills. On clear days the main tower was a beacon in the distance, the glass reflecting the light of the sun, making the entire complex seem alight with golden fire. Today it was hardly visible through the rain and against the charcoal sky.

Farren expected to see actual flames or smoke rising from

the tech park but, from this distance at least, things looked relatively peaceful at the southern end of town.

It took her more than half an hour to walk Pine Valley Road all the way to the tech park. By the time she reached the main gate, the storm had picked up in full. Thunder exploded overhead, ricocheting off the surrounding hills in deafening blasts. Lightning flashed and forked all around her. As if the entire storm was centered on the KnowMe Technological Park.

Aside from the storm, the tech park looked quiet. It had been years since Farren was here last but she remembered it being full of activity, with people coming and going like honeybees in a hive. Now there was no movement at all. She would have thought she was in the wrong place if not for the bright yellow school bus that had been driven into the side of the guard hut, blocking off the driveway. ZIIS was spray painted on the side of the bus in large, black letters.

She steadied herself with a breath and stepped around the bus, into the tech park.

46

Jasper groaned and tried to stretch out but, of course, he could not.

There was no moment of confusion spent wondering where he was or what happened to him. He remembered with perfect clarity being grabbed by Guppy and then Sasha covering his face with that stinking rag until everything went black.

Everything was still black, even with his eyes open, but he knew where he was. He wanted to scream but was terrified into silence by whatever lurked in the shadows of the Orchid Room.

Why was he still alive? Did whatever was waiting in the dark want him to be conscious before it struck? Would it torment him before destroying him? He knew very little about the place he'd imprisoned and doomed so many kids.

He deserved this.

The ropes he was tied with dug painfully into his wrists and ankles. Struggling only made it worse.

Jasper held his breath and listened, straining to hear if anything else was in here with him, nearby or otherwise. The only sound was his own blood pumping in his ears. He let his breath out slowly, silently.

Maybe the thing in here, the monster or whatever it might be, recognized him as the one who *brought* food and not the one who *was* food. He doubted the immunity would last long when whatever it was figured out there was no one else with him and that he wasn't going anywhere.

As if in response to that thought, there was a heavy thump from some distance behind him.

He resisted screaming, barely.

Half a minute later, another thump, followed by several more. Impossible to imagine what might be making such a noise. Farren's frog monster or some new horror? There could be a new nightmare at every stop of this lunatic carousel.

Now he struggled in earnest, feeling around for some weakness in his bonds but finding only tight, efficiently tied rope. It bit into his skin, scraping at his flesh with every twist.

*Thump, thump, thump.*

Closer. Like monstrous footsteps.

Figuring the thing knew he was here anyway, Jasper used his whole body to hop the chair forward. Paused. The noise didn't repeat itself, so he did it again, and again. No clue if he was making any sort of progress, or even going in the right direction. Another hop and the chair tipped forward. He threw his weight back, praying for an advantage over gravity. He overcorrected and the chair fell backward and slammed to the floor, causing him to bite down on his tongue. Blood immediately filled his mouth and he made himself swallow it, convinced his pursuer might be able to smell it.

He spasmed in a panicked last attempt to save his own life.

A heavy snuffing sound came from high above and behind him. It really could smell his blood. He imagined it opening its mouth to scoop him up. Hoped it would be quick.

As Jasper waited to be grabbed and eaten, the door opened —much closer than he hoped it would be—and a dull, gray light spilled into the room, affording him a glimpse of something enormous and pachydermic. A screech of pain or frustration or both came from the thing and it darted back with frightening speed. Out of the dark came the sound of a commotion, more screeching, an unsettling squelching sound, and finally a pained howl that was abruptly cut short.

Trying not to dwell on what those sounds could mean, Jasper looked to the source of the light and had to squint. In the gloom of the Orchid Room, the dull light of the overcast day looked bright as the sun itself. Someone stood at the threshold, indistinct.

"It's me," Kevin said.

Jasper sobbed as his assistant came to him, dropped to his knees, and cut the ropes around his hands.

"How?" he asked. He was shaking too violently to manage much more.

"I skipped out on the meeting this morning," Kevin said, cutting the ropes at Jasper's feet. "I was watching from my place when everyone marched out of there like a bunch of zombies. Saw them carry you out. Followed Guppy until I knew where he was bringing you then went back to see what happened with the tribe."

"What are they doing?" Jasper asked, sitting up and rubbing his wrists.

"They all armed up and marched out of here. The place is empty."

"They left?"

Kevin gestured over his shoulder with his chin. "Nick was standing guard. I hit him pretty hard in the head. Hope I didn't kill him. You want to tie him up in here?"

Jasper stood slowly. "Nick was just following orders."

"I don't know about that," Kevin said. "They all seemed—"

Something whipped out of the dark and grabbed Kevin hard enough to silence him. A tendril that looked comprised of solidified swamp muck wrapped itself around his body like a grotesque vine. Kevin's eyes went wide. Bones popped within him. Blood sprayed from his mouth.

Jasper made a grab for his hands just as the thing yanked Kevin up and backward, wailing, into the darkness. His cries were cut off with a series of nauseating crunches, followed by loud slurping.

Every one of Jasper's instincts told him to back out of the Orchid Room and nail the doors shut. How could he just leave Kevin here, though? He'd literally saved Jasper's life at the expense of his own.

He, Jasper, deserved to be the one devoured by some tentacled monster in the dark. He certainly didn't deserve to have anyone giving up their life for him. And for what purpose? It wasn't as if he had anything positive to contribute to the world. All he did is kidnap, steal, destroy, and kill. Just to have something exciting and different in life, to be someone who mattered. It would be easy to blame Sasha, but he was responsible for his own part in this. He could've turned away at anytime.

Part of him wanted to walk into the gloom and end it all;

save the world from whatever bad shit he'd do next. But that would render Kevin's sacrifice meaningless. Didn't he owe it to him to try to do some good with it? Or was that self-preservation talking?

At the very least, he could try to stop whatever it was Sasha and the tribe planned on doing, if it wasn't too late already. Once that was done, he could put an end to himself and whatever horrible things he might do in the future.

Mind made up, he turned to leave. He took a step toward the door and it slammed in his face, sealing him once more in the dark of the Orchid Room.

A voice like low thunder spoke in his mind.

*We need to talk.*

## 47

The KnowMe Technological Park wasn't abandoned after all.

Farren had made her way through the park, past all the shops, cafes, boutiques, and most of the offices without encountering any signs of life.

Plenty of death though. Bodies were strewn everywhere around the park; it had been a complete massacre. Just as in town, all of the bodies were adults, which at least made sense here, because of course kids wouldn't be hanging out in the tech park. But hadn't anyone tried fighting back? Or had the instinct not to hurt kids been so great in everyone that they simply fled, however ineffectively?

Along with the human bodies, the grounds were also littered with the smashed and smoking remains of various security robots used in the park. Some were aerial drones that appeared to have been shot out of the sky, while others were box-shaped, wheeled vehicles. Many of the latter looked as though they'd been hammered on with baseball bats or crowbars or whatever the kids were armed with. Some of the human bodies looked like they'd suffered the same fate. Farren tried her best not to look at them as she passed.

By habit from ages ago more than instinct, she made her way to her dad's old office. As it turned out, it was the right way to go. Beyond the lawn sprawling out in front of the building, hundreds of kids surrounded the low structure. Farren was mostly blocked from their view by the large trees on the lawn.

There were far more kids here than had been living in the Congo. This explained why there were only adult bodies in Maggie's Knee—the kids had all been recruited somehow. That could explain the graffiti all over town; a sort of siren call that apparently only affected kids.

Was that why only young people were recruited to the Congo to begin with? Before now, Farren believed it was because kids were easier for Sasha and Jasper to control. But what if the truth was more encouraging than that? What if the influence of ZIIS only extended to kids and adolescents?

Then how to explain her dad?

The best theory she could come up with was the hold was more powerful over young people. Maybe ZIIS could take a limited hold over an adult who had seen its name. Maybe her dad had simply had a more childlike mind, which made sense to Farren from what she remembered of him. He'd been a big kid at heart; fond of his video games and *Star Wars* action figures. And the more time he spent so close to that statue in the Museum—which ZIIS apparently lived in—the more powerful the hold became. Until her mother had broken it. The power of love or some gushy stuff like that.

None of which would help her get past all these kids. She needed a plan. Or a distraction.

She turned around, looking for something she could use, and found herself staring into the faces of half a dozen dazed looking people her age, one of whom she sort of knew.

"Priya?" Farren said.

The doctor's daughter didn't respond. She, along with the others she was with, had a far-off look in her eyes.

Three of the kids were big guys, two of whom stepped around Priya and grabbed Farren before she could make a move to evade them, not as if it would have done her much good. Looking behind her, she could see another dozen kids marching toward her, all armed with guns, knives, or blunt weapons.

Farren fought and twisted in the guys' arms but they were incredibly strong; she could hardly budge in their grip, even soaked as they all were from the pouring rain.

The third guy, a stocky, dark-haired kid, wrapped strong arms around Farren's legs, stifling her kicks. He lifted her legs up and Priya took hold of Farren's prosthesis.

"No!" Farren shouted at her. "Stop, Priya!"

The girl didn't seem to have heard—all of them appeared to be listening to a faint broadcast, heads almost imperceptibly cocked to one side.

Priya wrenched on the prosthesis, twisting Farren's leg and making something pop in her knee.

Farren screamed and thrashed uselessly.

The prosthesis socket dug into Farren's flesh as the other girl reefed the artificial foot back and forth. The boys joined in and pulled Farren backward as Priya yanked on the foot.

It finally came free of her leg in an agonizing final tug.

Priya lobbed the prosthetic foot over her shoulder and it landed with a single bounce on the lawn.

The guys holding Farren dropped her onto the grass. She landed on her left side, knee blazing.

Priya stood over her, looking down with that blank look that said something else was there with her, looking out at Farren through her eyes.

ZIIS.

"Fuck you," Farren said to it.

Priya took a step backward, wound up, and drove a foot into her face.

Pain exploded in Farren's head, and then she was on her back, staring up into the driving rain as her vision went gray.

Jasper was floating. At least it felt that way. He assumed it had to do with the complete lack of light, his mind conjuring the sensation in response to not being able to see, as if convinced this sort of blackness could only exist deep in space.

How long had he been drifting?

There'd been a voice. How long ago? Days? Weeks?

*You seek absolution.*

There it was again, a thunderous whisper in his mind, a hurricane gale with a tongue. There was power in the voice. He feared it but did not think it wanted to harm him. It was what he imagined swimming next to a blue whale might be like; fearsome enormity and power kept in check simply because there was no good reason to unleash it. Get in its way though ...

*I am no whale.*

The response to his inner thoughts didn't surprise him. By now Jasper was almost used to things reading his mind.

"What do you want?" Jasper whispered, though he was pretty sure he didn't have to speak the question out loud for it to be heard.

*Your help.*

Jasper almost laughed. "I don't know about that. The last bodiless voice in the dark that wanted my help had me kidnap and kill before locking me in here to die."

*You wish to make up for what you've done. To absolve yourself.*

Jasper kept silent.

*You can stop him.*

"Who?"

*The one calling himself ZIIS.*

Though he couldn't see whatever it was that spoke to him, Jasper thought he sensed an eye roll when the voice named the thing he'd been serving for the last couple of years.

Now he did laugh. "I wound up in here just for considering standing up to it."

*You considered running away.*

Ouch. But true.

*Bring him here.*

"How am I supposed to do that?" he asked.

*Bring his avatar.*

Jasper had no idea what this thing was talking about.

*In the Museum. The child.*

"What child?" Jasper shouted now, frustrated this thing had locked him in the dark only to bid him to do its dirty work.

Thunder roared, shaking the air around him, as if he was standing in front of the world's largest subwoofer.

*Bring him.*

"You said that," Jasper cried. "There's no child in the Museum, I've been there."

*You will see.*

"Bring him here and then what? You'll take care of him?"

*Not I. The portals will soon shift. Go now. To save her. To save everything.*

"Her who? Farren?"

Jasper wasn't sure why Farren was the first one who came to his mind but he had a feeling it must be who this thing was talking about. Everything started going to hell right around the time they'd brought her in. And Sasha said Farren's dad had helped prepare the Congo for them, which couldn't be a coincidence. Farren was gone though—had done exactly what Jasper couldn't bring himself to do. But this new thing in the dark said she was in trouble and, for whatever reason, he believed it. Wanted to help her if he could.

"I have some questions," Jasper said, trying to sound braver than he felt. "Before I do anything for you."

He thought he sensed a bristling, but mercifully tolerant, frustration with him.

*Ask.*

"What is he? ZIIS, I mean."

*A devourer. He feeds on suffering and death but also on his own vanity. To see or hear his name is to open the door of your mind to him. To acknowledge him is to give him power.*

It was a vague answer but Jasper was certain he wouldn't get much better than that.

"And who are you?" Jasper said. "Let me see you."

Even as he said this, goosebumps broke out on his arms and neck. Asking to see this thing felt akin to holding his hand out to a wild grizzly bear.

*To see me could render you useless.*

"I should just believe you've got all of our best interests in mind?"

*I've made no such claim.*

"I see you or I do nothing. I think I'm about ready to die anyway."

He didn't feel as courageous as he made himself sound and he was fairly certain the voice knew it.

*Glimpse me then and begone.*

Without further warning, the darkness exploded in a light so bright Jasper felt his eyes burning. He squeezed them shut against the radiance but it penetrated his eyelids, searing his retinas.

Something took shape in the afterimage behind his closed eyelids. It was mountainous, taller than any skyscraper by a mile, and vaguely man-shaped. Something circular spun and gyrated behind—but also within—the figure, which at the same time seemed to morph and contort. The man-shape changed to something avian, then to something with massive, curled horns protruding from the top of its head, and finally to something with countless pointed teeth.

In the image behind his eyelids—*through* his eyelids—the thing looked down at him and Jasper felt smaller than he ever had and knew his existence, his impact on all other existence was infinitesimal. Even if he decided not to do what the voice was commanding, he realized, something or someone else would. The question was how much time would pass before then? How much death would occur in the meantime?

He opened his mouth to tell the colossal, shapeshifting thing before him he would do what it asked. Before he could speak, it raised an arm and pointed at him. He felt sudden, intense pressure in his chest, as though he'd been struck with a hammer, and then he was soaring backward, hurtling away from the light cast by the thing.

The world went dark again. A different sort of dark than what he'd experienced in the Orchid Room. This was the natural dark of having one's eyes closed. He blinked them open and, at the same time, felt drops of rain pelt his face.

He sat up in the grass outside the Orchid Room, soaking wet. Wind whipped the trees around him, howling through the branches and joining in the chorus of the rain and thunder.

Nick lay next to him on the grass. His skin was pale, lips blue. The side of his head bore a deep gash the rain had washed the blood from. Jasper lay a tentative finger on his neck and knew immediately Nick was dead.

He felt bad about it, he'd genuinely liked the kid, but at the same time, he felt some relief that now he only had to worry about himself.

And ZIIS.

$$49$$

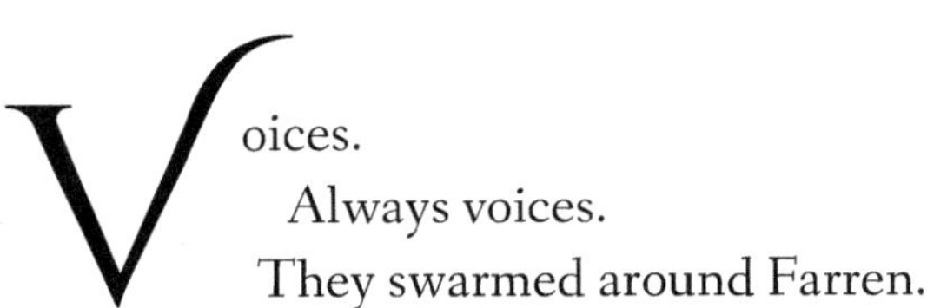

Voices.

Always voices.

They swarmed around Farren.

Her head hurt too much to focus on what they said. The pain came in waves, intensifying until she didn't think she could bear it, before receding just enough that she could form a coherent thought. She wondered vaguely about what level of brain damage she'd suffered since being kidnapped in the spring.

She shifted and was entirely unsurprised to find herself tied to a chair. Again. The movement awakened the nerves in her lower half and she remembered having her prosthesis ripped off. Her leg felt like it had been attacked with a cheese grater.

The pain in her head still jockeyed for attention, making her nauseous enough she thought she could puke at any second. Couldn't let herself do that, though. Had to focus, to stop the tribe.

Breathing slowly to prevent anyone nearby from noticing she was awake, she focused her breath and tried to center herself. A ghost of Anika's soothing voice whispered in her throbbing head, guiding her, telling her to seal the pain away in a little box and put it aside for later consideration. Slowly, the waves of pain in her head settled to a gentle lapping. Her vestigial limb still screamed in agony, but that too had already become a bit easier to bear.

The voices gained clarity and she wasn't surprised to recognize Sasha's among them. Three people were arguing; Sasha, another girl whose voice she didn't recognize, and a guy she thought might be Danny.

"Just get it done," Sasha snapped.

"Trying," the other girl said. "There's no button on here that says Hack System or Override All Security Protocols. I'll get it but I need some time. Maybe you should have kept the boss alive."

Must be Morgan, the tribe's hacker.

"There isn't much time," Danny said. "State police are coming. Who knows who else they'll bring in once they see the mess."

"We'll be protected as long as we need it," Sasha said without much concern in her voice.

Farren opened her eyes a crack but her head was down and all she could see were the tops of her own thighs. Scotch tape, a lot of it, was wrapped in a thick band around her legs—apparently, they'd forgotten to bring duct tape. Or hadn't planned on her showing up.

She lifted her head and opened her eyes the rest of the way, unable to help the gasp that escaped her lips.

They were in her dad's old office. Sasha and Danny stood

behind an enormous oak desk bare except for a quad-screen computer setup. Morgan sat in the chair, between Sasha and Danny, typing furiously, head swiveling between monitors. The trio were covered in blood. Only Morgan looked like she'd bothered to clean herself off, likely to prevent blood from gumming up the keyboard.

Behind the three at the desk, Jeremy Hrongar was pinned to the far wall with at least half a dozen random objects. A huge knife was buried to its hilt in one of his shoulders, what appeared to be the handle of a spear in the other. Someone had shoved a katana through his belly. Two smaller knives and a garden trowel were planted haphazardly in his torso.

Farren had only met the founder of KnowMe once, at an office party her dad brought her and her mom to. Hrongar—a blond, handsome man of average height and trim build whom Farren had long held a bit of a crush on—had shaken her hand and, in a soft Scandinavian accent, complimented her hair, which she'd been wearing long and full. She remembered him being an exceptionally nice grownup and knew her dad had been fond of him, even if the founder, president, and CEO of KnowMe was often vilified in the media. Seeing him pinned up like an insect added to her mountain of sadness. The violence of it, she was sickened to realize, did not affect her much. She'd seen so much already today.

"She's awake," a guy said from somewhere behind Farren, startling her.

Sasha and Danny looked up from the screens. Morgan didn't seem to have heard. Sasha grinned.

Farren ignored them and looked over her shoulder. The office behind her was crammed with kids from twelve to eighteen. They spilled out into the hallway beyond the office and watched through the windows and open door. Many stood or sat on furniture which had been dragged in front of the office, all vying for a glimpse at what Morgan was doing.

When Farren looked forward again, Sasha stood directly in front of her. She held a short-bladed hunting knife down at her side.

Sasha kneeled in front of Farren. "You know, when we first recruited you, I thought he wanted you more than me."

"Jasper?" Farren said, head still woozy.

Sasha cackled. It was a horrible, forced sound, not unlike a seagull with shards of glass caught in its throat.

"I had Jasper's balls so firmly in my hand, they've got my fingerprints embedded in them," Sasha said.

"Gross," Danny said from behind her.

She shot him a look then turned back to Farren.

"Morgan's working on the little treat your old man left for us," Sasha said, jerking her head back at the desk.

"Treat?" Farren said, genuinely confused.

"He put a bike lock on our update."

"It's more than a bike lock," Morgan said without looking away from the screens. "It's an advanced encryption standard. It's not a two-fifty-six but it's still turned this hard drive into a miniature Swiss bank vault."

Sasha rolled her eyes. "Morgan will get through it either way."

"Eventually," Morgan muttered.

Farren snickered. She couldn't help it.

"What's funny?" Sasha snapped.

"This whole thing," Farren said, feeling genuine laughter coming on. "This pathetic monster you all follow who hides in the Museum, in the dark, while you try to find friends for it on social media."

Sasha stood straight. "Watch your mouth."

She looked upset by what Farren said—threatened by it.

Farren decided to run with it. She craned her neck so she could see most of the kids behind her.

"You know the thing you worship hides in the statue of a little boy?" she said to them. "There's a giant fucking black bear in there. Why would he choose the little boy if he could be a bear? Unless he's scared of it."

Most of the kids still wore blank expressions but some now looked at Farren with a degree of thoughtfulness. She might be getting through to some of them.

Before she could open her mouth to cast more dispersions on their pathetic loner of a deity, a searing pain erupted in her right leg. She screamed and turned to see Sasha inches from her face, gritting her teeth in a ferocious grin. She clutched the handle of the hunting knife, the blade of which was stuck deep into Farren's inner thigh. An alarming amount of blood spilled out around Sasha's hand.

Sasha wiggled the blade back and forth, mincing the muscle in Farren's good leg.

The pain was blinding. Farren didn't think she'd felt anything like it since losing her left foot. And now, because she couldn't watch her mouth, both of her legs were rendered all but useless. But even through the pain, she held onto the knowledge that what she'd said had an impact on some of the kids in here with them.

A strange look came over Sasha's face, one that was almost wistful. It lasted a second before hardening into stony resolve.

Deep in her guts, Farren knew Sasha was finally going to kill her.

Morgan spoke from behind the monitors. "I'm in."

Sasha's face lit up. She stood and marched back to the desk, Farren's blood dripping from her hand.

The knife remained buried in Farren's thigh.

"Run it," Sasha said, leaning over Morgan once more.

"Done."

Morgan sat back and laced her fingers behind her head.

Danny put a hand over his mouth.

Sasha leaned in so her face almost touched the center screen.

"It's really happening," she said.

With their attention on the computer, no one appeared to notice Farren shifting in her seat, adjusting her legs, and bringing the blade of the knife in her thigh into contact with the tape, which didn't quite adhere to her wet jeans. She grit her teeth against the white-hot pain and moved her leg up and down. After a few agonizing attempts, the blade bit into the tape enough to make a small notch. Farren sawed at it, every movement its own torture. For a dizzying moment her vision wavered and she was sure she'd pass out. She focused on her breathing. Tried to cram this new agony in the mental box with all the other pain she'd already shoved in there. How much more could it hold?

More typing from Morgan as Farren continued to cut at the tape, a thousandth of an inch at a time, no doubt doing further permanent damage to her leg.

"What are you doing?" Sasha snapped.

Farren froze. But Sasha was looking down at Morgan.

"Forcing the update," Morgan said. "Instead of waiting for

everyone to perform it manually, this will push it through on all but the most secure devices, especially since the KnowMe platform has its own security protocols that supersede those of the devices it's installed or used on. Maybe one percent of users take the time to read the fine print and make the necessary adjustments before agreeing to terms and conditions. The other ninety-nine percent basically give the app permission to do whatever it wants, whenever it wants. Pushing an update through is easy."

"How long?" Sasha asked.

Morgan shrugged. "How often do people check their KnowMe? Most users will see it in a matter of minutes, maybe seconds. In this time zone anyway. Global integration will take some time. Less than a day before the majority are with us."

Without a plan or even knowing what her next step would be, Farren moved the knife faster, though the pain threatened to undo her. She wasn't even halfway through the tape.

The first KnowMe user to open the app once the modified Kraken update had been pushed through was fifteen-year-old Aubrey Mantel in Redford, Michigan. She was stretched out on the sofa in the living room rewatching *Wednesday* on Netflix but not really paying attention. She'd been thinking about Russel Tompkins at school and how his smile made her heart flutter and her skin tingle.

A ping on her smartphone alerted her to a KnowMe notification and she snatched it off the coffee table. Every notification was a possible message from Russel.

She looked at the phone and frowned. Instead of a message from her crush, she was treated to a notification saying the newest KnowMe update had been installed. Didn't they just do one? Whatever.

Aubrey tapped on the notification out of habit, not because she cared at all about whatever the update was for, then stared at the phone for a full minute, transfixed.

The phone fell from her hand as she stood and went to the

kitchen. On the phone screen was a black and white image. A single word.

Aubrey emerged from the kitchen carrying a knife in each hand—the two biggest in the block—a dazed look on her face. Through the living room, up the stairs, and into the office where her mother was wrapping up some accounting for the small business she ran out of their home.

Aubrey didn't respond when her mother asked her what was up. Simply closed the door behind her.

The screams went on for almost an hour.

z

KASIM SHIRANI, twelve years old, was playing basketball with his father, Liaquat, in their driveway in Elgin, Illinois when his father's phone dinged. Kasim's father was a busy man, so it was rare they got to shoot hoops uninterrupted.

"Time out," Liaquat said, forming a T with his large, dark hands. "Might be work."

Kasim took a swig of water from his bottle while his father frowned down at the phone, wiping droplets of sweat from his brow.

"Important?" Kasim asked without bothering to swallow first, water running down his chin.

His father held the phone out to him. "Just an update. Do you know what this means? A new rapper, maybe?"

Kasim took the phone and peered down at the screen. The word was strange; four letters that read the same backward and forward. ZIIS was certainly no rapper he'd ever heard of.

Staring at the word, it felt as though something was squeezing its way into his head, using sharp claws to find purchase and pull itself in deeper. For a brief second, Kasim thought about a burrowing rodent forcing its way into a tight space. Then things changed.

LIAQUAT WATCHED his son frown over the phone screen. He didn't think much of it when the water bottle fell from Kasim's hand, or even when the boy started walking toward the open garage; he had always been a distracted child.

When the phone fell from Kasim's hand and shattered on the driveway, Liaquat shouted after him but his son didn't seem to hear.

Even when Kasim emerged from the garage carrying a pair of hedge sheers, Liaquat didn't think anything was terribly wrong. Who knew what kids were thinking, especially these days?

It wasn't until Kasim came directly up to him and sliced through the meat of Liaquat's thigh with the sharp blades that the alarm bells began to ring. But by then it was too late. The blades had cut deep and the man fell hard and fast, splashing in a puddle of his own blood. Before Liaquat could even articulate a rebuke, Kasim brought the blades down into his chest.

Z

JUST OUTSIDE SEATTLE, Washington, in the Hoh Rainforest of Olympic National Park, the Seattle Junior Rangers, a baker's dozen of kids from fourteen to eighteen, gathered around a bigleaf maple tree, listening to Rod Parker, their longtime leader, drone on about the uniqueness of the biosphere they stood in. Most of the kids didn't give a shit about biology or ecology or any ology at all; they were in this for the survival training—the biology lesson was the necessary price to pay before being taught to make snares and build fires from scratch.

Phones were strictly prohibited on this trip so all but three of the kids had brought theirs. When Rod instructed them to bury the devices deep in their packs for the remainder of the trip, about a third of them listened.

Now, as he spoke in reverent tones about how a bigleaf maple could grow over 150 feet tall, Rod was mortified to note several of the older kids had their phones in hand. They weren't even being sneaky about it—he counted five of them holding devices in front of their faces, as if deliberately blocking him out. He'd spent most of his adulthood as an educator and was accustomed to being ignored. This level of rudeness and flat-out disobedience was not something he was used to with this group of kids, though. Sure, some of them gave him the gears every now and then, but they were all good people. They all *wanted* to be here; many had begged their parents to let them go. He stopped talking about maples when the rest of the group pulled out their phones. The kids who first had their phones out then passed them to those few who hadn't brought their own.

"Okay, what's going on?" Rod demanded. "Nuclear strike? It had better be big news for you all to be so interested."

He realized none of them had spoken during the exchange, which had gone on for about two minutes now.

"Rangers!" Rod snapped, clapping his hands twice.

Now they all looked up at him. Good.

He opened his mouth to continue his rant about the maples when he noticed the dazed look in each of their faces.

"Oh, God," he said, mortified that he'd made light of what could have been a terrible news update. "What's going on? Really?"

Brian Doeller pulled the hunting knife from its sheath on his belt. Jesse Nicklebee slipped his pack off, knelt, and unfastened his hatchet. Michelle Mason picked up a branch the size of a hockey stick from the forest floor. The rest of the kids were pulling out tools or picking up branches and rocks from the ground.

Rod chuckled. "Is this a prank? Which one of you is filming?" He looked for the camera lens pointing toward him so he could mug appropriately.

None of them held a camera. All of their phones were now on the ground—strange behavior for adolescents. A second ago they were all but glued to them.

He was about to call an end to whatever game they were playing when a rock struck him on the side of his head and fell to his feet with a soft thump. He looked down at the stone and his vision blurred. Was that his blood on it?

Michelle walked up to him and his last naive thought was she wanted to make sure he was okay. Instead, she clubbed him on the other side of the head with her stick.

The rest of the Junior Rangers moved in then, striking out at whichever part of Rod's body they could reach with whatever was in their hands.

Rod's last thought was at least he got to die doing something he loved, in his favorite place on earth.

He was an unidentifiable mess by the time the Junior Rangers were finished with him.

51

Jasper stood in the main hall of the Museum, truly seeing it for the first time. Gray daylight shone through the windows, illuminating what he had imagined until now as a vast, empty space; one filled with shadowy monsters. Looking at the cheesy but well preserved exhibits, he wondered if he'd imagined everything that went on here before, in the dark. But he knew better.

He'd gone around the outside of the building, throwing rocks at each of the blacked-out windows, allowing the light in before even thinking about going inside himself. Now the floors of the Museum were covered in shards of blackened glass glinting in the dull light. Rain poured in, soaking the walls and floors. Musty, stale air was displaced by the rich scent of evergreens and damp earth. Life replacing decay.

Exhibits in the Museum were remarkably well-preserved. The only sign of age was the generous layer of dust coating everything.

The Pilgrim boy stared out at a horizon only it could see,

painted eyes reflecting wonder and adventure. It looked so innocuous Jasper had trouble believing it could be home to anything other than the wood and wax it was composed of. This had to be the child the voice in the Orchid Room meant. It looked heavy. Should have brought the sled.

Reaching for the statue, he realized he hadn't so much as caught a whiff of ZIIS's presence. Had the light banished him? Was it that easy?

Or was he busy elsewhere?

No point waiting around to find out.

The base of the Pilgrim boy's display came up to Jasper's waist, so he leaned forward, grabbed the statue around the thighs, and heaved.

He was expecting resistance; the feet to be glued or nailed to the base. They weren't. All that kept the statue in place were two-inch-long pegs on each foot inserted into corresponding holes on the base.

The Pilgrim boy slipped easily from the display and Jasper staggered backward under the sudden weight on his shoulder. He only barely slowed his momentum enough to keep from falling on his ass; the statue weighed at least a hundred pounds.

Once he caught his balance, he turned with the Pilgrim boy braced over his shoulder and faced the exit, half-expecting there to be some slobbering monster waiting to eat him up before he could fulfill his destiny or whatever it was he thought he was doing.

The way was clear. No monsters or psychotic nouveau-goths.

His great commission was beginning to feel a bit like a dummy's errand. Sure, he still had to go back into the Orchid

Room with the mannequin—and that terrified him—but he had been expecting a full-blown cosmic battle over it. At least a minor struggle.

It occurred to him, as he bore the statue down the hall toward the exit, that perhaps ZIIS didn't *need* the statue of the Pilgrim kid anymore. Maybe he'd found a new vessel or whatever.

Either way, didn't seem likely the other, slightly more benevolent thing in the Orchid Room would instruct him to do this if there was no hope of it working.

Once outside, he leaned the statue against the Museum wall, stood under the awning, and smoked a cigarette from the pack that had mercifully been left in his pocket when he was put in the Orchid Room. He didn't much feel like smoking, but needed the time to muster his courage before stepping back into that nightmarish building for what he promised himself would be the last time.

He smoked the cigarette down to the filter, pitched it in the dirt, and hefted the statue up onto his shoulder with a groan.

When he turned toward the Orchid Room, Sadie McCallister stood on the path stretching between the two buildings, her deceptively young face watching him with an empty scrutiny he'd seen on the rest of the tribe's faces that morning. A curtain of silver raindrops fell between them.

Jasper struggled to find something to say. He felt nervous, though he couldn't say why; Sadie was a small girl and, at least up until very recently, he'd held a position of authority over her. Yet he still felt like he needed to provide an excuse for what he was up to.

As if she knew what he was thinking, Sadie said, "In a few

minutes, he won't need that anymore anyway." Her voice was husky and low, far from the bright pitch that usually came from her mouth.

Before Jasper could respond, Sadie raised her arm. She held something in her hand. Before he could register what it was, it went off with a *blam* that ricocheted between the buildings, bouncing off into the rest of the Congo and the forest beyond.

He felt the impact a full five seconds after the shot was fired. Looked down to see a ragged hole in his black T-shirt. Even then, he had trouble connecting it to the report of the gun. Still may not have clued in right away if it hadn't been for the blood streaming through the hole.

Sadie already had her back to him and was walking down the path to the creek, gun held in a loose grip at her side as if nothing had happened.

The ground rushed up at Jasper and he was semi-aware of it smashing into his face. Something heavy fell next to him and a blazing agony lit up his hand for a brief second before the fire in his stomach stole his attention back.

Cheek pressed to the hard-packed dirt of the path, he stared into the painted, blue eyes of the statue of the Pilgrim kid whose head had just broken several bones in his hand. The eyes stared back at him with cold, triumphant glee as if to say it had known all along Jasper's mission was one of futility.

Jasper felt cold. The hole in his stomach made breathing an exercise in torment. He could feel his blood pouring through the wound, soaking into the dirt to be feasted on by the worms and beetles that made the soil their home.

He didn't want to look into the eyes of the mannequin anymore, so he closed his own.

## 52

"What is taking so long?"

Farren jerked her head up at the sound of the voice. She had zoned out in her determination to saw through the tape holding her to the chair, focusing on moving her leg up and down, which distracted her slightly from the all-encompassing agony.

The voice belonged to Sasha. She was still behind the desk, glowering over Morgan's shoulder at something on the computer monitors.

"I can't force people to open the app," Morgan said, exasperated. She'd explained it half a dozen times already. "All users have been notified with an alert about the update. They have to actually open the app to see the message."

Sasha tapped Morgan several times on the shoulder. "Do that."

"Do what?"

"Send a message. To everyone. Make it look important."

Morgan chewed her lip. "What do I say to get people's attention? They've won a prize?"

Sasha looked around the office, then said, "Tell them Jeremy Hrongar has been murdered."

Morgan gave her a shrewd smirk and got to typing.

Farren checked her progress. Less than an inch to go on the tape. She flexed her legs against it to see if it would snap and the painful reply from her thigh was so intense she nearly blacked out. Back to cutting, forcing herself to take her time—it would be stupid to get caught now.

"Sent," Morgan said, leaning back and folding her arms over her chest. She leaned forward again after a few seconds and said, "Holy shit, that worked. Open rate just quadrupled."

There was a ruckus behind Farren, but she barely had the energy to focus on it. She was losing a lot of blood.

Wes shoved his way to the front of the room and shouted, "State police are closing in on us! They're at the tech park!"

Sasha shot him a withering look. "Why are we just finding out about this?"

"They switched channels a while back. We didn't figure it out until a few minutes ago."

"We?" Sasha said.

"Me." Wes looked at the floor.

Sasha strode to Jeremy Hrongar's body and pulled the sword from his stomach. She took half a second to adjust her grip and spun in a semi-circle, bringing the blade around with her. There was a shocked silence in the room. A red line appeared around Wes' neck, blood seeping from it. He grabbed at his throat but his fingertips only clawed weakly at the cut before his head slid off and hit the floor with a dull, wet *thump*. Blood fountained from his neck for a second before the rest of the young security chief's body joined his head on the floor.

"Fuck yes!" Sasha shouted triumphantly.

Morgan looked like she was going to throw up.

Which meant there was still some of her there. Maybe ZIIS hadn't fully taken over the kids' minds; there seemed to still be some part of them present, enough to be shocked by the murder of one of their own. What did that mean for the horrific acts they'd all committed? Had they been aware of what they were doing? Were they being controlled?

Two things happened while Farren considered this:

First, faint red and blue lights flashed in the window taking up much of the wall behind the desk. The lights reflected off raindrops, making the entire window alternate red and blue in a dizzying pattern. Sasha glanced over her shoulder at the flickering light and cackled.

"Ten at the windows here and the rest at the front and back doors," she barked, bending over and relieving Wesley's body of his rifle.

Sasha slammed the stock of the rifle into the floor-to-ceiling window. The glass exploded outward and immediately the air in the room was displaced by warm, moist wind from outside. It whipped into the building, spraying Farren's face with hard rain.

Farren hardly noticed. Had been too distracted by the second thing that happened at the same time. She'd cut through the rest of the tape.

She realized she was still moving her leg up and down and forced herself to stop. A fresh, aching pain welled up in her thigh as she ceased the sawing motion she'd kept up for what felt like hours, but realistically must not have been more than fifteen minutes. She forced herself to remain seated, not wanting to give away her success. Still had her hands to worry about, though it did feel as though cutting through the tape over her legs had been the worst of it.

Most of the office had emptied out as soon as Sasha issued her orders. The remaining tribe members were lined up at the window, aiming guns of varying shapes and sizes at a downward angle.

Someone shouted something into a bullhorn, likely providing the tribe with a final warning. Would the police march in here, guns blazing, and kill everyone in sight?

Sasha stood at the window, rifle in hand, apparently unafraid of being shot at.

"What are they waiting for?" she said to no one in particular.

She stuck the Marlin 336 out the window, peered down the sights, and started shooting. An instant later, the rest of the tribe joined in.

53

Jasper lay in the bottom of a canoe, staring up into clouds that swirled and billowed in a way that reminded him of milk poured into black tea. He was transfixed by them; had only seen such clouds in his dreams.

There was no way to see over the edge of the boat from where he lay, but he felt himself drifting steadily in one direction, which led him to believe he was floating along a lazy river. Eagle Creek? No, that trickle of water was barely suitable to float a paper boat down. The craft rocked gently from side to side as it meandered down the waterway. It was soothing.

Where had the boat come from? They might have some stored somewhere in the Congo ...

It all came rushing back to him.

The Congo, the tribe, the meeting, the Museum.

Sadie.

She had shot him.

He grasped at his stomach but, even though he could feel his hands moving, he couldn't seem to be able to touch himself.

He tried to sit up and was met with the same disorienting illusion—it *felt* like he was sitting up but he remained fixed in place, staring up at those frothing clouds.

Was he dead?

*Not yet.*

That voice. The multi-formed colossus he'd encountered in the Orchid Room.

*Your task is incomplete.*

Jasper tried to chuckle but all that came out was a weak cough. "You know I was shot, right?"

No response. The clouds danced and undulated above.

"You can't give me a hand?" he shouted. "Literally, I mean, 'cause I think that statue you sent me to fetch busted mine."

*She needs you to finish it.*

"Who?"

But he knew. This thing didn't seem to be on Sasha's side and, with the exception of the casual acquaintances she kept in the Congo, she and Farren were the only women left in his life.

"Where is she?"

*Waiting for you to do your part. She will die unless you do your job.*

Jasper said, "I put the dummy in the Orchid Room, and then what? How's that supposed to help her?"

Silence.

"Hello?" Jasper called.

He was alone again. Alone, adrift on some kind of spirit river, and expected to finish a job that could very well kill him, if it hadn't already.

The clouds became still all of a sudden, freezing and solidifying into typical patterns. They turned gray and dark.

Jasper felt the boat picking up speed. There was no wind

on his face, nothing moving past; he just *felt* the momentum of the craft.

Before he had the chance to speculate on where he was headed, the canoe came to a lurching halt that jarred him hard enough to send fresh gales of pain throughout his body. Along with those sensations came the feeling of raindrops on his face and body. Wet earth underneath him. He was lying on the path between the Museum and the Orchid Room. Had he ever been in that canoe, or had it all been a dying hallucination?

He closed his eyes. The darkness reached up and embraced him in warm, comforting hands. The pain slipped ever so slightly into that gloom, inviting him to join it. If he gave into it, the pain would disappear completely and he would die. He wouldn't mind dying.

An image from his memory shot up out of the ether and demanded his attention. Farren, standing in his cabin, staring at the books he kept stacked around the place as paper totems of his favorite genres. He recalled the moment they had shared, how she had listened to his story with a guarded warmth in her dark eyes, how happy she'd been when he procured her prosthetic foot. The unexpected kiss they'd shared.

She needed him now.

Before he could give it any more thought, he turned onto his stomach. Pushed himself to his knees.

He'd momentarily forgotten about his broken hand and immediately collapsed onto his belly, the gunshot in his gut teaming up with the broken bones to overwhelm his nerve endings with alarming agony. He puked brown, bloody mush onto the path and vaguely wondered what he'd eaten to make his barf look like shit.

This time he forced himself to his knees using only his left hand. He used the same hand to grasp one of the statue's feet and stood on shaky legs. His vision swam and went gray for a few seconds. There was no way he could do this.

The statue seemed to have doubled in weight since he'd been shot. It was slick with rainwater and his fingers ached as he struggled to grip it. Once he was sure he had it in as firm a grip as he could manage, he took a half step backward, dragging the statue through the mud.

His stomach lit up, like he was being shot all over again. Blood pumped from the hole in him and he wondered how much of it he had left before his body stopped taking orders. He looked up at the sky and let the rain fall onto his face, into his open eyes. Opening his mouth, he took what moisture he could, letting it trickle down his throat on its own, swallowing only when it felt like he might choke.

He had fewer than twenty feet to go, but the rest of the journey was the longest walk he'd ever taken. The statue slipped from his grip a dozen times, smashing his toes twice. Each time he had to stoop to pick the thing up, the pain in his stomach intensified to the point of being unbearable.

Somehow, he got it up the steps of the Orchid Room. Its cold blue eyes stared up at him in accusing rage, forbidding him from going any further. Jasper fully expected the thing to open its mouth and start shouting at him to put it back where he'd found it.

"Ssh. Almost done," he told the Pilgrim boy.

He shoved the door open and dragged it into the gloom of the Orchid Room.

54

The bulk of the shooting lasted only a few minutes.

Within seconds of Sasha opening fire, six of the kids at the window with her had been dropped by gunfire from outside. Four of them lay lifeless on the floor—one, a boy who couldn't yet be in high school, lay on his back crying and holding bloody hands to his equally bloody side. The sight broke Farren's heart; it was like something out of a war documentary.

The sixth person who'd been shot was a heavy teenage girl who had taken one in the shoulder. She clawed her way back up to the window and returned fire with a big revolver that bucked wildly with each shot. The big girl got off three shots before a chunk disappeared from the top of her head in a spray of blood and she fell to the floor one last time.

Sasha was laughing as she fired round after round into whatever forces were amassed below. Farren had no idea how many cops were down there, but it had to be a lot judging by the number of bullets coming through the window. The rounds ripped chunks out of the walls and ceiling, making plaster and insulation rain down on everyone in the office.

It was now or never.

Farren leaned forward in the chair and brought her bound arms around the back of it so they rested between it and herself. Then, whimpering at the pain in her thigh, she bent and looped her taped hands under her legs, musing that there was one positive thing to missing part of a leg. Hands in front of her, she brought the tape to the knife and swiftly sawed through it, ignoring the stabs of pain from the blade still lodged in her leg.

Stupid of them to have used Scotch tape to secure her. But what could she expect? They were kids. She had barely entered adulthood herself. None of them were versed in the complexities of warfare or taking hostages.

Farren felt bad for a lot of the tribe, most of whom appeared to be dead or dying at this point, sacrificed for some cowardly spirit who hid in the effigy of a little boy; an attention seeking sadist who had to prey on kids whose minds weren't yet capable of protecting themselves from it. And for what? All so it could be famous? ZIIS seemed to need the fame, to draw power from it.

Power.

The word sent Farren's mind reeling back to a day when she was just ten years old. Her dad had brought her to the office that afternoon; he had the day off but needed to pick some things up. When they got to the office, someone had a technological emergency they needed his eyes on so he'd asked one of his colleagues, a rail-thin woman in her thirties named Kim, if she could keep an eye on Farren. Kim had agreed enthusiastically and asked Farren if she would like a tour.

Most of it was stuff she'd already seen—desks, the big lounge, storage, the mop closet—but Kim also took her somewhere she'd never been before; the basement. Specifically, the server room.

"All of KnowMe's main servers are here," she'd explained to Farren, opening the glass door into a chilly room filled with rows of towering servers. Lights blinked on them, seemingly at random. "Millions of people's data is stored on each of these. If they ever went down, KnowMe would be done."

Farren asked what happened if there was a power outage.

Kim had laughed and said, "We have so many redundancies in this place—redundancies means back up plans in case things go wrong—that nothing short of an explosion right inside the room could do anything to hurt them. The room is surrounded by multiple firewalls, kept underground in one of the most secure private facilities in the state, and backed up by a dozen different power generator systems."

Now, sitting in an office alive with gunfire, Farren focused on one particular thing Kim had said. *Nothing short of an explosion ...*

Farren ripped the remaining tape away without trouble. She allowed herself to breathe, to cram all of her pain back into its box, and dropped to the floor.

The pain in her thigh was not to be ignored and she had to bite her cheeks to keep from screaming. She dragged herself forward in an army crawl, ignoring the glass and shards of plaster that tore into her.

Wesley's body was sprawled out behind the desk. The big girl with the revolver had fallen over the top half of his body and Farren saw what she needed poking out from underneath her.

Wesley's head stared at her with empty eyes from a few inches away, beads of red and blue lights from outside reflecting off his facial piercings. Trying not to look directly at the head, Farren slipped the red bandana from it and wrapped it around the wound in her leg without removing the knife—she'd heard somewhere it could make the injury worse if she took it out.

Leg bandaged, she slithered under the desk, through shallow pools of blood, barely clearing the gap between it and the floor, and scraping her back along the rough underside. The knife sticking out of her leg hit the floor more than once, making her nauseous with pain each time. She reached a hand out and was within a couple of inches of her goal when a running shoe came down on her wrist. She yelped and tried to pull it back. The foot held her in place.

Morgan sneered down at her. "Gotcha."

Before she could say anything else, a bullet entered her chest, dead center, in an explosion of blood. Morgan gurgled something and collapsed at Wesley's feet.

Farren reached for Wesley's belt, where what she needed was attached to a carabiner clip. She took the whole clip, snatched one more thing on impulse, and made her retreat.

Once out from under the desk, she forced herself to stand. Without her prosthetic foot, she had no choice but to put all her weight on her injured leg, which immediately protested. She hobbled out of the office, whimpering deep in her throat, muting it not because she was afraid of being heard but because she might break down in uncontrollable sobs if she let any of it out.

The gunfire had slowed considerably. How many were dead on each side? Faint pops came from below, the surviving tribe members shooting it out with the remaining police force.

"Hey!"

Farren had just limped through the office door when the shout froze her in her tracks. She turned to see Sasha pick a handgun up from the desk and aim it at her.

Farren kept her right hand behind the wall just outside the office, hidden from view.

Sasha's eyes dropped to what Farren held in her left. "It's too late for that. Even if you blow us up, he's won."

"I'm in it for the catharsis," Farren said, wriggling the carabiner in front of her, jostling the grenades attached to it. "You want one?"

Sasha smirked. "You won't get the pin out before I put a bunch of new holes in you."

They stared at each other for a long moment, long enough for Farren to steel herself against what needed to be done. It was a heavy thing to do, even with her life—and the lives of many others, she thought—on the line. She took a deep breath through her nostrils. Felt the air fill her lungs, the blood pumping in her veins, oozing from her leg.

Sasha took another step and that was all Farren needed. She raised the handgun she'd liberated from Wesley's belt along with the grenades. She'd flicked off the safety and cocked the gun as she'd been limping out of the office; it had been surprisingly easy to do, she'd seen enough action movies she knew what to look for, though she had no idea if it would work. Or if it was loaded.

The first report told her it was and that she was a terrible shot. No idea where the bullet had gone.

Sasha froze in her tracks, eyes wide. She bared her teeth. Took aim at Farren.

Farren fumbled with the gun, trying to figure out if she needed to cock it for a second shot. What kind of gun was it? Automatic? Semi-automatic? What did those things even mean? She'd been counting on taking Sasha out with one bullet, if she'd needed to use the gun at all.

Sasha laughed, obviously enjoying watching Farren fumble and fail.

Defeated, Farren met her eyes. Gripped one of the grenades, bracing herself to yank it from the carabiner, preparing herself for the bullets to rip into her, and hoping she could at least stop Sasha before dying.

But she couldn't do it. There were other kids bleeding out in here and she couldn't take them to the grave with her. She didn't owe them anything, but she was certain they'd had their minds screwed with and weren't acting entirely of their own volition. She lowered her hands, the clip of grenades dangling from her finger.

"Coward," Sasha said.

And then a hole ripped itself open in her chest. Sasha looked down at a red blotch blossoming on her shirt. Three more rounds burst through her torso. She wiggled her gun in front of her, as if waving Farren off with it. Then she collapsed.

Farren wasted no time. She took the stairs as fast as her leg could carry her. It gave out after the first step and she went down hard on her backside, sliding painfully the rest of the way down. Took every ounce of her will to pick herself up again at the landing. The staircase to the basement was even longer and she went down this one on her butt, not wanting to risk falling again.

The basement was as cool and dark as she remembered. Fortunately, its only purpose was to house the servers and she had no trouble finding the room they were stored in.

She'd just pulled the glass door to the server room open when something crashed into her from behind.

It wasn't a hard hit but Farren's thigh was beat up enough that, without her prosthesis, she wasn't able to keep her footing. She went down hard on her knees, the carabiner of grenades slipping from her grip and skidding across the floor, out of reach.

A feral scream ripped through the air. Farren turned to see Sasha, covered in blood, bringing her fist around in a cross-hook. The blow took her directly in the jaw. Stars exploded in her vision and she fell the rest of the way to the floor.

Sasha was on her in an instant, hands clawing at Farren's face and neck. One of her knees found the knife in Farren's leg, planted itself there, pushing the blade so it cut further into her. The pain was blinding. Farren slapped weakly at her attacker. Tried to buck Sasha off. But her strength had fled.

Hands clamped over Farren's throat, cutting off her airway. Sasha brought her face down so that it hovered only a couple of inches above her own.

"It's gonna be nice to finally kill you," she hissed through the exertion.

Farren's vision swam. It was over.

55

Jasper stood just inside the door to the Orchid Room for a long while, waiting for something to happen. The mannequin of the Pilgrim boy was too heavy for him to hold up, injured as he was, so he'd dropped it on the floor as soon as he was inside.

"What now?" he called, his voice too weak to carry far.

What did he expect, though, a celestial police force to bear the statue away in handcuffs?

It was getting harder every second to stay on his feet. He put a hand out to steady himself on the wall and almost fell right over. The wall was gone. The door too, which at some point shut without him noticing, had disappeared. The only solid thing he knew existed for sure in this room, besides himself and the dummy, was the floor. He turned in slow circles, breathing in loud, ragged gasps. Listened for the sucking sounds of whatever the thing was that had taken—and presumably eaten—Kevin.

He almost passed it off as hallucination when he spotted

the dim glow ahead of him. At first it was only an empty pool of light, as if an invisible streetlamp was pointed down at the floor. He took a step toward it and a vague form coalesced in the light.

Jasper bent over with a groan and lifted the foot of the statue. The sickening pain in his stomach intensified when he stood upright.

Took him longer than he thought it should to drag the statue to the pool of light. At times it seemed as if the shape under the light was getting closer, growing more distinct. Other times, it seemed to be moving farther away from him.

When he finally got close enough to see what the shape was, he dropped to his knees, the statue crashing to the floor next to him with a dull *thock*.

"Farren!" he cried, taking her face in his hands.

She lay with her eyes closed under the pool of dim, amber light, covered in blood, with a nasty hole in her thigh.

A cough escaped her throat and she pushed herself upright, whipping her head left and right, no doubt trying to figure out where she was. Finally, she looked at him, then down at the statue.

"Am I dead?" she asked in a faint, rasping voice. "Did she kill me?"

Jasper sat back on the floor to give her some space. "I honestly don't know." No need to ask who she meant.

Farren's eyes dropped to his stomach and grew wide in alarm.

"Just a flesh wound," he said.

She didn't laugh.

He wanted to say something reassuring but the pain in his

gut suddenly flared up, causing him to double over. He felt a hand on his back.

"You're not okay," Farren said.

"No shit," he muttered. "Sadie's a hell of a shot."

Farren sat next to him, put her arm around him. He lay his head in her lap.

"I think she won," Farren said. "Sasha, I mean. I think she killed me."

"You don't seem dead to me."

Farren stuck her legs out and wriggled her feet. Both of them. "I only have both feet in my dreams."

"What happened?" Jasper said.

"There was a shootout at the KnowMe park."

"The tech park? Why there?"

"I guess ZIIS feeds on attention," she said.

Jasper nodded weakly. It was the best he could do in the way of agreeing emphatically. "I've been told something similar."

Farren went on, "As he is, he's only strong enough to manipulate young people's minds and influence them to do his bidding. Having Sasha as his number one is a big benefit since she comes with her own commanding presence. For some fucked up reason, people want to do what she says. But ZIIS wants more than just a compound full of kids. So he gets my dad to set this place up, make it nice and easy for someone to just move in. Then ZIIS figures he might as well get this guy to do the whole job since he doesn't seem to be resisting. He sent my dad to manipulate a KnowMe update that would basically integrate with people's government ID, banking, everything; Orwellian levels of control over user information. ZIIS plans on piggybacking on the update, sending his name out to everyone who has it, and simultaneously getting access to almost anyone's information. I think the main thing was getting his name out, he just saw the Kraken update as icing on the cake.

"Then at the last minute, my dad flipped him the bird and destroyed it all, with the exception of the backup he hid at our summerhouse. For that, ZIIS had him killed and took my foot. Pretty sure he killed my mom too. He didn't kill me because he thought he could use me to find out what happened to the update, which he did by sending me back in time and watching along. No idea why he couldn't just go back himself. The only explanation I can come up with is that he's a little bitch."

Jasper snickered weakly.

Farren said, "I think he needs the weaker minds of kids to help him get more powerful and, once he has enough, he'll be able to upgrade to adults. Even then, I don't think he can do anything on his own. Not without his proxies. He can scare us, he can send other people after us, but he can't actually do anything to us himself."

It all made sense to Jasper. It explained why the giant, shape-changing thing he'd met in here spoke so derisively of ZIIS.

"Where are we?" Farren asked, looking around.

"Orchid Room," Jasper whispered.

He felt her go rigid next to him.

"Why are you in here?"

He nodded down at the statue on the far side of him. Apparently, she hadn't noticed it until now.

"You brought it here? Why?"

*I asked him to.*

Farren jumped.

Jasper recognized the voice. The big guy. He was glad she heard it too.

A man stepped into the pool of light. A normal sized man. Nothing close to the great, many-formed being Jasper had seen before. This man was a middle-aged Japanese guy with a wispy goatee and an old blue, red, and white baseball hat on his head with a logo that resembled the horns of a bull. It wasn't any team he recognized. The hat itself, though, he was sure Farren had worn during ballgames in the Congo.

"Dad?"

Farren pushed herself up to standing.

*You have a job to do, Kaeru.*

Jasper watched Farren's back. She and the man, who was apparently her dad, stared at each other for a long moment.

Finally, Farren said, "You're not really him."

The man gave her a warm smile Jasper would have done anything to receive from his own father.

*No.*

"You pretended to be him. To keep me here," Farren said, anger creeping into her voice.

The smile remained on the man's face. Jasper realized his mouth didn't open when he spoke.

*A necessary deception.*

Farren's voice shook, "You left me his hat."

Her father, or the thing appearing as her father, took the hat from his own head and wrung it gently in his hands. *A copy. Like this one.*

"You can copy hats and imitate my dead dad but you can't fix your own problems?"

He leveled his gaze on her. *The problem is not mine. I am*

*merely an arbiter. ZIIS has been allowed to play for too long in this place.*

Farren threw her hands out to her sides. "So you just let him kill my parents?"

*I don't decide who lives or dies. All beings are entitled to their own free will, to live or die as life dictates. I am allowed minimal interference, which even now I am stretching the limits of. But as I said, he needs to be stopped.*

"Why do you care?"

*That is my job.*

A long silence passed between them. Jasper wished he could see Farren's face. The expression on the man before her was impassive.

"Am I dead?" Farren asked, swiping a hand under her nose.

*You are outside of time. Practically speaking, you are still being strangled.*

"What?" Jasper meant to shout but could only croak. No one acknowledged him.

"So what do I do?" Farren asked.

*He has touched you, focused his energy on you. He is vulnerable to you. And to her. Only one of you can end him.*

Jasper assumed Sasha must be the other person he spoke of.

Farren said, "What do I do?"

*Touch his shell. You will be brought to him, to his true form.*

"Then what?"

*I have already helped you more than I am permitted. But hear me; it will only be yourself and him. You will be the only two beings existing in his plane. Do you understand?*

"Yeah," Farren said. "I'm on my own. As always."

She turned away from the man and almost immediately he faded into the darkness. Jasper could make out moisture around Farren's eyes. She knelt next to him and put a warm hand to his cheek. He leaned into it.

"Good job getting him this far," she said, looking into his eyes. "I don't think you're a bad dude. Maybe a little stupid sometimes, but all guys are."

He opened his mouth to respond, but it had become hard to catch his breath. An icy hand spread from his stomach up through his chest. His head was suddenly very heavy. The world canted to one side and he realized Farren was laying him on the floor, which felt like cold stone on his skin. He barely felt her soft lips on his own but when she pulled away from him, there was warmth in her eyes; something he wasn't used to seeing when people looked at him, not for the last few years anyway.

"Be good," she whispered.

He watched her turn to the statue and reach her hands out to it. She hesitated, pulled back slightly. Then she looked at him and grinned—a fierce showing of her teeth he'd witnessed when he'd watched her at bat. Without any more hesitation, she grabbed the statue's face in her hands.

As soon as she touched the Pilgrim boy, the light started to dim. Jasper felt himself dim with it. The pain was gone. He took a ragged, gasping breath and let it out in a final sigh.

While he breathed his last, he noticed Farren and the statue were no longer there with him. His last thought was of her, *for* her. If he'd been raised to know such things, he might have recognized it as a prayer.

56

Farren stood on the train tracks from her dreams. They spanned the same desert of smooth, round stones. The air was still as a tomb. She listened for the telltale shriek of the train's whistle but the world was silent. The desert stretched on forever in each direction, the tracks cutting through it in a straight line from horizon to horizon. The cloudless sky above was a sickly shade of purple, the color of a bruise.

With no better idea of what to do, she began to walk along the tracks. Her feet were bare and the only sound was them slapping on the smooth stones of the desert floor.

The whistle blared, a deafening, metallic scream. Right behind her.

She turned and came face to face with the thing she'd seen in her last dream of this place. Taller than any mountain. Taller than anything *could* be. The top of it somewhere in the stratosphere. It was miles away but even from that distance,

Farren could see its many eyes were focused on her. Mile-long, segmented limbs carried it along in a scurrying motion that should have been impossible for its size. It raced toward her, the ground quaking in response to the enormous, bladed feet smashing against the tracks. It shrieked, the warped train whistle slicing into her ears. At the same time, she felt the thing scratching around in her mind, looking for a way in.

How could she possibly make a dent in something like that? It was tailored to maim and destroy. Could crush her without effort.

Maybe the thing posing as her dad overestimated her. Or, more likely, it had sent her here to die. How did she know it wasn't working with ZIIS?

Thinking its name seemed to intensify the invasive, almost perverted sensation of it prying inside her head. Along with the scratching of claws, she sensed—could almost physically feel—a rough tongue desperately licking around the edges of her mind. It took power from her attention.

Understanding came like a hurricane.

The answer was at once obvious and ridiculous. There was no other choice. Any stand she tried to make against the thing would get her killed. The voice in the Orchid Room said she and ZIIS would be the only things in existence. If nothing else existed while she was here, it stood to reason the thing towering before her relied on her attention for sustenance. If she could cut that off entirely ...

She turned her back on it.

The thing shrieked. Coincidence?

Farren stopped moving altogether. Took a shaking breath. Counted to five.

The monster, ZIIS's physical body in this place, bellowed in obvious rage. The feeling of something scratching to get inside her head had stopped.

She bent over and brushed imaginary dirt from her feet. Could sense the thing directly behind her, towering over her. The track shook and she had to plant her hands on the ground to keep from toppling over.

It was stomping its feet. Throwing a tantrum.

She focused on her left foot, enjoying its presence.

ZIIS shrieked

Something long and sharp pierced Farren's back. The pain was absolute and she cried out, arching her back. She could feel the thing pushing through her flesh, past her ribs, separating them, boring its way to her heart.

The ground fell away from under her. She was being lifted. Air rushed past as she went ever higher; two dozen feet, fifty, two hundred. It was going to eat her, she realized with unshakeable certainty. It was raising her to its mouth, somewhere above the clouds.

Panic, which could be the death of her, snapped its fingers for her attention. She needed to calm down, to put ZIIS out of her mind, even though it was killing her here while Sasha was killing her in another reality.

Farren closed her eyes. The thing stuck inside her scraped against her rib cage, poked into her lungs. She ignored it, breathing slow and deep.

She commanded herself not to think of what was happening to her. Crammed the pain into that overstuffed mental box.

Farren concentrated entirely on her breathing. Convinced

herself she was alone. Conjured white noise in her mind. Focused on it. Pushed out all other sensations until there was only the imagined static and her breathing.

In.

Out.

She felt herself drifting instead of being lifted. Gave in to the sensation. She was in a river, on her back, just drifting.

The white noise resolved into the babble of water splashing against the edges of a shore. She allowed herself to be carried down the river, utterly alone, at peace.

A smile crept across her lips and somewhere far off, itself alone and unacknowledged, ZIIS screamed.

Z

THE PEACE WAS SHATTERED by an intense pressure on her throat. Gunshots from somewhere above. Blinding pain in her thigh. Smoke burning her nostrils. And someone grunting on top of her.

Farren's eyes flew open. Sasha's face was an inch from her own, teeth bared, lip jutting, spittle dripping.

Farren grabbed her by the ears and ripped with every remaining ounce of her strength. Sasha bellowed and released her grip. Farren bucked her hips, throwing the other girl off.

Sasha fell to her hands and knees. Looked around wildly as if she'd lost something.

"What did you do?" she screamed.

Farren wasted no time. She scrambled to where the carabiner of grenades lay on the floor.

"Stop!" Sasha screeched.

Farren pulled herself to her foot and hopped to the door, ignoring the pain in her thigh.

She yanked the door open and pulled one of the grenades from the clip. Tore out the pin.

Her head was jerked backward.

Sasha had a handful of her hair. She slammed Farren's face into the metal frame of the door. Stars exploded in her vision. Sasha pulled her back for another strike and Farren yanked her head away, short hair slipping easily from Sasha's grip.

She tossed the grenade through the door.

"No!" Sasha screamed, throwing herself after it.

Farren yanked the pins on the other two grenades and lobbed them into the room. She took two big hops toward the staircase before the first grenade went off, shattering the glass door of the server room.

An agonized howl came through the door and Farren wondered how badly Sasha had been maimed by the first explosion.

The blast from the other two was enough to send Farren crashing into the wall. The collision knocked the wind from her and she sank to the floor gasping.

Sparks and flames shot from the destroyed server room door. Black smoke billowed from it, filling the hall.

She should get out of there but she suddenly felt so weak, all of her strength having left her. Lost too much blood. Even if there was enough in her for her to survive, the smoke filling the basement would soon suffocate her. She tried to push herself up but could hardly lift a finger, let alone stand.

That was okay. She didn't want to die, but she was okay

with it. Thought she'd done a good job. Whatever came next, she hoped she'd absolved herself of the bitterness she'd been living with for the past few years.

Farren closed her eyes and drifted away.

## 57

She woke in a hospital bed. Warm sunlight streamed through the window next to her, casting golden rays over her body, which was covered by a thin, powder-blue blanket. The room was silent; none of the monitor beeps you heard in movies.

A man in a shirt and tie sat in the chair next to her bed, looking bored. She'd been around Gordon long enough to know he was a cop. He saw her eyes were open and straightened up.

Several more state police joined the plainclothes detective soon after Farren woke up. She was subjected to a battery of questions and was told her official statement could wait until she was out of hospital.

She'd been one of only a few survivors of the incident at the KnowMe Technological Park, which was now little more than a smoldering wreck, according to the news. The police didn't seem to have any trouble swallowing her story, which she told truthfully, only omitting the Museum, the Orchid

Room, and everything about the things living in them—she didn't want to spend extra time under observation for a suspected mental break.

When the police asked her if she knew anything about the graffiti sprayed all over town or what the word ZIIS meant, she told them she assumed it was a gang name and they nodded in agreement. She found out later, on the news, the word had been found at the sites of dozens of other grisly murders across the continent, all committed by kids between twelve and eighteen.

The official explanation wound up being that a highly organized and secretive collective of young people had gathered online, using the social media platform KnowMe. Nobody could figure out what ZIIS meant but assumed it was the word used to mobilize the kids when the time came for them to take action. What baffled the media and all the experts they could get their hands on was many of those who had taken part in the killings were known as good, well-behaved kids. Many came from stable homes, did well in school, and took part in extra-curricular activities. There were also a decent number of regular troublemakers in their ranks, but they by no means made up the majority.

There was no mention of Sasha or Jasper in the news—Farren kept a close eye out for any word on either of them.

After a week of its name being everywhere in the media, it seemed safe to assume ZIIS had lost its power. Farren thought she'd feel it if it came back.

The kids who were brought in all claimed to have no recollection of what happened after the KnowMe update went live. Each was being held under close watch at mental facilities across the country. Books were written about them by doctors, cops, lawyers, and conspiracy nuts, and most immediately made it to the top of the bestseller list. It was a mystery the world relished taking part in.

A service was held for Gordon and the rest of the Maggie's Knee police who had been killed on what the media quickly started calling Z-Day, which Farren thought sounded a little too much like something from a zombie movie.

The funeral was an elegant affair, with state officers in dress uniform performing a twenty-one-gun salute for Gordon.

Farren's grandparents flew down from Seattle but neither they nor Farren wanted to stay in the house where Melinda and Bonzo had been slain. They got a couple of hotel rooms in town and stayed there with Farren until after the funeral. Her grandparents were made executors of her parents' estate and offered to have her come live with them. She met them halfway and agreed to move into her own place in Seattle with plans to enroll at the University of Washington.

The day before she was to fly to the West Coast, three weeks after waking up in the hospital, Farren went for a walk. At first, she told herself she would just walk out to Jessop's Bridge and back, to exercise her recovering leg—the knife wound had required a dozen staples, which were eventually switched out for stitches. Her prosthesis had been recovered, unscathed, from the lawn of her dad's old office and was comfortably attached to what she now thought of as her good leg.

When she reached the bridge, she found herself sliding down the embankment to Widow's River and walking along its shore. Soon she was hiking along a nearly invisible path that branched away from the river.

So deep was she in her own thoughts she was almost

completely surprised when she found herself standing before the front gate of the Great Forest Outdoor Discovery Center. It looked decrepit and rundown.

Inside was no different. The Congo-that-was had an entirely different feel without anyone living in it, without the near-constant traffic of kids bustling about. It was almost sad to see. In spite of how she'd wound up there and how things had turned out, her experience hadn't been entirely miserable. She could have done without the evil spirit bent on world domination by popularity contest, but she thought she would miss some of the people. A bit.

Before she could stop herself, she was walking through the grounds, to the far end. She stood at the small bridge for a long time before working up the courage to cross Eagle Creek. Nothing happened when she reached the other side.

The windows of the Museum were all broken. Farren stepped through the front doors and caught a whiff of mold and dust. She didn't bother exploring the building any further. The place was dead.

She went out the door of the Museum and walked the path that connected it to the Orchid Room. The door to the building stood open and sunlight poured inside, illuminating an empty room with plain wooden floors and bare walls. She didn't go inside.

A thrush flew down from somewhere overhead and landed on the point of the roof. It thrust its spotted belly toward her and sang loud and clear, as if in defiance of the structure it stood on. She watched it for a long time before it flew off again.

Her thigh was beginning to throb. She swallowed a painkiller with a mouthful of water from her bottle and turned to go when a splash of color in the grass along the outside of the Orchid Room caught her eye. The old Osaka Kintetsu Buffaloes hat. She picked it up, turned it over in her hands, studying every thread. It was identical to the real one, the one her dad had worn all her life. She tossed it back into the grass. The real hat was buried with her dad.

On her way out, Farren was passing a group of cabins when she heard the unmistakable sound of crying coming from one of the smaller ones. Its door stood open. Farren stepped up to the threshold and held her breath.

Sadie McCallister sat on the floor with her back to the door, face in her hands, sobbing.

Farren watched her for a long time.

Sadie had shot Jasper. Killed him. Sure, it hadn't been entirely her fault, technically speaking, but she'd pulled the trigger.

A war raged in Farren's heart. Part of her wanted to shoot Sadie in the guts and watch her die slowly, the way Jasper had. Another part of her felt bad for Sadie, alone in the woods, abandoned by her friends.

Eventually the crying stopped and Sadie only sat with her back to Farren, facing the far wall.

After a long while, Farren pulled the cabin door closed.

And left the Congo for good.

# ACKNOWLEDGMENTS

I first need to thank my superhero of a wife, Annie. Without her constant support and encouragement, none of this could have been accomplished. I imagine it isn't easy being married to a writer of fiction. Overactive imagination, anxiety over completely unrealistic situations, obsessed with imaginary characters and situations—it must feel like living with another child at times. Annie bears all this with tolerance and, dare I say, enthusiasm. She eagerly reads my early, garbage drafts and attacks the revised versions of my stories with an interest I often find myself in disbelief of. There is bolstering magic in having a partner who is as enthusiastic about your work as you are. Thanks, Annie, for giving me the time and space I needed to get this thing finished and for all your valuable insights.

Big thank you to all who took the time to read earlier drafts of this beast, when it ran almost ten thousand words longer. Mom, Courtney, Nancy, Tomas, and Michael; your feedback went a long way to informing my later decisions regarding this book.

And to you, the reader of the finished product, I extend my most heartfelt gratitude. Not only for investing your money, but your time. For opening your mind and your heart to me. Without you, the work would grow stale.

Thank you.

# ABOUT THE AUTHOR

Christopher Sweet is the author of the horror / magical-realism novel *The Boy in the Canvas* and the occult horror novella *Something Sweet*. He has worked as a freelance writer, manager, waiter, bartender, event DJ, actor, children's entertainer, truck driver, shopkeeper, call center operator, concierge, office assistant, barista, and a campground manager. He is an avid reader, a lover of movies, and a fan of almost anything horror related. A nature hound at heart, he isn't above crawling through the dirt to get a closer look at a particularly interesting beast, bird, or bug.

Christopher lives with his growing tribe of people and pets on a peaceful river in New Brunswick's Acadian Peninsula.

You can catch him online at: www.authorchristopher-sweet.com

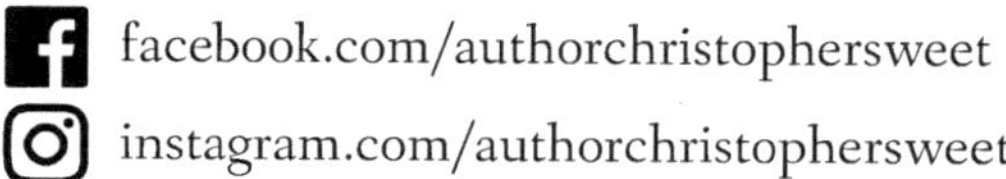